A SHERLOCKIAN QUARTET

Rick Boyer

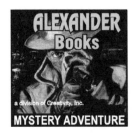

ALEXANDER Books

a division of Creativity, Inc.

MYSTERY ADVENTURE

Publisher: Ralph Roberts

Vice President/Publishing: Pat Roberts

Cover Design: Gayle Graham

Editor: Susan Parker, Pat Roberts

Interior Design and Electronic Page Assembly: Susan Parker

Printed in the United States of America

10   9   8   7   6   5   4   3   2

ISBN 1-57090-084-1

Library of Congress Catalog Card Number: 99-62051

Alexander Books™—a division of Creativity, Inc.—is a full-service publisher located at
65 Macedonia Road, Alexander NC 28701. Phone (828) 252-9515 or (828) 255-8719 fax.

Alexander Books™ is distributed to the trade by Midpoint Trade Books, Inc., 27 West 20th Street,
New York NY 10011, (212) 727-0190, (212) 727-0195 fax.

This book is also available on the internet in the **Publishers CyberMall**™. Set your browser to
http://www.abooks.com and enjoy the many fine values available there.

CONTENTS

PREFACE

by John H. Watson, M.D.

No one since my great-grandfather and namesake has chronicled the adventures of Sherlock Holmes so well and so vividly as Richard L. Boyer. *Authenticity*, I believe, is the word I seek in summing up his efforts in this book.

Indeed, a strong albeit true statement, and I thank Mr. Boyer's publisher for the opportunity of making it here in these pages. More about Boyer and his four most excellent Holmesian adventures shortly.

First, I must say my family has long been involved with the undisputedly greatest of fictional detectives–Mr. Sherlock Holmes, late of Baker Street in London. As a literary character, Holmes has taken on a life of his own, gaining popularity and faithful fans as the decades roll onward to the new millennium. A brief perusal of the Internet (*how* Holmes could have used *that* tool) shows there are currently more societies worldwide devoted to his exploits than those of any other character in literature.

Look up Sherlock Holmes in most references and you'll find he was supposedly created by the British writer, Sir Arthur Conan Doyle. The first Sherlock story, purportedly by Doyle, was published in 1887, and the last in 1927–a span of some 40 years.

Most aficionados of Holmesian adventures are well aware that Conan Doyle was little more than my great-grandfather's literary agent. Certainly this is intimate knowledge in our family. Manuscripts yet exist in the hand of the original Dr. Watson–some unpublished; but that's for a later book.

To Conan Doyle's credit, he certainly acknowledged my great-grandfather's role in relating the cases of Sherlock Holmes. For example, in *A Study in Scarlet,* below Doyle's byline as purportedly the author are the words: "BEING A REPRINT FROM THE REMINISCENCES OF JOHN H. WATSON, M.D., LATE OF THE ARMY MEDICAL DEPARTMENT."

There was, alas, also a dark side to Conan Doyle. He actually resented the initial success of Great-grandfather's stories, even though *he* was getting the credit for them! Doyle even said he felt "entirely identified with what I regarded as a lower stratum of literary achievement."

As preposterous as that position might seem, it was this feeling which caused him to modify one of the original Dr. Watson's stories to *kill off* Sherlock Holmes. Doyle accomplished this dastardly and unauthorized deed in 1893 by rewriting a story which sent Holmes over the Reichenbach Falls in Switzerland, locked in a fatal embrace with the arch-villain, Professor Moriarty.

The results of this literary treachery astounded Conan Doyle. Great-grandfather, ever the gentleman, took no revenge. Holmes' many fans were less restrained. They wore black crepe bands around their hats in mourning, and marched in protest. Worse, they wrote letters of condemnation to newspapers and even more threatening ones to Doyle himself. Needless to say, Sherlock Holmes was quickly resurrected and has gone on to rather ironically outlast Doyle's own fame.

Conan Doyle did little to disguise Great-grandfather's stories, other than to prominently place his own byline at the top. Otherwise, he passed them along to the publisher verbatim. Take again *A Study in Scarlet* and its opening:

"IN THE YEAR 1878 I took my degree of Doctor of Medicine of the University of London, and proceeded to Netley to go through the course prescribed for surgeons in the Army. Having completed my studies there, I was duly attached to the Fifth Northumberland Fusiliers as assistant surgeon. The regiment was stationed in India at the time, and before I could join it, the second Afghan war had broken out ..."

Great-grandfather was describing here his military experience and the events leading up to meeting Sherlock Holmes. The former is true; his relation of Holmes' marvelous detection, naturally, fiction and quite *good* fiction at that.

His experiences in the military involved considerable hardship. Again, from *A Study in Scarlet*:

"The campaign brought honours and promotion to many, but for me it had nothing but misfortune and disaster. I was removed from my brigade and attached to the Berkshires, with whom I served at the fatal battle of Maiwand. There I was struck on the shoulder by a Jezail bullet, which shattered the bone and grazed the subclavian artery. I should have fallen into the hands of the murderous Ghazis had it not been for the devotion and courage shown by Murray, my orderly, who threw me across a pack-horse, and succeeded in bringing me safely to the British lines.

"Worn with pain, and weak from the prolonged hardships which I had undergone, I was removed, with a great train of wounded sufferers, to the base hospital at Peshawar. Here I rallied, and had already improved so far as to be able to walk about the wards, and even to bask a little upon the veranda, when I was struck down by enteric fever, that curse of our Indian possessions. For months my life was despaired of, and when at last I came to myself and became convalescent, I was so weak and emaciated that a medical board determined that not a day should be lost in sending me back to England ..."

He goes on to relate his return to England and a search for lodgings. This leads into the wonderful Sherlock Holmes stories penned by Great-grandfather and whose origination fools no one.

No man is immortal and, in the normal course of events, both Dr. John H. Watson and his literary agent, the reluctant A. Conan Doyle, passed the bounds of this mortality. Holmes, however, lives on to this day because so many other writers have refused to let him die, nor would his countless legion of fans accept such an unthinkable end result.

My grandfather engaged in a long military career, as did my father; emigrating to the United States after World War II. My own service has been with the Navy of our family's new country. None of us have had the time to pursue literary endeavors, yet a number of writers have attempted to pick up the torch and carry on Great-grandfather's work.

These new Holmes stories—crafted by others than my great-grandfather—have not always been up to par. Even the collaboration between Doyle's youngest son, Adrian Conan Doyle, and the renowned mystery writer John Dickson Carr was allowed to collapse as the collaborators themselves were displeased with the quality of their product.

Some have exceptionally strong opinions about any of the Holmes stories written by other than Great-grandfather (referred to generally as Holmes *pastiches*). In the introduction to the Nero Wolfe mystery by Robert Goldsborough, *Death on Deadline* (1987), it is stated that "As for the avalanche of Holmesian pastiches that followed, with the exception of Rick Boyer's *Giant Rat of Sumatra*, the results have been so flawed that many readers can sympathize with Nicolas Freeling, who effectively closed out his Inspector Van der Valk series by shooting Van der Valk through the heart."

Despite my family interest in preserving the high position of Great-grandfather's work, I am disinclined to take as strong a stand as the above. Yet—while having read other Holmes pastiches and even enjoying them—I most certainly do subscribe to the opinion that Boyer's are best.

Boyer's first Sherlockian pastiche was *The Giant Rat of Sumatra*; included in this book but first published as a separate book in 1976 by Warner's. Now rare, this volume helped establish Rick's career as one of America's most promising mystery writers.

Rick Boyer went on to win the prestigious Edgar Allan Poe Award for the best mystery novel in 1983, *Billingsgate Shoal.* His popular Doc Adams series of novels continues regular publication today and Boyer enjoys his own legion of fans.

Since *The Giant Rat of Sumatra* had become so rare, the publisher of this book prevailed upon Mr. Boyer to grant reprint rights. To the publisher's considerable joy, Rick announced that he had *three more* Holmes unpublished pastiches. Hence the concept and creation of *A Sherlockian Quartet.*

I am sure Great-grandfather would have approved of the high quality of those three new stories—"The Adventure of Zolnay the Aerialist," "The Adventure of Bell Rock Light," and "The Adventure of the Eyrie Cliff"—as he would have *The Giant Rat of Sumatra.*

May I say, you are indeed in for a treat as you savor this quartet of Sherlock Holmes adventures.

No, Holmes is not dead—Rick Boyer has breathed exciting new life into the old boy!

—*Captain John H. Watson, M.D.*
USN (retired)

THE ADVENTURE OF ZOLNAY, THE AERIALIST

THE ADVENTURE OF ZOLNAY, THE AERIALIST

"Whoever our mysterious visitor is, he is certainly an impressive physical specimen," observed Sherlock Holmes as he doffed his overcoat.

"Whatever do you mean?" I asked. It was a blustery spring afternoon in mid May. Holmes and I had just returned from a brisk walk in Regent's Park; our cheeks were flushed from the fresh air. His comment had taken me entirely off guard.

"Come now Watson, don't you see that new pair of gloves he left behind on the sofa cushion? Here they are, now let me show you something ..."

So saying, he took the right one and plunged his hand into it in a twinkling. Then he clenched and unclenched his fist inside the garment, twirling his thin fingers about.

"Loose fit eh? *Quite*, I'd say. But my hands are extraordinarily thin. So let's try one of yours. There, try it on for size."

I did as instructed, and was amazed to discover how easily my hand slid in. Once inside, there was still half an inch of finger room left.

"Hmmmm! Amazing Watson. You are a perfect mesomorph in the prime of life, yet you now resemble a child trying on his father's glove, correct?"

"Yes, it certainly is large. The man must be a giant."

"Let's see what else he is. Grab the mate, will you, and bring them over to the window—let us see what these mis-laid items will reveal about the man who came calling while we were away."

He examined them for some time, checking the label sewn inside, and finally turned them both inside out. Upon seeing faint red blotches along the upper extremity of the palm of the right glove, a cry of satisfaction broke from his lips.

"Hah! You see that Watson? Surely these stains tell us quite a bit about our absent friend."

"Is it blood? I don't see how—"

"Let us start at the beginning. First, as you can see, the gloves are new—probably not more than a few days old. I can tell by the odour and texture of the flannel that they have not been cleaned, for the sizing is still present. But they show no signs of dirt: therefore they are quite new. There is, however, a trace of wax along the index finger of the left glove, so we can assume our man wears a moustache. Observe also the label: E.J. Stanhope, Ltd. It's one of Bond Street's most exclusive shops—far too posh for the likes of us eh? Therefore the man is rich, or well off anyway. It is here that a curious anomaly emerges ..."

"What anomaly? So far all your observations make sense Holmes; it appears you're putting together quite a portrait of the fellow."

"The quirk is this: he is well-off financially and well-dressed, yet he is *not* a gentleman. In fact, it appears he makes his living by performing physical feats of the most prodigious sort ..."

"A labourer?"

"No. Remember he is wealthy, or relatively so. I draw your attention once more to the faint bloodstains on the inside of the right glove. Obviously they are the result of extreme trauma to the palm of the hand just below the fingers. You know that this is the spot on the hand most subject to abrasion or callouses—"

"Which again would suggest the man is a labourer who swings a hammer or plies a shovel."

"Let's not be too hasty. Would a workingman earn the money to buy gloves like these? Certainly not. Furthermore, as I showed in the case of the apprentice Smythe, a workingman's hand soon becomes coated with callouses that are thick and shiny, and very hard. Yet these bloodstains show us that the skin has been ripped off by extreme trauma, a force so great as to destroy even hardened callouses. What sort of activity would cause this kind of terrific strain to the hand? And while you're pondering that question, let us consider another possibility: that the man does not ordinarily wear gloves—at least not dress gloves of fine grey flannel like these."

"How do you know this?"

"I do not know it, I *infer* it as a probability. First, he left the gloves behind. Now he could be extremely agitated, yet a gentleman who is in the habit of wearing dress gloves regularly would not forget them, and this fellow has. Also, the fact that they are new is suggestive. Perhaps he has bought these fine gloves for a special occasion, or as a result..."

He pondered the facts and possibilities before him for a few minutes, then fetched the morning's newspapers and retired to the sofa with a pipe. I had settled myself comfortably with a cigar and the most recent issue of *Lancet*, when there came a series of heavy bounds upon the staircase, followed by a robust knocking upon our door. Holmes, putting aside the paper with a gleam in his eye, rose and went to the door. But before he opened it, he turned to me and proclaimed in a loud voice: "Ah Watson, I see *Mr. Gregor Zolnay* has returned. Come in Mr. Zolnay, and welcome!"

With this he threw open the door, and revealed a personage with the most awesome physique I have ever seen. He was a full head taller than either of us, with broad shoulders, a piercing face set off by green eyes and a giant brown moustache. All in all, his appearance was striking in the extreme; he seemed to exude strength and vitality. And when he spoke, it was with a booming baritone voice, modulated somewhat by halting speech and a thick accent.

"Mr. Holmes, yes?" he enquired, stepping into the parlour and extending a huge hand wrapped in bandages.

"Yes Mr. Zolnay, and this is my friend Dr. John Watson. Tell me, what brings you back from the circus grounds so soon?"

Our visitor was so stunned he nearly reeled into my armchair with amazement. I must confess that, accustomed as I was to Holmes' feats of observation and deduction, my wonder almost equalled that of our caller.

"Mr. Holmes you are *mizand*, eh ... eh ..."

"A sorcerer?"

"Yes! You are magic Mr. Holmes! You have been to the Chipperfield's? No? Then how do you know me? I leave no card; I speak with no one! Gregory Zolnay comes and goes, and *pfffffft!* Sherlock Holmes knows who I am even before he sees me— *mizand!*"

"Come now my dear sir, it wasn't really all that difficult, eh Watson?" said my companion, filling his pipe.

I mumbled an assent, but for the life of me was at a loss as to Holmes' thinking processes.

"You see Mr. Zolnay, you forgot your gloves earlier this afternoon, and they served very well as your calling card."

"Yes I leave them. I forget. Zolnay does not wear gloves except in wintertime ..."

"Or except to hide his injured hand," continued Holmes, winking in my direction.

The giant bounded back, drawing the hand under his coat.

"Zolnay is not injured!" he cried, and then added thoughtfully, "It is only to *myself* I am injured, not to others."

"I think we understand, don't we Watson? You have a reputation to uphold. But guessing your identity was not hard. Watson and I were discussing the possible occupations of the man who owned these gloves. We concluded the man was well-paid, yet evidently possessed great strength, and *used* it too, as we saw by these bloodstains. Now what sort of job would it be that pays a nice salary for physical exertion? There is only one: a performer of some sort. Focusing my efforts along this line, I seemed to recall a notice for the circus in this morning's *Telegram*. Finding it, I scanned the advertisement for a lead. Certainly the performer was either a strongman or acrobat, but odds favored the acrobats especially a trapeze artist who would undoubtedly subject his hands to incredible abrasion. You see Mr. Zolnay, I do a bit of boxing in my spare time at Sullivan's gymnasium, and so am familiar with the torn hands of the gymnasts who train there–"

The huge man stared dumbstruck at Holmes, glowing with admiration and wonder.

"Prominently featured in the advertisement was a reference to 'Gregor the Great–Aerialist Supreme,' alias Gregor Zolnay."

"But how did you know it was Zolnay behind the closed door?" I asked.

"Ah yes Herr Doctor," joined Zolnay, wagging a huge finger in Holmes' direction, "you have magic eyes too, eh?"

"There are seventeen steps leading to our flat," returned Holmes. "You bounded up in four leaps plus a step. Would an ordinary man be able to ascend a staircase four at a time? No. Could an acrobat? With ease, as you have proven. Now sir, what is it I can do for you?"

Recollecting his reason for seeking assistance, Gregor Zolnay's strong face assumed a forlorn expression. He sank wearily into my armchair and sighed deeply.

"Mr. Holmes, Herr Doctor ... I have much sadness in my heart. My dear Anna is crippled, she–"

Here the man, so outwardly strong, buried his head in his hands and rocked to and fro in grief. Holmes, after waiting some time for the man to continue, began to ask him questions.

"Is her condition the result of illness or injury?"

"She fell. It was two nights ago, during the time we rehearse. We were doing the triple pirouette. It is very difficult, and dangerous, and demands much attention. Also Mr. Holmes, the net was down, as it must be during the performance."

"I take it the stunt miscarried, and as a result she fell to the ground–"

"Yes, forty feet down into the ring. When I saw her fall I grabbed a cable and slid down after her. So *this*," and he held up his bandaged hand.

"I see, that would be the natural thing to do. Anna is your wife then?"

"No, we are to be married–that is we had planned to be married. She may never walk again. She can barely talk. It is very sad."

"You mean she is unconscious?" I asked.

"Sometimes she wakes, sometimes she sleeps–mostly she sleeps–"

"Is she hospitalized?"

"Yes, Herr Doctor, at the London Hospital. When she wakes she talks nonsense. Always it is the same thing she says. She grabs my head and whispers in my ear: 'Gregor, the elephant man, *it is the elephant man!*'"

Holmes and I exchanged bewildered glances. I assumed Zolnay's rather cryptic phrase was due to his heavy accent and marginal command of English.

"Surely," said Holmes, "Anna was referring to the man who cares for the elephants: their keeper. Is this not the case?"

The giant shook his head dumbfoundedly

"No, Mr. Holmes. I ask her this. *Is it Panelli who feeds the animals?* No, she says. I don't know what she is trying to say gentlemen. Until this morning I think she is mad with fever and talking nonsense. But then this morning I remember something odd, and come to see you."

Holmes leaned forward eagerly.

"I am remembering that just before she fell, she said too: the *elephant man.* I think too she screamed a little just before–"

"–just before the accident?"

"Yes, Herr Doctor. Let me explain please. I am catcher who hangs on centre bar–"

"On the trapeze?"

"Yes, I hang head downwards by my legs, swinging. Anna leaps from platform holding onto her bar. She releases, pirouettes three times–quick like this–then extends her wrists for me."

"Then you grab them."

"Yes, and after one, maybe two swings, she releases to grab again the bar held by Vayenko. Then she swings to other platform."

"Who is Vayenko?"

"Vayenko is third man in team. A Russian, from Kiev. He is long time with Chipperfield's. He is now too old for much performing—he holds bar for Anna. When we are in correct place on the swing, he releases it from far platform so it will be there for Anna to catch. We are not friends. He loved Anna before I joined Chipperfield's in Buda-Pesth three years ago."

Holmes shot a keen glance in my direction.

"Naturally, he was disappointed, and angered, that Anna should abandon him for you," I pursued.

Zolnay remained silent for a short while before replying. He looked down at his hands, assuming almost a guilty look.

"He does not talk of his feelings, Herr Doctor. But I think they are as you say. He proposed to Anna after we met, and she refused him."

"Can you relate the details of the accident?" asked Holmes, changing the subject.

"It is as I say: Anna on the platform, I am in the middle, hanging upside down on the bar, Vayenko is on the far platform holding the other bar..."

"Yes," I said, recounting, "and Anna leaps from her platform, releasing the bar at the height of her swing—"

"Yes, then turning like this you see—"

At this point the huge man jumped from the chair and turned around three times with amazing quickness and grace.

"—then she was to extend to me her arms so—then I to grab her wrists, but she did not do this gentlemen. She went into a ball and fell."

"And you remember her crying out?"

"Yes, she cried out something about the elephant man ... I think she said the word *horrible*, or *horrid*... but I am not sure now because then I am watching her fall—going fast down away from me and I cannot think—"

Here the aerialist winced with the memory of the tragedy.

"And Vayenko never left his place on the far platform?"

"No, Mr. Holmes. He never moved, from the time we start the rehearsal until Anna is falling ... and afterwards he is at my side as I am leaning over her."

Holmes pondered what had been said for some time before responding.

"And you have come to me solely because of Anna's strange talk about the elephant man?"

"It is not much perhaps Mr. Holmes. But Anna is a great flyer. She would not miss the triple like that—bent over, like a baby who sleeps in a little ball. It was something ... something horrible that frightened her so that she could not think of the triple."

"And there was nothing unusual in the ring, or tent? Nothing strange about the gounds?"

Zolnay shook his head.

"No. In fact, Vayenko fastened the tent so that no one could enter during the rehearsal—so there would be no interference."

"And I take it that was the usual procedure."

"No. Only then was the tent fastened."

"That is interesting ... decidedly so. Feel like taking in the circus Watson? Shall we shed our middle-age stuffiness and become boys again?"

He fetched his coat and flung mine across the armchair.

"Come on man! Can't you hear the steam whistle blowing? You're encamped on the fairgrounds at Wimbledon I suppose, eh Mr. Zolnay? Good, then let's have a look around the grounds before going to visit poor Anna at London Hospital."

Inside of an hour's time, we were standing at the edge of the *tober* (as Zolnay called it) or field at Wimbledon. In its centre rose the immense tent, an elliptical mountain of cloth over a hundred yards in length. Pennants fluttered gaily from its summit while, as predicted by Holmes, the robust tones of the steam piano could be heard from afar. Long queues of anxious people streamed to the centre tent, while throngs of curious onlookers packed into the "sideshows" that ringed the circus grounds. Encircling the show, so as to form a crude fence round it, were scores of wagons and caravans, all painted red with "CHIPPERFIELD'S" painted in huge silver letters on their sides. Drawing closer, the heavy odour of animals and the smell of hay reached us, and a wave of nostalgia passed over me.

Soon we were inside the ring of wagons, and our famous companion was besieged by countless admirers. Zolnay informed us that this area was the "back yard" where the performers congregated between acts, and where the properties and wardrobes were kept. Many people came to offer their condolences and best wishes for Anna's recovery. Among the interesting people we met were Bruno Baldi, the strongman who could lift a horse. "Black Jack" Houlihan could swallow a scimitar, bending the trunk of his body to accommodate the curved blade. Several clowns approached and offered their best wishes too, and it seemed strange to hear normal, sober voices emerge from the grotesque faces. Zolnay hailed one fellow, a slight little man with a twisted body who limped along the sawdust like an urchin.

"Sidney, Sidney Larkin!" he called, and the stunted figure stopped, turned and bounded over to us. Zolnay, who had to prepare for the afternoon show, instructed him to take us to Panelli's caravan. The man complied instantly, obviously an indication of his affection for the aerialist. He led us, with his hobbling gait, to a caravan that resembled the ones owned by Gypsies and Tinkers. It was immediately apparent that someone was home; we saw the plume of grey smoke rising from the tin stack that projected through the wagon's roof. Drawing closer, the delicious aroma of onions and garlic frying in olive oil issued from the open window.

Larkin lurched up the rear ladder and rapped on the door.

"'ey Panelli," he said under his breath, "couple of flatties out here to see you ..."

"What the devil is a *flattie*?" I asked Holmes.

"I believe it's circus parlance for 'outsider.'"

"You in a kip? Eh? Allright mate, we'll wait a bit."

Shortly afterwards the caravan's owner appeared in the minute rear doorway, and motioned us all inside. Panelli was a short, stout man with an enormous drooping moustache and swarthy features. He wore a tattered hat, and most strange and engaging of all–had a small black monkey riding on his shoulder. The monkey too wore a tiny hat, and a bright jacket, which gave him an almost humanoid appearance. Already I was glad to have accompanied Holmes on this errand, since I had always been most curious to see the inside of a traveling caravan. We ducked in and were surprised to find not only Panelli, but his wife and five children too! How they could survive in those cramped quarters I couldn't say, yet the place, crowded as it was, certainly had a cozy air about it. Mrs. Panelli stirred the iron pot on the stove, and offered us tea.

Panelli, who was sprawled on a cot feeding his monkey (whose name was Jocko), was most cooperative in answering our questions. It was a curious experience sitting on a steamer trunk in the tiny traveling home, listening to the babble of the throng outside as the noise entered through the windows that were cheerfully decorated with curtains of blue gingham.

"You will come with me please gentlemen," said Panelli, who

bade his family goodbye and led us back down the ladder and towards a large tent.

Lifting the flap for us to pass through, Panelli led us around a haystack. I was met with a sight that fairly took my breath away, and made me take several steps backwards.

"Not to be afraid gentlemen, they will not hurt you," said the Italian, and walked calmly into the midst of a small herd of elephants that stood eating not ten feet away from us. One huge tusker caught my attention as he flicked the heavy chain which fettered him to and fro with his trunk as if it were a piece of twine. The beasts flapped their ears and swayed rhythmically as they ate. I could hear the grinding of their molars.

"Now Mr. Panelli, am I given to understand that when the accident occurred you were in this very tent with the elephants?"

"Yes, it was late when they were rehearsing. I remember it was dark outside. The elephants were all as you see them now. Sidney sees me here then, also Rocco the clown. Panelli here the whole time."

"And all of the elephants too? None amiss?"

"No, all here, all twelve, as you can count now—"

At that instant the big bull, head swaying, backed up three steps and would have stepped on Holmes had he not backed off.

"Hannibal!" shouted Panelli, and the bull resumed his original place.

"They are easy, you see. Now gentlemen, I go eat my lunch?"

"Certainly. Thanks you for your help," replied Holmes.

We stared at the great animals for perhaps ten more minutes, but then the big bull showed signs of restlessness again so we departed the tent and resumed walking around the grounds.

Holmes, as was his custom, walked slightly hunched over peering downwards in thought, his hands clasped behind his back.

"Well, did you observe anything remarkable either about Mr. Panelli or his elephants?"

"I'm afraid not Holmes. Everything seemed to be entirely above board. Besides, Panelli has several witnesses to attest to his presence in the tent."

"I concur. I think we can rule him out ... and the beasts too."

"But why then Anna's constant referral to the elephant man?"

"Humf! That is why we must see her personally. It is good you are a physician Watson, for it will make our visit to London Hospital much easier. Of course this means that we must miss the show. Let's look up Zolnay and—good heavens, what's that?"

A piercing cry reached us over the din of the crowd. It came again, and I recognized it as the scream of an elephant. We made our way back to Panelli's tent in time to see him scurry out of the caravan, a driving hook in his hand. Jocko the monkey rode chattering on his shoulder.

"It is Hannibal again," he said to us as he hurried toward the canvas flap. "He is near musth, and restless lately, as you saw. I must chain him apart from the others."

Having dispersed the crowd that was beginning to gather, we followed the trainer back into the tent. The animals were restless. Their rocking, swaying motion had increased, and they swung their trunks about with hollow blowing noises. The great bull Hannibal raised his head and trunk upwards and walked deliberately into the young bull tethered next to him. That animal in turn trumpeted and prepared to charge back. It was then I realized how frail indeed was the canvas tent that enclosed the animals. Panelli rushed between the huge beasts, goad upraised. I couldn't help but admire his courage. The monkey shrieked with rage and delight. The animals backed away from each other and the massive chains straightened, then sprung into the air, thrumming like guitar strings. Holmes and I watched fascinated at the incredible strength and energy being displayed. Talking softly to the animals—whose behavior had much improved since his arrival—Panelli then crept round behind Hannibal and in a twinkling had affixed another chain to his right rear leg. This he then fastened to an enormous iron stake (its head flared like a mushroom from countless hammer blows) at the rear of the tent. After several minutes of tricky maneuvering, he had succeeded in isolating the bull between two stakes—far away from the others.

All seemed in order, yet there occurred the next instant one of the most violent and ghastly spectacles I've ever witnessed. And though it involved no human life, the incident remains grimly marked in my memory for life.

Panelli had finished drawing tight the rear chain and was walking past the animal towards us when Jocko, seeing the elephant's tail swinging a few feet away, was overcome by temptation. Whether the huge tail resembled a rope or vine I cannot say, but they monkey sprang from the trainer's shoulders and grasped the tail, then scrambled up along the huge back. There it pranced delightedly, turning backward somersaults and flinging about the straw that lay upon the elephant's back. But in an instant the excited chattering was replaced by a muffled groan as the enraged beast's trunk found the interloper and wrapped tightly round him. I heard Panelli cry out an admonition to Hannibal, but it was too late. The trunk snapped downward like a gigantic buggy-whip, and the monkey was slammed to earth. It tried to flee, and rose spastically for an instant, but was then blotted out by the descending grey foot. Before the trainer could call off the elephant, it had drawn up the small limp form again in its trunk and flung it through the tent flap.

We all stared dumbstruck for a few seconds, so great was the shock and violence of the occurence. Then, recovering our wits, the three of us raced outside the tent to meet the gathering crowd that had formed a circle around the tiny furred carcass that lay sprawled upon the sawdust. The dead monkey lay on its back, its mouth, full of gore, opened in a horrid mocking grin which exposed the large teeth.

"Hoodoo!" cried Rocco the clown.

"Hoodoo!" echoed Black Jack Houlihan.

"Oh lord! It's the *hoodoo* sure enough!" responded Sidney Larkin, looking with horror on the dead monkey.

"Holmes! The *'hoodoo?'* What's the *hoodoo?*"

"I take it to be an ill omen, a Jonah," he replied.

"Aye sir, that it is—a Jonah! And the worst sort," said Larkin, backing off in fear. "The worst sort of sign there can be, for if a monkey is killed, it means that *three people shall die!*"

"Humph!" I exclaimed in disbelief, as we watched the elephant trainer sadly gather up his departed friend and wend his way back to the wagon. But despite my incredulity, I noticed the look of fear and wonder on the faces of the circus people, and the comment I heard more than once: "I hope it ain't me!"

We paused in the tent yard long enough for a pipe. At the end of that time, Holmes frankly admitted to me that the case appeared confusing. Since we'd struck a dead-end at the circus grounds for the tine being, he thought it best to go to Anna's bedside directly and have Zolnay join us there at the performance's close.

"Perhaps we'll learn more at the hosptial Watson, though I must say this is not an auspicious beginning."

The ride to London Hospital was not a long one, and before half an hour had elapsed we were at its entrance. Sir Frederick Treves, the brilliant doctor and surgeon who was one of the hospital's directors, was an acquaintance of mine. I therefore approached the head nurse and informed her of my relationship with Treves, and said we wished to see a patient in the hospital.

"I'm sorry Doctor, he's not to be seen unless so directed personally by Dr. Treves, we've had enough of the curious—"

"I beg pardon Miss," I pursued, "but the patient we wish to see is a woman: Miss Anna Tontriva ..."

"Oh I'm sorry. I thought it was ... another matter entirely. This way please."

I was shown into the chamber alone whilst Holmes waited outside. We had agreed that if she were in sufficient condition, he would join me in asking her questions. But upon examining the lady for only a few seconds, I uttered a sigh of despair, for I knew she would not live. I again checked her vital signs to make certain, but I had not been mistaken: the woman was in a deep coma, and runing a high fever. Moreover, from examining her chart and palpitating her abdomen, I could tell that peritonitis had set in. There was nothing to be done ...

"What is it then old fellow?" enquired my companion as I emerged dejected, "Come on man, raise up your head—"

I shook my head sadly.

"Fetch Zolnay. I'm afraid there's much unpleasantness ahead for us. I'll get the physician in charge, or his assistant. But believe me Holmes, she hasn't a chance."

Holmes said nothing, but his expression told me that he too was thinking of the monkey.

"The '*hoodoo*,' eh Holmes?"

"Bah! Rubbish!" he cried, and spun off to bring the acrobat.

* * *

I needn't relate to you, dear reader, the painful events that followed. We saw the gigantic Hungarian, Gregor the Great, reduced to a weeping hulk as the body of his beloved Anna was borne away on a litter. We summoned various people from Chipperfield's to comfort the man, and to arrange for the funeral. Leaving the hospital to continue our investigation, we passed Treves in the hallway. He was speaking to an orderly as we approached, and I heard a snatch of the conversation.

"... so fortunate that he has quarters *here* now don't you see, for he won't have people gaping at him all the time. Yes, women have been known to faint—oh hullo Watson, what brings you here?"

I briefly explained our grim mission to Treves, who extended his sincere sympathy, and we made our way back to the circus grounds. We had no trouble finding Sidney Larkin and Rocco, for they were in Rocco's caravan, heads bowed in grief. All claimed it was the hoodoo working, and shuddered at the thought of the two additional deaths to follow. Panelli, feeling he was somehow to blame—would see no one. The show had been over for several hours and we were at liberty to examine the main tent. We entered and were immediately overwhelmed by the enormity of it. With the assistance of Larkin and Rocco, Holmes lighted several of the big carbon-arc lamps that served as spotlights. These he aimed upwards at the flying bars and platforms. Then, much to the amazement of all present, he approached the rope ladder that hung down into the centre ring and began to climb.

"Halt!" came a voice. "What are you doing here?"

We turned to see a powerful-looking man approach the centre ring and glare up at Holmes, who was almost to the top.

"Vayenko, this man is Sherlock Holmes, a detective who is helping Gregor discover the cause of Anna's fall—" began Rocco, but he was cut short.

"Get down!" cried the Russian, shaking his fist.

"Mr. Vayenko, I am here at the request of Mr. Gregor Zolnay. I would be most anxious for your assistance in this matter," said Holmes coolly. "However, it you do not wish to cooperate, I would request you not interfere."

Holmes continued climbing toward the aerialist's platform. He had almost reached the platform when Vayenko, with a curse, started up the ladder in pursuit with a speed that was unbelievable. In short order he had overtaken my comrade and seized him by the ankle.

"See here!" I shouted and ran to the ladder, Larkin and the clown at my heels.

Holmes assayed the situation calmly, and asked the acrobat to release his grip. I was appalled at the aerialist who, of all of us, should have been the most keenly aware of the danger to which he was subjecting Holmes. Yet I watched terrified as the Russian began pulling at his leg, and drew Holmes' other foot from the rung on which it rested. My friend dangled there, forty feet up, carrying not only his own weight, but much of the other man's as well. However, just as I thought his grip would fail, I saw his free foot snap back and the boot drive into the Russian's hand. The man let out a howl of pain, and allowed Holmes to reach the platform.

"What is going on here?" cried a deep voice. We saw an elegantly dressed man approach the ring and look up.

"Vladimir, is that you? Who the devil is that up there with you?"

The man made himself known as Lamar Chipperfield, the owner and manager of the show. Upon hearing the nature of our business, Mr. Chipperfield gladly consented, and instructed Vayenko to dismount the ladder immediately. Upon receiving this order, the man's demeanor changed markedly; he assumed a meek and dutiful manner, and went to great pains to assure Mr. Chipperfield that he was acting only out of concern for the circus—preventing a stranger and trespasser from damaging the apparatus.

"You know Mr. Chipperfield that our lives depend on the wires. To have them damaged in any way ..."

"I fully understand Vladimir. You made an honest mistake. Kindly wait in your wagon until these gentlemen are through, for they may have questions to ask you. Goodnight."

The Russian moved off most humbly, even bowing slightly in my direction. But my loathing for him remained, and I felt that his servile attitude was a sham, for I saw him glare again in Holmes' direction just before he departed the tent.

I returned directly beneath the platform and spent the next several minutes helping to direct the spotlights in the directions Holmes indicated.

"A little to the left and up," he would say, peering about the tent from his lofty perch, "no, not so far—there, hold it steady for a moment ..."

Apparently tiring of this, he amazed us by drawing the middle bar over to the platform by means of a light rope. In a few seconds we saw him swinging in a wide arc over our heads. We were all afright for his situation, but he displayed that remarkable coolness which was his hallmark; he sat on the bar as if enjoying himself tremendously, gazing about and shouting directions to us.

"Don't be a moron Holmes!" I cautioned. "You'll break your neck! I say, come down at once!"

But he stayed up another ten minutes before returning, bright-eyed, to the sawdust ring.

"I say Larkin, what's that?" he enquired, pointing to a canvas canopy that emerged between tiers of wooden benches.

"That sir, is the *run in.*"

"The *run in?*"

"Yes sir. The animals make their entrance through it. It's a canvas tunnel that runs out to the backyard and wagons. It's kept sealed until showtime, for the children would sneak in through it to avoid paying."

The three of us examined the cloth-covered entranceway. It was about four feet in diameter. We entered the tunnel, stooping low as we walked, until we came to a wall of canvas tightly laced. Larkin undid the laces for us and we passed out into the night air. Sure enough, we were in the midst of the menagerie of wagons. The faint growling and acrid stench indicated the presence of lions.

"And this is always kept laced?"

"Yessir. Until the middle of showtime. As you can see, there's nobody hereabouts mosttimes—since the performers gather over near the front line tent for tea and a chat ..."

"I see. And not only is this area deserted, but remarkably near the outer fence too," observed Holmes as he walked slowly about, eyes glued to the ground. "It may interest you to know, Watson, that the entranceway of the run in is visible from the platform, but not from the centre bar..."

"You don't say," I replied, unable to follow his train of thought.

"Larkin, are the flaps to the run in kept closed also?"

"The inside ones? Yes sir. It allows the trainers to lead their animals into the run without them being seen."

"And how are the flaps raised?"

"By means of stout cords, which are held by the ringmaster—Mr. Chipperfield, the gentleman you met. After announcing the act, he gives a sharp pull to the cords see, which raises the flaps, signaling the animals to prance into the ring. It's a pretty sight sir, ain't it Rocco?"

"I see," mused my companion, and returned through the tunnel of canvas to the grounds. There he requested a lantern, which Rocco promptly brought. He spent the next half hour, lantern in hand, tracing wide half-circles over the "pitch," or grounds. I seated myself on an enormous coil of rope and smoked three cigarettes during this procedure. Finally I heard the yelp of satisfaction that announced a discovery.

"Like a hound eh?" I said to my companions, "his cries tell us he's found the scent."

Holmes, thirty yards distant, was kneeling upon the earth, eyes and face aglow with excitement.

"You see here Watson ... you *see?*" he cried tensely, pointing at the ground.

I saw nothing save a rough scrabbling on the earth that seemed to repeat itself at regular intervals. It certainly did not resemble footprints of any sort I had ever seen. Yet the regular repetition of the strange pattern indicated a locomotive motion, albeit a strange one.

"Ah look here," said Holmes, pointing to a small round depression in the earth that was likewise repeated with the pattern.

"A cane?"

"Yes, or a crutch. So it is a human—or is it? Certainly it leaves no ordinary footprints. Let us follow them ..."

The track led to the outer fence, and there, fastened upon a slat of wood that formed the fence, was a cloth object that Holmes removed from its perch and examined with much interest.

"What is it Holmes?"

"I'm not yet sure, but it appears to be some kind of garment ..."

He held the weird object under the lantern's beam, mumbling to himself. He then made additional efforts to pick up the strange track on the other side of the fence but, owing to the darkness was forced to relinquish the chase.

"The track was clear enough in the earth and sawdust of the pitch, but will be extremely difficult to follow in the meadow that surrounds it. It's a wonder we ever found it at all considering the enormous traffic flowing over the grounds. However, as you saw, I discovered it only by circling far out towards the fence. Whoever, or *whatever* it was clearly headed straight for the fence, and over it. No Watson, we'd be wasting our time to search further tonight. Better to return tomorrow in full daylight. For the present, I think we've learned all we can from our inspections. Tell me Larkin, is it true the flyers were alone in the main tent the night of the accident?'"

The stunted man hobbled alongside us in the darkness for several minutes before replying.

"Yes sir, to the best of my knowledge. I think we was all in the side tent, or tending to our own affairs in our caravans. As you know, I was with Panelli and Rocco."

Holmes spent another half-hour questioning the remaining circus people: had any of them been in the main tent during the ill-fated rehearsal? Was it true that the flaps were fastened shut so no one could enter? Had they seen a strange animal amongst the wagons, or loitering near the big tent? The answer to these questions was no. Therefore we boarded a hansom and within the hour found ourselves once again at our quarters. Saddened over Anna's death, we sat for some time before the fireplace in silence. Then Holmes retrieved the strange article of clothing he had found on the circus fence. It resembled a huge sleeve, yet one end was sewn up in heavy canvas, which was blackened with dirt and macadam. He drew it over his arm; his hand was then encircled by the canvas end, which he inspected carefully with the aid of his lens and the glare of the student lamp. After twenty minutes of scrutiny, broken only by occasional sighs and grunts, he flung it nonchalantly into my lap.

"What do you make of it?"

"It looks like some kind of slipper," I replied at last, "since we can see by the condition of the canvas end that it has had repeated, even constant, contact with the ground."

He nodded his head in agreement as he drew on his pipe, expelling clouds of smoke into the lamp's glare.

"The strange part is, it is not shaped like something that would fit over a leg and foot," I continued. "In fact, from its dimensions, I would say it was made more for a fin, or flipper, than for a human limb–"

"If it were made for a normal human foot, even disregarding its intense size and grotesque shape, we could assume that the *footprint* on the canvas–the dark stain that has been produced by the limb within pushing the cloth onto the ground–would bear a roughly elongated shape comparable to a foot. It would show a series of smudges at one end corresponding to the balls of the feet and perhaps the toes–"

"Yes!" he interrupted, "and a slightly smaller smudge at the other end which would be made by the heel ..."

"Of course. But in this case, we see that the stain is an irregular blob. Instead of delineating a foot, even roughly, it delineates nothing."

"Or nothing that is a foot," he corrected.

"Then *what is it?*" I enquired, the horor growing in me.

"I don't know Watson, except to say that it is perhaps human, or half-human, as the case may be. I can tell by the remnants of sawdust stuck to the tar that this was on the limb–one of the limbs rather, that made the strange track near the tent."

" ... the elephant man ..." I mused.

"My thoughts exactly. Is it possible? What sort of man–if such he could be called–would require a boot like this one eh? He would have to be terribly–"

"Deformed?"

"*Yes!* Only–I say, wait a minute! I seem to remember a column in the *personals* of about a month ago ... let's see here..."

He flung himself down upon his knees and began rummaging like a pack rat through the stacks of newspapers that littered our floor.

"Drat Watson! I see you've been housecleaning again–shame on you! How am I to solve these puzzles if you persist in raiding my stores of information, eh? Neatness is a loathsome trait Watson; never forget it!"

I spent the better part of an hour convincing him that, were it not for my 'housecleaning,' our flat would soon become a jackdaw's nest. As a further balm for his distress, I offered to buy our dinner, and soon we were off to Morley's Chop House. Throughout the meal he plied me with questions. As a medical man, was I aware of any disease or condition that would result in horrendous deformities? I replied that there were a few, like *elephantiasis*, that could result in unbelievable swelling of the flesh and lymph glands, and a corresponding ulceration and scaling of the skin.

"By Jove! And the correct name as well! Surely then that is the answer, and yet ..."

He fell silent again, and we finished the meal talking of other subjects.

"Tell me Watson," he pursued as we left Morley's, "does elephantiasis, damaging though it is to the flesh and glands, affect the bones?"

When I replied in the negative, Holmes observed that we had best rule out the disease.

"As you yourself stated after examining the strange slipper we found, the *limbs* are misshapen, not just the tissue on them, correct?"

I nodded. "I must say I'm entirely at a loss Holmes. If indeed it is a human afflicted with a malady, the malady's identity escapes me. I don't see how you expect to find the answer to this puzzle either, unless you plan to continue following the strange track in tomorrow's daylight ..."

"There may be an easier way Watson. Tomorrow morning shall find me at the *Times* office. I'm quite sure it was in that paper—in the agony columns—that I saw the notice a month ago. Well, shall we return directly to Baker Street or would you rather stop by Drury Lane on the way?"

* * *

I had scarcely dressed next morning when Holmes burst into my room full of excitement.

"Your surgeon friend at London Hospital Watson, his name is *Treves* is it not?"

"Yes. Sir Frederick Treves. You saw him yesterday in the hospital corridor, if you recollect—"

"—of *course* I recollect," he snapped, "but, though the name was faintly familiar to my ear, I failed to assemble all the pieces ..."

"Eh? All the pieces?"

"I take it that until yesterday you had not spoken to Treves in some time? That would seem plausible, since you work at different hospitals. It is unlikely then, that you have heard about his recent charge."

"No, I confess I haven't."

"A unique charge, to say the least. Come along, there's a cab waiting at our kerb. No! You must skip your tea old fellow—one of the penalties for being a slugabed!"

He half-dragged me down the staircase and flung me into the waiting hansom. We dashed off in the direction of London Hospital.

"Now Watson," said he, drumming his fingers on his knee impatiently, "don't you recall that yesterday when you introduced yourself as a friend of Treves the head nurse assumed you were visiting another patient ..."

"I think I do remember ... she said they had seen enough of the curious ..."

"Yes!" he beamed. "And also, you may recollect that Treves himself, whilst speaking to a colleague in the hallway, mentioned that *women have been known to faint!...*'"

"... since time immemorial, I'm afraid! ..."

"Dash it Watson, you really are slow sometimes!"

"I beg pardon—"

"At first I thought it coincidence that Anna Tontriva should be confined in the same building that contains the solution to our problem. But upon reflection it makes sense, since London is the closest hospital to the circus grounds ..."

"Whatever are you talking about Holmes?" I said with a yawn, for I was not entirely at my best without my morning cup.

"Never mind Watson, you'll see the answer for yourself soon enough. Here we are. I'll meet you inside directly I pay the cabbie."

Shortly afterwards Holmes joined me at the head nurse's station, where he enquired for Treves.

"Mr. Holmes? He is expecting you. Yes, Doctor Treves received your wire. This way please."

She led us to the rear wing of the hospital, where, set off by two sets of doors from the remainder of the building, was a suite of rooms which looked out onto an enclosed grassy courtyard. Being vaguely familiar with the hospital, I had heard this referred to as Bedstead Square. It was an isolation ward, and usually used to house lunatics temporarily before they were transferred to asylums. The nurse bade us sit down in the first of the rooms, and after several minutes wait, Treves entered the room and drew up a chair opposite us. "Hullo again Watson. Mr. Holmes, I received you urgent wire this morning. Surely your keen powers are much as Watson has proclaimed, for we've done our level best to keep Merrick's confinement here a secret."

"I'm sure you have sir. And may I express my sincere admiration to you and Mr. Carr Gomm. Your advertisement in the *Times*, I take it, was successful."

"Oh quite. Merrick now has the means to sustain himself in comfort here for the remainder of his life, thanks to the generosity of the British public. He was unaware of his newfound fortune until yesterday, for we didn't want to disappoint him were it not to materialise. But now he knows he can stay here for good, and is most joyous. Now you, Watson, have not heard of John Merrick?"

"Not until this very minute."

Treves paused for a moment before continuing.

"Are you familiar with *neurofibromatosis?*"

"Recklinghausen's disease?"

"Right you are! It's known by both names. As you no doubt know, it causes a proliferation of cells around the delicate connective tissue surrounding nerve endings. It usually affects only the nerves and skin."

I nodded. It was indeed a rare disorder; in my dozen or so years of practice, I'd seen half as many instances of it, if that.

"But in the strange—and tragic—case of John Merrick, the disease has run rampant over his entire body with alarming consequences. Not only that, but it has affected his *bones* as well, with the most monstrously deforming results ..."

"Doctor Treves, is Merrick free to come and go as he pleases?" asked Holmes.

"In what sense do you mean? Certainly in the legal, or medical sense he is free to go wherever he pleases at any time. He is not bound here. Yet, considering his frightful appearance, he remains a voluntary recluse in these chambers since even a brief glance at his form has caused people to go into shock."

"Was Merrick here three nights ago?" pursued Holmes.

"Now that you mention it, Mr. Holmes, that night he made one of his rare nocturnal excursions. He goes about after dark, and clothed in the most amazing rig of garments you have ever laid eyes on."

"Is this part of the wardrobe?" enquired my companion, holding up the strange slipper he had found the previous night.

"Dear me, so it is! Where did you find it? Merick will be most grateful I'm sure. But come along, you may see him now, if your nerves and stomach can take it."

He led us to a closed door and turned the knob. He was about to open it when he hesitated, turned to us, and spoke.

"I know you two gentlemen, considering your many dangerous adventures together, have stronger nerves than most people. Still in all, I must caution even you Watson, who have seen so many medical oddities and loathsome sights, that you surely have never seen a human so horribly disfigured as the man who lies beyond this door. Likewise Mr. Holmes, even considering the myriad smashed corpses you have examined closely—the countless maimed and injured on either side of the law—the person you are about to meet is all the more horrid and pathetic because he is *alive*, trapped inside his own monstrous form."

He then opened the door and led us in. In the centre of the large room was a bed with a hospital screen round it. We approached this, and Treves drew back the screen partially, revealing a foot that was so hideous that, despite my inner steeling and Treves' words of warning, I could not suppress a short gasp.

The foot didn't in the least resemble a human one, as Holmes and I had surmised from inspecting the slipper that had covered it. It was a flat slab of lumpy flesh. The skin was of a warty texture, resembling a head of cauliflower.

"You can see gentlemen, the extent of poor Merrick's plight. When he was first confined here the attending nurse, who was not forewarned of his appearance, fainted dead away at the sight of him."

With this, Treves then slowly slid the screen back to reveal the pitiable wretch who lay stretched upon the bed. His skin throughout was of the same lumpy, fibrous appearance as we had observed on his foot. But in addition, the limbs themselves were grotesquely twisted and gnarled.

The back was bowed as a hunchback's, and from his chest, neck and back there hung great masses of lumpy flesh. The head was most gruesome of all, for it was nearly twice normal size, and had protruding from it—where the face should have been—a number of bony masses, loaflike in shape and covered with the same loathsome, fungeous-looking skin. The projection near the mouth was huge, and stuck out like a pink stump, turning the upper lip inside out, leaving the mouth a cavernous fissure. This singular deformity gave the appearance of a rudimentary trunk. It, coupled with the cauliflower-like skin, was obviously responsible for the epithet of "elephant man."

"Dear God ..." I murmured, against my will, and found myself involuntarily looking away. But the next moment, I observed Sherlock Holmes, and felt ashamed at myself. For my companion, although obviously revolted by this disgusting specimen of humanity, bore not the look of loathing upon his face, but pity. Obviously, whatever personal reaction he had to viewing Merrick was eclipsed by his pity for the poor wretch. Once again I was struck by the compassion and sympathy that so clearly marked his character, and which lay so close under the surface of his cold exterior.

Treves asked us to shake hands with Merrick who, he assured us, despite his strange appearance, enjoyed meeting people from the outside world, particularly when they showed no fright at meeting him. Holmes, typically composed, strode forward and extended his hand in greeting. To my amazement, I saw that one part, at least, of Merrick's body was completely free from the scourge that had transfigured him. It was his left arm, which he eagerly thrust in my companion's direction.

It was not only normal; it was beautiful. Finely shaped and covered with skin of a delicate, glowing texture, it was a limb any woman might have envied. The other arm, by contrast, resembled the rest of Merrick's body. In fact, there was no distinguishing between the palm and the back of the hand. The thumb looked like a stunted raddish, whilst the fingers resembled twisted carrots.

Holmes grasped the normal arm and shook Merrick heartily by the hand. The wretch babbled something unintelligible, but it was obvious from general tone of the reply, and the excited twitching of his prostrate form, that he was delighted to meet my companion. I followed suit, and found that, once having become accustomed to the hideous appearance of the man, being in his company was not at all unbearable.

"As you can no doubt surmise," said Treves in an offhand way, "Merrick's facial deformities render normal speech impossible. You can see that his speech has a slurred quality, and seems to issue from a deep cavern rather than from a mouth. I therefore, will translate his responses to you Mr. Holmes, as I have grown accustomed to his utterances and can discern their meaning."

So for the next hour Holmes plied the man with questions. The man answered willingly enough, with a boyish enthusiasm and desire to please (he was, in fact, a very young man, though telling it from looking at him was, of course, impossible).

"Now John, I want you to remember all you can about the last several days," began Holmes. "First of all, where did you go Monday night, and why did you go there?"

The wretch babbled and snorted an unintelligible reply which Treves quickly translated.

"He went to the circus grounds to seek a job. Ah Mr. Holmes, that would make some sense. You see, up until recently John was forced to make his 'living,' if such it could be called, by exhibiting himself as an oddity at local fairgrounds and circuses, right John?"

The man nodded his huge head slowly in sadness.

"But now, thanks to the public's concern and generosity, he need no longer worry about being gaped and jeered at. Obviously, he went to the circus unaware of his endowment, and reluctantly, yet he reasoned it was that or starve. Well you needn't worry any longer my friend ..."

Here Holmes and I stared dumbstruck as the man threw his head down upon his deformed chest and wept with joy and relief, the tears covering his monstrous face. I could almost have wept myself, so pathetic was the sight of this poor creature who had endured so much, without a friend or comforter in the world. And yet, were tears to come to my eyes, they would also have been tears of joy and renewed faith in the human heart: for now clearly John Merrick *had* friends and comforters, and his life as a public horror had drawn to a close.

"He went to the grounds that night," Treves continued, "alone and in secret, as strictly instructed by the circus representative—"

Holmes and I glared at each other. We had little doubt as to the identity of the "representative."

"And did you meet this man at the edge of the grounds?" pursued Holmes.

"Yes he did," continued Treves. "He was helped over the fence and led into a narrow tunnel in the tent. There he was told to remain, squatting in his great cloak, which conceals him in public, until the signal was given."

"And what was the signal?"

"When the flaps were raised, Merrick was to fling off his cloak, rise up and wave his limbs about. Thereupon, he was told, the flaps would immediately close again, and he was to refasten his cloak and scurry outside again the same instant—returning to the hospital secretly, and telling no one of this 'audition.'"

"Was he paid, or offered employment?" I asked.

"He was paid two pounds for his appearance which is, as we know, remarkably good pay. If the owners decided to hire him, he was to be notified in a week. Otherwise, he was strictly instructed to keep the matter quiet, accepting the generous payment for his efforts."

Merrick answered all the questions in a forthright manner, obviously blissfully unaware of the nefarious purpose to which his "appearance" had been put.

"Finally John, can you please describe this representative who approached you?"

When we heard the description, which fit Vladimir Vayenko in every detail, we knew the last piece of the puzzle had fallen into place. However, so as not to upset Merrick, Holmes and I departed without further questions.

"Well, we've truly met a *monster* on this case Watson," remarked Holmes as he hailed a cab, "although it's not the poor follow who lies yonder ..."

"The coward! Rather than face his rival directly, he chose to seek revenge by killing his loved one!"

"Yes. But I'm sure the revenge was *direct* as well. Love can turn quickly to hate as you know. He never forgave Anna for throwing him away for Zolnay."

"And to use poor Merrick as the means—after all the wretched soul has been through ..."

"It is ugly in every respect, Watson. Also, considering his recent actions towards me, I'm convinced that, like most cowards, Vayenko is a bully."

"Lucky for him he didn't choose to confront you on the ground!"

"I was thinking the same thing. Like most heavily-muscled men, he would be slow to the punch and block. But we digress. The question is: what to do now?"

"Why summon the police of course! It's clear now that Vayenko caused Anna's death: he somehow rigged the flaps so they could be opened from the far platform. Then, just as Anna began her difficult stunt, he opened them quickly, revealing a sight so horrid that she lost control—"

"Yes, of course. *We* know that's what happened. But who else would believe us? Zolnay, due to his position high up on the centre bar saw nothing. Anna is dead. We have poor Merrick, who can scarcely speak. Can you imagine his appearing in a public court-room against Vayenko? On whose side would the jury's sympathy lie? Also, who would believe such an outlandish tale? The only evidence that Vayenko was directly related to a *planned* act was his closing of the tent before the rehearsal. No Watson, it won't do. Vayenko is a coward and a blackguard, but a deucedly clever one. Somehow, probably in connection with his career, he became acquainted with the whereabouts of Merrick, the *elephant man*, and has used the unfortunate man in a diabolically clever murder."

"Is there nothing we can do then?" I asked with a curse.

"Yes," he answered after several minutes of deep thought. "That is why we're headed for Chipperfield's."

* * *

Once again we found the circus people, usually so gay and sociable, downcast in clouds of fear and gloom. To add to their woes the weather had turned cold and rainy with heavy winds. This is the worst possible weather for the circus, and attendance had fallen to a mere trickle. Accordingly nobody seemed surprised, in fact most seemed relieved, when Lamar Chipperfield announced the afternoon show postponed. Holmes and I ambled along the back yard, splashing through puddles and watching the performers idle about. Most were snug in their caravans, and from the noise issuing from many of them, we could tell that the ale and calavados were flowing freely. Passing close by some of them, we heard more talk of the *hoodoo*, and how the ugly weather was but one manifestation of the dead monkey's curse.

We found Zolnay in his wagon, brooding over a bottle of *schnapps*. He welcomed us warmly, and managed to keep a composed exterior for several minutes before breaking down into a fit of weeping. We comforted him as best we could. Then my companion, fixing his steely gaze upon the Hungarian giant, said in a low whisper: "Mr. Zolnay, Dr. Watson and myself are close to finding the solution to your beloved Anna's death. But there remains one matter that must be attended to. Will you help us?"

As expected, he complied fully and eagerly.

"Good," continued Holmes. "Now tonight, the doctor and I shall return here to your caravan. We will arrive late, when everyone should be asleep. Do not tell anyone of our intended visit, not even Larkin. Is that clear?"

"Yes, Mr. Holmes. But is there nothing more you can tell me about my poor Anna?"

"Not at this time, I'm afraid. Just be here at one o'clock fully dressed. *Adieu.*"

To my surprise, we retraced our route back to London Hospital. There, Holmes dashed from the cab, telling me to wait. In less than ten minutes he came bounding back, a hospital laundry bag slung over his shoulder.

"Marvelous fellow Treves, and most cooperative as well," said he after directing the cabbie to Baker Street.

"Eh, what's in the bag Holmes?"

"Tut! You shall find out soon enough dear fellow. I think I have devised a rather clever way for Vayenko to confess his guilt, as you shall see tonight. Now where shall we dine? It's my turn to treat, is it not?"

* * *

Shortly after mid-night Holmes roused me from my fitful dosing in front of the fireplace.

"I must say I sometimes envy your lethargic nature Watson," he remarked, drawing on his coat, "you seem to be able to sleep anywhere at any time, regardless of impending action. Well, up you go and let's be off. But first, will you lend me your leather coin purse?"

We arrived at the circus grounds shortly before the appointed hour. I was dumbstruck to see that Holmes had brought the laundry bag with him, as well as a walking stick. It certainly had my curiosity up. We were about to scale the fence when the sound of measured footfalls reached our ears.

"Watchman!" cried Holmes in a hoarse whisper. "Drat! I'd forgotten him."

But we scurried behind a wagon until the man passed, then scaled the fence without difficulty. Slinking from shadow to shadow, we worked our way to Zolnay's caravan. We were careful to avoid the menagerie wagons, for if aroused, the lions would certainly betray our presence.

We entered the wagon and Holmes instructed Zolnay to light a single taper, keeping the curtains drawn tight over all the windows. He then stood before Zolnay's bunk and proceeded to empty the contents of the laundry bay upon it. Out tumbled a ragged pile of clothes, including the strangest, and largest, cap I have ever seen.

"Good Lord Holmes, what on earth–?"

"John Merrick's walking apparel, Watson. Treves is correct, a most amazing—not to say *outlandish*—bit of haberdashery eh? You see how clever it is? Not a bit of the person can be seen. Notice especially the hat. See the canvas visor that hangs down on all sides? The eye slit is the only opening. Now the cloak, as you can see, actually is more of a tent. The long sleeves conceal the arms. These mittens somewhat resemble the coarse 'slipper' we examined at our quarters ..."

Zolnay stared silently in amazement as Holmes held up each strange article.

"Finally," he continued, "we have these baggy trousers, which I shall now draw on over my own ..."

I was beginning to follow Holmes' scheme, and had an inkling of the purpose to which he would put my leather coin purse.

"Now the two of you must help me. Master of disguise that I am, impersonating the 'elephant man' will surely be my most ambitious enterprise to date. Now Watson, fetch those two rolls of sticking plaster will you. Zolnay, if you'd be good enough to wad up that newspaper yonder and stuff it into this great hat—hardly a task worthy of your strength—that's a good fellow."

Next he brought out an empty snuff tin from his coat. I noticed that its bottom had been removed so that, with the lid off, it became a metal tube about four inches in length. To my utter amazement,

Holmes placed the tube against his mouth and, with my help, fastened it there securely with the sticking plaster. When next he spoke, it was in a hollow, distorted voice remarkably similar to Merrick's!

"This miniature megaphone does the trick eh? And the cap's visor will keep it well-concealed."

He then drew on the grotesque slippers and gloves, finally topping off the disguise with the giant peaked cap, from which hung down, from all sides, the curtain of cloth. And when he hobbled about the caravan with his cane, bent over in the strange costume and babbling incoherently behind the visor, the transformation into Merrick, the "elephant man," was complete. Zolnay continued to gape in confusion until Holmes, unable to keep him in the dark any longer, explained our night-time mission: Holmes, impersonating Merrick, was to go to Vayenko's wagon—in the dead of night as Merrick would have been forced to do—and ask for more money for performing his "feat." Hopefully Vayenko's reaction would implicate him. As expected, the Hungarian trembled with wrath, and almost burst from his wagon in fury to seek the Russian. Holmes and I restrained him with difficulty.

"There, there old fellow! I've gone to much trouble to arrange this nocturnal visit. If properly carried off, Vayenko will hang. Seek revenge now, and *you* could hang, and Anna's killer will go free."

The man saw our logic and restrained himself, yet I could hear that his breathing was heavy and fast, and he swore an oath under his breath as we departed the wagon.

We ambled about in the dark with Holmes in the lead. I was surprised that he headed towards the fence instead of Vayenko's wagon. But his intentions were made clear by the silent approach of a figure who had been waiting near the fence. In a moment, Lestrade was standing beside us.

We made our way to Vayenko's wagon. There Holmes bade us crawl underneath it and sit behind the rear axle. From there, we had a clear view of Holmes as he stood at the foot of the ladder. I felt the excitement growing in me, and noticed that Zolnay's agitation had increased still; he clenched and unclenched his huge fists and ground his teeth in rage. We hadn't long to wait. The "elephant man" hobbled up the steps and rapped upon the wagon's door with his walking stick. A long silence followed, and Holmes rapped a second time. We then heard a thumping and stumbling above us, and the door opened with a curse.

"Who's there?" cried a voice still heavy with drink. "What do you want?"

Holmes backed down the ladder and held up my coin purse. We could hear the unintelligible, hollow groaning that issued from his mask.

"Oh it's *you* is it?" said Vayenko in a threatening tone. "What have you come back for? I told you not to return!"

Yet Holmes remained, holding up the purse and groaning.

"You monster! You have your nerve, you hideous beast! What are you trying to tell me eh? What?"

Holmes was busy gesticulating with his arms and mumbling. We could see he was trying to indicate a fall from a high place.

"Ah, so you know of *that* do you?" said Vayenko in a low voice. "So you saw her fall. You have discovered my little scheme, eh? And you now want more money to keep quiet ..."

There was a period of silence. Holmes stood still, as if to indicate that that was indeed what he wanted. When Vayenko spoke next, his voice was full of treachery.

"See here man. People will hear us talking out here, won't you come inside my wagon? There we can share a bottle and discuss the payment ..."

Holmes backed off, still holding the purse upraised towards Vayenko, who began to descend the ladder towards my companion.

"No need to be afraid Merrick. I'll pay you five pounds not to tell anyone about Anna's death ..."

At that instant, the Russian lunged at Holmes, who would have raised his stick in defence were it not for the cloth that covered his face and so affected his vision. For the night was dark to begin with, and the small eye slit rendered him almost blind. Likewise the loosely draped clothes hindered his normally quick limbs, and Holmes fell beneath the rush of the heavy man.

Vayenko was no doubt surprised that the man he supposed to be stunted and clumsy was in fact a sinewy boxer of tremendous strength. After recovering from his momentary disadvantage, Holmes dealt his attacker two quick punches to the face. His blows staggered the acrobat, who seized the cane Holmes had dropped. Although we three had already sprung from our hiding place and were racing towards the two combatants, we were too late to prevent Vayenko from striking Holmes on the side of the head and knocking him to the ground. The man turned in time to see us, and went pale with terror at the sight of Zolnay bearing down on him.

I knelt down over Holmes, who was not seriously hurt, though he had a nasty welt on the side of his face. We heard the din of running feet and shouted oaths as he removed the awkward disguise and joined me in pursuit. Before we had gone ten steps however, there came a scream that froze the blood in my veins. It was filled with terror and agony, and ended abruptly in a hoarse choke.

Owing to the darkness, it was several minutes before we discovered the body. By this time scores of people had joined us at the site, as we gazed at the twisted figure that lay bent backwards over a wagon tongue. Vayenko's eyes were open, and showed the ghostly white of death. His head was flung backwards at a grotesque angle, the back of the neck resting on the wooden beam. A quick inspection with my hands revealed what I had thought from the first: his neck was snapped entirely through. We called for a lantern, and in the light Holmes pointed out four great bruises upon the dead man's forehead. Each was the size of a shilling. Holmes attempted to place his fingers upon them but they were far too wide apart. In my mind's eye I swiftly recalled the great gloves that had enveloped my hand, and had no doubts as to how Vladimir Vayenko had met his death. Holmes shot a knowing glance in my direction.

"You see Watson," see whispered softly, "using this projecting wagon tongue as a fulcrum, and placing his hand along Vayenko's forehead, he bent the head back—"

"Yes I know," I said shortly. Certainly only a man with superhuman strength could have broken the massive neck of Vayenko. Yet I felt no remorse for the scoundrel who lay at our feet. Moreover, my concern was for the Hungarian giant, who was no doubt at that very instant in flight for his life across the fields of Wimbledon.

I felt a jostling at my side and saw Lestrade, recently arrived, peering down at the corpse.

"How did this fellow meet his end?" he enquired. "Did he fall in the dark and break his neck?"

Holmes and I glanced at each other momentarily.

"That would certainly seem possible," admitted Holmes noncommittally.

"And the other fellow, where is he?"

"We've no idea," I replied. "I say Lestrade, shouldn't I call a hospital van? Eh? Yes, I'll do so directly whilst you and Holmes see to matters here." By the time the van arrived Lestrade, still assuming Vayenko's death was accidental, had lost all interest in Zolnay. Holmes and I suspected that he was hiding in one of the many caravans belonging to his friends, or else was flying from London, and the horrendous events he was part of—aboard an express train.

"Wherever he may be," mused Holmes as we made our way back to the flat as dawn was breaking, "I wish him Godspeed."

EPILOGUE

But in the end, the *hoodoo* claimed its final victim.

Scarcely two months after our adventure with Zolnay the aerialist, Holmes interrupted our morning tea with the announcement that Merrick was dead. The piece in the *Telegraph* was brief, and obviously devoid of the pain and pathos that had marked the tragic life of young John Merrick:

"Elephant Man" Dies in Sleep

London, August 24—John Merrick, the human monstrosity known also as the "Elephant Man," died in his sleep last night in his private room at London Hospital. According to Dr. Frederick Treves, the physician in attendance, death occurred around 3:00 a.m., and was caused by a dislocation of the neck. Dr. Treves explained that Merrick was accustomed to sleeping in an upright position, yet, perhaps to fulfill his lifelong dream to "be like other people," he had this night attempted to sleep recumbent, with the result that his massive head—over three times normal size and weight, must have fallen back upon the soft pillow in such a fashion as to dislocate the vertebrae and sever major nerves. All evidence seems to point to a peaceful, if untimely death, since the coverlets weren't in the slightest disturbed. In accordance with a voluntary arrangement with the hospital, the body shall be donated to the Medical School of the University of London. Merrick was 27 years old.

"Poor chap," I said. "At least his death was quick and painless."

"I suppose that adds to the irony. The poor fellow seems to have been fortunate only in death. The more I ponder upon it Watson, the real hero of this adventure was Merrick. He bore his pain and suffering stoically, with tremendous fortitude and bravery. Think of it! Think of his childhood Watson! Abandoned as a horror by his mother—sold to a local fair at the age of four. Treated as a living monster by the human race, mocked and scorned by children his own age—shut up for days on end in dreary closets and cold compartments! And after this living hell, he emerges not only unscathed, but *grateful* for his last few months in Bedstead Square! Was there ever in human history a tale of greater courage?"

I glanced out the window and sighed.

"Thank the Lord for people like Treves, and the British public," I said at last.

"Amen Watson. And now, on a cheerier note, I have a surprise for you which I know you'll like. I received this package yesterday. You notice the postmark?"

"... Salzberg ..."

"Open it Watson," said Holmes, gleefully rubbing his hands.

I tore off the brown wrappings and found within a cardboard box containing two leathern cases, each the size of a butter loaf.

"One is for you, the other for me," he said. "Would you prefer the fullbent or the bulldog?"

His question reached my ears as I was opening one of the leathern cases, revealing the handsomest meerschaum pipe I'd ever laid eyes on. Its bowl glowed with a creamy lustre, and the amber mouthpiece was a radiant golden hue.

"Holmes, a pipe like this is worth a fortune! Who wishes to bestow gifts like these upon us?"

"I've no idea Watson," he answered with a twinkle in his eye, "yet he enclosed his calling card—here it is—"

He flung a grey flannel glove in my direction.

"Now let's see if we can discern his identity: he is rich, yet not a gentleman, and seems to make his living by performing physical feats of the most prodigious sort ..."

AUTHOR'S NOTES FOR THE STORY
"THE ADVENTURE OF ZOLNAY, THE AERIALIST"

John Merrick, "The Elephant Man," actually lived. His disease, and consequent deformities, were as described in the story. Furthermore, the history of his life was, for the most part, as it was told. Frederick Treves was the greatest London physician of his time—with the exception of course, of John H. Watson. It was Treves who befriended Merrick and, with the assistance of Carr Gomm (the director of London Hospital) obtained private quarters in the hospital and an endowment to sustain Merrick for the rest of his days which were few in number. Aside from this gallant show of philanthropy, Treves is perhaps best known for removing the inflamed appendix of Edward VII on the eve of his coronation.

For a detailed account of Merrick's life, see Treves' book "*The Elephant Man and Other Reminiscences,*" or the excellent review of the book (and a capsule summary of Merrick's unfortunate life) by Ashley Montagu that appeared in the March 1971 issue of *Natural History* magazine.

This story was written with my friend Tom Zolnay especially in mind. He knows "Vayenko" only too well, having escaped from Hungary in 1956.

RLB

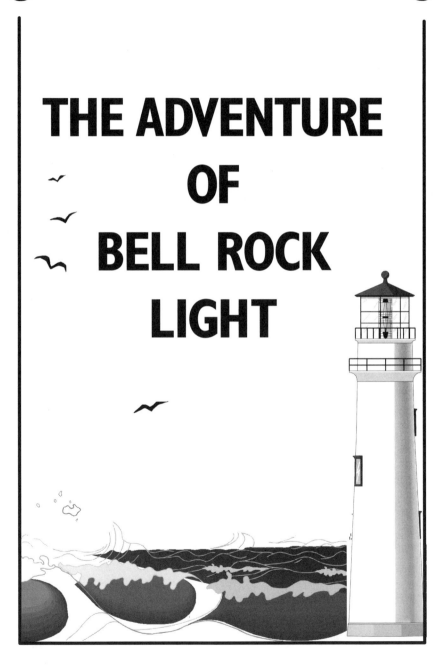

THE ADVENTURE OF BELL ROCK LIGHT

PART ONE: THE PROBLEM

I t was I, not Sherlock Holmes, who suggested we holiday in
Scotland.
"The choice is yours, Watson," he remarked as he lighted his
after-breakfast pipe. "Really, it's only fair, since you're the one who's
convalescing."

It was true: the thigh wound inflicted by Killer Evans a month
earlier was still a trifle sore.* Still and all, I considered myself hale
and hearty compared to my friend, who was affected by the Prescott
Forgery case far more than one would have suspected. Perhaps he
felt it was through his actions that I was wounded. Whatever the case,
he was clearly more in need of a holiday than was I. Considering his
needs, I felt compelled to name Scotland as our place of respite. With
its cool streams bursting with trout, its fragrant heather-clad meadows and highland vistas—surely this North country was the spot for
us.

As I had supposed, Holmes gave in to my suggestion eagerly.

"Capital idea Watson! I've a friend named Clive Wallace who
lives in Arbroath on the Firth of Tay. I haven't seen him in years.
Would you object if we put up with him for a few days? He's been
after me to visit him for some time now, and has a lovely sea cliff
cottage—"

"Say no more," I returned, "It sounds splendid. I need to exercise
this leg regularly, and shall do so now by stopping round at the ticket
office and booking our passage on Thursday's Scotch Express.
Meantime I trust you'll notify Wallace."

*At the close of the *Adventure of the Three Garridebs*

Holmes wired his friend, who the following day returned a cordial invitation. Holmes brightened as he read the wire.

"Aha!" he exclaimed.

"What is it?"

"Oh nothing," said he, quickly folding the scrap of paper into his pocket. "Well then, are you all packed and ready? The express departs at dawn you know. Mrs. Hudson, dear woman, has packed us a lunch of cold tongue and plums, and has further volunteered to arise at the ungodly hour of four and fix our breakfast."

Early next morning we were rattling northwards in a carriage all to ourselves. Our holiday gear, including fishing rods, tennis racquets, golf clubs, and two bulging carpetbags, were piled high on the neighbouring seats.

"Ah Holmes, to think of the quiet countryside! Hundreds of miles from the nearest criminal. Surely this is what we both need, eh?"

"Exactly. And our visit should be enlivened by this."

He leaned forward and handed me the crumpled wire he had received the previous day. It read as follows:

DELIGHTED YOU AND WATSON COMING UP.
SHALL MEET YOU AT TRAIN. HOPE YOU CAN
SHED LIGHT ON MYSTERY AT BELL ROCK.
YOURS, WALLACE.

"Saints Alive! Is there no escape from it? Both of us are in need of rest, yet on the advent of this much-deserved holiday you receive a wire from your old school chum inviting you in on another case! I tell you we shall go to our graves early, and none but ourselves to blame."

"Ah, you are too hasty Watson. You and I both know there is no rest like enjoyable work. This problem may prove interesting. I haven't seen Wallace in years, but know that he is in the government service with the Commissioners of Northern Lights. Now Bell Rock–"

"–Bell Rock. I've heard of it. It sounds like a famous bit of granite, like the Blarney Stone perhaps?"

"No. Bell Rock is a treacherous reef lying twelve miles off the east coast of Scotland. You may have seen me poking into my atlas and almanacs just before we quit our flat. But you weren't far off the mark when you guessed it was a 'famous bit of granite,' for Bell Rock Lighthouse is a famous granite tower. Built directly on the reef, it is in a very precarious situation–exposed to the horrendous winds and waves of the North Sea ..."

"It sounds too strenuous for my blood," I said, snuggling into the cushions in preparation for a nap. "What I long for is a calm stroll on the cliffs, a day's fishing in a mountain brook, a full morning's tennis, at half-pace if you please ..."

I dozed fitfully for the remainder of the journey. The swaying of a railway carriage and the muted thumping of its wheels are generally a fine producer of sleep. However, I confess I was alarmed by the wire sufficiently so that I found sleep hard to come by, however needed. In strange contrast, my companion seemed elated by the promise of adventure and mystery. He rubbed his hands in anticipation, and would have fairly danced with glee had the carriage been large enough. I was appalled.

It was mid-afternoon by the time we quit the train at Dundee. True to his word, Clive Wallace met us with a carriage. I was glad it was not an open one, for although it was midsummer—towards the end of July—a chilly sea wind was up.

Wallace was the picture of a Scotsman: large and rugged with a kindly smile, he wore huge mutton-chops and had the glowing, ruddy face that comes with a life spent out-of-doors. He was dressed in thick tweeds, from his Norfolk jacket to his knickers, and topped off his apparel with a tam. He greeted us pleasantly and we commenced the three-hour jaunt to Arbroath.

Holmes, unable to contain his curiosity, prodded him for the details of the mystery.

"Ah Holmes, I see you haven't changed at all. But stay if you please till we arrive home. It will be much better to explain the circumstances warmed by the fire and a dram. Besides, it is rather complex, and will require the aid of drawings, and paper and pen."

And so we watched the rugged beauty of Scotland sweep by as we jounced over the gravel roads to the seaside town of Arbroath. We stopped there only long enough for Wallace to jump from the coach and return a few minutes later, arms overbrimming with good things to eat and drink. In a very short while the carriage swung to a stop. Wallace paid the driver and as the rattle of the wheels died away, I became aware of the sound of surf. In the fading light of day, we wound our way down a footpath. At its termination stood a white-washed cottage, perched on the summit of a seacliff that fell away sharply to the beach one-hundred feet below. It was utterly charming: the perfect place to live. We stowed our parcels and went for a walk before returning to the cottage at sunset. Wallace lighted a roaring fire in the corner fireplace. Like the rest of the cottage inside and out, it was whitewashed–but blackened with the smoke of a thousand fires. He drew out a bottle of single-malt whiskey and poured liberal portions for all. Perhaps it was the cold sea air or my recent wound, but it was some time before I stopped shivering and the warmth of the whiskey and fire went through me.

"Now then," said Holmes with an authoritative air as he lighted his pipe, "here we are all settled, and it's time for you to tell two eager listeners–pardon me Watson–one eager listener, the story of the strange occurrence at Bell Rock."

"Quite so," mused our friend. "Now let me start by telling both of you that I am in the employ of the Commissioner of the Northern Lights. In Scotland, this body has the responsibility for the location, construction, and maintenance of the scores of lighthouses that dot our rugged coasts. As the district supervisor, I have direct responsibility for all buoys, channel markers, fog signals and lights within this region. *Dear Holmes! I'm at my wits end–.*"

Here I was most profoundly struck by the change in Wallace's expression. He looked at my friend with a face full of pleading and desperation.

Holmes grasped his arm in reassurance.

"There Wallace. Steady old fellow! Now tell us all, and we'll set off at once to try and set things right, won't we Watson? There now, please proceed."

With a heavy sigh, our friend continued his narrative.

"You should first know that on the eighteenth of June, Robert Ross, one of the three keepers of Bell Rock Light, was found dead. There are reasons to think it was murder."

There was a moment of stunned silence.

"But before I proceed further with this recent event, I feel it necessary to provide both of you with some important background information regarding lighthouses, and Bell Rock in particular. For when you are fully acquainted with the facts surrounding this famous structure, you will be lead, as I was, to the inescapable conclusion that Robert Ross was murdered by one of his fellow lightkeepers."

Holmes' face bore a look of rapt attention. His eyes shone with excitement and eagerness. From that moment forth, I knew there was to be no turning back; we were entangled in the mystery of Bell Rock.

After stirring the fire and throwing on two slabs of fragrant peat, Wallace excused himself and returned a moment later with a pile of papers and drawings.

"Now gentlemen, much of this case hinges on the fact that the murder, death, occurred in a light tower. As will soon become apparent, the location and structure of Bell Rock tower is unique, and forces us to several conclusions, as I have already hinted. First of all, let me explain that there are basically *two types* of lighthouses: land-based and waveswept. As one might imagine, the land-based structures are situated on hills or cliffs overlooking the oceans–locations very similar to the one this cottage occupies. Safe from the pounding of the seas, they are buffeted only by the wind and weather. Consequently, they may be no stronger than a house, and in fact assume all sorts of shapes and proportions. Also, they are mostly made of brick masonry, but occasionally of wood..."

I felt that Wallace's digression was a trifle lengthy, but my companion, ever-diligent when it came to details, leaned forward on the edge of his chair in profound concentration. Watching him for only a second, I was instantly aware that his previous lethargy and depression had vanished in a twinkling. How foolish of me to suppose that what Holmes wanted was a leisurely fishing trip!

"... now the *second* type of lighthouse ... the second type is far, far different. It has perhaps occurred to you that places where the need of a guiding light is greatest are also sites where it is most difficult to construct light towers, and the most inhospitable areas in which to live. I am speaking of course, of the treacherous and deadly rocks and shoals far at sea."

"And these are the wave-swept lights?" I asked.

"Yes, Doctor. And to give you an example, I have here a rare photograph of Bell Rock tower under heavy surf, so you can judge for yourself the meaning of the phrase 'wave-swept.'"

He handed me a cardboard print.

"Good gracious Wallace! I can scarcely see the light!"

Holmes, looking at the photograph over my shoulder, gave a low whistle of amazement. The print was somewhat blurred, owing to the fact that the photographer was forced to ply his craft from a small boat rather than steady ground. But however imperfect, the photo was dramatic to say the least. The huge lighthouse was engulfed in water and spray. The sea swirled and foamed white round the tower's base. High fingers of spume arched up and away from the sloping walls and gallery. The massive wave was a mountain of solid water on the windward side of the tower, and a seething cavern of current on the other. The only visible part of the lighthouse was a portion of the lantern, at the very summit of the tower.

"Good heavens man, and people live in these things?"

"I can assure you they do indeed Doctor. And it is my job to see that they perform their vital duties well—and, if possible, with a happy heart."

He assumed a sad and forlorn look.

"My dear Holmes, the principle reason I'm so desirous of a solution to this problem is to discover what I've done wrong. How did I fail these men? What wish was left unfulfilled so that they would feud and fight, and eventually destroy each other? What conditions were so wretched that these carefully selected people should be enemies instead of supportive comrades in a noble calling? If it is not resolved I have sworn on my honour to leave the service—"

His voice trailed off in a broken sob of despair.

Once again Holmes showed his second-greatest strength which was, after crime detection, the setting-at-ease of the unfortunate.

"Now Wallace, no time for remorse! Continue please with your interesting discourse on wave-swept lighthouses. I'd no idea they were so awesome and romantic ..."

After a deep swallow of soothing malt whiskey, Wallace continued.

"The pressure of the wave stroke upon the structures is immense. It has been measured at Bishop Rock light, in the Outer Hebrides, to be several tons per square foot. You can well imagine the incredible lateral forces that act upon a light tower a hundred feet tall and thirty feet wide ... It was at Bishop Rock, bye the bye, that a fog bell weighing two tons was swept away from its mountings on the gallery, a hundred and forty feet above the sea, by a giant wave! It was flung away as a bug is flicked off a leaf ..."

Holmes and I looked at each other in awe.

"It is a wonder the towers don't collapse!" said I.

"Many have Watson, and would still today, were it not for an engineer named John Smeaton, who built the first great granite tower at Eddystone. Now Smeaton knew that it was a simple matter of physics that heavy objects are more difficult to dislodge than light ones. So he built his tower of huge granite blocks that were dovetailed on all sides to one another. All wave-swept towers since have borne a striking resemblance to this one. In fact, the oldest tower still standing is the one at Bell Rock, built by Robert Stevenson in 1811. Now here is a diagram of it which will illustrate the points I wish to make:

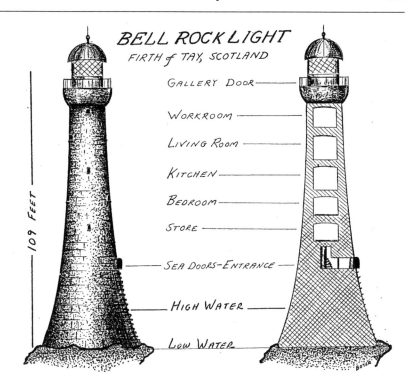

BELL ROCK LIGHT
FIRTH of TAY, SCOTLAND

GALLERY DOOR

WORKROOM

LIVING ROOM

KITCHEN

BEDROOM

STORE

SEA DOORS-ENTRANCE

HIGH WATER

LOW WATER

109 FEET

"Now gentlemen, mind how this tower embodies the *three basic principles* Smeaton incorporated in his first tower. They are these: *First,* the tower be massive and have a low centre of gravity. You will notice that the bottom third of the tower is solid granite–the entranceway being located thirty feet up the side and reached by a ladder. *Second*: the tower should be circular, which it is, to offer minimal resistance to the wave strokes from any direction. *Finally,* the outside of the tower should be absolutely smooth–free from any projections and appurtenances that would offer additional resistance to the waves. Notice also that in the interests of maximum weight and strength, the tower windows are tiny–far too small for a man to pass through. Now note please the five rooms inside the tower, placed one above the other. Most keepers of shore lighthouses may live in dwellings nearby with their families, and ascend the tower only to tend the lights. But of course in wave-swept towers the men are forced to remain in the structure for as long as their tour of duty lasts. The crews consist of three men. They are, as someone once said, voluntary prisoners in vertical dungeons."

"How long does a tour of duty last?" I asked.

"Two months. Then each man is granted a month's shore leave before returning. But sometimes, if there is continued heavy weather, the men must remain without relief and oftentimes without adequate food and supplies. Now it is interesting to note that the tower is an up-side down house. That is, the bedrooms and storerooms are the lower chambers, since they should be located furthest away from the workroom—the scene of daily work and activity—whilst the living room and kitchen are, as you can see in the drawing, located high up, just under the lantern.

"An important point is this: the rooms are connected by a spiral iron stairway that passes from one level to the next. *It is impossible to go from one end of the tower to the other without passing through each and every room.* Do you follow me?"

We nodded in silence.

"Now gentlemen, let me again stress the following points: first, the *isolation* of this structure and the danger involved in approaching it in even the mildest weather; secondly, the *single entranceway*, thirty feet above the raging currents and roaring surf, which is secured by two heavy iron sea-doors; and finally, the *smooth face* of the tower, broken only by several tiny windows. Do you see what I am leading up to?"

"Of course. The three men were, as you put it, prisoners in the tower. There were no other parties involved—there couldn't have been," I said, "so if indeed there was murder done, then the culprit is one of the remaining two lightkeepers, or perhaps both."

"Excellent! There is really no other possible explanation. But *which one*? Ah, that is the puzzle. Now let me relate in greater detail the events of last June 18th."

Holmes and I drew our chairs yet closer to the Scotsman. We sat upon the edges of them and leaned forward intently. The only sound was the faint purr of the fire.

"The two survivors, John Cormack and George Hay, both agree that the last time all three men were together was in early evening of the day in question, just after supper. Now for lightkeepers, the day is divided into six four-hour watches, the day beginning at noon. Thus it was at 8:00 p.m. that the murdered man Ross took the third watch—the one commencing at that hour and ending at midnight— and ascended the stairway from the kitchen to the lantern to light the lamps and set the revolving clockwork in motion. The man to follow him was Hay, who remained in the kitchen two levels below the workroom to smoke his pipe and read a novel. The third man Cormack complained of sleepiness and announced he was retiring to the bedroom, one level below the kitchen, for a rest. It should perhaps be mentioned here Holmes, that this was not Cormack's usual custom, for he and Hay were in the habit of playing chess after supper unless one of them had the evening watch."

"Ah Wallace, a small point," interjected Holmes. "If one of these two were to have the evening watch, would the other one engage Ross in a game?"

"I think it unlikely," said Wallace after reflection, "although I was never there to observe directly, you understand. But it has always been my impression that Cormack and Hay were on quite friendly terms, while Ross was a bit stand-offish. But this would be the natural thing you see, since he was the eldest by ten years or so."

"I see. Ross had been with you for some time then?"

"Almost three years. He became a keeper when his young wife died in childbirth He was, I must admit, a morose and ill-tempered man, though efficient."

"I see. Pray continue."

"The last contact Hay had with Ross was when he climbed halfway up the stair to the workroom and called out to Ross, asking him if he'd like a cup of tea. Ross answered that he didn't. Then all was quiet for the next three hours. Cormack claims to have been asleep for all of this period and remembers nothing. Hay claims to have been reading his novel. At least Holmes, when first questioned he claimed to have been reading. But he changed his story subsequently—"

"Ah! Let me guess: he now claims to have fallen asleep also."

Clive Wallace dropped his jaw and stared dumbstruck at my companion.

"Holmes! My Lord Holmes, that's exactly what he says! How in the world could you know—"

"I didn't say I knew Wallace. I said 'let me guess.' My guess proved correct. It's fairly obvious. Watson here can tell you why I'm sure."

"Why certainly," I replied after brief reflection, "you see Hay was accustomed to the stimulation of chess—matching wits with an opponent, that sort of thing. With the opponent absent, so was the stimulant. Ergo: he fell asleep."

Holmes shook his head impatiently.

"No, no, Watson. Really, I had higher hopes for you."

I sank back into my chair and remained silent. I could not help reflecting that Sherlock Holmes, for all his fine points, could be remarkably ill-mannered at times.

"Then how did you guess the correct answer?" asked Wallace.

"Well it's absurdly simple. You yourself said that to pass from one end of the tower to the other, one must go through each and every room. Correct? Now, supposing Ross, on watch up in the work-room is point A. Hay, in the kitchen two levels below, is point B. Then Cormack, slumbering in the bedroom beneath both of them, is point C. How can point C reach point A without the knowledge of point B? Impossible. So George Hay, having first admitted forth-rightly that he spent the entire third watch reading, later is faced with the proposition that to have done so places his neck in the noose: for if Cormack has *not* left his bedchamber, then the murderer *must* be Hay himself, correct?"

"Why Holmes, that was exactly his statement! He told me, and the inspectors too, that he did not actually remember John Cormack climbing the staircase to the workroom, but, says he, 'I was probably asleep by the warm stove for a short while, and Cormack undoubt-edly seized this opportunity to sneak past me to Ross, where he did away with him!' Holmes, you're a genius!"

"Umf," said my friend, puffing his pipe. "And what then was Cormack's story?"

"Well it was quite simple, and remains unchanged. He fell asleep shortly after suppertime and was awakened by Hay, who shook him up in the dead of night with a story of murder. Half asleep, Cormack followed Hay up the winding stairs to find the body of Ross sprawled over the workroom table. The cause of death was the inhalation of cyanide fumes. The broken glass vial was found on the floor nearby."

"What time was this?"

"At midnight, at the change of the watch."

"And did they both fly into mutual accusations?" asked Holmes.

"Curiously, from what I have gathered they did not, but assumed each other to be innocent. This was obviously a master ploy by the guilty party, whoever it is."

"But Wallace, why are you and the authorities so certain it was murder? I don't know much about lighthouses beyond what you've related to me. But I *have* heard of the terrible, lonely lives the keepers lead. You say Ross lost his wife three years ago. Perhaps he never got over the depression that followed her death ..."

"You are then suggesting suicide?" I asked.

"Certainly. It seems far more logical than murder. Where's the motive? Also, were there even a strong motive, would either keeper be foolish enough to commit the crime in a place where he knows he'll be one of *two* suspects? Also consider the method. Cyanide is a favourite vehicle for suicides because it is quick and virtually painless. On the other hand, it is an unpopular murder weapon in the gaseous form, since the murderer is equally endangered if he is at all nearby ..."

"These points are well-considered, but there's a final element in the case that I was leading up to Holmes, that makes it look very much like murder. Also, I'm afraid it draws a dark picture indeed for young Cormack. Just before he died, as he felt his strength leaving him and he began to slump over the worktable, Ross wrote a final message. He grasped the keeper's logbook and hastily wrote in big block letters, as follows."

Wallace drew a message in thick pencil on the reverse of the photograph, then handed it to us. It read:

KILLED BY CORM

"Well, well," I responded with a sigh. "That seems to settle the matter doesn't it?"

"One would think so," answered Wallace, "especially when one is made aware of the fact that two days previous to Ross' death, he and Cormack had a quarrel. Sharp words, even threats, were exchanged. Surely these two things together seem to sew it up."

"And what," asked Holmes after a short silence, "does Mr. Cormack say about this piece of damning evidence?"

"He keeps to his original story: he was sound asleep during the period in question. He's convinced it was suicide, and professes to be amazed that Ross would pen such a message, despite their recent quarrel."

"And Hay?"

"Hay claims that whether murder or suicide, he is innocent. He adds that the quarrel between Ross and Cormack that preceded Ross' death was by no means the first one. Apparently the two men had grown to hate each other, and each vowed never to serve another tour in the same company. This would seem to lend weight to the theory that Cormack is the culprit. The authorities lean toward this as well evidently, for they have Cormack in custody, yet have released Hay on bail."

"And no one," pursued Holmes, "has considered how unlikely it would be for the murderer to allow the victim to write his name in the logbook–thus pointing the accusing finger? On the other hand, thc printed message left by the dying Ross seems to exonerate Hay. Thus, isn't it more likely Hay wrote it? In short, does not the message intimate Hay rather than clear him, especially considering his proximity to the victim?"

Wallace received this line of reasoning with incredulity, then remained silent for some time.

"By George! It seems this possibility wasn't considered. Dear God, they're holding the wrong man!"

Holmes held up his hand.

"Stay Wallace. I'm not certain murder was committed in the first place. Certainly we should not jump to conclusions at this point–"

"But the authorities–"

"*Pshaw*! The *authorities*! You needn't tell me about the 'authorities' my friend. It seems I spend as much time untangling the 'work' of the authorities as I do apprehending criminals, right Watson? Now then, there is a series of possibilities, which I'll attempt to set forth here.

"*Number one: Cormack killed Ross.* He crept stealthily up the iron stairs, passing the dozing Hay in the kitchen. He discovered Ross busy at the worktable, perhaps with his back turned–"

"Yes, Holmes, the granite floors are noiseless ... It would be quite possible to sneak behind whomever sat there ..."

"Well he approached to within, say, a dozen feet of Ross, flung the glass vial at him and at the same instant, turned and fled back down the stairs to escape the deadly gas. Considering the nature of the murder weapon, and the fact that the body would remain in the tower, people would assume it was suicide. But he misjudged, for Ross, after turning to see who it was, still had a few seconds of strength in him. Enough time to pen part of a message telling of the deed."

"It fits perfectly!" I cried. "Then the police do have their man! And he had the motive as well ..."

"*Number two*," continued Holmes, "*is that Hay killed Ross.* He knew he could probably do the deed uninterrupted since Cormack was asleep in the depths of the tower. He ascended the stair, killed Ross in the same manner as previously described, then returned to the kitchen. In all probability, it would be considered suicide. However, a thought intruded to shatter his sense of triumph: what if the authorities were to doubt it was suicide? What if there were some shred of evidence, noted by a shrewd inspector, that would show it was definitely *not* suicide? Then Hay due to his proximity to Ross, would be the prime suspect. So he again climbed the stair and wrote the false message in hopes of casting blame upon the innocent Cormack."

"That also seems to fit the facts ..."

"All except two important ones," said Holmes. "One was the *first* statement given by Hay that he never fell asleep, which is tantamount to admitting Cormack's innocence. The second is the fact that Hay did not accuse Cormack immediately, as he undoubtedly would have done had he wanted to cast suspicion upon him."

"Now the *third possibility* is that *Ross killed himself,* and wrote the message out of spite to put his enemy Cormack in the dock..."

"That would seem to fit the facts, but I think it's out of character for Ross," said Wallace. "Besides, if he indeed wished to implicate Cormack with a message, why not write it out before breaking the vial, so as to complete the incriminating note?"

"An excellent point!" remarked Holmes, "which brings us to the *final possibility*–actually a combination of the previous two: Ross killed himself with cyanide and his body was later discovered by Hay. Hay starts to dash down the stair to tell Cormack, but on the way he re-considers ... Although Ross took his own life, others, including Cormack, may not think so. Accordingly, he re-climbs the stair, *etcetera* as previously described. Although he was loath to implicate his fellow keeper, he saw it as either Cormack's neck or his."

"The scoundrel!"

"Exactly Watson," said Wallace, "If Hay acted as you describe, surely I am a miserable judge of human character–for it was I who hired him. I cannot believe he would act in this fashion."

"Could he have murdered Ross, based on your knowledge of his character?"

"I think it unlikely, Holmes. Furthermore, he had no motive, or at least no visible one. Yet Cormack had a motive of sorts in that he hated Ross. Frankly, although I also find it hard to believe that Cormack would be capable of murder, I think that of the possibilities you have briefly outlined, the first is most probable: Cormack, as a result of his quarrel with Ross, vowed to kill him. He saw his chance on the night in question. The events happened much as you have related them. Above all, it explains the message left by the dying man."

"Quite so," added my companion, "but the one detail that troubles me greatly is Hayes *original* statement to the police that *he did not fall asleep* during the third watch. He changed his story, as I correctly presumed, only when he saw that the original version placed him in jeopardy. Then too we have the vial of cyanide. How long did Cormack contemplate the murder deed? If the plot rose in his enraged brain midway through a tour of duty in an isolated lighthouse, how did he procure the fatal vial? Did he spirit it up out of thin air, as Hamlet did the dagger? Hah!"

"Then what do you think, if I may ask?"

"I think, my friend," said Holmes leaning back languidly in the stuffed armchair and gazing dreamily at the ceiling, "I think it is a pretty problem. A pretty problem indeed. I am most grateful for your invitation, both to your cottage and to the case. Obviously it intrigues me. I am ashamed to admit it elates me. A better holiday one could not ask for. But personal tastes aside, Wallace, it is a grim business. A man is dead, another's life hangs in the balance. Your well-being is threatened."

Holmes broke off impatiently and sprang from the easy chair, pacing to and fro before the peat fire. In a twinkling the dreamy theorist had been transformed into the eager sleuthhound that paces and whines at the kennel fence, eager for the chase.

"Let me say at the outset I'm not satisfied with any of the explanations. I feel there are, there must be, some externals we are not aware of. Clearly, a visit to the lighthouse is in order. We shall start tomorrow at dawn. The first thing to do is procure a launch–"

"But the weather–" protested Wallace.

"D– the weather!" he retorted. "Watson and I have seen worse, haven't we old fellow? After supper I'll retire early, and suggest you both do likewise. Ah, speaking of supper Wallace, the leg of lamb's aroma has me on the verge of madness... Now where's the corkscrew?"

PART TWO: THE TOWER

I shan't ever forget the rude awakening that was in store for me the following day.

Snug in my feather-bed, I was jostled awake by Holmes, already clothed in a woolen jacket and his familiar deerstalker cap, who prodded me like a stern schoolmaster.

"Up, Watson, up! We've no time to lose; we must be at Bell Rock at high water and that's not far off. Moreover, the sea is quiet, or relatively so. Now up you go, that's a good fellow ..."

I mumbled an assent and, the moment he quit the room, drew up the feather bed once again and was off. I dread few things as much as arising early, especially on a chilly morn. I fear the condition is congenital and without cure. An accompanying symptom of this disorder is a thorough hatred of those hardy souls who bound about at unreasonable hours barking brisk commands and exuding false cheer.

The weather was not encouraging. The sky was dull grey in colour, resembling hammered zinc. A cold seawind swept through my chamber, riveting me to my bed, which was delicious. The surf sound was many times louder than it was the previous evening, which lead me to suspect that my friend Sherlock Holmes had not been altogether truthful in his maritime reportage. It sounded heavy and forbidding.

But there was no relief, for soon again I felt the prodding and shaking, heard the same admonishings, to which I replied "Go blast your silly lighthouse!"

Surprisingly enough, my friend left without another word. Seconds later I heard him say to Wallace, in a loud voice, "Watson won't be coming with us. It seems his constitution is too delicate nowadays. Pity. Some of us seem to age faster than others ..."

If this were a ploy, then it was successful. Incensed by his deprecating words, I sprang from the covers and was dressed in an instant.

"Changed your mind Watson?" asked Holmes with a wry grin as he piled his plate with kippers and scones. "Now eat hearty dear fellow, for we'll be in need of all the strength and warmth we can muster, eh Wallace?"

His friend agreed, and bade us put on two extra layers of woolen sweaters. Once outside the snug cottage, I was instantly aware of the necessity of the hot breakfast and warm clothes. The sea wind cut through me like a blade of cold steel. We walked along in great discomfort for the mile and a half journey that brought us to the wharf. There we boarded a vessel, a sturdy coaster with wide beam and shallow draught. Wallace knew the boat's captain, as the vessel was oftentimes engaged in service and charter for the Northern Lights. Our skipper posited himself in the tiny wheelhouse aft whilst the three of us stood in the bow. As usually the case with coastal lighters, the *Petrel*–so she was named–had a high stem and bow. Behind this raised superstructure we stood and smoked, and watched the rocky shoreline fade into the distance. Soon the measured dip and roll of the craft told me we were in "big water," and making our way from the Firth of Tay into the North Sea. From the open hatchway in the centre of the deck came the hissing of steam and clanking of metal. Occasionally we could also hear the ringing of the fireman's shovel and whistling of the engineer. But the sounds most in evidence were the thump and wash of seawater and persistent mewing of the gulls as they glided past, or halted in mid-air with delicate rowing motion of their slender wings.

Somewhat chilled, I descended the main hatch. There, amid the din of pounding metal, I heard the engineer and fireman talking.

"I tell ye Johnny, we're riskin' our necks! It's death sure to make for Bell Rock in a blow ..."

"Aye," the other answered, "the *Petrel's* a sturdy old gal, but she'll smash to splinters out there–you mark me!"

My spirits were somewhat dampened by this dialogue, and the odours of hot metal and burning grease did not improve them. I returned topside where I found Wallace pointing over the bow. Holmes stood at his side looking through a pair of massive field glasses. Without their aid, I could barely see a dark vertical splinter on the horizon. Curiously enough, the next instant it was gone!

"Gracious!" exclaimed Holmes, "that last wave fairly engulfed the tower!"

A moment later, the faint splinter was again visible.

"It may be too hazardous to land," warned Wallace. "We might be forced to wait on for a spell until the sea calms. If it remains high, we'll have to abandon the visit altogether."

And so on we went, standing in the pitching bow of the boat, making for the dark sliver in the distance. It continued to vanish and reappear as the huge waves, which were not yet discernible, battered it in clouds of spray. I watched the tower for many moments, and it did not seem to grow larger. I took this to be evidence of its great size, and I was not mistaken.

These many years later, as I sit recalling the great and varied adventures Holmes and I were a part of, I can think of no incident more exciting, more eerie, than viewing Bell Rock tower from the bow of the *Petrel* that stormy summer day. It was huge, rising up a hundred feet above the roaring water. But the impression upon one's mind, indeed one's *soul*–was not merely the immensity of the structure, but its *isolation.*

Sticking straight up out of the sea–miles from shore and without any visible rock nearby–it had a chimerical, fantastical appearance. It was as if the Devil himself had built it. The lines were graceful, yet the dull, dun-coloured stone of which it was made, the look of desolation and the utter silence, these were oppressive to the spirit, and, I might admit, not a little frightening.

As we drew to within a hundred yards of the tower, its size seemed to overwhelm us. The silence was broken by a series of deep rollers which struck the reef–invisible at high water–obliquely. They broke in furious plumes of spray long before they reached the lighthouse. It was as if a score of organpipe fountains had been set off in quick succession–one after the other.

The next instant, the waves struck the tower. There came a thunderous crash and the water, after striking the sloping sides of the structure, then proceeded to climb it in great licks of spray. Up, up went the plumes, till they reached the gallery ninety feet up. There, they were turned away by the granite lip, and curled back in graceful arches to fall back towards whence they had come. The entire tower was engulfed in seething, climbing water. It seemed to spurt upwards ever-so-slowly, and I was reminded of a waterfall. For if one watches a waterfall carefully, he is soon fascinated by the various plumes and tongues of white water that fall earthward in slow cadence. This was the reverse, and it was a sight as thrilling as fireworks to see the climbing water arch slowly upwards.

"A sight we won't soon forget, eh, Watson!" shouted Holmes above the roar. "What say you Wallace, can we make a landing?"

"Only a madman would attempt it," he shouted back. "I'll signal the captain to lay off to leeward. If we're in luck, we can land in an hour or so."

It was a two-hour wait, during which, as the result of the violent pitching of the boat, I began to feel ill. It was with a sense of relief that I heard the shriek of the *Petrel's* whistle–the signal for the keepers that we were preparing to land. The sea had subsided, and soon a tiny figure appeared at the gallery railing. With a full head of steam we approached the base of the tower with caution. Ten yards out I saw the iron door, twenty feet above the waves, open. A man clad in oilskins leaned out and flung a coil of rope to the deck of the *Petrel.* This was made fast to a cleat, and the captain reversed the screws. The *Petrel* backed off, tightening the rope. Then a small sling, called a "bos'un's chair" was lowered down the rope by means of a pulley. Into this contrivance each of us in turn seated himself, then was hoisted up towards the small doorway in the sheer granite wall. Once inside, Wallace's earlier description of a lighthouse as a "vertical dungeon" came immediately to mind. I found myself in a tiny cylindrical room. The walls were of cold stone, and the light was faint. The hole in the rock through which we had passed was secured by two massive steel doors, each over two inches thick and swinging on hinges that bore a strong resemblance to those used on bank vaults. I realized firsthand the necessity of these, having seen the waves working against the tower.

"Good Heavens, Wallace," I cried when we were all safely aboard and the doors had been secured, "it's no wonder lightkeepers have been known to go insane. The rooms are certainly cramped and dreary enough ..."

"No, Doctor, the rooms are above us. We are standing in the entrance room which is considerably smaller than the others. Beneath our feet, the tower is solid. Come, let us follow Hutchenson up–this way please ..."

"The doors," mused Holmes as we wound our way up the spiral stairs, "I noticed that the outer one appears to open from either side, while the inner one is secured only from within."

"Quite so. I assume both of you noticed the iron rungs that lead down to the water? The outer door may be opened from without—this to offer shelter for any poor soul who chances to swim to the rock and climb the ladder. But you are correct about the second door: when fastened from within, it is impenetrable from the outside."

"And on the night of Ross' death both doors were secured?"

"Yes. And the sea was up—much as you saw it this morning. In such instances, no boat can safely approach the tower. Add to this the darkness, and we can rule out any outside parties."

"It would certainly seem so, eh Watson? Ah, and this, I presume, is the storeroom?"

We had reached the first of the rooms. Here the stone stairway ended, and the large iron one commenced. The room was circular, twelve feet in diameter. The steel shutters, having been closed to keep out water, were opened. Even so, the light afforded by the two tiny windows was meagre indeed. It was some time before my eyes accustomed themselves to the dim light. I could make out piles of crates and sacks, heaping coils of hempen ropes, and a wooden bin for coal. But the principle commodity present was oil; great drums of it lined the walls. The place, as one might suspect, had a close, musty odour, and I was happy to leave it.

"Our new oil vapour lamps burn a gallon of fuel every two hours, and there are four of them. Since the lamps are sometimes lighted up to sixteen hours a day, you can see that the chore of carrying oil up these stairs is considerable. No matter what you've heard, being a lightkeeper is not an armchair job."

"How is the oil brought here?" I asked.

"The tender vessel visits here every other month, during which time the crews are changed. Now here we are: the bedroom."

The room was the same size as the other, but seemed immeasurably more cheery. The windows were somewhat larger, and the walls were hung with heavy cloth to take the chill from the cold rock. Three bunks were placed alongside the walls, alternating with sea-chests and dressers.

"And it was here that Cormack claimed to be taking his rest?"

"Yes. He claims not to have stirred from his bunk until awakened by Hay. As I mentioned previously, the windows are no means of exit ..."

Holmes, ever curious, stood upon a dresser and looked out one of the minute, rectangular windows. I followed suit, and found myself peering down a narrow tunnel in the rock four feet long.

"By Jove the walls are thick!" I exclaimed. "It's a wonder any light gets in at all. No man could pass through here, that's certain. I cannot even see the water, merely a patch of sky."

We continued our upward, circular journey on the spiral staircase to the kitchen. Here we met the two remaining keepers, Mitchell and Evans, who were taking mid-morning tea. We joined them, and chatted for a few moments over the steaming brew. I was glad for the rest, since my leg wound had begun to throb from the stair climbing. I stretched out my legs near the tin stove and let the warmth work its magic. The room was delightful, though a trifle crowded with the six of us. As we rose to depart, I heard a dull thud and felt the tower vibrate ever so faintly. A second later came a rushing, washing sound, followed by a stream of water through the window!

"Sea's up again!" shouted Mitchell, and flew down the staircase.

"You *did* make fast the doors, Sir?" asked Evans with a worried smile.

"Have no fear lad, they're both shut tight," said Wallace with a twinkle. "Holmes, I remember once out at Skerryvore Light, the sea came up and, for some reason, my assistant keeper forgot to close the entrance doors. With the first wave, the tower flooded. The seawater roared up the stairway like an express train!"

I paused with the teacup midway to my lips. Would I never cease to be amazed at these unique and lonely buildings, and the dangers they were subject to?

"Now I assume Wallace, that this is the very table that Cormack and Hay used for their chess games? Very well. Then I further assume that Hay would sit in either of these two chairs, since they're far more comfortable than the others–"

"That's correct Holmes. The one Watson is reclining in. He has admitted as much."

"And it was in the same position?"

"Absolutely."

"Now Watson, facing straight ahead, what do you see?"

"The staircase."

"Exactly. So it would be impossible for anyone to pass this room on the stair without your knowledge unless, of course, you were asleep. Are you ready Watson? Let us continue our climb."

We quit the kitchen and, after a brief inspection of the living room with its bookcases, maps, and easy chairs, made our way to the work-room. Situated at the tower's summit directly below the lantern, it consisted of polished wooden cabinets and a long worktable. Strewn on the table were four huge parabolic mirrors, which Hutchenson polished with jeweler's paste and a chamois cloth.

"You may think a lightkeeper leads an idle life, but you'd be mistaken," said Wallace. "It demands constant work and unfaltering attention to detail. Failure, as you know, can mean peril for those at sea. Each day the mirrors and lenses must be cleaned and polished. The lamp reservoirs must be filled and the air chambers pumped up to pressure."

He paced the workroom with an air of authority, like a general inspecting his barracks. The keepers moved about quietly, as if in fear of reprimand. For although Wallace was a gentle man, he was strict and demanding professionally.

"And now gentlemen, the light," said Wallace leading us up the final flight of stairs. In contrast to the rest of the tower, which was massive and gloomy, the lantern room was delicate and airy. In its centre, mounted upon an enormous iron pedestal, stood the lens. It glowed in all the colours of the rainbow, for it consisted of scores of prisms set one above the other. The room was spotless and reminded me of a hospital surgery station. Besides the giant Fresnel lenswork and its pedestal, there was a clockwork to rotate the lamps (which required winding every two hours) and a pressure pump that led to the oil reservoirs. After a brief look about, we returned to the workroom below where Ross' body was found. Holmes cast his sharp eyes about and, seeing the logbook which rested upon the table, seized it immediately, only to fling it aside with disgust.

"Now Holmes, you certainly don't think an important piece of evidence like Ross' scrawled message would remain here do you? It's been impounded by the court."

"I feared as much," groaned my companion. "And I assume the same is true of the glass vial?"

Wallace gave the same answer, but was interrupted.

"Excuse me sir, perhaps it's a trifle ..."

"Yes, Evans?"

"When I was called to duty here after the, eh, death of Ross I swept out this room thoroughly. Curiously enough, I found several splinters of glass, which I saved in an envelope upon the remote chance they would be of interest—"

"My dear fellow!" cried Holmes. "Evans, you have rendered an invaluable service. Have you the fragments?"

Replying in the affirmative, Evans led an eager Holmes down to the living room. Meanwhile for lack of anything else to do, Wallace and I re-climbed to the lantern room, then strode out onto the gallery. The instant we were outside, I was smote full-force by the stinging wind and spray. Looking over the railing, my head swam with dizziness. Far, far below, seething in spray and waves, was the tower's base. But from our lofty perch it looked no bigger than a penny. Indeed, the structure was so tall it seemed to shrink towards its base, which gave the most unsettling impression that it was disproportioned and top-heavy, and was teetering on the brink of falling over into the sea. For a moment I thought of nothing save retreating back into the lantern room. But my pride held me to the railing. Soon my initial trepidations vanished, and I began to enjoy the view. What a vista was the lightkeepers! The cliffs of the mainland, invisible from the *Petrel's* deck, were seen as a low purplish line on the horizon. We saw the tall masts and billowing sails of barques, and dark plumes of smoke from the steamships. But of course the greatest spectacle was directly below us, as the water crashed madly against the tower and slid up its face towards us. Adding to the din was the piercing cry of the gulls as they swirled round the light. Many of them perched on the copper dome itself, no doubt welcoming this firm perch at sea.

"Lightkeepers have mixed feelings about the birds," said Wallace. "On the one hand, they're a nuisance, as they foul the glass and ironwork. On the other hand, they're visitors, and any visitor to a lighthouse is a welcome one."

Before I could reply, there came a whistle blast, and the stout *Petrel*, forgotten by us, steamed round into view. The captain came out on deck and began gesticulating and shouting. Unfortunately, his voice could not be heard, but Wallace soon understood his message: the sea was so high the boat could no longer remain safely nearby. By means of flag signals Mitchell, who was summoned by Wallace, made it clear that the *Petrel* should depart and pick us up the following morning. With a heavy heart, I watched the boat grow smaller and smaller, until only its black plume of smoke was visible. We were now truly isolated, and I would come to know first-hand the life of a lighthouse keeper.

Holmes received the news amiably.

"Capital!" he exclaimed, looking up momentarily from his magnifying lens, "I couldn't be more pleased. This is as snug a retreat as anyone could wish. There are books a-plenty, and fine company. Here gentlemen, what do you make of this, eh?"

He pointed to the tabletop, upon which rested two piles of broken glass.

"The remains of the vial?" asked Wallace.

"Yes, the overlooked fragments found by Evans. Do look here; you'll note, upon close inspection, that the curvature of the fragments varies. See the pieces in the first pile, and note the radius of the curve, use the lens if you like ..."

We did as he instructed.

"Now if you will, examine the pieces in the second pile—"

"The curve is tighter ... noticeably so," said I.

"Which indicates a vial of smaller diameter. Therefore there were *two* vials—not one. And one was smaller than the other. Does anything else strike you Watson, upon examining all the fragments?"

"No, I cannot see anything unusual."

"I am surprised, considering your occupation. Of course, I perhaps deal with laboratory apparatus more often than even a physician. The oddity is this: the glass is thin. *Extraordinarily* thin. I've seen enough broken test tubes in my life to know that most laboratory glass is !/16 of an inch thick. This is much thinner—perhaps twice as thin ..."

Here he paused in thought for a moment, then continued.

"It would be interesting indeed to have a more accurate picture of the size and shape of these vials. Perhaps they aren't vials at all ..."

He sank back into thought. Wallace and I, seeing further communication with him was out of the question, selected books from the bountiful shelves and settled down into the armchairs, one on either side of the stovepipe, and read until teatime. Outside the weather intensified; the tower shook at regular intervals, and the wind whined and shrieked. The tower's vibration had terrified me earlier, but I had grown used to it gradually. The living room was warm and cozy, and made even cheery by the glow of student's lamps and the heat radiating from the metal pipe. We might just as well have been inside a London club. After tea we descended for supper. Hutchenson was on duty, which left five of us to wedge ourselves tightly round the small table. Evans and Mitchell had of course heard of my companion's many adventures and successes, and they prodded him with questions regarding Ross's death.

"I must confess the puzzle grows more intricate," said he. "I have no final theories yet."

"Which of the two suspects is the more likely?" enquired Mitchell. "It's Cormack I'll wager. I think he'll swing for it, sure."

"Ah no Phil, it's too obvious—far too obvious I say. When the truth comes out, it'll be Hay who swings."

The talk grew heated, and the men resolved it by laying a large wager and shaking hands on it. Holmes said nothing, but the look in his eyes told me he was amused. He asked if any of the men had known Ross. Wallace replied that Hutchenson had served with him for several tours at Bell Rock three years previously. After our meal, Holmes eagerly led me up to the workroom where Hutchenson was preparing to light the lamps. We helped him carry the reflectors up to the lantern and place them over the founts. After checking the oil level and air pressure in the reservoirs, he opened the valves. We heard a hissing sound, then a popping of flame as he lighted the mantles. They glowed dull yellow, then gradually rose in brightness until the entire room was filled with brilliant bluish-white light. Looking into any of the reflectors was like looking at the sun. Releasing the gearwork, he set the four lamps slowly turning.

"They will complete the circle every forty-eight seconds," he told us, "which means that Bell Rock shows a one-second flash every eleven seconds. Now Mr. Holmes, you wish to know of Ross?"

"Was he the sort to consider suicide?"

"I would say so, sir. Of course, you must know that when I was on tour with him it was directly after his wife died. He was in a severe state of depression ..."

"How long had they been married?"

"Only a year. She was a local girl, and up until she met Ross, betrothed to another."

"Oh?"

"Yes. But her man was away when Ross arrived in Arbroath. He was in the government service, you see, in China, I believe ..."

"And his name?"

"Hayne Edwards. He's spent his life in the government service, and is now a local magistrate. It was he who was engaged to Lucille MacCarg. But during his absence in China, she met Robert Ross and fell in love with him. They were married before Edwards returned."

"And what was Mr. Edwards' reaction when he returned home from the East?"

"Well, he wasn't pleased, as you may imagine. However, he was gentleman enough. What enraged him was Lucille's death. He placed the blame square on Ross. Said Ross killed her."

"Most interesting. And this accusation, I presume, merely added to Ross's woes?"

"Yes, sir. Drove him into the Northern Lights, where he could live the life of a hermit. He spoke of Lucille often on that tour, and Hayne

Edwards too. He'd go out on the gallery and point to the mainland. 'There lives the man who would have my death,' he used to say."

Holmes' eyes shone in the brilliance of the room. The blazing glare swept his hawk-like features, and seemed to exaggerate the keenness of the face.

"And you think Ross had been threatened by Edwards?"

"I'm not sure, sir. In any case, Ross never mentioned a direct threat–just that Edwards held him responsible for the death of the woman he loved. And sometimes ..."

"Sometimes what?"

"Sometimes, Mr. Holmes, I got the impression Ross tended this light not only out of remorse, but also for his own safety."

"I see. Thank you Hutchenson, you've been most helpful."

We left him tending the light to the measured click and roll of the revolving lamps, a sound not unlike that produced during a game of billiards.

"Well Watson," said Holmes as we descended the iron stairway, "it certainly seems that Mr. Hayne Edwards had reason enough to kill Ross."

"Perhaps, but why three years after Lucille's death? Besides, while he may have had the motive, he hardly had the means. You're forgetting this tower, are you not? We know it was one of Ross' fellow keepers, or both acting in concert. So it won't do to drag Edwards in, will it?"

My companion remained silent and, entering the living room, we let the matter drop.

The night we spent in the tower was most memorable–and punctuated by the roaring pounding water, the vibrations of the structure, the ever-changing watches, and the beautiful dawn that sent white rays of sunshine sloping down into the gloomy chamber from the tiny windows. I climbed to the gallery for a last look about. The morning was warm and lovely; the sea sparkled in the sun and the wind was soft and pleasant. A plume appeared on the horizon, growing larger each minute. Before long the *Petrel* was churning her way round the tower's base, hooting impatiently. This time with Mitchell as our guide, the three of us wound our way down into the dismal depths of the lighthouse. With a grinding shudder, the iron doors were opened and in a few minutes, we were again upon the *Petrel's* deck and heading for the mainland.

I looked back at Bell Rock tower. Although it appeared less forbidding than when I first saw it, it still had an awesome, desolate appearance. I was glad to be leaving, and knew for certain that the lightkeeper's calling was not for me.

PART THREE: THE QUEST

Our journey back was uneventful; we arrived at the cottage in plenty of time for lunch. Deep in the throes of a quest to the solution, Holmes remained silent and aloof. Consequently Wallace and I engaged each other in conversation and spent the afternoon in an enjoyable round of golf. It was on the twelfth tee that I discovered the answer to the mystery of Bell Rock. The idea came upon me gradually at first, then with increasing suddenness and clarity. So agitated was I that my game fell apart utterly.

"My dear Watson, that's the third rough shot in a row. Whatever's the matter?"

I exclaimed that I'd solved the problem, and proceeded, by drawing with a stick in the sand, to explain the solution.

"By George, you've done it, Watson!" he exclaimed open-mouthed. "I see some of your friend's genius has rubbed off on you. Come, let us hurry back. Holmes should be overjoyed."

We found our friend out behind the cottage, hands thrust deep in his pockets, his bulldog briar clenched between his teeth. He was gazing out over the sea in the direction of Bell Rock.

"You may put aside your conjectures Holmes!" I cried as we strode to meet him. "For once you are outdone! As Wallace here can tell you, I have found the solution to Ross' murder. Would you care to join us over a glass of port while I explain it?"

His face shone with surprise, and I confess I couldn't help gloating a bit over my discovery. After years of playing second-fiddle to my friend, I relished leading him into the cottage. As we sat down, I delighted in the reversal of roles.

"Now Holmes," I began, "it is you who have so often told me that when the impossible is eliminated whatever remains, *however improbable*, is the truth ... correct?"

He nodded, and a flicker of an amused smile began to play upon his lips. Sensing he was about to deride me, I drew myself up and with a level stare, proceeded to unravel the mystery.

"And you won't be so smug," I warned, "when you see the keenness of my logic. Now then, to briefly re-state the possibilities: Ross was murdered by either Hay or Cormack, or both. The dying man's scribble incriminates Cormack. Yet Cormack's retreat to the bedroom below Hay and his absence on the stairs tends to clear him ..."

Holmes nodded.

"Now this is the important point, you see. Viewed in a slightly *different* fashion, one sees Cormack's want of a nap—something he did not usually need—is an *alibi*. We know he and Ross did not get on well. There was friction, animosity. Cormack wanted Ross' death, and so set about contriving the perfect alibi. We have seen how the stairs, being of iron and suspended in the stone tower, vibrate and ring with the slightest tread. This plus the fact that Hay's chair faced the stairway—"

"Of course. Hay's first statement, as we all know, tended to absolve Cormack and jeopardize Hay himself."

"Precisely," said I. "Now the question that remains is this: how then did Cormack reach the workroom? The answer is as follows: Cormack reached it from the *outside*. He did not ascend the stairs, but rather *descended* them!"

"Watson—amazing ... I congratulate you dear fellow! I see your logic. If he did not go up the stairs, and the windows are too small for a man to pass through, then the only route left is *down* to the entrance doors, correct?"

"*Exactly!* But the question that now arises of course is *how* did he climb up the tower's face? It is smooth vertical stone, and sixty feet separate the sea doors from the gallery railing ..."

"Now Holmes," interjected Wallace, "here is the ingenious part of Watson's explanation—"

"I'm dying to hear it. Come on man ..."

"The idea struck me as I remembered the many coils of rope in the storeroom of the lighthouse. Sometime during the day preceding the murder, Cormack surreptitiously carried a long rope up to the lantern. Concealment would be an easy matter; wrapped about his waist, it would be invisible under an overcoat. Stepping out onto the gallery, he walked round it until he was directly over the sea doors many feet below. Fortunately for his foul scheme, the sea doors and gallery door are on opposite sides of the tower. Therefore, it was a simple matter for him to tie the rope to a railing stanchion and let it fall. From the gallery it would be visible only as a knot at the base of the railing—assuming that either Ross or Hay would even venture onto the far side of the gallery. Although plainly evident from a passing ship, the rope would hang invisible to those within ...."

Holmes' eyes sparkled.

"Dear Heavens, Wallace!" he cried, "in letting Watson in on my methods, I'm in danger of doing myself out of a career!"

"The best is yet to come," I said immodestly. "The evening arrives. Neither Hay nor Ross has discovered the length of rope tied to the gallery railing. Ross goes to the workroom, Hay remains in the kitchen, and Cormack says he's going to sleep in the bedroom—"

"But he actually passes the bedroom and proceeds down two more levels to the entrance room," continued Wallace, "opens the iron doors, feels in the darkness for the rope he knows is waiting—"

"And, closing the outer iron door after him—remember it opens from either side—climbs hand-over-hand up the rope, bracing his feet against the tower face. Any noise he might make is muffled by the surf and the cry of the gulls. Finally reaching the railing, he draws himself over and pauses to regain his breath. Then, silent as a cat, he enters the lantern room by the gallery door. Slowly, softly, he creeps down the staircase 'till he's almost above Ross, hunched over the table in the workroom. Ross, engrossed in the logbook on the table, is unaware of his arrival ...."

"In an instant," added Wallace, "Cormack has flung the deadly vial onto the floor near the table and retreated up the stairs and back onto the gallery—safe from the noxious fumes. After waiting a few minutes to make certain his victim is dead, he returns to the rope ...."

"And at this point, Cormack's evil genius becomes evident," said I. "For now he *unties* the knot. Drawing up the dangling length of rope, he passes it round the same railing stanchion, letting the free end fall seawards again. The rope being *twice* the distance from railing to doorway, Cormack has *looped* it double, so that the two ends fall at the door. Cautiously, he climbs over the rail and, gripping the two falling lengths of rope—one with each hand, he lowers himself down back to the door. After he opens it and is standing firmly inside, he pulls one of the free ends—"

"–drawing the other one upwards," added Holmes.

"–yes, until the end passes over the railing and falls into the sea ..."

"Brilliant Watson! He has thus disposed of his means of climbing the tower–"

"Of course! There is no incriminating rope left. He either lets the other end go into the sea, or else retrieves the entire length, coils it neatly, and deposits it amongst the others in the storeroom on his return to the bedroom."

"Where he waits, feigning sleep, till Hay rouses him with news of Ross' death," continued Wallace. "But he's made the mistake of allowing Ross to scrawl the message identifying him as the culprit."

There was a moment of silence. I basked in the euphoria of it. Holmes rose at last and came to my side. Clapping his hand upon my shoulder, he fixed his steely gaze upon me.

"Watson, I say in all earnestness that is the finest bit of detective logic I have seen in some time. You are pleased with yourself, and deservedly so. I must confess your acumen has set me slightly on edge."

I flushed at his praise.

"However," he continued, "as brilliant as your explanation is, it would be a mistake I think, to jump to the assumption that Cormack is guilty–"

"Now Holmes," I interrupted sternly, "I must say your behavior is rather unbecoming. You, who are so quick with your judgements of others' intellects, are finally in a position of having been outdone. Rather than accept this graciously, you choose to be childish in your failure. For my part, I shall go straightaway to the local authorities and explain this crime. For the sake of justice, it is my obligation."

In hauteur, I turned on my heel and left the cottage. Although I instantly regretted my show of temper, Holmes' acid comments of two evenings earlier had stayed with me. It is ironic, but it seems that in so many instances those who so readily offer criticism are most reluctant to accept it. Upon hearing the door close, I was surprised to see Wallace joining me.

"Difficult," said he, "decidedly difficult. He was the same way at school you know."

We left him much as we'd found him–staring out over the ocean in the direction of the lighthouse.

The jail was easily located, and after a short interrogation we were admitted to the cells. We found Cormack in the last one, cowering on his tiny cot. He had the helpless and forlorn look of a trapped animal. At our approach, he sprang to his feet and embraced Wallace.

"Thank God you've returned Mr. Wallace," he cried, "I'd all but given up hope. Surely you believe, sir! Surely you know my innocence of this murder!"

His lower lip trembled; he was on the verge of breaking down completely. When Wallace informed him that I had discovered the method he had employed, and that his conviction now appeared a certainty, he collapsed on the bunk and buried his face in his hands, sobbing and protesting his innocence. I was instantly struck by the appearance of his left arm.

"Hold on, Cormack," said I. "Would you kindly rise and remove your shirt?"

He did as I bade, and my suspicion was confirmed. His entire left arm was stunted and gnarled. He held it awkwardly and half turned, as if to hide the grotesque limb in shame.

"Good grief, dear fellow!" cried Wallace. "I'd no idea the injury was that serious. You said it was a minor inconvenience..."

"Really sir, I can manage quite well despite it, as long as I don't attempt any heavy lifting—"

"Raise your arm over your head," I commanded.

He drew up the shrunken arm level with his shoulder, then winced in pain.

"I'm afraid it won't go any higher, sir," he said apologetically.

"Just as I thought," I returned. "How did it happen?"

"I fell from a horse when I was nine. The arm broke in two places. It never did heal correctly—as you can see. Since then I'm weak as a kitten in it I'm afraid."

The young man drew his shirt on again and sat down on the bench. We recanted our earlier statements, to his visible relief.

"You've a sharp eye doctor," said Wallace as we began the long trudge homeward, "to have detected the severity of the lad's handicap."

"I only wish my mind were as sharp," I replied bitterly. "In a fit of vanity I nearly cost the boy his life. Holmes was so right—jumping to false conclusions can be disastrous. What a fool I've been, and my berating Holmes—ah! It adds to my shame!"

We walked on in silence. My ears burned when I thought of what Holmes would say.

Surprisingly, he was all kindness and understanding.

"Well it appears that Cormack didn't kill Ross," said he packing his pipe, "at least by climbing up sixty feet of rope, eh?"

"It certainly does not! I've been an ass Holmes."

"On the contrary Watson, you have been a doubly shrewd fellow: once for originating your ingenious theory, and twice by your astute observations, which cleared the boy. However, I shall tell you both that I doubted your theory from the outset."

"You knew of Cormack's withered arm?"

"No. Your explanation has the same weaknesses of all the others in that it fails to explain a few basic questions."

"Such as?"

"Well for one, why would either Cormack or Hay wish to kill Ross? Even if he were unbearable they would merely have to wait until the tour was up—then never see him again. A second question is this: even assuming either or both suspects wanted his death, why kill him in a remote tower where they would certainly be the only suspects? Of course, the final question is most puzzling: why was Ross's body left in the workroom, when, with only a little effort, it could have been dragged up to the gallery and flung into the sea? A better means of disposing of evidence cannot come to mind. The tower being a dozen miles from land, the remains probably would never be recovered—"

"And his death would be presumed accident or suicide," added Wallace.

"Precisely. You see all the theories we have answer the little questions, but none deals with these larger questions."

"Then Ross killed himself," mused Wallace, "but then why the scrawled note?"

"To find the answers to these and other questions, I think a good place to start would be the residence of Hayne Edwards. I plan to call there first thing in the morning. Would you care to join me?"

The Edwards' house was a large stone affair in the centre of Arbroath. The bell was answered by an elderly housekeeper, who asked us to wait. So we stood before the great oaken door and smoked. Holmes commented that Edwards was receiving a handsome salary indeed to afford such a house.

"I think the family has been wealthy for some time," said Wallace, "certainly his post as clerk doesn't pay him much."

The housekeeper returned, and curtly informed us that Mr. Edwards was not in.

"When will he return?" Holmes asked.

"I've no idea sir. I shall tell him you called. Good-day to you."

"Then we shall wait here until he returns," said Holmes firmly, seating himself on the stone bench near the door. We followed suit, and after staring at us in disbelief, the woman withdrew.

"A small wager," Holmes said winking, "says that Mr. Edwards is home. His walking stick was plainly visible in the hallway. I wonder why he is so reluctant to see us ..."

A quarter of an hour later the door opened and a gruff-faced man thrust his head out.

"What is your business?" he asked in a clipped tone.

Holmes explained our errand. His face grew pale at the mention of Ross' death.

"Very well then, come in. But I tell you I know nothing of the matter. As a matter of fact, I believe I was on holiday when it occurred. Wasn't it in the middle of June?"

"On the eighteenth actually."

"Well I was either on holiday or just returned–"

"Where did you holiday?"

"I don't see what it matters, but since you ask, Isle of Tyree. Here, let us talk in my study, but I warn you now, I haven't much time."

"And were you visiting relatives there?" pursued Holmes.

"No I wasn't," he remarked irritably. "Does one always need relatives to visit? Besides, it is no concern of yours I'm sure."

He led us into a wainscoted room that was luxuriously furnished. The walls were hung with oriental silk screens and tapestries–souvenirs no doubt from Edwards' tenure in China.

We seated ourselves in the overstuffed chairs that flanked the fireplace. Edwards lighted a cigar and puffed at it nervously.

"It's no secret that I held no love for Robert Ross," he admitted.

We indicated that we were familiar with the story of Lucille MacCarg.

"He killed her," Edwards grunted, "and although I certainly am not responsible for his death, I cannot say I am sorry he is dead."

"As unfortunate as it was," I interjected, "you are foolish and bitter to hold him responsible–death in childbirth is all too common ..."

"You obviously have not been told the whole story. Lucille probably would not have died if Ross had been with her to take her to the hospital. As it was, he was twelve miles away on business when she was taken with labour. She died from hemmorhage. He killed her."

"We don't approach you as a suspect, Mr. Edwards. We thought you might be able to give us some useful information as to Ross' character and personality. The police are fairly certain young Cormack is the murderer. In all likelihood he'll hang for it."

A sudden change came over Edwards. He grew pale as death and, springing up from his chair, dropped his cigar and clutched at his breast–his breath coming in short gasps.

Holmes quickly reached for the decanter that rested upon the table. Together we forced the brandy between Edwards' clenched teeth. In a few moments, his breathing returned to normal and he again seated himself in the chair. His brow was damp and his face deathly pale.

"A momentary spell," said he, "I am all right now."

"My mentioning the suspect's name seemed to send you reeling," said Holmes eyeing him keenly. "You are surprised that they have found the murderer?"

"Of course not, it's just that I, I was of the initial *impression*, after reading the account in the newspapers, that it was suicide ..."

"Ah no. Definitely *murder*. But justice shall run her course, eh gentlemen? The young man protests his innocence, but the weight of evidence is too strong. He has but a month left on this earth–"

"What evidence?" sputtered Edwards. "Are the police quite certain? There is no mistake?"

"No mistake. His conviction and execution are certainties. Well, I had not intended to upset you sir; there's really no point in continuing this interview. Come Watson, Wallace, we must be going, it's–"

Holmes stopped in mid-sentence. His eyes were fixed upon the silk tapestry on the wall. It was a large picture depicting a river scene in China. Boats plied up and down the swirling current, polled by men in flowing robes and wide, conical hats. Sea birds and ducks swam about the boats, while women prepared meals under straw canopies. It was a pleasant scene, and ordinary enough to my eyes.

Holmes, however, was transfixed by it.

"Tell me," he said at last, "is it true you lived in China for some years?"

"True indeed, as deputy ambassador," said Edwards, still fighting for breath.

"And is it possible you lived near a river like the one depicted in this print?"

"Coincidentally Mr. Holmes, I lived near that very river."

"How interesting. Well, we must be going. Good-bye Mr. Edwards, and for Heaven's sake, put the death of Robert Ross out of your mind:

it is over and done and the culprit is doomed. So there's an end to it. Adieu."

Hayne Edwards seemed to have a recurrence of the seizure as we left him, sitting in his fireside chair with a look of dread upon his face.

"He is not a happy man," I observed as we boarded the cart.

"Nor would you be my friend," said Holmes, "if you had the weight of guilt upon your soul."

"You infer that Edwards is the killer?" asked Wallace.

"I infer nothing at this point. Yet his Chinese print was most inspiring ... most inspiring to be sure ..."

His eyes assumed that far away look, and he lapsed into a deep reverie from which it was useless to rouse him.

He remained in this comatose state until we arrived at the cottage. Declining a whiskey, he sat gazing into the peat fire, tobacco smoke surrounding him in blue wreaths. He remained thus even through dinner, much to Wallace's consternation.

"How long will he be like this?"

"For as long as it takes."

"As long as it takes?"

"To solve the problem of course. I say Wallace, it won't do to remain here this evening. Holmes' state casts a deathly pall upon this place, and he'll become nasty as a viper if disturbed. I noticed a pub in town, the Three Caltrops?"

"Ah yes! They serve McGewan's porter. Many good lads frequent it. Are you keen on darts?"

"Say no more, let us be off! We'll leave our sombre friend to his own devices."

So off we went, and spent a jolly evening at the Caltrops. Wallace's skill at darts was unbelievable and, as we played for pints, I found myself treating him all evening. Of course this delighted me all the more, since he was a gracious host. The place buzzed with talk about Ross' murder, and several times Wallace was beseiged with questions and theories. But, responsible commissioner that he was, he declined comment. We returned to the cottage shortly before midnight to find Holmes anxiously pacing before the fire.

"Ah Wallace, I'm so glad to see you," he cried.

"But not your friend Watson, I take it," he returned dryly.

"Oh yes, you too, Watson. I say ..."

He advanced and eyed me closely.

"Really, Watson, a bit on the intemperate side this evening aren't you? I see you've had four pints of ale. Your head shall be heavy come morning. Shame on you Wallace, you know we English cannot keep pace with you Scotsmen ... not to mention our neighbors to the West ...”

“I say Holmes! Are we that unsteady? How on earth did you know we’d had four?”

“By Watson’s waistcoat.”

“What? Well, I’m dashed! His waistcoat?”

“Certainly. It’s really quite simple. Watson wears his waistcoat a bit tighter than most, which means a snug fit indeed. I have often observed him during a large meal unbutton the lower two buttons. If the meal is yet larger, he’ll un-do three. I see three unfastened now, and made a rough calculation on that basis.”

“Incredible! Aren’t you amazed Watson?”

“I’ve grown used to it. Well perhaps a bit on the excessive side Holmes, but a splendid evening–especially after the trying experience of this afternoon. It’s a pity you didn’t join us.”

“I had graver things on my mind than raising a glass,” he said reproachfully. “But I’m happy to say I’m on the verge of a solution to our little problem. Now Wallace, the reason I am so happy you’ve returned–finally–is that I want to ask you some questions about your country. You recall Edwards mentioning he was on holiday?”

Wallace nodded.

“He was on the Isle of Tyree, was he not?”

“Yes. Now what is the place like?”

Wallace reclined in a chair and knitted his brows.

“I would say,” he said at last, “that it is much like here–for it lies in the same latitude exactly, being on the West Coast instead of the East ...”

“Aha! Now we are getting somewhere. I tingle with anticipation,” cried Holmes, pacing all the faster and puffing furiously at his pipe. “And would you say,” he continued, “that the terrain and coastline are similar to the ones hereabouts?”

“It’s a bit more rugged, but otherwise quite alike.”

Holmes stopped and drew near to Wallace. He leaned over and peered intently into his friend’s face.

“Now Wallace, consider carefully. Is there anything on or near the Isle of Tyree of interest to you?”

“Why certainly. *Skerryvore* is there.”

“And Skerryvore is ...?” asked Holmes, his eyes shining.

“A lighthouse–wave swept, lying twelve miles offshore.”

“Hah! How *similar* is Skerryvore light to Bell Rock?”

"It's interesting you should ask. They are remarkably similar, both being Stevenson lights ..."

"I beg pardon?"

"The Scottish engineer. Robert Stevenson—grandfather, bye-the-bye, of Robert Louis Stevenson—and his sons Thomas and Alan built most of Scotland's wave-swept towers. Skerryvore was built by Alan, and though taller, is the twin sister of Bell Rock."

Holmes fairly danced with glee.

"You see Watson, you see! Ah how the pieces come together!"

I confess that my brain, never as quick as Holmes', was a bit slower than usual due to our festivities at the Three Caltrops.

"Whatever do you mean?" I sputtered

"Consider for yourselves gentlemen: a man goes on a holiday. That is usual enough—yet he sojourns in a place *remarkably similar* to the area he's left. Moreover, he has no relatives there to visit. Why then, does he choose to spend his vacation in a place so devoid of change or variety? Watson, would you care to spend your holiday in Liverpool?"

"I should say not. I have no friends or kinfolk there. Besides, it is a big city, and I live in a big city. You know yourself we sought the change of scenery and clime that Scotland could offer."

"Precisely: everyone wants a *change* as well as a rest. Edwards has forgone the change, for whatever strange reason. I had a suspicion there might be a lighthouse nearby too—but I had no idea it would be almost identical to the one the murder was committed in. If I do say so my friends, I think this case shall be one of my most memorable. Now Wallace, are you acquainted with any of the keepers at Skerryvore?"

"Douglas Burnham is my counterpart on the Isle of Mull. We are old and dear friends."

"Then you won't object if I refer to you in a wire to him?"

"Not in the slightest. I'll give you his address."

Next morning Holmes left early for the telegraph office. Upon his return the three of us played golf. It was a lovely day and for the first time in weeks, I saw Holmes utterly enjoying himself. The afternoon was spent fishing. In this pastime Holmes excelled, and before teatime he had killed five plump trout. Stopping on our return journey, Wallace purchased fresh butter, a half-dozen lemons, and a clump of parsley. I bought a bottle of Chablis. Needless to say, our dinner that evening was superb. But after the meal, Holmes again grew anxious. Murmuring something about "proof and evidence," he borrowed a pair of field glasses and left. When Wallace and I retired at eleven-thirty there was still no sign of him. He repeated the maneuver the following evening, and no amount of questions would draw an explanation from him.

On the third day after our visit to the Edwards' residence, a letter arrived for my friend via the morning post. He took it outside and opened it. It was a long letter apparently, for his cry of delight did not reach our ears for some time. Then he paced to and fro along the cliffside for half an hour before returning to the parlour to announce that he was again off to the telegraph station. In late afternoon, he received an answer which he showed us. It read as follows:

SHALL ARRIVE TOMORROW WITH McPHERESON
AS YOU HAVE INSTRUCTED. TELL CLIVE HE
CAN REQUEST CORMACK'S RELEASE. IT WILL
BE AN HONOUR TO MEET YOU SIR. BURNHAM

"Request Cormack's release? How so?"

"Because I shall prove his innocence tomorrow. With the help of your friend Burnham—who bye-the-bye strikes me as a tremendous chap—I shall disclose one of the most ingenious and diabolical murders in history."

We received this news with gladdened hearts, for fresh in our minds was the vivid picture of the young man sobbing in his tiny prison cell. I, of course, deeply regretted I had ever suspected him. That night, Holmes again amazed us by pursuing a nocturnal errand. To top it off, he carried with him not the field glasses but Wallace's landing net!

"I deeply appreciate this," he said lighting a last-minute cigarette before departing. "I've brought along a small net, as you saw yesterday. But this one, with its long handle and wide mouth, is just what I need. Farewell, I'll see you in the morning."

And so we watched him disappear up the path in the twilight, walking in his loose, swinging stride with the large net over his shoulder—as incongruous a sight as I ever witnessed.

PART FOUR: THE CULPRIT

Burnham and McPhereson arrived as promised the following afternoon. The three of us were at the station to meet them and drive them back to the cottage. Holmes had said nothing all day either about his solution to the Bell Rock murder or his solitary adventure of the previous night.

Since the weather was pleasant we sat in wicker chairs on the cliff while Wallace served sherry. Holmes looked tanned and fit after the day's fishing. Moreover, his countenance glowed with satisfaction—obviously the solution to this perplexing riddle had put him in a good frame of mind. And so he sat, his legs crossed in a jaunty fashion, the sea wind whipping at the cuffs of his flannel trousers and catching strands of his brownish hair. I had seldom seen him looking so well. He sipped his sherry and began.

"First of all, my deepest apologies to you Wallace and Watson. You have been most patient in putting up with my erratic—even *strange* behaviour of late. Furthermore, I've kept you both in the dark as to my theories and conjectures on this matter. As a matter of fact, even as we sit here both Burnham and McPhereson are more informed than either of you. This was unavoidable—but soon all of you shall be let in on the true nature of the deed, and the culprit. Ah, I see Inspector Drummond has arrived if that's the sound of his trap yonder. If I'm not mistaken, he'll have in tow a somewhat reluctant guest."

Drummond was a tall hefty fellow who commanded instant respect. He approached, removed his helmet and bowed slightly. As we rose to greet him, I was surprised to see the portly figure of Hayne Edwards appear from the pathway. A dour look was set upon his florid face; it was obvious he'd rather have been elsewhere.

"I have come on my own volition," he announced immediately, "and intend to remain only as long as I wish. You, Mr. Holmes, have now twice disturbed me; I request that you dispense with your business directly, as I am a busy man."

"Yes, of course, Mr. Edwards. Thank you so much for coming. I hope your presence here will help us get to the root of the problem."

Edwards face darkened still more.

"Eh, you say? I thought you told me the problem was resolved. The murderer has been identified ... is that not so?"

"I'm afraid I made a mistake, sir. As it happens, new evidence has come to light which clears the fellow. Now we must find the true murderer, and so I have summoned you. Let me ask you Mr. Edwards, which chemical did you employ?"

"Eh? What on earth are you talking about? You're talking rubbish man!"

"Come, come. Your scheme was clever–deucedly so. But I see through it. I am still curious however, as to the chemical used for the dispersant. Was it Calcium carbonate? That would be the most likely it seems to me. Then the cyanide was dissolved in an acid solution. Yes! That would do the trick, wouldn't it?"

Edwards' face flushed bright crimson. He weaved upon his feet and gasped for breath. Falling into a vacant chair, he regained his composure at last.

"I don't have the slightest idea–"

"What I am talking about? That is curious sir. These two men here have a rather strange account of an occurrence at Skerryvore lighthouse in the middle of June. Didn't you say that was when you were visiting the Isle of Tyree?"

His face assumed a look of fury, and he jumped clear of the chair.

"See here, Mr. Sherlock Holmes! You may be a clever man, but that does not give you the right to make slanderous statements about decent citizens. I shall take legal action against you sir! You have not the slightest shred of evidence or proof against me. At the time of the murder I was here in Arbroath. My housekeeper can vouch for that. Ross was killed in an isolated lighthouse miles from shore. There is no possible way I can be linked with his death. Good-day to you."

He was halted by Drummond, whilst Holmes excused himself for a moment. He disappeared into Wallace's barn, to return a few minutes later, walking with the net again over his shoulder. Under his arm was a strange, brightly coloured bundle. As he drew near to us, I saw it was an argyle stocking slipped over something that quivered and shook. I heard a gasp at my side and saw that Edwards, hands to his lips, had resumed trembling. Holmes drew up, and I was amazed to see a pair of yellow scaly feet protruding from the stocking's mouth. Holmes grabbed these in one hand, and the toes of the stocking in the other. With a flip of the wrist he had removed the cloth, and a scrawny, greenish-black bird with a hooked beak stood croaking and flapping in his grasp.

"You! Thief!" shouted Edwards, and lunged at Holmes. Being quite the stouter man, he knocked my friend to the ground, catching him unawares. With a shriek, the bird flew up. The next instant, Hayne Edwards had begun to run along the cliff path as fast as his thick legs would carry him. The bird followed, beating its greasy wings against his shoulders and crying.

"Is he the man you saw?" asked Holmes quickly.

"The very same," said Burnham. "He came to our headquarters inquiring about the bird. I'll swear to it in any court you name–"

The six of us started along the path in pursuit. The man ahead of us struggled furiously for flight, but his feet slipped on the loose sand. Meantime the bird continued flying round him, uttering hideous shrieks and beating at the running figure with its large wings. More than once Edwards reached up with flailing arms, yet still the bird pursued him like the Furies of Hell.

When we were but a few feet away, Edwards cried out, clutched at his chest, and staggered backwards. With a strained, purplish face he fought for breath, then slipped sideways off the path. We could not reach him in time, and the next instant he tumbled over the edge.

We saw him fall thirty feet, strike a projection, then fall again to land on the beach. The bird followed, circling slowly earthward.

* * *

"It would be difficult to say whether he died from the coronary arrest or the fall," said I, after examining the body.

"In any case," said Drummond officially, "he's dead, and it appears–deservedly so."

"*Here is the culprit gentlemen!*" said Holmes plucking the bird from the corpse. It rode willingly enough, and Holmes carried it back to the cottage. Drummond stationed himself by the shattered body of

Hayne Edwards—waiting for the help we would summon. By the time we returned to the cottage, I was bursting with curiosity.

After dispatching McPhereson to get the police, we returned to our chairs.

"Holmes!" I exclaimed. "Would you kindly tell us your explanations?"

"Certainly. I shall begin by showing you this letter I received yesterday from you, Burnham. We may as well start with it."

He took the letter from his breast pocket and handed it to me. It ran as follows:

Isle of Mull
July 27, 1902

My Dear Mr. Holmes:
Let me say at the outset that I am delighted and heartened that a man of your acumen has elected to take up the defence of Mr. Cormack. I do not know him personally, but am certain he is of noble character and therefore falsely accused. I say this because I am a lifelong friend of the man who selected and trained him, Clive Wallace. Am I given to understand that you too are a friend of his? If this be the case, then you know as well as I that Clive would never choose a man of less than the finest scruples and temperament.

As to the second point in your wire sir, I confess I am somewhat puzzled. You recall you asked if there had been any curious disturbances or incidents at Skerryvore Light within the past two months. Upon reflection and consultation with the keepers, we all agreed there had been none. But shortly after our talk one of the keepers, a chap named McPhereson, recalled for me the strange episode of the bird. His relating this curious tale, trivial though it was, immediately struck a chord with me, for reasons that will soon become clear to you. McPhereson reported that late at night in the second week in June, he'd been visited in the tower by a sea bird, a common cormorant. While he was on watch, the bird appeared sitting in one of the windows. It croaked, as if beckoning him. When he approached it, it opened its mouth and disgorged an object which then fell onto the floor. Seizing it, McPhereson saw it was a small pocket watch. Obviously, the blow caused by striking the rock floor of the workroom had shattered its crystal. Nevertheless, the watch, though smaller than most, seemed to be repairable. McPhereson delighted in his find. However, thanking his strange benefactor was impossible, for immediately upon letting the watch fall, the bird turned and flew off.

But sad to say McPhereson's gift was not to be kept, for the very next day a stoutish man appeared at our mainland office. He made his inquiry to my assistant but, watching them unseen from the next room, I overheard every word that was exchanged.

'Dreadfully sorry to trouble you,' the man began, 'but last evening, as I was fishing from a small boat, my watch was curiously plucked from my hands and stolen by a large duck. He appeared to fly towards the lighthouse yonder. I know it would be an un-thinkable coincidence, but perhaps one of the light tenders there has seen the bird.'

The assistant of course thought the man insane, and made a general excuse to be rid of him, whereupon the stranger's manner assumed a sterner tone. 'See here young fellow, I am quite serious. The bird stole my watch—I've often heard that birds are attracted to shiny objects. Now I saw it fly to the uppermost window in that tower. Could you please contact the tender there upon the chance he has seen my watch? I am willing to pay him a handsome reward for it if recovered, for it has tremendous sentimental value.'

To our astonishment Mr. Holmes, McPhereson came ashore bearing the broken watch in his hands. The stranger, who would not give his name, paid him five pounds for it—far more than it's worth I'm sure. But why do I go on with this foolish narrative? Surely it has nothing to do with Mr. Cormack's guilt or innocence. I report it only because you asked me to report any or all curious incidents, however trifling. So I report this occurrence because it is curious—made more so I think by the fact that the stranger, upon recovering his treasure, seemed delighted the crystal face had been broken.

I regret I have not been of greater assistance,

Sincerely,
Douglas Burnham

We sat in stunned silence after reading the letter. The quiet was broken by a hoarse croaking and flapping as the bird fought its way free from Holmes' grasp and fluttered to the ground, glaring balefully at each of us in turn with its demonic yellow eyes.

"A clever man Edwards, and deadly," said Holmes. "Of course to the trained mind, his account to the assistant is suspect. What man goes fishing off the Scottish coast in a small boat at night? Why would he look at his watch in the darkness—let alone carry so fragile an item with him? Finally, how could he possibly see the bird enter the tower window? But his plan eventually worked: he killed Robert Ross with diabolical ingenuity, and from a distance of many miles ..."

"I take it then," said I, "that Edwards trained the bird to fly in the direction of lights, to enter small windows in towers and drop objects—deadly or otherwise, into them? Then of course, the charade at Skerryvore was merely the *rehearsal* to see if the training were complete."

"Certainly. And using a pocket watch as the training dummy was a stroke of genius. What other small object can be sought after the following day without drawing undue attention? Also, the timepiece's fragility was a splendid test of the operative conditions. By some means Edwards ascertained the dates when Ross would be on duty the third watch. All he had to do was prime his weapon: place the deadly vial in the beak pouch of this bird—face it towards Bell Rock's flashing beacon, and release it. It wended its way unerringly, on silent wings of death over the stormy ocean to its victim."

I looked at the animal in horror. Yet it paid scant heed to my stare, and continued to preen itself and jerk its sharp head about on its long, snake-like neck. Holmes again picked it up and, placing thumb and forefinger beneath its jaws, drew down a thin, membranous sac.

"There's room for several vials in here—no danger of the bird accidentally dropping it before accomplishing the mission. As you may know, these birds are remarkably intelligent, and are trained in China to retrieve fish for their masters—"

"Ah, so *that* was the significance of the Chinese print in Edwards' study!" cried Wallace. "You noticed the cormorants thus engaged in the river scene."

"Yes, and knew he had seen the birds operating first-hand during his tenure there. Ah McPhereson, are they on their way? Splendid! I think we should all go round to the lock-up and oversee the release of young Cormack, who has the misfortune not only of a crippled arm, but a name that begins with the same four letters as our friend's here. Shall we be off?"

EPILOGUE

"Really Watson," said Holmes irritably putting aside his split-bamboo flyrod, "you mean you still haven't filled in the details of this case? Well then," he mused, "I suppose it's a blessing too, knowing after all I shan't be outdone by you. You Wallace, drawing up your ottoman, you wish to hear this too? Very well. Let me say at the outset I was fairly convinced, even before we departed for Bell Rock, that neither Hay nor Cormack was guilty for the following reasons:

"*One*: murder by civilised men is an act of final desperation, not the result of petty grievances. I wasn't convinced by your narration Wallace, that either man hated Ross sufficiently to end his life.

"*Two*: As I stated earlier, the tower's isolation rendered it a poor place to commit murder. The killer could not escape becoming suspect.

"*Three*: Despite the fact that disposal of the body would have been simple and permanent, it remained in the tower. The scrawled note was puzzling, and for some time I was convinced Ross committed suicide and vented his general depression and frustration by implicating Cormack with it. However, as you know, it was mere coincidence, unfortunate for John Cormack, that the villain bird had a similar name in the initial syllable ..."

"But what led you to suspect outside causes?"

"The broken vial. You perhaps remember my earlier doubts concerning this. How could a lightkeeper who decides upon murder suddenly procure a vial of cyanide? He cannot. Either Ross brought it with him—intending to kill himself all along, or else it was introduced from the outside. I was assuming the first possibility until—through Evans' foresight—I was able to examine the fragments first-hand. You recall the glass was very thin, and of two diameters. These details led me to the theory that the vial was really a double container: a larger glass tube enclosing a smaller one. They were filled with chemicals that react violently when mixed. As you may suppose, when the apparatus shattered on the stone floor of the work room in which Ross was sitting, the release and dissemination of lethal gas was terribly swift. In fact, I may venture that Edwards was relieved indeed to see his partner in crime, the cormorant, return from the grim mission unscathed."

"And when did you begin to suspect Hayne Edwards?"

"When I interviewed Hutchenson and discovered that he alone had sufficient motive for Ross' death. You see, the pieces fit well. I knew by examining the glass fragments that the vial was not a suicide weapon but in fact a bomb, a missile—obviously having come from outside the tower. Hearing Hutchenson's story, I knew the likely candidate was Edwards. The only question that remained therefore, was the means of transport. How did Edwards inject this lethal glass bottle into an isolated, dangerous tower a hundred feet high? It was then that the swirling gulls took on a new significance. Obviously, the only feasible means was through the air–thus a bird was employed. Still, stupid as I was, the scrawled message misled me. It wasn't until I saw the Chinese river scene in Edward's house that I recognised the identity of his accomplice."

"Incredible!"

"Not in the slightest. An interesting case, but an easy one. You might recall my telling Edwards twice during our visit that the murderer was caught and as good as dead. His reaction was dramatic to say the least. Villain that he was, he still had enough fibre in him to reel at the thought of causing an innocent man's execution. He'd carefully planned the murder, you see, to appear as a suicide. When I observed his reactions I knew he was the culprit. But who would believe my weird tale? I needed proof! So I took the field glasses and surveyed the house at night. The first night I drew a blank. But sure enough, the second evening Edwards emerged and brought food to the barn on his property. That meant he visited the bird every other night. Accordingly, if my reasoning were correct, the following night I would be left undisturbed to gather the final evidence. I took your wide landing net Wallace, and a dark lantern. Stepping inside Edwards' barn, I held up the beam in one hand, and the net ready in the other. As per my conjectures, the trained bird flew directly at the beacon. Snaring it was no problem, and I was frankly amazed at its timidity and friendliness."

"It should have been destroyed Holmes!" I spouted, "How foolish of you to release it–Lord knows what havoc it will cause–"

"Watson, I'm surprised! You know animals merely reflect the mind that employs them. Our many adventures together bear this out, especially those known as the Speckled Band and Giant Rat of Sumatra, the latter from which we scarcely escaped with our lives and reason."

"I suppose you're right; the cormorant is harmless without the poison bomb in his beak. He may as well join his fellows in one of the coastal rookeries. But I–"

"Hush Watson–you hear it?" said Holmes quickening.

I cocked my ear. Before long came the unmistakable sound of Scotland that sets one's hair on end, and causes one's throat to swell in a tight ache.

"It's the family of John Cormack," said Wallace. "He's a local fellow, and his kin have come to show their gratitude. They're giving you a piping, Holmes."

And so we went out into the evening air. The soft wind brought the skirl down along the cliffside. At last we saw the four of them silouetted against the golden sky. They say pipes can be heard over a mile, and I'm convinced it's true. As they marched up towards the cottages, their kilts swinging, the three of us gazed spellbound in silence. The sound grew piercing. It seemed to surround us, indeed to go through us. The pipers paced to and fro on the cliff walk, their regimental medallions gleaming in the sun's last rays.

"They're playing *Loch Rannoch*, a tune of victory," said Wallace at last.

"I am honored, and moved," said my friend. "What a fitting end to our trip, eh Watson—standing here in the golden gleam of evening listening to the rousing wail of bagpipes. It is glorious. Shouldn't we invite them in for a whiskey when they've finished?"

THE ADVENTURE OF THE EYRIE CLIFF

THE ADVENTURE
OF THE EYRIE CLIFF

The Spring of 1917 came cloaked in grief and drenched in blood. England watched horrified as her young men, so recently sent off to France to the tunes of brass bands, returned in ragged heaps bled out from hospital trains, torn and dying.

To make matters worse, the war dragged on and on without any resolution in sight. Furthermore, with the Imperial Navy's resumption of unrestricted submarine warfare in February, British trade had ground to a halt. We were losing over twenty ships a week. At that rate, all imports would soon stop and the Isles would be starved into submission.

Like most physicians too old for field service, I spent fifteen hours a day in surgery or at the dressing stations. As the end of March drew near, my spirits ebbed lower and lower. On the night of the 27th, I collapsed in surgery. Awakening in a military hospital, I was informed I was suffering from acute nervous exhaustion. So I lay upon my back for two days recovering, surrounded by the groans and cries of the wounded and dying. Upon my release I was advised—ordered would be a better word—to take a short respite from my duties.

"Do not feel you are deserting England by taking a holiday Watson," said my colleague Davies. "On the contrary, I'm certain you'll be doing her a *disfavour* by remaining, for if my diagnosis is correct, you'll not last til summertime if you keep up this pace, and the war may last for another two years. So off you go now John, and *no arguments*! Neither I, nor any of the hospital staff, want to hear from you, or know your whereabouts, for at least a fortnight." So I tottered out of the hospital and hailed a cab. Rattling away to my lodgings in the West End, I was seized by a sudden fit of nostalgia; I threw up the trap and shouted to the driver to go along Baker Street. Upon spying our old quarters, I felt a quiver of excitement race through my weary soul. Instructing the cabbie to wait, I stepped from the cab and climbed the stone stoop to the doorway. There were the faint gilded numerals: *221.* How many times had Sherlock Holmes and I returned to this very doorway, bone-weary, yet flushed with the success of solving another adventure! And how many times had we then retired to our chairs before the fireplace to recount the evidence, Holmes' brilliant observations and deductions, and the final apprehension of the criminal!

I entered the hallway and climbed the seventeen steps. It struck me as odd, yet the intervening years seemed to vanish in a twinkling and, my rheumatism notwithstanding, it was as if I were once again the young practitioner who, in 1881, would be returning from my day's work to the companionship of my strange roommate, newly acquainted, who indulged in his grotesque experiments and startling pronouncements. As I reached the landing, I could almost hear the plaintive violin melody issuing from within.

Ah, but the illusion vanished in an instant! From behind the door came the sound of a woman sobbing—in grief no doubt, for her son or husband recently killed in France. Impulsively I knocked at the door, instantly regretting my action. It was opened by a young woman who stood in a tattered dress, staring at me with tired eyes that stood in her pale face like hot coals set on baker's dough.

"I am Doctor John Watson," I began awkwardly. "I used to lodge in these very rooms—"

"We haven't the money," she said in a flat voice.

"You don't understand," I interjected.

"We haven't any money!" she wailed. "My Tom's crippled. We've no food! Clara's got the consumption ... go away *please*, we haven't the money!"

The door slammed in my face. I heard a series of fast footsteps, then the muffled sound of crying into a pillow. Above rose the high sound of a child's wailing. In the instant I was afforded a look into our old quarters, I was appalled at its appearance. The peeling plaster and paint, the dilapidated furniture, the heaps of rags strewn about— Holmes would have been shocked.

I raised my hand in an attempt to knock again, but realised the futility of it. I had turned on the landing to start down when an idea struck me. I drew a ten pound note from my wallet and placed it under the crack of the door.

"God Bless you," I murmured, then returned to the cab.

During the ride hone, it became clear to me that, rather than lifting my spirits, the visit to the old quarters had only deepened my despair. As I trudged wearily up the flights of stairs to my lodgings that evening, I felt more alone and sad than I had ever felt in my entire life. Later that night, after my evening glass, as I sat staring into the purring fireplace, the recollections of the old days with Holmes rushed upon me with unexpected clarity and suddenness. This *déjà vu* at first elated me, but then, as I juxtaposed the old memories with my present state—alone and sick in a dying world, the disparity proved too much. All the rage, sadness and frustration of my recent life bore down upon my weakened spirit like a steam hammer. I wept.

I must have dozed while I sat, for I awoke, chilled to the marrow, at four in the morning. The cold, dark room and the spent ashes of the fire reminded me painfully of what my life had become.

"I have fallen into the sere and the yellow leaf," I murmured, "and that which should accompany old age ..."

I was on the verge of another bout of self-pity when the voice of Reason rose up from the depths of my being and set things right.

"Dash it!" I cried. "Enough of this sulking sorrow. Davies says a holiday's in order, and a holiday I shall have. I shall wire Holmes tomorrow morning and seek him out!"

So saying, I retired to bed, and slept more soundly than I had in months.

But I was unable to deliver my telegram to my old friend, because first thing in the morning I was awakened by the delivery boy tugging at the bellcord.

"A wire sir. Do you wish to send a reply?"

Seeing the *Eastbourne* office mark at the top of the wire as I opened it, I felt my heart jump with anticipation and hope.

"It couldn't be," I whispered aloud as I raced towards the mantle to fetch my reading glasses, "surely this would be a tremendous coincidence, since I was about to wire him!"

But my fondest expectations were granted as I read the following message:

MY DEAR WATSON, CAN YOU SPARE A WEEK? THE BIRD WATCHING HERE IS LOVELY. SHALL AWAIT YOUR REPLY. HOLMES.

Overjoyed at this happy turn of events, I replied immediately that he could expect me at the Eastbourne station the following day at 1:00. I spent the remainder of the day preparing for my journey, packing my valise, checking through my closets for various objects that might be of value: golf clubs, fishing rods, field glasses. I must confess I was excited as a child on Christmas Eve as I made my preparations. But what was the cause of Holmes' sudden invitation? I hadn't heard a word from him in almost a year—and had not seen him for much longer than that. Had Davies wired him up and arranged it all? My heart sank at the thought ...To make matters worse, I looked at the date affixed to the wire and saw to my horror that it was All Fool's Day! What if it were a monstrous joke?

But, realising my unfounded fears were getting the best of me, I put aside such thoughts, and looked forward, in high hopes, to my holiday on the South Downs ...

Next day at the station, my new-found optimism vanished in a twinkling. As I waited to board my train to Eastbourne, a hospital train from Southampton pulled into Waterloo, discharging its grim cargo. The stretcher bearers toiled endlessly to and fro, taking the wounded from the train to neat lines along the station platform. Again there came to my ears the horrid sound of the past several years: the moaning and weeping of the men, their plaintive cries for help and loved ones. Almost from habit, I set down my luggage and began attending them. So engrossed was I that, ninety minutes later, I realised I had missed my train. Holmes will be angry with me, I thought as I trudged along the platform and boarded the next train. Knowing his natural impatience, I spent the greater part of the journey fretting that my late arrival would throw him into a temper and so ruin our holiday.

One had only to glance out the carriage window to see the grim evidence of war: the home guard in their helmets, directing traffic and manning sandbagged posts; the long queues of townsfolk waiting for ration cards, and most of all, the total absence of young men.

I arrived at Eastbourne in the late afternoon. As I expected, Holmes wasn't there, so I began the five mile trudge to his cottage at Birling Gap. Due to my recent illness and advancing age, the grip seemed heavier than it might have been, and the walk more arduous.

I had reached the countryside and was making my way along the shoulder of the road when I heard behind me a great commotion—a series of popping coughs and the drone of a petrol engine. Next instant, a motorcycle shot past me.

Through the bluish haze that remained, I could just see the driver, clad head to toe in leather, glance back in my direction. With his helmet and dust goggles, he resembled an aeroplane pilot. The motorcycle, dragging its sidecar, shot forth in a shattering roar. Yet to my surprise, it turned about half a mile up the road and came back, bearing down directly at me. Just before I jumped aside with fright, the contraption braked to a halt and the driver sprang from the saddle. He approached me and grabbed me by the shoulders.

"Watson! Where the devil have you been?"

"Holmes! Dear God man, what are you doing with that infernal machine?'"

"Don't you like it? I must confess it's now my favourite possession!"

He led me over to the motorcycle, which sat puffing and snorting, and belching clouds of blue smoke. It had an aura of malintent, as if it had a life of its own—a poised dragon—and I approached it warily.

"Isn't she a beauty? A Douglas twin cylindre, and capable of sixty miles an hour ..."

"I say Holmes! Take that silly outfit off and let's take a carriage. Really, I'm shocked—"

"No need to be. You know I'm in the Home Guard, and so must have transportation ... *fast* transportation. A car is expensive for one who lives alone. A horse requires constant care, and I am away for long periods on government business. So you see the Douglas is perfect. Come on, climb aboard. I'll go slowly—word of honour ..."

With some difficulty I posited myself in the tiny "sidecar." It was fastened to the frame of the motorcycle, and held level only by a large spoked wheel which, judging by the appearance of the car, was a mud-flinger *extraordinaire.* Holmes tied my grip to the rear fender, climbed once again aboard the Douglas, and we were off. After the initial sensations of bewilderment and fear, I enjoyed the ride immensely. It was like flying. Also, I was amazed at the smoothness of the ride—much preferable to a coach.

After a while we left the main highway and turned onto a narrow dirt road that was lined on either side by tall hedges. We skipped and bounced along in this tunnel for several miles, shouting our conversation the whole time. Holmes looked as trim and fit as ever, which meant he had not been idle. Presently the road opened onto a broad sloping meadow. Far in the distance I could glimpse the sea. Now on a gravel path, we rode over the gentle hills of the South Downs for another mile or so until we came to a neat stone cottage with adjoining courtyard. It was set halfway down a long slope that was dotted with trees. Trees and bushes were thick round it, which afforded some shelter from the sea winds and weather. Up the slope and to the side of the cottage was a medium-sized orchard. My vision unobscured by the newly-budding trees, I could see the many hut-shaped straw beehives that were placed within. My companion braked to a stop and helped me extricate myself from the tiny car. On cramped legs, I managed to wobble the twenty yards to the front door of Holmes' cottage. It was lovely. All stone, it had an immaculate slate roof, two tiny gables, and matching bow windows on the ground floor. The windows were leaded, and decorated with coloured glass round the edges. The name *Finisterre* was done in lead above them. The more I saw of *Finisterre*, the more apparent it was to me that Holmes, after leading an arduous and spartan life in London for so many years, had chosen to retire in the style and comfort that befitted his distinguished career. Though small, the cottage was richly appointed, and lacked not one single comfort or convenience. I noticed that Holmes, always fond of gadgets and things technological in general, had a telephone installed in the hallway.

The downstairs consisted of four rooms: parlour, living room, kitchen, and study. Upstairs were two bedrooms—one of which I was to occupy. Also, there was a small glass greenhouse that abutted the study and opened onto the courtyard. Housed within were easels and canvasses as well as a myriad of plants. I noticed the plants looked different from common house and garden varieties. I gazed about in awe at the strange collection of flora.

"Come, come Watson, don't tell me you fail to recognise our old friend *Conium maculatum*, which is responsible for the death of so great a man as Socrates, to say nothing of Clayborne the canal lock-keeper. Then of course you are familiar with *curarae thanadensis*, over yonder in the corner—a mere speck of its resin under the skin and a man has only seconds to live. Needless to say also, his final moments are not pleasant ones. The tail spurge vine over your head is *mimosa euphorbia delacanses*, whose milky juice, you'll recall, played so important a part in the episode of McCauley, the Idiot-Savant. Yes, that's correct: its ingestion causes the victim to babble incoherently for days ... It may interest you also that in the root cellar below us I am cultivating some remarkable fungi: several species of deadly

Amanitae, a toadstool called the Devil's Drinking Cup, not to mention the famous—"

"Enough Holmes! I see you haven't changed, despite your declining years ..."

He winced at my comment then, after reflecting briefly, answered earnestly.

"On the contrary, Watson. Though in my sunset years, I feel that my time here on the South Downs is being put to better use than ever. As you can see, I have taken up painting, and spend many a carefree hour at the cliffside."

"So I see. Well, your keen powers of observation, coupled with your fine taste lead to excellent results. This one of the approaching storm is superb."

"It's called 'A Clear Day ...'"

"Oh, sorry—"

"But thank you for your kind words, none the less," he said patting me on the shoulder. "Bye the bye, I believe I mentioned *birdwatching* in my wire, did you bring your fieldglasses?"

"Yes, of course—but when did you take up ornithology?"

"The same time I took up painting, and I'm glad for your fieldglasses too. Let me explain. Look here ..."

He led me back into the study which was, as was immediately obvious, the only room in the cottage untouched by the housekeeper. Like our flat of old times, it was strewn with newspapers, souvenirs, artifacts, weapons, sporting equipment, and chemical apparatus.

"It looks as if a typhoon struck it," I mused. "Thank God this place is large enough to have a few rooms left uncluttered. Now what is it you wish to show me?"

Holmes pulled down a chart that hung rolled on the wall. It was a diagram of a submarine, showing side and front views, a silhouette, a silhouette with darkened background and, finally, an internal view of the vessel, showing the compartments, engines, and so forth.

"This is the *UB-2*, the new German boat that is killing England."

I looked at the machine with horror and loathing. Even its appearance was menacing. The raked bow, the closed metal hull, devoid of ports or stacks, its fishlike, serpentine configuration: all spelled evil, stealth, and death.

We spent a few minutes discussing the war's horror and immensity before Holmes returned to the submarine. He took the chart from the wall, and the large map beneath it—which was of the English Channel and environs—and bade me follow him to the living room, where he lighted the fire. There we sat, exactly as in the old days, while he poured over the charts explaining significant points to me.

"So now you see the significance of birdwatching and painting on the cliffs, eh Watson? It's the Home Guard's duty to keep channel watch, and a periscope wake that is reported may save lives and ships."

"It's like the Zeppelin scourge of last year."

"Exactly. A new weapon with monstrous potential. But we found the answer to the zeppelins with the explosive bullet. Thank heavens for that! It's no longer a threat. Now we must do the same for the UB-2. But until that time arrives, we must do the very best we can."

"And you sit on the cliffside with your glasses, or your easel...but *why*? Why the ruse Holmes? Surely most people know you're in the Home Guard..."

He leaned back in the chair and drew on his pipe contentedly.

"My role in England's defence is perhaps a bit more involved than you realise."

"Eh? How so?"

He paused reflectively before answering.

"I'm afraid I cannot tell you."

My head sank involuntarily. "... I see..." I whispered.

"Heavens Watson, don't take on so! Lord knows it's no reflection on our relationship. You are the closest, dearest friend I've ever had, or ever shall have. In fact, it is your reassuring presence that I find so soothing in these troubled times–"

"Likewise!" I interjected, brightened by his remarks.

"But state secrets are state secrets my friend, and oaths are oaths."

"I quite understand. So you're doing more than watching for periscope wakes."

"To be sure. Now I can, I think, tell you about certain strange occurrences that have taken place recently on this coast without betraying my oath of secrecy."

"Pray, don't place your oath in jeopardy because of me."

"I shan't. But you should know the basic nature of my investigations here, since you're likely to be involved in them yourself."

I felt a thrill of excitement surge through me. On the chase once again; how like the old times!

"Now you of course recall Lord Kitchner's death last year aboard the *Hampshire*. It was a doubly tragic blow. On the one hand, he was a symbol of British military might and cunning. Also, as you may recollect, he was one of the first persons in high authority to predict that the war would be long and arduous, and urged that England prepare herself accordingly—"

"How true his warning! If only more had heeded it—"

"*Exactly!* In addition, he was enroute to a meeting with Czar Nicholas. Perhaps had he met with success, the Russians would still be fighting with us, instead of amongst themselves. So you see how Kitchner's death was a terrific benefit to the enemy ..."

"Obviously of enourmous consequence."

"Now Watson, there's reason to believe that word of Kitchner's errand was leaked to the Germans, and that they know he'd be aboard the *Hampshire* on her voyage past the Orkneys. The ship was deliberately singled out on the chance of killing the illustrious passenger."

"How was the word leaked?"

"Wait a second. There are other events since then that I should briefly relate. Do you recall the mysterious disappearance last fall of Sir Nigel Crittenden, the armaments engineer?"

"I believe so. Was it not he who designed the new breech-loaders at Gibralter?"

"The very same. And he was in the midst of perfecting coastal fortifications for Dover when he disappeared."

"Isn't it generally supposed that he fell from the cliffs while on a solitary walk?"

"Yes. And that supposition is only further evidence of the cunning and audacity of the Hun, who will strike us at home as well as on the fields of France and Belgium. You also recollect the death of Henry Shutcliffe?"

"Yes, of course. His Bristol accidentally overturned on the Isle of Wight. He was crushed under it ..."

"Humph! I'll wager you *five to one* it was no accident! It was certainly convenient for the Triple Alliance that Shutcliffe died within a few weeks of perfecting the Dragonfly rotary engine for our S.E.5 aircraft. Here are three more, quickly: the death of Clarence Upham, the Oxford cryptologist, while visiting Brighton on Holiday. The abduction of Sir George Wexler from his country home in Hastings in February. And finally, think on this Watson: just night before last Geoffery Cardwell, while out for a stroll on the shore not more than eight miles from here, *vanished into thin air.*"

"Extraordinary! But who is this fellow? His name is the only unfamiliar one of the lot."

"Cardwell is a brilliant young naval strategist. Some say he's the best since Nelson. My brother Mycroft, who works with him, shares this opinion. And he's hard to please. His importance to our cause now is paramount, since he appears to be the world's leading authority on countering submarine attacks. He led in the development of the convoy technique, which may prove to be the best anti-submarine tactic yet. Also, he assisted in the creation of the magnetic mine, which can be set off by the mere *proximity* of a metal hull. He has even mentioned the possibility of using airships to track down—well, I've said enough to give you the general idea, have I not?"

"Of course. And you have been engaged to discover his whereabouts?"

"Yes. And that's another reason I sent for you, old fellow. The game's afoot once again, and I shall appreciate your help."

"Delighted Holmes! But surely you have been active since Von Bork's arrest, why you yourself told me—"

"Pshaw! Of course I've been involved in problems now and then Watson, and actively sought them out to keep in form. But the unravelling of Cardwell's disappearance ... well, I shouldn't be exaggerating if I were to say that *the fate of our country is at stake.*"

"Beg pardon, but if the matter is as urgent as you say, why have you waited an entire day to commence?"

"A good question. To begin with, I heard of it only yesterday since I have been in Oslo for a fortnight—"

"What were you doing there?" I asked.

"Let us say ... state business. To continue, I returned here Tuesday and was met by the awful news. Mycroft wired me direct from the Admiralty! I, in turn, wired you. First thing tomorrow we shall meet two persons who were close to Cardwell just before his disappearance: his cottage housekeeper and his school friend."

"And they are coming here?"

"No, Watson, we'll take the Douglas and drive up towards Hastings where it occurred. Now look here. Notice that I have placed a small cross in ink upon this map of the coast to show where each incident occurred. You see them? Ah, your eyes, like mine, have grown weaker, eh? I'll turn up the light, and here's a lens ... now, see them? Hastings, Hyde, Brighton, Dover ... you see any pattern?"

"None except that they are all along the south coast ..."

"Yes. And another rather interesting thing. The very geographic *centre* of the web of incidents seems to be—"

He tapped the map with his pencil.

"*Eastbourne,* that's right here!"

"Yes. Curious, is it not? Now then old fellow, would you like a whiskey to take the chill from your bones? I'll fetch the bottle directly I pop the beef pie in the oven."

* * *

Early next day Holmes fueled up the Douglas and we shot off towards Hastings. We roared and thumped along the small roads for several miles before alighting at a rustic seaside inn for breakfast. Over our meal Holmes briefly recounted the information he had presented to me the previous evening. Cardwell's cottage lay near cliffside a quarter mile from the beach. He had disappeared on his evening stroll along the cliffs.

"Much as Sir Nigel disappeared."

"Yes, Watson. The two incidents are remarkably similar. But see here," he continued, tracing his finger along the map, "this has caught my eye: do you see this narrow indentation on the coastline? It's a small cove—it cannot be more than a hundred yards across..."

"*Ballow's Wash,*" I said, reading the print that covered the little bay.

"Yes. Note it is the only such shallow bay 'til one gets to Hastings proper, four miles further up ..."

"And you think there is a connection between this small wash and Cardwell's disappearance?"

"I say nothing yet, except that its presence is interesting. We'll no doubt know more when we inspect the site firsthand."

We arrived at the Cardwell cottage near Bexhill-on-Sea. Miss Simmons the housekeeper and Cardwell's friend Stanley Gaines came out to meet us. Miss Simmons was a trim elderly woman who had known young Cardwell all his life. Gaines was a large, blandish fellow, who looked as though he'd played some football at college. He appeared open and frank, and greeted us warmly despite his obvious agitation. We followed them into the cottage and seated ourselves in the parlour. Holmes asked them to describe the events leading up to Cardwell's disappearance.

"We'd come down together," began Gaines. "Geoffery rang me up last Thursday night. 'Let's pop down to the cottage for a week,' he said, 'I'm in need of a rest from all this war business.' Well, I was as tired as he, and had a leave due, so I agreed to accompany him—"

"Pardon me," said Holmes, "but may I ask which branch of the service you're in?"

"Engineering," Gaines replied.

"And you went to school with Cardwell?"

"Yes, we've known each other since the Cambridge days, and were in military engineering together until he transferred to intelligence."

"And were you aware of the projects he has been working on recently?"

The big man grimaced slightly at Holmes' query, and, with an air of annoyance, answered.

"Well he did confide in me that he'd been involved in anti-submarine warfare ..."

Holmes' eyes narrowed to slits as he examined Gaines. "Did he mention anything more *specific* with relation to submarines?"

Gaines hesitated, then replied: "He mentioned ... he did talk of the possibility, the *possibility* mind you, of a mine barrage—"

"Yes—?"

"—a mine barrage extending from the Orkneys to the Norwegian coast—"

"*Drat!* Oh callow youth, Watson! Brilliance and wisdom are so rarely joined! Tell me Gaines, what did he say of this mine barrage?"

"Nothing else, Mr. Holmes."

"And to the best of your knowledge," continued Holmes earnestly, "he mentioned this to no one else?"

"I'm sure he didn't."

"Miss Simmons, you have known Cardwell longer than anyone except his parents. Can you in any way account for his strange disappearance?"

"Oh, no sir! And that's what makes it all the more disquieting. Geoffery was always so punctual; he never went anywhere without leaving word. I'm so afraid ill's befallen him—"

She buried her trembling face in her hands, unable to continue.

At Holmes' signal, I sat down next to the woman to comfort her while he returned to Gaines.

"Exactly what time did he leave for his walk?"

"After dinner. About eight or eight-thirty."

"And why did you not accompany him, if you don't mind my asking?"

"Of course not. In fact, I had gone with him on the three previous walks. But earlier that day—it was Monday—I turned my ankle slightly climbing up the cliff walk, and that afternoon it began to throb. So when Geoffery asked me if I cared to go with him, I naturally declined the invitation, and waited at the cottage with a book, my foot propped up before the fire ..."

"It's as he says," added Miss Simmons, who had managed to pull herself together. "And we waited for Lord knows how long before going out to look for him."

"When he failed to show at ten, I went out along the cliffs in search," said Gaines. "I walked perhaps half a mile in each direction, but saw no sign of Geoffery or Tinker—"

"Who is Tinker?"

"Geoffery's Airedale. He vanished as well."

"Interesting ..." observed Holmes. "Cardwell kept the dog with him in London?"

"Oh, yes. They were together always."

"And they disappeared together too eh? That could tell us something perhaps. Well Mr. Gaines—your ankle's had two days to mend, are you fit for a hike? Splendid, then come along Watson, we'll have a look about the place and see if we can catch a scent, though it'll be difficult considering the lapse of time."

The Cardwell cottage commanded a view of the sea that was even more splendid than Holmes enjoyed at Finisterre. The cliffs were not far away, and we soon stood at their summit looking down to the beach far below. There the surf rolled and broke in steady rhythm. Above the booming of the water came the high mewling of the gulls and shorebirds beneath us as they whirled about or perched upon the crags and crevices of chalk.

"What was the weather like Monday evening?" Holmes asked Gaines.

"A heavy mist, Mr. Holmes—almost a light rain ... but surely it was no different at your lodgings ... do you not reside on the South Downs also?"

"I was out of the country."

"I see ... well it was quite damp."

"And next morning, did you see Cardwell's footprints, or those of the dog?"

"I'm sorry, but I didn't think to look."

"Yes, that's not surprising, but still unfortunate. However, we're in luck, it seems, because we've had no rain or dew since then. The tracks, made in damp earth, should still be easily visible. Now which direction did you usually go when you walked with Cardwell after dinner?"

"Either one. But I think he generally preferred to turn right and walk south ..."

We'd scarcely gone twenty feet before Holmes picked up the track. Considering its age, it was remarkably clear; one could see the imprint of a heavy boot and the scraped print of a large dog. Kneeling, Holmes swept his eyes in all directions.

"I say Gaines, did Cardwell tell you how far away the nearest neighbors are?"

"He mentioned that the cottage is very isolated Mr. Holmes, likewise this stretch of cliffs."

"Then we might safely assume," muttered Holmes, "that these tracks are either Cardwell's or yours, Gaines. But if you've worn those shoes all along, then these cannot be yours."

Gaines' shoes were dress brogues with pointed toes. He replied that he had indeed worn them on the walks with the missing man.

"Also, the night of Geoffery's disappearance, I did not venture this close to the cliff edge. The night was dark and wet, and I am unfamiliar with the area."

"A prudent course. Now Gaines, it is imperative that we establish the identity of this track. Tell me, are you familiar—quite familiar—with the appearance of Cardwell's boots?"

"Yes, sir. I could give you quite an accurate description of them."

"Splendid! But don't you do it my good man, let *me* do it. Let us devise a little test. Let me see if I can recount the general appearance of Cardwell's footwear to you, Gaines, by studying the prints left behind ... If my description is at all accurate, then we'll have satisfied our test, will we not?"

"Well, I suppose so," said Gaines in a bewildered voice.

"Now first off, can you tell me if Cardwell complained of a bunion, ingrown toenail, or planter's wart on his right foot?"

"No, I don't recall any such complaint."

"Fine, then let me proceed. First, the boots are *brown*; they can be no other colour—"

"Holmes!" I cried. "A cheap trick surely! You know it's quite *impossible* to tell a boot's colour from the *footprint.* You're simply guessing this tid-bit in hopes of impressing Gaines, and hoping you're right because we all know most boots *are* brown, rather than black."

Holmes ignored me totally, continuing to stare closely at the impressions in the earth.

"*Brown*, Mr. Gaines?"

"Yes sir, but how on God's earth—"

"Now this is a bit trickier. I would also venture that the *laces* don't match. I could be mistaken I'll admit, but tell me, are the laces on the right boot borrowed from dress shoes?"

Gaines weaved before us, dumbstruck.

"Mr. Holmes sir! I don't know what to say ..."

"Say yea or nay man—well?"

"Yes sir, *yes*! It is exactly as you say: Geoffery broke the laces on his right boot Monday afternoon and, having no spares, took those from his dress shoes. You are a *wizard* sir!"

"Thank you Gaines, but it's hardly news to me. Ah, but that's not the *only* difficulty Cardwell had with his footwear eh? Just as you turned your ankle, he seemed to have had an accident too, correct? Yes? I'll venture it was either on Friday evening, or the following morning. Of course, he had the new heel put on locally, rather than in London. Finally, he's used these boots for riding now and then, which shows his unconventional streak. You may or may not be familiar with this habit, but I must say I rather admire him for it. I say, are you all right man?"

By this time, poor Gaines was beside himself with wonder. He had settled himself on a ledge of outcropping rock, and was wiping his damp brow with trembling hands.

"You must explain this to me Mr. Holmes, you really *must*."

"Tut man, once I reveal to you the method and the process, you'll shrug it off as sheer drudgery, right Watson?"

"I must say Holmes," I answered, "accustomed as I am to your observations and deductions, I am completely at a loss as to how you can tell things such as the colour of the boots, and the condition of the laces, *etcetera*, when all you've to go on are the imprints of the soles. Now if—"

"Then I shall lift the veil of mystery now. First of all, these soles are familiar to me, and to astute inspectors and policemen as well. They are as well-known, I would submit, as the treads of famous tyres, like Palmer, Dunlop, and Michelin, for they belong to a famous brand of hiking boots. *McFarren's Country Squires* are sold everywhere, and the tread is unique and quite distinctive. Moreover, while they are now offered in both brown and black uppers, the black variety was introduced only this year. By examining these severely worn treadmarks, one can easily see that the boots in question are several years old at least. Ergo: they are *brown*."

"But how came you to know about all the different boot treads, and their imprints?" asked Gaines.

"The same way I came to know about all the cigar ashes, tyre treads, mud splashes, poisons, tattoos, and everything *else*," responded Holmes with irritation, "because it is my *business* to know them. Now, let me describe the boots further: did they not have octagonal brass eyelets, and double waxed stitching round the heels?"

Gaines nodded his head in disbelief.

"Now as to the laces. Brilliant as the deductive leap was, I consider myself fortunate; I'll admit I was on rather thin ice. But remember, I asked you if Cardwell had complained of foot pain. You replied he had not. Yet, as evidenced by the sloppy presentation and exit of the right footprint, I knew the right boot wasn't laced on tightly as it should have been. The condition was not momentary; we see the same pattern for quite a distance. Therefore he did not stop to tie the lace that had come undone. Now an improperly laced boot means one of two things: a sensitive foot, or an inadequate shoelace. Since I doubted the former, I assumed the latter. Also, would it be natural for a man to go on a hike with a sensitive foot? In addition, what more obvious solution to the problem of a broken shoelace than to cannibalise one from a pair of dress shoes? These of course would be scarcely adequate, being too short and fine for tight lacing."

"It all seems to make sense now," said Gaines.

"Naturally," returned my companion cynically.

"Just a minute Holmes," I protested, "how did you know that Cardwell met with a minor accident? And why is it so clear that the repair was a local one?"

"As I stated at the beginning, the boots were several years old. As the result of some sudden blow, the left heel was dislodged. We see by the footprints that the right boot still carries the proper McFarren's heel–designed especially for the shoe. Yet the left heel is new and different. Also, the fit is poor, not to say *abominable*. Now obviously a person able to afford McFarren's Squires is particular, and would want them to be properly re-done. In London, given the wide variety of shops, this would be no problem. But out here, it's catch as catch-can. We know then that the mishap occurred locally, and obviously before Sunday, when the shoe repair shops would be closed. Now have I quite satisfied your curiosity, or must I also relate the obvious inference derived from the stirrup marks on the soles? No? Thank you Watson–the headway has been slow over the years, but you're progressing. So we've passed our test gentlemen. We can assume this is Cardwell's print. He's heading south then, his dog at his side. Let's continue our stroll, and see where it leads."

After ten minutes, Gaines indicated that we had reached the terminus of Cardwell's usual evening stroll. Yet the ground showed that the tracks went on. Holmes therefore continued following them.

"Who knows?" said he, "perhaps something along this way drew his attention, and he went to investigate."

Holmes led the way for another twenty minutes. At that time we came upon a small cove with vertical sides that was undoubtably Ballow's Wash. It cut into the sheer rock in a semi-circular curve. Looking down from the cliff-top, we could see that the beach below was of fine gravel, and wide and deep. But we could scarcely hear one another's speech, for every square foot of cliffside was occupied by shorebirds, which screamed and cried with an ear-splitting din.

"This may be what you call Ballow's Wash," shouted Gaines, "but Geoffery referred to it as the *eyrie cliff—*"

"That is the name he gave it?" I asked.

"He mentioned 'the eyrie cliff,' I imagine it could be no other place, though we never came here."

"In what context did he mention it?" inquired Holmes.

The big man lowered his head in thought, absently kicking pebbles over the precipice.

"I think," he said slowly, "he mentioned that the beach was particularly fine, and also ..."

"...yes?"

"Oh yes! He mentioned the eagles' nest. It's a great place to watch the eagles. Look, is that not one there now?"

We watched a huge brown bird soaring over the ocean. Almost immediately, another dropped from the far cliffside. I could see the huge mass of matted sticks that was its nest. The two great birds circled together for a moment, then drifted seaward in wide arcs. We watched fascinated as they approached a flock of shrieking gulls, twenty yards offshore, which wheeled and perched above a dark object in the water. At the approach of the eagles the gulls fled, protesting. The big birds then settled themselves, wings outstretched, upon the semi-submerged object.

"Humph!" I snorted. "So much for the mighty eagle! I've heard before that they'll eat carrion if nothing else is easy, and there's the proof of it."

"I don't like the look of it," said Holmes warily. "There must be a pathway cut into the hillside. Let's find it and get down to the beach quickly. Whoa Gaines! Just a second if you please, let me inspect these footprints first ... Do you mind if I take the lead?"

We found the pathway commencing at the centre of the cliffside. It was hewn from the rock and, at intervals, constructed on iron stairs and platforms fastened to the rock face, as a fire ladder is fastened to a building. Holmes led the way carefully, noting each and every mark left in the fine dirt covering the path. In ten minutes we were upon the beach. We walked across the wide stretch of gravel. The cacophony of the birds was increased tenfold by the high rock walls round us, which seemed to form a natural amphitheatre. Holmes stood at the water's edge, gazing at the rolling surf. The eagles, having apparently satisfied their appetite, had departed. The gulls returned, and were mewing and fighting over the mysterious carcass that seemed to float closer to shore with each heave of the water. Yet, after waiting some minutes, we realised the object was stationary.

Losing patience, Holmes fetched a long stick and, doffing his shoes and stockings, rolled up his trouser legs and waded into the sea. Using the stick as a wading staff, he negotiated the rolling current with the expertise of a fisherman long familiar with fast-running streams. He approached the object and pulled at it with the stick. However, it remained fastened in the mass of floating kelp. Holmes waded out further—up to his waist in the frigid water and tugged at the object itself. After some effort, he steered it towards us. Even before the object lay at our feet at the water's edge, I could discern the black and tan colouration that distinguishes the breed. Soon we were all staring down at the remains of the dog. Fastened to it was a long leash that had evidently caught in the seaweed, and had in effect anchored the carcass in the sea.

"Cardwell's Airedale," I said.

"So it would seem," answered my companion. "Gaines, does this appear to be the remains of Tinker?"

"I regret to say it does, Mr. Holmes. In fact, I'm dead certain of it, because there is no other Airedale about these parts ... And yet the body is so disfigured—"

"Your point is well taken; it has been in the water perhaps two days, and the birds have been at it as well. But you feel certain these are Tinker's remains?"

"Yes, I do—that's his leash and collar too. I'd say there's no doubt at all, Mr. Holmes. Which doesn't look good for poor Geoffery, I'm afraid."

"I'm forced to agree," returned Holmes, gazing out over the

ocean. "I shall spend a few more minutes here examining the beach, then we'd best return to the cottage. I have a feeling that a naval chart of the coastline would also be helpful."

While Holmes scoured the beach, Gaines and I watched the eagles and sea birds on the cliffs. Presently we saw an old man in a macintosh appear on the summit. He carried with him a telescope and tripod, which he set up on the cliff edge and began to scan the rookeries.

"That's old Mr. Helgeson the birdwatcher. Geoffery mentioned him several times; he's the only other regular visitor to the cliffs hereabouts. Look, he's waving at us."

We returned the old gentleman's wave and started up the steps. At the top we met Mr. Helgeson, who rubbed his hands together with enthusiasm.

"Aren't they a pretty pair? Aren't they beauties eh?" he chortled, pointing to the eagle's nest. We agreed, and waited 'til Holmes ascended the cliffside and joined us. He shook hands with Helgeson and plied the old man with questions. When had he last seen Geoffery Cardwell? Did he know him well? Had he seen anything strange on the sea or around the beach lately? Helgeson responded at length, saying he'd known young Cardwell for years (though, from his recounting, we assumed he was *unaware* of Cardwell's importance to the war effort), though he'd not seen him for over a week. As to any strange occurrences, he'd noticed none.

"Except of course, the blowing in the night," he added after a reflective pause.

"Blowing in the night?" I asked.

"Yes, a blowing sound ... a curious loud snort, if you will, like a whale spouting—"

Holmes and I listened intently at this revelation, while Gaines, obviously beside himself with worry, gave a cry of shock and seemed to weave before us.

"Are you all right?" asked Holmes, catching the big man by the elbows.

"Y–Yes," he managed at last, breathing deeply. "Pardon me for appearing shocked ... it's just that my concern for my friend—"

"Of course Gaines, we understand, I'm sure. Now Mr. Helgeson, when have you heard this noise?"

"At night sir. In the dead of night. I suppose it's the whales surfacing off Ballow's Wash—"

"And have you heard whales before sir?" asked Holmes.

"Oh, no sir, but I imagine that's what they sound like—a deep puffing and blowing."

"Were you at cliffside then?"

"Oh, of course not, but in bed—"

"Nearby?"

"Oh yes, my cottage is just over the ridge yonder."

"And did you by chance hear this sound on Monday night?"

"That would be three nights ago, yes?"

"Yes sir, yes! I remember hearing the sound then, around ten o'clock."

"I see. And is there anything else that has caught your attention lately? Any other visitors or birdwatchers on the cliffs?"

He replied in the negative, and, after searching the ground for more footprints, we returned to the cottage.

There Holmes addressed the housekeeper.

"Tell my Miss Simmons, has Mr. Helgeson resided long in the area?"

"For four or five years, Mr. Holmes. A very nice gentleman he is."

"So he took up residence here in 1912 or thereabouts? Well that's something to keep in mind I suppose. Now then, I'd like to examine Mr. Cardwell's personal effects—I assume the proper authorities advised you of this?"

"Of course, sir. Ever since Mr. Cardwell's disappearance in fact, I have been expecting you, or Mr. Mycroft."

"Yes, of course. It was he who advised me of Geoffery's disappearance. I know they had become close personal friends as well as compatriots. To be befriended by my brother, Miss Simmons, is a rare honour indeed, since he is yet more solitary and strange than I am, right Watson? He even confided to me that he felt he had become an uncle to Geoffery. Well—may I look about the house?"

We examined the entire cottage but turned up nothing of interest.

"Can either of you tell me," asked Holmes at the doorway as we prepared to depart, "if Mr. Cardwell said anything out of the ordinary just before his disappearance?"

The two thought for a while and then both replied in the negative.

"But there is *one* strange thing, though perhaps it's a trifle," said the housekeeper as an afterthought.

"And what was that?"

"The episode of the picture, Mr. Holmes. I know it's nothing—"

"Pray tell me. The picture?"

"Yes sir. Do you recall the picture in Mr. Cardwell's bedroom sir? The young gentleman with a fancy suit on—"

"–oh, you mean Gainsborough's *Blue Boy*?" I asked.

"Yes, doctor, I believe that's the name of it. Mr. Cardwell was fond of that picture. He said it reminded him of his younger brother, who died years ago. But the day before he disappeared, he took it down from the wall, saying it had to be repaired–"

"Oh?" replied Holmes. "Then I take it the glass was broken, or the frame cracked?"

"That's the odd part of it," continued the housekeeper in a half-whisper, "there appeared to be absolutely nothing wrong with it; it looked the same as always."

"And yet he took it down off the wall? Why then, is it hanging there now?"

"Because I replaced it yesterday sir. It looked so odd leaning backwards against the mantel ..."

Holmes led us back to Cardwell's room, where he instructed Miss Simmons to re-arrange the print exactly as Cardwell had placed it. The housekeeper, ever cooperative, took down the picture and placed it on the mantelpiece, leaning the face towards the wall. Holmes took down the picture and examined it. Miss Simmons was correct; it appeared in fine condition.

"And what did Geoffery say, *exactly*, if you can remember? Please madam, it could be quite important."

"He said 'Miss Simmons, I'm afraid this painting is not what I thought it to be. I cannot bear to look at it any longer, and must have it fixed as soon as possible.'"

Holmes and I stared at each other in puzzlement.

"Did he mention this in passing, or deliberately call for you to draw it to your attention?"

"Oh, he sent for me sir, and then made his strange speech. That's why it so sticks in my memory."

"Thank you ever so much madam—you've been most helpful. May we take this with us? Yes? Thank you and good-day! Oh, one final thing, Miss Simmons. I regret to tell you we found Tinker's body on the beach in Ballow's Wash ... yes, I'm sorry too ma'am. We shall see that the animal's remains are taken care of, and shall return the collar and leash to you."

"That's curious ..."

"What is curious?"

"Did you say the dog was wearing a leash? That's odd, because Geoffery never used a leash with Tinker, Mr. Holmes. He was well trained, and came to heel upon command."

"Oh really? And he usually left the leash behind?"

"I can't remember him *ever* taking the leash along sir; no, not for a stroll hereabouts ..."

"A most interesting point ma'am. Really, you've been *most* observant and helpful. Doubly so, I'm sure. Adieu."

Picture in hand, we left the cottage and returned to Holmes' lodgings at Birling Gap, stopping on the way at a cartographers, where Holmes purchased a navigation chart of the south coast from Hastings to Eastbourne. We sat in his study over pipes and coffee, Holmes reflecting grimly on the morning's expedition.

"Well, it does not look good for Geoffery Cardwell I'm afraid," he said at last.

"You think he's dead?"

"Yes, Watson, the odds favour it. Certainly the dog's body paints a dark and violent picture. Additionally, there is the pattern of disappearances and deaths that I related to you yesterday. But let's review this case in a thumbnail fashion now, and see if there are any singular shreds which strike our attention. We know definitely that the track left along the cliff walk was made by Cardwell. After closely examining the stairs and pathway to the beach, I am convinced he never returned up the cliff path. I examined the cliffs closely, and there appears to be no other way up them save for the path we used. He then disappeared from the beach.

"Now there are several curious incidents Watson, which I'll mention: one is Cardwell's strange statement concerning the Blue Boy picture. It is curious and, coming so close upon his disappearance, deserves our attention. Secondly, the fact that a leash was found on the dog shouldn't be passed over, since Miss Simmons has informed us Cardwell never used one. Also there is Helgeson's talk of hearing whales spouting in the night, Now I've lived here for over ten years and have heard nothing of whales. Either his tale is a hoax or simply imaginary, or else—"

"Yes, go on ..."

"Or else it was something that *sounded* like a whale and wasn't ..."

"He called it a blowing, puffing sound ..."

"Yes, and at about ten o'clock at night—just about the time Cardwell was overdue from his evening stroll. I fear that the strange noise could be linked to this final piece of ominous evidence: I found it on the beach after you and Gaines departed. Here, what do you make of it?"

He reached into his pocket and tossed a small shiny object at me.

"A cartridge," I said, turning the brass cylindre round in my fingers.

"To be more specific, a seven millimetre parabellum pistol cartridge."

"*German!*"

Holmes nodded grimly.

"The Hun on our *shores,* Watson! Ironic, is it not, that we are only a few miles from Hastings, the site of the only successful invasion of England?"

A chill shot through me at the thought.

"Does that chart tell you anything?"

For a reply, he pointed to a section of the coastline with his pipestem.

"–Ballow's Wash–you see how familiar it looks? Now note the depth of the ocean as expressed in fathoms on the chart. Do you see anything interesting?"

"It seems to be a good deal deeper in the vicinity of the wash ..."

"Yes, noticeably so. In fact, I would venture to say that Ballow's Wash resembles a miniature harbour."

"But surely a ship could not enter it; it's much too small for that."

"Certainly. But what about a U boat? Their length is one hundred twenty feet. They may remain submerged, and therefore *invisible,* in water forty feet deep. We can see from this chart therefore, that such a vessel could approach to within sixty yards or so of the beach. Moreover, the tall cliffs that surround the cove would provide further concealment to the raiding party. And finally, there's *this,* Watson–"

He turned quickly to the chart of the German U boat, and pointed to a hole in its side.

"As a submarine surfaces, she must expel ballast water from her tanks. This is done by forcing compressed air into them–"

"By Jove, Holmes, then that could have been the *'blowing in the night'* heard by Helgeson!"

"I fear it could. Certainly a U-boat blowing her tanks would sound like a spouting whale."

"And the pistol cartridge you found on the beach adds the final confirmation. Then the gruesome tale runs as follows: through their agents in London, the Germans learn of Cardwell's specialized knowledge and his vital importance to the allied war effort. They decide to abduct or kill him. Learning of his sojourn to the seaside, they plan a nighttime raid to effect their goal–"

"Your explanation would seem to be the logical one, Watson—one I have myself considered. If it is but partially true, we have a serious security leak in high places. Yet ..." He seemed momentarily to lose himself in thought.

"You were saying?" I pursued after a lengthy wait.

"I was just thinking how dashed *convenient* it all is ... how rationally *simple*. It's as if someone wrote the script. And of course Helgeson ..."

He again drifted off, and remained in that state of suspended animation that had been so familiar a part of his behavior ever since I had known him, until just before teatime.

Next morning I arose and, walking about the house, failed to find my companion. It was only upon glancing out the study window that I saw him in the courtyard, perched upon a raised wooden platform that seemed to be—judging from the coloration of the wood—of recent manufacture. I had not noticed it earlier. Holmes stood upon this contrivance peering over a disc, which was set upon a wooden tripod.

"Hullo Holmes, what's this?" I enquired jovially. "Another of your experiments?"

"Come up, Watson," he said grimly, "and you'll see for yourself."

He returned to the instrument, and scribbled figures on a notepad. I climbed the stairs. On the platform, I could see over the courtyard wall and had an unobstructed view of the sea. Instantly, I saw the ominous brown blotch on the horizon. The ugly smudge grew by the second, and elongated in the direction of the wind.

"Torpedoed only minutes ago, Watson," he said, "and with a blaze like that, it's a wonder anyone will survive. That's the third this week I've seen. Can you imagine the ghastly total."

Cursing under his breath, he dove down the stairs, leaving me on the platform to stare in wonder at the spreading cloud of smoke. I heard him inside telephoning the bearing he had taken. Shortly afterwards he rang off and rejoined me at the observation post. To our horror, the smudge on the horizon suddenly vanished. As the last brownish blur was dispelled, there remained nothing visible, even with the aid of powerful field glasses.

"Too late," whispered Holmes in anguish. "They've gone to the bottom ..."

We stared for some time in silence, the rage growing in us. He turned and faced me solemnly.

"You see now the importance of Cardwell, and why my statement that this would be our most important adventure was not an idle one?"

I nodded in sadness and we departed the lookout platform. We entered the study and Holmes stood before the print of the *Blue Boy*, which he had placed upon his easel. Chin in hand, he examined it whimsically. Next he took it over to the window and re-examined it with his convex lens. He carefully noted every detail of the picture itself, then studied the frame and back. He was about to set it down upon the laboratory table when an idea seized him.

"Of course! Oh Watson, what a dunce I've been! Fetch that penknife will you?"

Seating himself at the window, he placed the framed picture face down upon his knees, and began deftly cutting round the edges with the skill of a surgeon.

"It's obvious now why he turned the print around Watson—as we'll no doubt see in short order ..."

With a gleam in his eye, he tore off the brown paper and cardboard backing, and removed the print itself. But I saw the look of disappointment which immediately clouded his face; apparently whatever he was looking for had failed to materialise.

"*Drat*! I was, of course, expecting a note or sealed envelope to be hidden here—but as you can see, I've drawn a blank."

He examined the paper and cardboard, and reverse side of the print with no success.

"There's nothing here at all Watson. Then perhaps his strange action has no meaning ... and yet ..."

"If Cardwell felt the impending danger and wished to leave a note of warning, then why not leave it with Miss Simmons, or his school chum?"

"A good question. Well, with the point you've just made, coupled with the blank I've drawn, perhaps we'd be wisest to forget the picture and prepare for Mycroft's arrival. He's due in an hour's time."

"Will you fetch him in the Douglas?"

"Heavens no, Watson, are you forgetting his girth? He'd never fit in the sidecar, nor wish to. You are also possibly forgetting my brother's high position in the government—a niche few have attained. He'll be arriving by limousine direct from the Admiralty ..."

"And he'll be staying here?"

"Of course not; there's no room. Besides, baronial as *Finisterre* is to me, I'm afraid it wouldn't do for Mycroft. His tastes over the year have, I fear, grown even more partial to the comforts that only an inn with a full cellar and complete kitchen can provide. We'll meet him and his party at eleven over at the *Fox and Hounds*. Are you up to it?"

At exactly the appointed time, the black Rolls limousine whispered up the drive of the *Fox and Hounds*, a rustic, yet well-appointed country inn on the outskirts of Eastbourne. We had arrived on the motorcycle shortly beforehand, and were clad in moleskins and thick sweaters. All in all, we resembled gatekeepers or farmers. What a difference indeed from those who emerged from the limousine! First, the driver exited and opened the rear door. I noticed he was a soldier in uniform, and fully armed with a pistol. From the rear seat came an official-looking gentleman in impeccable dress, followed by Mycroft, who extricated himself from the car with some difficulty and soon stood puffing before us.

"Hello Watson," he said jovially. "You're looking fit enough. Lost some weight eh? Wish I could. Hello Sherlock, how did you find our Nordic brethren? You must fill me in soonest. I assume you both remember Howarth, my secretary."

The fellow greeted us warmly. Of course we both recollected him; he had served Mycroft loyally for the past dozen years as secretary and personal valet. The other man, Abercrombie, was the uniformed fellow we'd seen driving the limousine. His greeting was more reserved, in fact almost cautious, yet the cordiality showed through.

"Abercrombie here is in charge of my personal security, so you'll pardon him I'm sure if he's a bit stand-offish."

Certainly they were an official-looking pair, Howarth with his intense eyes behind wire glasses, his stooped shoulders and thinning brown hair. He gave the impression of sobriety, diligence, and total dedication. Abercrombie, a tall Scot, had the rough look of a guard dog. His piercing blue eyes were constantly on the move, hunting any signs of the furtive, the out-of-place, the suspicious ...

"Bye the bye," continued Mycroft in a more jocular tone, "young Allistair gives his best to both of you."

We were delighted to hear about the promising military career of young Peter Allistair, whose father had passed away the previous year. It was largely through the generosity of the senior Peter Allistair that Holmes was able to purchase *Finisterre*. We saw Mycroft and his companions to their quarters, then joined him in the dining room for luncheon.

"It beats me how Cardwell allowed himself to be taken," said Mycroft sullenly between mouthfuls. "Lord knows he's a clever chap—smartest I've seen in quite a while. They must have had knowledge of his coming along the cliff before hand, and lay in wait in the shadows of the cliffside ..."

"But if a U-boat were employed," said I, "wouldn't he have seen it if it were surfaced? And this being the case, would he not have been foolish indeed to descend the stairway to the beach?"

"A good point doctor," said Mycroft. "Of course he wouldn't have. And the German UB-2 is far different in appearance from our E. type, especially to the eye of an expert like Cardwell. The other possibility is that he was set upon some distance from the Wash, then dragged down to the beach forceably ...."

"No chance of that," said Holmes. "I examined all the footprints closely and there's no sign whatsoever of a scuffle. No, he went down the stairway of his own accord I'm afraid, foolish or not. Of course the remaining possibility is that the U-boat was in the cove, but submerged. It would then be invisible to Cardwell as he went down to the beach. The enemy officer could however, observe the beach through his periscope and, upon seeing a prearranged signal from the shore—such as a lamp or flare—could then surface to take on the prisoner."

Mycroft held his chin in hand, scowling.

"Dash it, I think you're right. But then how did they know for certain Cardwell would come down? How did they pre-arrange for his evening walk? I assume it was not his usual custom ... how was he lured down? This fellow Gaines was not with him? Then someone else must have been involved, perhaps to give a cry of help from below? Surely Cardwell, being the fine lad he is—"

Here Holmes' elder brother caught himself short, wincing with pain at the thought. This show of emotion stunned both of us, for we were long accustomed to Mycroft's stony rationality. To consider that he would ever form strong emotional attachments would never have occurred to me. Yet the grief on his features was plain enough, indicating his great affection for the missing young man.

"... we must find him Sherlock..." he said at last. "They'll win the war in four month's time if we don't."

It was then I realised the true, deeper source of Mycroft's agony. I had seen it before, curiously enough, in another case involving submarines: the adventure of the Bruce Partington Plans ...

"If we limit our discussion to those people immediately around the area," said Holmes, "then the only person left besides the house-keeper and Gaines is Helgeson, the retired gentleman who lives above the Wash. It might interest you to know Mycroft, that he came to reside there in 1912. Also, he has a faint accent to his speech–"

"He's Danish; that is what he told Gaines and me," I said.

"Possibly Watson, or perhaps–"

"*Intriguing!*" interrupted Mycroft.

"Then you think perhaps Helgeson is a plant, and a deucedly valuable one at that. Here on the South Downs he happens to be Cardwell's neighbor. And on a certain night, he plays the decoy that brings him into the trap..."

"It's a possibility, surely. The scenario might go something like this: Helgeson, a German agent, has taken up residence at about the same time others of his ilk have done, that is to say 1912, or early 1913. Knowing Cardwell's strategic importance to Britain, he keeps a close eye on him and his activities–also his friends and associates. All of this is valuable information which he transmits–by means unknown–to the Triple Alliance. Meantime, he has managed to become friendly with Cardwell and his family, or at least on good enough terms so that his call for help brings Cardwell running down to the beach at Ballow's Wash without a second thought. Either alone or with help he overpowers Cardwell and holds him ready for the captors, who come ashore from the U boat just surfaced. The only flaw in this theory is its failure to explain how Helgeson descended to the beach without leaving footprints on the path ..."

"And the pistol cartridge?" I asked "What of that?"

Holmes explained the finding of the object to his elder brother, and they thought in silence.

"Since it is German, we must assume the enemy fired the shot. And it is a Luger cartridge, so the weapon was not a revolver. The spent cartridge was therefore expelled automatically upon firing. They probably wished to retrieve it so as to leave no traces of their raid behind, yet were unable to find it in the dark ..."

"You are saying then Sherlock, that Cardwell is dead–"

"Perhaps Mycroft. But not for certain. It's possible they used the pistol on Cardwell's dog–"

"Oh, Tinker was with him? Then that's the likely explanation! Tinker was a fine guard dog as well as companion to Geoffery. I'm certain that if his master were set upon, he'd lose no time in springing to his defence."

"And yet," pursued my companion, "when we examined the corpse of the dog I was unable to find a bullet wound ... though I'll admit this: the animal's body was sufficiently decayed and mangled that its death by shooting could have occurred."

"Despite the fact that I *want* very much to believe Cardwell is alive, I think all the evidence *supports* my contention that he *is* alive," said Mycroft deliberately. "For what value would he have to the enemy dead?"

We mulled over this proposition in silence while we finished our meal. As we returned out of doors, Mycroft suggested a good place to begin our search was Helgeson's cottage, and Holmes and I agreed. We set off in the limousine accompanied by Mycroft's assistants, with Abercrombie and Howarth in the front seat and the three of us in the rear one. Fortunately, Mycroft's bulk was somewhat offset by his brother's narrow frame, so we proceeded comfortably. Within half a hour we were at Cardwell's cottage. We gave Mycroft a brief tour of that place, then walked, slowly in deference to Mycroft, up along the cliff path.

The two aides, ever alert, walked some distance behind us. When we reached the Wash, Mycroft was forced to rest for twenty minutes, and even declined to descend the stairway to the beach. But he looked down and saw the carcass of the dog, which had by this time almost been reduced to a skeleton by the birds.

We all decided to arrange to have the body buried at earliest convenience, and Howarth and Abercrombie agreed to the grim task.

"After all Sherlock, it's the least we can do for old Tinker."

"Ah, you were familiar with the dog? Tell me then, did he have any quirks of nature, or unique habits?"

"None I can think of. A pleasant dog, and loyal to the death, as we can see ... no, he had a fondness for knuckle bones and, like most Airedales, he seldom barked. But I don't see what you're driving at."

"Are you rested? Helgeson's cottage is just over that ridge yonder."

We found the place deserted, and sat down on a stone bench to await his arrival. Our wait wasn't a long one, for presently we heard the sound of a car and the vehicle swung round the drive and stopped before us. We rose and greeted Helgeson, but, not expecting us, he seemed nervous and put off–far different from the congenial man we had met earlier. He seemed particularly distressed at the presence of Howarth and Abercrombie.

"Are you in the habit of arriving unannounced?" he said in a clipped tone as he stepped off the running board, glaring at the two aides.

His tone changed abruptly however, when confronted by Mycroft. In his most official voice, Holmes' elder brother made it clearly understood that we were to interview Mr. Helgeson on official government business. Was he to cooperate fully now or would he rather be detained into custody?

"Oh please forgive my shortness," he said cravenly. "I've been out on errands and have overtired myself. I would offer you tea gentlemen, but I'm afraid my cottage is rather untidy–"

"The tea won't be necessary sir, though the offer's appreciated," said Mycroft. "But we'd like a look inside if it's not too much trouble ..."

"I'd rather not, actually," returned the widower, visibly colouring.

"I see ..." said Mycroft softly, "though you must realise sir, that your uncooperation cannot be construed in anything but a negative light, especially considering the gravity of the situation, and the state of war which now exists between Great Bri–"

"Excuse me, Mycroft," interrupted Holmes. "But perhaps we are being a bit brusk with Mr. Helgeson. After all, England is a civilised land *because* a man has the right to deny entry into his dwellingplace, not *despite* this right. Mr. Helgeson, when would it be convenient for us to return, or should we wait outside for a few minutes? Whichever suits your fancy sir ..."

To Mycroft's amazement, the man's demeanor changed instantly. He told us "That, provided the aides waited outside," a few minutes' wait would be sufficient, and scurried into his cottage. I was again impressed with Holmes' smoothness and sagacity when it came to dealing with people. Clearly Mycroft, brilliant though he was, could take a lesson or two from his brother in dealing with the human race.

In less than ten minutes' time, we were ushered into "Smuggler's Rest," a charming and cozy coastal retreat if ever I saw one. We seated ourselves in the tiny parlour made cheery by the crackling fire, bright curtains, and hunting prints. Both Holmes and his brother walked about, shooting their keen glances everywhere. I was convinced, seeing them thus engaged, that any foul play or skullduggery would be swiftly unearthed–for if these two men of genius failed to uncover Helgeson's evil, what mortal could?

After a short while, the brothers returned to the small parlour and joined the two of us round the fire. Helgeson had served tea after all, and it was most welcome.

"I see you're a Dane, as you have claimed," began Mycroft.

"And a sailor too," added Holmes.

"I extend my sympathy regarding your deceased relative," continued Mycroft.

"Yet the pain is somewhat lessened, no doubt, by the fact that he was old ..." said Holmes.

Helgeson rose from his overstuffed chair, staring open-mouthed at the two men.

"What you say is true gentlemen, but my uncle Jans died in Copenhagen two weeks ago, how could you–"

"Oh, of course, we knew he wasn't *here*–don't be absurd ..."

"Still in all, to die in a city hospital, away from his country farm ..."

Holmes and Mycroft mused silently over the poignant details. Helgeson, meanwhile, remained distraught with fear and wonder.

"Don't worry," I said comforting him, "it's all really quite simple. They will explain it to you presently."

"I say Watson, would you care to follow me about this place for a quick tour? It's most charming, I assure you."

I rose and followed my companion through the halls and rooms of the cottage. Though small, it was substantially built, the floor being constructed of heavy spruce planking that was doweled into place.

"Come along man, hurry up," urged Holmes, and I had to fairly run to keep up with him as he plunged through rooms and hallways. I was frankly surprised at his pace; it surely wasn't in line with his usual sleuthing habits, in which he strode deliberately about, bent over, his eyes sweeping methodically about him.

"Stop lagging Watson!" he admonished, "I want you two steps behind me–just so, there, now shall we try the kitchen?"

Puffing from exertion, I followed him into the final room on the first floor. After walking briskly to and fro across it, Holmes led me back into the parlour, where Mycroft and Helgeson were chatting.

"Ah Sherlock, it seems that this cottage was in fact, a 'Smuggler's Rest,' eh Helgeson?"

"I was just telling your brother," he said to Holmes, "that a hundred years ago, this house was built by a smuggler, a retired sea captain named Traviss. As you can see, in many ways it resembles a ship ..."

We talked pleasantly for another twenty minutes before we rose to go.

"Ah, but tell me how you discovered all about me," enquired the widower. "How did you know my uncle had died?"

"It was a simple matter to observe the sheaf of papers under the glass paperweight on your writing desk," said Mycroft. "Sherlock and I both noticed it at once. Without prying, it was clear that one letter stood out. We could only see a corner, but the black margins of the death letter were salient, to say the least ..."

"Ah yes, the *letter edged in black*. But I assume you do not read Danish, despite your combined genius. How then did you know it carried news of my uncle?"

"First, death letters, though rather uncommon nowadays, are sent only to relatives. Second, the script, though in Danish and therefore undecipherable to us, was in a woman's hand. We could tell the woman was very old. What more natural announcement than that her husband had passed away?"

"It was also interesting," continued his elder brother, "that the corner of the letter visible was the upper left, in which the greeting was penned. It refers to "Benje," which is obviously a diminutive, or nickname given you when you were a small boy. The man was then either your father or an uncle–"

"The latter, as you told us. Furthermore, we assumed he died in Copenhagen, since that city is penned at the top of the letter along with the date, yet it's doubtful the couple lived there, for the letter edged in black is a custom almost extinct nowadays in all European countries, except amongst the rural farming folk ..."

"This is wondrous," said Helgeson. "Well, it's easy now to see how you knew for certain I was a Dane, but I recall telling no one about my love of the sea–perhaps you guessed this from the fact that I own a seaside home ..."

"We guess *nothing*," said Mycroft sternly, "but we can *infer* a great deal. Certainly, the emblem of the Royal Danish Yacht Club upon your china plates in the kitchen is as good a starting point as any. And now sir, good-day to you, and thanks. Come Sherlock, Watson."

"Oh bye the bye sir," said Holmes as we paused at the door, "do you own a dog?"

"No."

"Thank you. I assume then that it died some time ago. Yet I just thought it curious that the leash is still hanging near the back door ..."

The man scowled and fidgeted with the door handle. It was obvious Holmes had caught him off guard.

"Eh ... quite right Mr. Holmes, the dog died over a year ago and I haven't put the leash away ... sentimental of me I suppose ... yet when a man loses his only source of companionship ..."

"I quite understand Mr. Helgeson. Tell me, what breed was it?"

"...eh...cocker spaniel ..."

"Thank you again sir, we look forward to seeing you soon."

Followed by Mycroft's ever-present guardians, we walked back to Cardwell's cottage along the cliff path.

"It strikes me as odd Mycroft, that Helgeson would keep a dog leash handy when he has no dog. Also, the leash I examined was quite large for a cocker. Moreover, the snap was shiny."

"Been used recently? Hmmm ..."

"And you, Watson, were an *enormous* help."

"Now don't jape at me Holmes, really. You know all I did was clump around after you through the house."

"And that was the enormous help. Well, here's the eyrie cliff again—my, but doesn't the ebb tide make a difference!"

Mycroft and I peered down at the cove, and were amazed to see a huge stretch of beach where there had only been water before. Furthermore, the cliffsides appeared taller, as indeed they were; there was a dark ring of rock that comprised the lower eight feet of the cove walls. Thick with barnacles, mussels, and sea plants, they nevertheless appeared dark because of the dampness and total absence of sea birds.

"The beach extends a good deal further during low tide, eh Watson? In fact, the whole place seems to take on a new appearance. It's interesting too, the way the beach extends itself round the edges of the cove, almost like a narrow pathway ..."

Holmes observed the scene below carefully, his eyes narrowed to mere slits. After some time, Mycroft grew impatient and suggested we return to Cardwell's cottage. Here, Holmes took him upstairs and explained the episode of the picture. Mycroft listened intently, and expressed a desire to examine the picture personally.

"I don't doubt your acumen Sherlock, quite the contrary. I admit it's always been sharper than mine, which is considerable. Still, a fresh pair of eyes is always helpful, eh?"

"To be sure. Watson and I shall start for *Finnisterre* directly you drop us off at the inn; we'll return in an hour's time with the picture."

So we proceeded accordingly. But halfway home we grew hungry, and Holmes suggested we stop at an inn for supper.

"After all Watson, I've planned nothing for tonight's meal—we'd just as well get a bite here. But it's apt to be a bit crowded at this hour, so why don't you be a good fellow and jump out now and get a table. I'll see to the Douglas and find you in a wink."

I did as he bade, and secured a comfy table near a window. He joined me, and after our soup, he pulled out the naval ordnance map of the seacoast he'd bought the previous day, and asked me to go over it with him. However, I discovered I'd left my reading glasses in my coat, which was tucked into the toe of the sidecar of the Douglas, so I excused myself and went to retrieve them. Imagine my surprise a moment later when, approaching the motorcycle in the gathering dusk, I saw the sidecar was gone!

"Holmes! Someone's *stolen* your sidecar," I panted to him as he peered up incredulously from his map. He rose and followed me outside. In less time than it takes to tell, we were standing before the Douglas, its sidecar in place.

"You were saying Watson ..." he said acidly.

"I was mistaken Holmes, but look here," said I as I led him round the corner of the building. Sure enough, there stood our machine's twin, distinguishable only by its lack of a sidecar.

"Ah, a natural enough mistake my friend. You did not see where I parked the motorcycle, and therefore assumed this one *here* was ours. They do look alike don't they, both being the same make–"

"Yes. After all, I wasn't expecting *two* of them at the same place. Well I shall go collect my–I say *Holmes*, are you all right man?"

My companion was staring thunderstruck at the motorcycle before him. He clapped his hand to his forehead in an exclamation.

"Of *course!* The same make ... *indistinguishable!* Oh Watson what an ass I've been not to see it! I say, when you next hear my admirers singing my praise, would you kindly jerk me back to reality by reminding me of this episode? Thank you. Now let's be off. Pay the chit will you, and I'll pick you up in front."

We arrived at *Finisterre* a short time later. Holmes' first act was to telephone Mycroft and say we wouldn't be returning to the *Fox and Hounds* that evening.

"No, don't fret over the picture," I overheard him remark. "If what I now think is true, as an object it has no importance; it was used *symbolically*–but really, I haven't time now..."

"Now Watson, it's just after six. I've some urgent errands to attend to, and shall be gone until around nine. Can you make yourself comfortable 'til I return? Splendid. By the way, I urge you to take a long nap in the meantime, since we're liable to be up all night. Low tide is at 2:12; we'll be down at the Wash then. It's best we're going in the dark to remain unseen–yet there's almost a full moon, so we'll have some light. Have you any rubber boots? No? Then you'll have to do without. See you later on."

I heard the sputter and roar of the motorcycle outside, and lay down on the sofa to doze until Holmes returned.

* * *

I was awakened at half past 12 by Holmes, who stood shaking me. He offered me hot coffee and a cigarette.

"Come on man, wake up! When one gets older, it's hard to shake off the sleepy fit, eh? There, have another cigaret–they're pure Turkish leaf, that'll get you going. Now put on this country jacket too, the night is clear but chilly."

"You're late Holmes," I murmured. "Where have you been?"

"To every butcher shop and veterinarian in the county, I'll wager. But it was worth it. What's true about motorcycles is true with dogs as well ..."

"Eh? Dogs, motorcycles? Butcher shop? Have you lost your mind?"

"I should have considered the *tides* much earlier on," he remarked changing the subject. "Of course I was aware of them, but I failed to consider how crucial the tidal change is to this case. Consider first Watson, how unlikely it is that a U-boat would enter the wash at low tide, which is when Cardwell disappeared."

"A good point. But still, isn't it possible? The wash is big and deep. Not an optimal time, but it could have happened. And also there's Helgeson's recollection of the sound of the boat blowing her tanks."

"I fear Helgeson is lying Watson. Well, let us be off. Did you bring a pistol? Well of course not, assuming you were coming here only for a rest. I have a spare which you'd better put in your jacket pocket. Also, take this walking stick."

We boarded the motorcycle and re-traced our route to the Cardwell cottage in the darkness. There was no traffic whatsoever on the country roads; no one saw us, and at medium speed, the Douglas purred over the dirt paths and gravel stretches quietly. In order for our noctournal mission to remain unnoticed, Holmes parked the machine some distance from the Cardwell cottage. When we approached that building, Holmes whispered to me to avoid the gravel and stay on the meadow. Thus we skirted the cottage without a sound.

"I say Holmes," I whispered, "if there's liable to be trouble, why not knock up Gaines? He's a stout young fellow, and I'm sure he'd be eager indeed to help us ..."

My companion chuckled softly.

"You may be amazed later on at your suggestion," said he.

As we arrived at the cliff path, the moon emerged from behind a wisp of cloud. We ambled along in the eerie half light, our forms casting long shadows over the gravel. Any sounds we might have made were drowned out by the boom of the surf below us. It was almost two when we reached the top of the stairs. We found our way down to the beach without much problem owing to the moonlights The rookeries were quiet and the surf was faint, for at ebb-tide the beach was extended fifty yards farther out.

"Now imagine you are Cardwell, Watson. How would you get off this beach?"

"If I did not return up the path behind us, I would certainly employ a boat. That's why I think the U-boat theory makes the most sense. Remember too, that Tinker's body was found out in the water—you waded out yourself to fetch it."

"True enough. It all seems to fit perfectly. And yet, let's see what this gravel spit to the right has to offer. Now mind, these rocky ledges are slick with moss; use your walking stick and don't rush."

We made our way warily along the mushy gravel and beds of seaweed, under the towering rock wall that rose up directly on our right side. The cliffs were high and sheer—impossible for anyone save a mountain climber to scale. Occasionally, during a lull in the waves, the faint flutter of wings or croaking protests of the birds on the eyrie cliff could be heard. Presently though, after walking forty yards or so further, a new, strange sound came to our ears. It was a slapping, popping sound, followed by a hollow chuckle of spouting water. It resembled the sound that would be produced by thrusting a bucket mouth-downward into water, then pulling it back up. Holmes showed not the slightest surprise. In fact, he quickened his pace.

"Come along Watson; that's what I've been waiting for—"

Another thirty yards further and I realised we were rounding a small point. Whatever it was we were seeking was therefore invisible from the beach. The strange gurgling grew noticeably louder, and, skirting round a giant projection in the cliff face, we were forced momentarily to wade through icy water knee deep. On the other side of the boulder, and therefore totally hidden, was a hole in the cliff face two yards across and three feet high. As the waves struck it they produced the curious sound that was audible for some distance. Clearly though, the grotto entrance was low enough so that it was above water only for an hour or so each tidefall. Holmes and I, washed in the waves, bent over and peered inside. It did not look inviting, and even less so when Holmes drew an electric torch from his raincoat and shined the beam inside. In the instant the dismal chamber was flooded with light, I saw myriad tiny sea crabs prancing under rocks, their delicate antennae and shiny eyes twitching with fright. The floor was a shallow pool of tidewater, and the interior of the gruesome tunnel was lined with barnacles, mussels, rockweed and kelp. This plethora of marine life, most of it waving or dancing about, lent a ghastly and nightmarish quality to the place. The smell was thick with brine and dampness. I might add that visiting the spot in the middle of the night in search of a man who was probably dead did not increase the attractiveness of our quest.

"I'm not going in," I said.

"Oh yes you are, old fellow. Come on, we've been through too much together. Just a wee step inside, there we go. It's really a shame you forgot your rubber boots ..."

"I wasn't instructed to bring them," I replied with irritation.

Once inside, we were somewhat sheltered from the waves. Still we were fairly soaked and cold. Also, as the waves thumped against the mouth of the grotto, the effect on our eardrums was most painful. Holmes remarked that the resultant rise in air pressure indicated the grotto had no outlet. Further evidence of this, he added, was the curious popping noise produced by the waves.

"If there's no outlet, then why are we here?" I asked. "If whoever killed Cardwell wished to hide his body here, surely they would run the risk of having it wash out to sea again unless it were weighted down."

"Let's walk a bit further up. Note how the cavern slopes upwards, that is interesting. In addition, it seems to branch outwards into several smaller tunnels ..."

I certainly did not like the idea of being trapped and drowned in the dreary place when the tide rose, and likewise informed my companion. He agreed with me, and quickened his search of the damp tunnels. But after an hour's time we seemed to be no further along in our search. To make matters worse, we returned to the entranceway to find it submerged!

"Dear me," said Holmes, "the tide has turned and locked us in. We'd best find what I'm looking for, and soon too, for here we are!"

I scuttled about the grotto after Holmes, and watched dismayed as the water crept ever higher up the slimy rock floor.

"And are we to die here Holmes?" I cried, the terror growing in me. "Are we to drown here, trapped in this dismal place ... our remains to be picked at by crabs and water snakes?"

"Steady, Watson, steady old fellow. I'll admit this venture was a bit foolish of me—certainly not as well planned as it could have been. Of course, it may be still possible to fight our way out through the water, though the current is strong ..."

"Well, we'd best do something quickly Holmes, your torch is running low. We should have brought a carbide miner's lamp instead of the electric one—it would last far longer."

We searched for another quarter of an hour for a continuation of the grotto—without success. When we returned to the mouth of the marine cave, we were dismayed to see the water had risen another foot, and we had no idea where the entrance was to be found. In fact, the appearance of the place had so changed that we were totally disoriented. For the first time, I noticed fear in Holmes' manner. The cold seawater slapped about our ankles, numbing our feet. It splashed mockingly round our legs.

"Oh Watson, what a fool I've been to lead you into this!" he cried. "Well, we shall do what we can. Let's seek out the highest passage we can find and burrow up in it in hopes the water won't reach us. I'll switch off the torch to save the light. I *did* think to bring a candle butt along. The light it gives is faint, but long-lasting."

So saying he lighted the candle. After allowing our eyes to become adjusted to the dim light, we made our way slowly up towards the large passage. The water followed us.

However, just before we were to enter the passage, Holmes stopped dumbstruck.

"Watson! Look at the candle will you? What do you notice?"

"The flame is inclined ..."

"Yes, and in which direction?"

"To the left."

"Ha! Don't you think that's interesting? It indicates a draught, obviously. A draught indicates the flow of air, which further indicates—come on man! Let's see where the flame takes us."

We walked on a few steps to our left, but to Holmes' dismay, the flame flickered in several directions alternately. Again, the fear that had subsided welled up inside me again. Holmes thought for a moment, then asked me to light a cigar.

"Dammit Holmes! This is hardly the time for levity!" I retorted.

But he repeated his request, and I soon discovered the wisdom behind it. When great bluish clouds of the pungent smoke were roiling forth, he again drew his electric torch. Shining the faint beam on the smoke, we could see it weave and flow about like a school of fry.

"Keep puffing Watson, that's it. Now follow me. This way!"

We advanced far to the left side of the grotto, following the drifting clouds of smoke. We came to the rock wall that was the side of the cave, and were amazed to see the clouds swirl quickly about and disappear behind a giant icicle of rock.

"We walked past this very spot twice before," I said.

"Yes indeed, and missed the crevice which lies concealed behind this stalactite. Come on."

We wound our way behind the rock pillar and found ourselves in a steep passage that turned upwards in a wide spiral. Soon I felt the dry walls of the passage and knew the ocean never reached it. At any rate, we would not drown in the watery trap. We continued our way upward, and I heard the hollow thump of Holmes' rubber boot and his curse echo in the near darkness, to be followed almost immediately by a shrill cry of joy.

"Watson, look at this!"

I gazed in awe at a crude staircase hewn in the rock. It was no wider than the tunnel, about two and a half feet across. After a short flight, they changed somewhat in character and I realised that they were built up of flagstone. I reached the top puffing with exertion (for my legs had not yet recovered from the cold seawater) and brimming with questions. How had Holmes predicted the grotto and the inner passageways? Who built the steps, and when? Where were we going?

"I shan't answer your questions yet Watson, except to ask you one: do you still have the pistol I lent you? Very good; it might be a good idea to have it ready. See how the cavern widens up here....? I would not be surprised if we were within a few feet of ..."

His voice trailed off as he lost himself in concentration. The draught was more noticeable now, and we felt it on the backs of our necks as we made our way along the wide tunnel for another fifty yards. Though still a natural cavern, it appeared in places to have been altered and widened by tools. At last we found ourselves in a high-domed room filled with broken barrels and casks. At the far end of the room was a line of light. As we approached it, we could see it was light coming from behind a doorway. Still inwardly reeling from the danger and the many recent strange events, I was taken totally off guard by this, not to mention the sound of voices issuing from beyond!

Holmes put his finger to his lips, and beckoned me forward. Pistol in hand, my heart thumping wildly, I followed close behind him towards the door. But in my excitement, I grew careless and stumbled over one of the barrels that lay invisible in my path. In my fall I upset several more, and sent them flying. The underground chamber of rock resounded with the thump and clatter of rotten wood, and the next instant light flooded in upon us as the door was flung open. In the blindness that followed, I could scarcely see two dim figures in the room beyond, and a low shape that came bounding into the cavern with terrific speed. The animal hit Holmes with full force and sent him reeling into me. The next moment we were in a heap upon the ground rolling and struggling amidst the barrels–the dog growling and thrusting himself at us from above.

"*Tinker*!" came a voice. "Tinker *hold!*"

The animal instantly obeyed, and went to his master's side. The young man stood over us, shining a powerful electric beam into our eyes. I heard the cocking of a pistol.

"Drop the gun," he said quietly, and I realised the pistol was still in my hand. For half an instant I thought of shooting the man, though it would mean my own death as well. But before any decision could be made, a familiar voice called from behind him.

"Hold on Geoffery, it's Mycroft's brother."

Helgeson rushed up to join the young man who aimed his pistol at us. Hearing these words from his confederate, he put his revolver up and helped us to our feet.

"By Jove, Helgeson, I see Mr. Sherlock Holmes is a clever chap! He seems to have discovered our little secret, eh?"

"And discovered that Geoffery Cardwell is a *traitor* of the first water," I cried, "and not fit for the friendship of a man like Mycroft Holmes."

"Easy Watson–don't jump to conclusions," said Holmes taking me by the shoulder. "There, can you walk? Did Tinker bite you? No? That's good–I have likewise escaped. No Watson, there *is* a traitor lurking about, but it's not Cardwell."

"But you told me Helgeson *lied*–" I stammered confusedly.

"And so he did. And a deucedly clever story it was too. But let us follow our hosts upstairs; I'm sure we'll be more comfortable round the fireplace with a dram and a pipe. Come on."

In a perfect fit of bewilderment and confusion I followed the three men and the dog–whose manner had changed miraculously, I might add–through the cellar room that adjoined the cavern. It was an ordinary cellar, lighted by paraffin lamps, and full of the usual garden implements, trunks, overcoats, and what-have-you. However, in the centre was a low table upon which rested a large-scale map of the coast. Cardwell paused before it, and I could see he was a good looking chap of medium size with a trim moustache. And despite his obvious intellect and acumen, he appeared an amiable, sociable sort of fellow. Helgeson paused only long enough to scoop up the map in his arms and continued leading us to the far end of the room to an open stairway of wood. I noticed Cardwell's boots as he mounted the stair. They were *exactly* as Holmes had described earlier! We followed them up, and at the top Helgeson swung back a trap door. The next moment, I was standing in the kitchen of *Smuggler's Rest!*

"By George, Holmes!"

"Isn't it clever? And now, dear fellow, you know why you were of enourmous help to me yesterday ..."

"You mean when I clumped round the house after you?"

"Of course. You were wearing the same boots you now have on. Leather soles with hobnails—perfect sounding instruments. As you know, my soles were of crepe rubber. Also, I am much lighter than you are. How could I expect to discover a hidden cellar underneath the floor? But with my friend in his heavy boots two paces behind me, how easy was the task!"

"But what made you suspect it in the first place, if I may ask?" said Helgeson, as he drew the parlour drapes with caution.

"Your manner showed you obviously had something to hide. I must confess that until quite recently I suspected you as the guilty party. Anyhow, when I learnt the cottage's name, I decided on a quick 'walking tour' to see if I could discover any hollow spots in the floor, since there was absolutely no indication the place had a cellar. Of course you recall Watson that the same method, with a slight variation, was used in one of your more popular recountences: the story of the Red-Headed League ..."

"Then of course," added Helgeson, "when I told you and Mycroft this place was once used by smugglers—you knew. Of course you *must* know Mr. Holmes, that it wasn't you, Dr. Watson, or your brother whom I mistrusted—"

"I've gathered that. You seemed quite put off, however, by our aides from London."

"That's closer to the point, but still not the principal villain."

"Then *who is it?*" I asked.

"Mr. Cardwell, may I assume you and Mr. Helgeson are full compatriots?" asked Holmes.

"Yes, you may," replied the young strategist.

"Then am I correct in assuming that the *Blue Boy* picture points the way?"

"Right you are! I left the clue for Mycroft, but obviously you are every bit as brilliant as he—"

"While I have no doubts as to that affirmation, I nonetheless enjoy hearing it," replied my friend. "As a matter of fact, I doubt if Mycroft has yet discovered the message you intended by your strange actions ..."

"Hold on!" I cried. "I fail to see how you made any sense of that dashed painting, Holmes. I saw you examine it thoroughly—even take it apart in hopes of finding a hidden message ... the search was absolutely fruitless."

"Yes, indeed. Which set me thinking. There *was* nothing wrong with the picture, physically at least. Yet you, Cardwell, plainly told Miss Simmons you had to have it fixed. Furthermore—and this stuck in my mind afterwards—you told your housekeeper that the *painting was not what you thought it to be, and you could not look upon it any longer*—correct?"

"Absolutely!" Cardwell cried approvingly.

"At that point, I began to wonder why you had gone to the bother of taking the picture down—a perfectly good picture—and placing it face against the wall..."

I shook my head slowly in confusion.

"Obviously, viewed in a *symbolic* way, this was meant to indicate betrayal of some sort ..." continued Holmes.

"I see now," I said. "You mean Cardwell was attempting to portray a turncoat, or traitor."

"Yes, Dr. Watson," he replied.

"But *who* betrayed you? And why did you choose so roundabout a way of leaving a message?"

"A good question Watson; you asked it earlier, if you'll recall. I must confess it helped me onto the solution of this little puzzle."

"But whom does the painting implicate?" I asked. "I remember Miss Simmons saying, Cardwell, that the picture reminded you of your brother ..."

"But he's been dead for years Watson, so that would seem to rule him out. Tell me, what does the *artist's* name suggest to you?"

"... Gainesborough ... *Gaines!* By Jove!"

"Now you see how insightful your question was my dear fellow, when you wished to know why, if Cardwell wanted to leave behind a message, he did not do so directly with either his housekeeper of many years or his old school chum."

"Bravo!" I cried.

"Shhhhh!" whispered Cardwell. "It's way past midnight, but we daren't give ourselves away no matter how small the chance. Yes Mr. Holmes, you are clever indeed. I had to leave behind an indication for Mycroft, and at a moment's notice too. I had to point the accusing finger at Stanley, but do so in a way subtle enough to preclude his discovering it."

"But why not tell Miss Simmons directly?" I asked.

"Ah, my good doctor, you are obviously unfamiliar with the elements we're facing. A state of war is a state of war I'm afraid; to inform Miss Simmons would have been to endanger her life. The message was left safe and sound, with my assurance that only Mycroft, or his brother, could decipher it."

"But how came you to suspect Gaines in the first place?" asked Holmes.

"I'll show you," said he, and after rummaging in the back of Helgeson's writing desk, produced a small scrap of paper which he showed to us. It ran as follows:

STOAT: HAVE HEARD FROM OSTENDE. HOUSE IN LONDON. BOAT IN BAY 4.3. GUARD YOUR CHARGE. – OTTER

Holmes seized the paper eagerly and began examining it minutely, but was told by Cardwell not to waste his time, as it was merely a copy of the original note that he had discovered.

"Where?" asked Holmes.

"Inside Gaines' hat band. It was quite by accident, since I obviously don't go round snooping on my friends. But how fortunate that I noticed a corner of it sticking out from behind the leather as his hat hung on the coat tree! As you might well imagine, I was dumbstruck at first. Yet certain odd things about Stanley–things I'd grown used to over time–suddenly leaped out at me. I needn't go into them all–the most obvious was the sudden warming of his friendship when I joined the staff at the Admiralty. Well I almost called the note to his attention, certain it was meant as a joke–how glad I am now I didn't, but rather copied the note quickly and replaced the original. I was none-too-soon either, for next instant he'd bounded down the stairs from his room and retrieved the hat, taking it back up with him.

Knowing he had no legitimate use for it up there, I made the obvious conclusion."

"Most interesting," observed Holmes. "Gaines no doubt didn't wish to leave the note unattended for even an instant, yet he momentarily forgot it, and wished to retrieve and destroy it immediately. From the message, I gather he is 'STOAT.' Who then, is 'OTTER?' Also, have you deciphered the meaning? I think it noteworthy that Ostend is spelled with the final *e*, which means whoever wrote the message–or OTTER–is European, perhaps German."

"Yes, I'd thought the same thing. Also, the 'Boat in bay' probably refers to a U-Boat. What is the Bay? Well, I speculated that it could be Ballow's Wash–the place I call the eyrie cliff that you have just come from. I don't fancy it's self-puffery to suspect the note dealt in some way with me–"

"Absolutely not, Cardwell. Considering your importance to the war effort on the one hand, and the proximity of Gaines to you, on the other, it was a sensible inference. Yes, I think we can assume you are involved. Therefore, you suspected an abduction ..."

"Or assassination. I sensed I was in danger. Ostend is the principal U-Boat base as you may know. I took the words 'BOAT IN BAY 4.3' to signify a submarine raid on the third of April. As for the instructions 'GUARD YOUR CHARGE,' I think they are clear: Gaines was to keep a sharp eye on me and see that I remained in or around the cottage. What good fortune then that, having been forewarned, I was able to plan my *own* abduction and serve two ends: guarding my safety–and England's, and also causing Gaines to think his communication with 'OTTER'–whoever he may be–had gone awry. I would venture to say gentlemen, that Gaines' mind is in a pretty state by this time! Who took him? he is thinking. If it were our fellows, then why two days early? Oh, it was a splendid All Fool's Day prank! How lucky he sprained his ankle that day–and allowed me to take my nighttime walk alone!"

Cardwell had a hearty chuckle at his "friend's" expense.

"Today was the fourth," I mused, bringing him back to the subject at hand.

"Yes. Helgeson and I watched from the cliffs last night, and there was no raid. I daresay they got word of my disappearance and called it off. But tell us please, Mr. Holmes, how you were able to discover my escape? I thought we'd worked it out quite cleverly."

"A bit *too* cleverly. The parabellum cartridge set me thinking.

Surely it was too obvious a clue. That coupled with the painting episode left me wondering if the script weren't too carefully worked out. From your statement, Mr. Helgeson, that you had heard blowing sounds in the night, I first suspected what you intended me to: that a U-boat had surfaced. But when I began to doubt the authenticity of Cardwell's disappearance, you became a natural accomplice. I must confess the most authentic touch was the dog's body in the water. That had me puzzled for a deucedly long time, until I realised that one Airedale looks almost identical to another. This plus the fact that 'Tinker' was conveniently anchored in the kelp with a leash that wasn't usually used—"

"Ah, so you discovered that ... yes, I knew that to keep the animal's body in place, we would have to fasten it—"

"A master stroke, Cardwell, for everyone would naturally suppose a man wouldn't murder his own dog for the sake of falsifying a disappearance. But the planting of a dog that was *already dead*, and procured, I might add, Mr. Helgeson, from Clyde Witherspoon, the veterinarian in Eastbourne—"

"Dear me, Mr. Holmes," piped the old gentlemen in awe, "you've certainly been thorough."

"I have. And for further proof that the real Tinker was still alive I consulted a dozen local butchers. I take it Mr. Helgeson, that Arrowsmith's has the finest knucklebones? He tells me you've been in twice already ..."

"Extraordinary—"

"No, just logic and hard work. Now I assume, Cardwell, that once having decided to 'capture yourself' down at Ballow's Wash, you approached Mr. Helgeson?"

"Yes. Mr. Helgeson befriended me when he first arrived here at *Smuggler's Rest*. He taught me all about birdwatching, and even showed me the hidden passageway to the beach—making me vow to keep it secret, as I have these many years. In the few days prior to my departure, I sought him out. He was an immense help. We secured the dead Airedale from the veterinarian you mentioned, and took the remains to this cottage. On the night of my disappearance, Helgeson met me at the entrance to the grotto. We fastened the dog in amongst the seaweed, exactly as you found him. Then, leaving the cartridge on the beach to give further credence to the plan, we left the beach exactly as you and Dr. Watson did—up the grotto and into *Smuggler's Rest*, where we now sit.

"It was our plan for me to remain here in utter secrecy—for two weeks at least, or until my death or disappearance was believed in unshakably round the country. We did not plan on the likes of you, Mr. Sherlock Holmes."

"Hmmm. I see. And I take it Mr. Helgeson, that you deliberately stationed yourself at the top of the stairs to watch us when we examined the beach ... and to tell us about the strange noises?"

"Yes, Mr. Holmes. But you are no doubt wondering why we have chosen not to inform your brother Mycroft, about whom Geoffery speaks so highly ..."

"You distrust his aides—is that not correct?"

"Yes sir," answered Cardwell. "Mr. Holmes, as fond as I am of your brother, it has become quite noticeable lately that he's ... well, getting on in years ..."

"He is seventy years old—"

"Quite. And his faculties, while still immense and sharp in the larger sense, are sometimes a bit fuzzy when it comes to matters of detail."

"One would suspect so anyway," replied my companion.

"In any event, it has become evident—painfully so I'm afraid—during the past year that there is a security leak at the highest levels of the Admiralty ..."

"Good God man! You're not saying that *Mycroft*—"

"No, Dr. Watson. Absolutely not. But there is nevertheless a leak, and I fear that Mycroft, honest and steadfast as he is himself, could be overlooking—"

"I might say at this point Cardwell," interrupted Holmes with irritation, "that your revelation to Gaines about the mine barrage was hardly in the national interest."

"A good point. Were it not for the fact that our counter-intelligence has revealed that they already know about it, it would have been imprudent. As it now stands, it was a good ploy to make him and his cohorts think I suspected nothing. But to continue, I have for some time felt there was an agent near Mycroft, perhaps one of his personal aides—"

"But they have top security clearance—" I interjected.

"*Of course*, as do all good agents. Else what use would they be? No. When I think of the cunning behind the planting of Gaines ... I tell you nothing would surprise me."

"Nor I," confessed Holmes. "Well, is it Abercrombie or Howarth? Have you the slightest clue?"

"No. It was our plan to remain hidden, and to skulk about my cottage either at night, or in disguise in the daytime to discover 'OTTER's' identity. Since we trust both of you to keep this to yourselves, telling not even Mycroft, we shall proceed this way."

Holmes, chin in hands, thought for a full minute before replying.

"A noble scheme, but ineffectual. It might take a month to bring results, and time is precious. What you say about agents in high places is well-founded, I fear. Also, I admit that Mycroft's zealous patriotism, coupled with his advancing age, make him a sure mark for a cunning agent. But we cannot wait for them to appear, we must *seek them out!*"

Holmes rose and paced the floor furiously. He asked once again to examine the message Cardwell had copied. He studied it at length, asking Cardwell to remember if he could recall any distinguishing features of the original.

Our new friend replied in the negative. Holmes then inquired about the opening words on the note.

"House in London ..." he mused to himself. "*Whose* house? *What* house? Could this be the agent's headquarters?"

"It would depend I think, on whether there is a period after *Ostende*, or a comma," said I. "If a period as it now reads, then we are to assume there *is* a special house in London, or the fact that there is a house there is newsworthy in itself. But if the word Ostende is followed by a comma, then we obviously must assume that 'OTTER' has heard *both* from Ostende and the house in London, which means that the house is definitely the agent's headquarters."

"Brilliant Watson! A remarkably lucid explanation. Well Cardwell, a period or comma?"

"I'm fairly sure a period. I examined it for some time before copying it."

"All right then. Besides the boat in the bay, there is a house in London—or rather a house that's unique from all the other thousands or ordinary ones ... but now it's time to make a plan. To ensure secrecy I would suggest we retire to the hidden cellar of *Smuggler's Rest.* Is this agreeable Mr. Helgeson? Fine. Also, a pot of strong coffee would be most welcome, for I wouldn't be surprised if we were up 'til dawn."

Just after daybreak on the following morning, April 5th, a heavily-bandaged Geoffery Cardwell arrived at his seaside cottage. As his physician, I answered all queries relating to his health, and also gave strict orders that he was to lie flat upon his back in bed, and be disturbed by *no one.*

As might be supposed, Holmes helped me carry him upstairs and put him to bed. Only a sly wink from our patient, as we drew up the covers in mock gloom, betrayed our plot.

"Now Gaines," I remonstrated to the traitor—doing my best to conceal my loathing for the villain—"Geoffery specifically requested to be brought back here, rather than be confined to a hospital. This is against my better medical judgement, I'll have you know. But he expressed such a strong desire to be here with you and Miss Simmons, in a familiar place—yes I agree Gaines, I think it will be beneficial to his recovery ..."

Holmes then went on to explain how we'd discovered him wandering about in a daze in the next county—temporarily deranged by a head injury.

"But he's much better already," I added as planned. "In fact, I can state with absolute certainty he'll be his old self in a day or two. He still cannot remember what happened. He descended the stairway at Ballow's Wash for a walk upon the beach. His dog Tinker ran after something in the water, breaking loose from his master and dragging the long leash behind. The dog then got stuck in the kelp. Hearing the animal's cries, he ran along the spit to reach the dog, but fell forward violently after slipping on the seaweed. He remembers nothing afterwards, but we surmise that, disoriented by the blow to his head, he was awakened by the rising tide and swam away from shore rather than towards it. He thus swam clear out from the Wash to the next beach, leaving his dead pet behind. It's a miracle he's alive—and how fortunate for England! Well, we've said enough. Please allow no one to enter Gaines, that's a good fellow. And remember, he is not to be disturbed at all for the next four and twenty hours, until his concussion abates. We shall be at Mr. Holmes' cottage at Birling Gap if needed. Adieu."

"Bye the bye Gaines, there will be a guard sent round directly to help you," added Holmes as an afterthought as we climbed into the Douglas.

"I hope that should prevent his acting hastily, Watson. Yet if Gaines is the kind of fellow I think he is, he'll seek out 'OTTER' directly, instead of worrying about Cardwell. After all, according to our tale, Cardwell is helpless and stationary. I take it you noticed Gaines' joy at seeing his 'charge' back, eh?"

"Yes but I tell you Holmes, I fear for his safety."

"And I too, somewhat. Cardwell is a brave man. Yet if all goes well, we should soon have all the herrings in the net. Now as we discussed, we'll need some help following Gaines, and I wonder how long Helgeson can stay at his telescope in the woods yonder without falling asleep ... We'd best seek out Mycroft immediately. Bear up Watson, I know you're tired as well—"

The next instant we were again bouncing along the countryside in the motorcycle towards the *Fox and Hounds.* At Holmes' direction, I settled myself low behind the sidecar's cowling whilst he opened the throttle wide, and how we flew along. The vibration and noise were terrifying. When we hit the slightest hump in the road the machine took wing, only to land again in a series of bouncing leaps. We took the curves at a dizzying pace, and more than once the sidecar was tipped high in the air, its wheel spinning freely above the road.

Needless to say, we arrived at the inn in a matter of minutes. Holmes sprang from the machine, ran across the lawn, and bounded up the stairway with a speed and agility I found amazing. I followed as best I could, and soon joined him in the large, well-appointed room which housed his brother. The latter was sitting bolt upright in bed, obviously a bit surprised at being knocked up so early.

"Well, what have you to say Sherlock? Pray to God it's good news. I am in sore need of it I can tell you."

"Would you consider it good news if I were to tell you Geoffery Cardwell is alive?"

The heavy man sprang from his bed and grasped his younger brother by the elbows, beaming into his face.

"You don't say! Well I'm dashed! How do you know, and where is he? You must tell me all—"

"Yes, but not before you dress and join us outside."

"Why on earth—"

"That will be apparent enough before long, dear brother. Now please, do as I instruct. Where does that door lead?" Holmes asked, pointing to the wall on his left.

"Abercrombie and Howarth share the adjoining room, so there's nothing—"

"Yes, to be sure. Well Mycroft, Watson and I shall await you out on the lawn. We expect to see you soon as possible ... *alone.*"

We were not forced to wait long before the stout form of Holmes' senior brother, hastily clad and grunting irritably, strode into view.

"Well?" he intoned imperiously.

"Sorry to inconvenience you, but we've reason to suspect that either Abercrombie or Howarth is an enemy agent."

Without even replying the portly man turned on his heel and

started for the inn. But I grabbed him by his shoulder, turning him round, and Holmes quickly explained our midnight adventure to the statesman, and the message found by Cardwell. Mycroft listened intently to this string of events, then stroked his chin in bewilderment. He then paced to and fro in a distraught fashion.

"Damn!" he shouted at last, striking his open palm with his huge fist. "I think you're right, and I'll tell you why. But first, let us walk a bit further out, and talk as we walk ... there, that's better. I must say Sherlock, it was wise indeed of you to come out here before revealing your suspicions—"

"You have something to add then?"

"I think so. The word *house* in the message, was it capitalized?"

"Yes. But the entire message, as copied by Cardwell, was done in block letters."

"Still in all gentlemen, I think we can assume the word was meant to be capitalised, since it refers to a *person*, not an edifice. 'Colonel' House arrived in London March 28. What gives credence to your suspicions is the fact that his visit is a top state secret, since it concerns the possibility of America's entering the war. Only four men in all the Kingdom knew of it. I was one, Churchill another—the other two I assume you know. But even Cardwell wasn't informed—thus his bewilderment at the message. So if word were leaked, I fear I must bear the responsibility—"

He lowered his huge head to his chest in grief and shame. But, always an indomitable spirit, he soon regained his regal composure.

"So it would follow," he said in a breaking voice, "that either Howarth or Abercrombie is the man called OTTER. Off hand, I would guess Abercrombie to be the plant. He's less known to me and newer in my service, and generally has a more sinister mien—but no matter which one, we've not a moment to lose."

Holmes then explained to Mycroft the trap we'd hastily set in hopes of catching Otter, and any other agents who might have been involved.

"And you have only poor Mr. Helgeson to watch the wily Stoat? He must be relieved as soon as possible! But by whom? The natural thing would be to send either Howarth or Abercrombie, but if indeed one of them is the enemy we shall defeat ourselves. You say you told Gaines there would be a guard sent round? *Excellent!* He would suppose, in light of what's happened, that we would be anxious to guard Geoffery at all costs."

"But again, the question remains as to who will help us," said

Holmès. "Help cannot arrive from London in time. Furthermore, any such official request, if carried through your aides, would further impede our strategy. To circumvent the aides will arouse their suspicions—yet it is the best alternative. Let us place the fate of this operation in the hands of that institution so many Britains depend on: the rural police constable."

Mycroft agreed, and within an hour's time Holmes and I, armed with a state document provided by him, secured the services of two policemen who were proficient in the use of sidearms. One we stationed at the Cardwell cottage; the other surreptitiously relieved Helgeson at his lookout post in the copse of tall trees that overlooked the cottage. In accordance with our plan, we also informed Gaines that Cardwell would be moved the following day, April 6th, and taken to a military hospital in London. As we suspected, he showed great agitation over this piece of news, though he did his best to conceal it. As for the aides, Howarth and Abercrombie, they appeared no different whatsoever. They both seemed pleased and relieved that Cardwell had returned and would soon be well. Neither of them went near the Cardwell cottage, but stayed round the *Fox and Hounds* all morning. We supposed therefore, that there had been no communication between either of them and Gaines. So unassuming was their manner in fact, that I began to doubt their culpability.

"But if they wish to steal him away, they'd best make their move soon, or at least get in touch with one another," said Holmes to us as we sat on the terrace of the inn overlooking the driveway. Mycroft's limousine sat imposingly at the far end of it. "It was for this reason that I informed Gaines of Cardwell's imminent departure from the seacoast ..."

"And how do you suppose they will communicate?" asked Mycroft.

"I'm assuming they don't have a wireless, so that leaves three options: telegraph, telephone, or personal visit. The first is out of the question unless done in code. The second is possible, but the Cardwell cottage has no telephone. Therefore, Gaines cannot communicate with OTTER without leaving the cottage, and from all reports he has not done so."

"But can OTTER communicate with *Gaines*?" I asked.

"An excellent question Watson," he replied. "If the method employed is a note, then I don't see how they can communicate without a physical conveyance—a drop of some sort. I cannot at present imagine what other sort of signal they would have. It seems we've caught them off guard, at least momentarily."

"But don't forget Sherlock, we are not dealing with petty thieves or cutthroats, but with enemy intelligence. Think again of their cunning in placing Stoat and Otter ..."

"To be sure. Well, the best we can do is to keep watch on all of them without being too obvious."

We were interrupted, however, by the approach of Howarth, who informed Mycroft it was time to collect the dispatches from London at the railway station.

"Both Abercrombie and myself will go, if it's all right with you sir."

Mycroft, with feigned casualness, waved him off with his hand. As the two of them departed in the car, he turned to us with an air of resignation.

"What else to do? To forbid them going would be to arouse their suspicions. However, if they're gone longer than necessary it would be best to collect Cardwell directly and proceed to London."

But we hadn't long to wait; the two aides returned in less than an hour's time with the sealed Admiralty dispatch box. The three of us exchanged knowing glances; it was unlikely any real mischief could have occurred in that length of time, especially since the two men went together. Mycroft dismissed them, and opened the case. To his dismay, there was an urgent cable, top secret, commanding him to return to London immediately. With a groan, he threw up his hands in despair.

"Don't fret Mycroft. Watson and I can manage with the help of the local constabulary. But if go you must, pray don't take your aides with you, for then how will we spring the trap?"

Grudgingly, his brother agreed to take the train, though he knew it was strictly against regulations for so important a personage.

"I doubt you'll be needing to take the train, since the Eastbourne police have volunteered the services of a car and staff should the need arise. I would suggest that this unexpected emergency fills the bill nicely. I shall telephone them directly and arrange for them to pick you up. We shall notify Howarth and Abercrombie only after you're an hour upon the way."

Though disgruntled at being recalled at this hour of suspense, Mycroft was nevertheless slightly mollified at the prospect of a pleasant and private ride back. For as the few people who knew him are aware, Mycroft Holmes was an exceedingly private person. Within an hour the car, as instructed, pulled up near a yew hedge behind the Inn. Mycroft boarded the vehicle unobtrusively, settled himself comfortably in the rear seat with his dispatch boxes, and was off.

"Rum luck, eh Holmes, his being called away at the last minute."

"Not luck, but careful planning. While you were bandaging Cardwell in Helgeson's living room just before dawn, I was telephoning young Allistair in London, arranging for him to send the cable Mycroft received. He carried it off perfectly, as only a man in his position could. His late father would be proud indeed ..."

"But why—"

"Surely Watson, you *know* why! Think of the plot against Cardwell. Then ask yourself if there's anyone *else* in the vicinity yet more important to England's survival ..."

"Dash it, of course!"

"Mycroft has been in danger for months. The only reason they've spared him 'til now is his value as an information source. But you can rest assured, my friend, that once OTTER discovers he is unmasked he will put a bullet in my brother instantly. No, I'm breathing much easier now Mycroft is gone. Also, I made other arrangements this morning. Arriving at the Eastbourne station at one is a remarkable assemblage of cunning and brawn. Do you perchance recall the colorful career of Logan, the Lion of Leeds?"

"*Do* I? The meanest scrum half who ever played for England!"

"Well he's in the army these days ... in the special brigade. He'll be there, along with Crusher Calahan, late of Newgate Prison. Two other noteworthys are '*Fandango*,' the Basque sharpshooter and assassin, and Mad Mike Higgins ... whom I'm sure you've heard of ..."

"Dear God in heaven, that's a rough lot!"

"Pray to God they'll *be* rough—I didn't invite the special brigade down here for a cricket match ..."

"Shall we meet them?"

"Yes, and straightaway, for it's now almost noon. Tell me old friend, how are you holding up? As you know, I can go for days without sleep if the fit is upon me, and we are now in the midst of the jolliest chase in years. But you Watson, are of sensible disposition. We've been thirty hours without sleep, and won't be worth a farthing if we don't rest. Can you go with me or would you rather I drop you at *Finisterre*?"

"No, I'm fit as a fiddle," I lied. "Let's go meet the train first, then take a nap."

And so we made ready for the trip, but first telling Abercrombie and Howarth about Mycroft's sudden departure.

"He had a car at his disposal don't you see," said Holmes in his most soothing manner. "So he bade me tell you to join him in a few days after you've enjoyed yourselves thoroughly down here in the South Downs ... and helped us see Geoffery Cardwell to safety."

"But why did he not wish us to drive him back?" asked Howarth nervously.

"Good question Howarth. Why not, Mr. Holmes? Is he dissatisfied with our service?"

"Not at all, I assure you. He thinks you're two of the most remarkable men he's met in quite a while. In fact, he weighed the decision for some time before electing to return to the Admiralty unobtrusively, leaving us to see to Cardwell and perhaps enjoy ourselves a bit. You're free to use the limousine, by the by, anyway you choose."

"We assume then Mr. Holmes, though you're not officially in charge, that you will be in some way directing the transfer of Cardwell?" asked Abercrombie dryly.

"I'm not actually sure, but I believe Mycroft arranged for his transfer tomorrow or early the following day. Now if you'll excuse us, Dr. Watson and I have some personal errands to attend to. You may reach us at my cottage in Birling Gap, at the phone number 221. Farewell!"

By half past twelve we were at the station. The train arrived on schedule, but I saw none of the notorious crew emerge from the carriages. I had begun to think that a terrible miscalculation had been made when a hard-looking chap approached my companion and nodded quickly.

"Good afternoon, Mr. Holmes," he said in a half whisper, "we're all here sir, ready to be of service."

"Excellent Ainsley! This is my friend and colleague Dr. John Watson, whom I'm sure you've heard of ... Watson, this is Captain Henry Ainsley, commander of the Fourth Detachment, Special Brigade, King's Light Rifles."

We greeted each other briefly and then Ainsley disappeared unobtrusively along the platform.

"Hmmph! He scarcely looks a military man to me Holmes. He's not even in uniform."

"Exactly. Nor are the eleven others. See that big chap yonder with the scarface and scowl? That's Mad Mike Higgins. You recall I'm sure how he wiped out a whole platoon of Huns single-handedly at Ypres, with nothing but a trenching spade and bayonet ... Now that unassuming fellow over there with the long satchel is Derrick Flemming, nicknamed *Death Dealer*, and I'll wager that's not a fishing pole in the case he's carrying...."

I then examined the milling throng more closely, and could discern many mean looking fellows who ambled about innocently enough, yet they were set apart by a certain grimness of expression, a vacant look about the eyes that made one's blood run cold. A few coming near us slipped Holmes a sly wink or a nod, but to the casual observer, nothing at all was different about the milling crowd of train passengers. One man in particular appeared pernicious. A slim chap of short stature, he slunk cravenly at the crowd's edge. He was obviously a loner; a man who had little use for people. He was dark complexioned, and had sunken cheeks, but his black eyes danced bright in his weak face with insane energy.

"I say Holmes, I hope he's not one of your men. Merely looking at him gives me the *jim-jams.*"

"Don't look too long or hard Watson, for your own good. That's *Fandango.* I've heard quite a bit about him, none of it good, except his fantastic skill at long range shooting. He's a bit homicidal, so it's best not to rouse his nasty temper."

The men left the platform in groups of two or three—a few singly. Most carried long cases or satchels slung over their shoulders. When the station was almost deserted Holmes, rubbing his hands with satisfaction, led me back to the Douglas.

"We'll have a surprise for them all right!" he chuckled grimly as he started the engine. "They'll drift over the countryside separately so as not to arouse notice. We'll all rendezvous at Helgeson's cottage in three hours. They've been issued maps and complete instructions. Now I suggest we return to Birling Gap for a nap."

Upon arriving at *Finisterre,* Holmes immediately telephoned Helgeson at his cottage (where he had gone after being relieved by the constable) for word. Told nothing had changed, and that Gaines had not left the cottage, he settled himself comfortably on the divan, and I retired upstairs in my room. I fell asleep quickly, and later amazed myself by waking before my companion. Looking at my watch, I saw it was almost four. We were late! I hurried downstairs and awakened Holmes, who cursed himself for oversleeping. But to me there was no mystery as to the cause of his fatigue, and I reminded him that prior to our midnight visit to the wash, I had slept whilst he scoured the countryside for clues.

"Well we'd best hurry," said he, drawing frantically on a cigarette, "take your pistol and an entire box of cartridges. Neither you nor I have ever killed a man Watson, but there's a possibility we may tonight, or," and he turned me round to look me directly in the face, "or be killed ourselves. I should warn you of that possibility."

I shrugged him off and, placing the revolver and ammunition in my coat pocket, strode for the doorway.

* * *

We arrived at *Smugglers' Rest* shortly afterwards by a route that did not take us by the Cardwell cottage. The scene that met my eyes as I entered the snug abode is one I shan't ever forget. Round the parlour sat seven of the fiercest looking men I'd ever laid eyes on. All were dressed as rural laborers, wearing coarse jackets, rough trousers, and heavy boots. None of them rose to greet us save Crusher Callahan, who fairly embraced Holmes with joy, for it was he who was largely responsible for securing the "Crusher's" release from Newgate prison. All the others nodded and grunted an assent, and returned to their weapons. And what a display of deadly artillery!

On the oval rug, in various stages of assemblage, were three machine guns. All were mounted on tripods. There was a 30 calibre Lewis gun, an eight millimetre Hotchkiss, and a heavy Vickers. Four men hovered over these awesome machines, oiling the breeches, checking bolts, firing pins, drum and belt feeds, etc. I was, I must admit, repulsed in the extreme, having spent the previous two years of my lifetime trying to counteract the effects of guns such as these.

Before I could recover from the shock of seeing *Smuggler's Rest* transformed into an armoury, there came a deep roaring and vibration from underneath. The very floorboards and walls shook with the terrific din. Within seconds, however, I was informed of the origin of these noises when the trap in the kitchen was thrown up and three men scurried up the ladderway, dragging a huge water-cooled machine gun with them. It was a 50 calibre Browning and required three men to lift it. In their wake, a bluish cloud of acrid smoke flowed, and made its way into the parlour where we sat.

"*She's on the money, she is!*" chirped one of their number as he rubbed down the smoking barrel with grease.

"I say Steve, take two turns on that leaf sight will you? That's a good lad ..."

This fourth gun was set up with the other three, and the men sat back and lighted cigarettes. Obviously, they had been using the underground cavern as a shooting gallery in which to sight in and test the weapons. I examined the various belts and drums that were being filled with rounds of ammunition. Curiously, the ammunition for the big Browning looked different. The rounds appeared longer as well as thicker, and every sixth one had a blunt tip painted white.

"Them's armour-piercing rounds Doctor—explosive bullets. Them white ones, they're tracers—phosphorus tipped—best not get a fag near 'em sir ... whole place go up in a heap, if you get my meanin'—"

"Oh quite," said I, stuffing out my cigarette and backing away from the little man who stacked the drums and belts into canvas bags. I noticed also there were many haversacks lying about, filled with lumps the size of cricket balls. I had an idea what they were, but didn't ask. My inner question was indirectly answered by the little man (called "Weasel Williams" by his compatriots), who said, when he'd finished loading the gear: "we'll have a surprise for 'em when they show up mates! They'll be sorry blighters indeed when they pay the *detachment* a visit!"

It was getting on towards five o'clock, and the men grumbled they were thirsty and longed for a pint, but Captain Ainsley refused them, saying they must stay at their keenest for the duty which would surely arise within the next twelve hours. This put the crew in an ugly mood, and I was glad Ainsley had the integrity and force to instill the discipline necessary. Truly, this was a rough bunch.

Helgeson and I repaired to the kitchen to put the tea water to boil. But on the way, there came to our ears a sad, haunting sound—a dirgeful wailing song that filled us with wonder and sadness.

"It's the *fado*," said Helgeson. "I heard it once before, in Portugal ..."

In the kitchen we found Fandango, sitting alone, his eyes downcast. From his lips issued the melancholy folk hymn of Portugal. He sang softly, hardly moving his lips, and he did not sing words but rather sang only the melody in a soft alto voice. He looked down at the rifle he was cleaning, and caressed the weapon with an adoration that was sickening. The rifle looked far heavier than the standard military issue, and moreover had a long telescopic sight affixed to the barrel. The deranged sniper did not even look up at us from his beloved instrument, but continued polishing the weapon and singing.

Leaving the kitchen later with the tea, I told Helgeson under my breath that the fellow made me uneasy. He replied he had the same feeling, but that the Basque sharpshooter was only different from his comrades in degree, not kind.

"They're all professional killers Watson, the whole lot of them ..."

Returning to the parlour and looking round me at the grim-faced group packing their deadly array of equipment, I was forced to agree with him. These men certainly weren't common soldiers; one could immediately sense the difference in carriage and mood they exhibited on the eve of battle. Unlike the average soldier, poised in the trench ready for the offensive, they showed no nervousness or dread whatsoever. On the contrary, they sat quietly joking, engaged in light banter as if in a pub after a day's work. In fact, they seemed eager for the action and excitement soon to come. Three of them busied themselves sharpening double-edged combat knives on whetstones. Others took a last inspection of their personal arms: sten guns, Browning light carbines, and automatic pistols. A few even wore brass knuckles! And here too, in the very equipment they carried, one could see a striking difference between the common soldier and men of the Special Brigade. Absent were the cumbersome rifles, heavy packs and helmets of the infantry. The detachment carried a bizarre assortment of light automatic weapons that were highly portable and produced enormous firepower.

"All right lads, it's time!" chirped Ainsley, draining his cup. "On your feet and move out as planned. Remember, only squad two can open fire before my flare. Colours as follows: red for the cliff, yellow for the cottage, white gather to, blue stops it–got it? Right ho' Derrick, take your boys down to the cottage first. Then you Logan, to the cliffside. Billie, outside and guard the hedge. We'll go last. Off you go now lads."

The men rose and slung their gear across their broad backs. I was amazed at how the incredible assemblage of weapons and ammunition again "disappeared" into the canvas haversacks and satchels as the men formed teams and left the cottage in the fading light with scarcely a sound. And again I saw their faces: the hard mouths, the bored, vacant eyes ...

The entire group left, divided into four three-man squads. One squad was to cover *Smuggler's Rest*, which was to serve as the general headquarters and field hospital with Helgeson remaining in charge. They would also defend the cliff walk if and when a battle got underway. Their machine gun was placed hidden directly opposite the cottage, covering the front approach. A second team crept surreptitiously in the gathering twilight to cover Cardwell's cottage. They were instructed to storm the building, guns blazing, at any sign of violence from within. Otherwise, they were to remain absolutely hidden from view. The third group stationed themselves atop the

Eyrie Cliff, and placed the heavy Browning machine gun in a crevice in the rock wall so that it commanded the entire wash below. The men then hid themselves likewise in the rock. The final group of men, known as the "flying squad," was to join Holmes and me, and was commanded by Captain Ainsley. I was distressed to see that Fandango, resplendent in his Basque beret, was part of it. This team was to temporarily station itself on a high knoll overlooking the coast and the entire cliff walk, from Smuggler's Rest to the Cardwell cottage. It also commanded a fine view of Ballow's Wash and the Eyrie Cliff which surrounded it. The five of us lay on the far side of the slope, our heads above the summit. With the aid of our field glasses, we could observe the Cardwell cottage closely, and also members of two of the squads, which now and then communicated to Captain Ainsley with hand signals, signifying that all was quiet. Each squad had its own machine gun, but ours was the lightweight and highly-portable Lewis. We were to keep watch, overseeing the entire operation, and direct the soldiers to where they were needed by means of a Very pistol which Captain Ainsley wore on his belt. If the Cardwell house were attacked, or if we detected any commotion whatsoever, a yellow flare would be fired into the sky, a signal for everyone to converge there. If a red flare were sent up, the men were to proceed to the Eyrie Cliff as quickly as possible. In the event of another type of raid, our group was to rush wherever needed, firing a white flare as a signal. These flares were the small signal type, but after the operation had begun, Captain Ainsley was to continuously fire white phosphorus flares to illuminate the scene of battle.

"I'll feel foolish if nothing happens," whispered Holmes to me. "But if there is even a remote chance of breaking this ring of espionage it's worth it."

We waited for almost an hour before Fandango tapped the Captain on the shoulder and pointed seaward. We could see nothing; night was falling and the sea appeared deserted. I raised my field glasses and could barely see a crescent of white moving slowly towards us down the coast. Truly, the Basque rifleman had the eyes of an eagle! In the space of a minute, the white "V" revealed itself to be the bow wave of a small steam cruiser. She was painted white with a green stack, and clipped along nicely, the heavy black smoke trailing behind her like a plume.

"Not a warship," observed Holmes as he peered through his glasses. "It appears to be a private yacht, and a well-furnished one at that..."

The boat appeared to be slowing down; the bow wave almost

disappeared. We could now see several crewmen on the deck walking about. One raised his binoculars and looked landward. Soon, he raised his arm, and the boat stopped in the water. Pretty as she was, the yacht, perhaps half a mile off the coast and idling along, had a sinister look. I switched my glasses back to the Cardwell cottage and saw Gaines emerge from the double doors. He was almost a mile away and the light was faint, yet the flash of his blond hair, illuminated by the light behind was unmistakable. To my amazement, the next instant I saw two more figures appear at his side.

"Abercrombie and Howarth ..." said Holmes in a musing, almost philosophical tone. "So OTTER has joined STOAT at last ..."

"Yes, Holmes, but *which* is OTTER and *which* the loyal aide?" I asked. "We must not kill the wrong man."

"The men are instructed absolutely to hold their fire unless there's evidence Cardwell is being killed or hurt," interjected Ainsley. "They are to remain totally concealed otherwise. Hopefully, the local constables Mr. Holmes has dispatched will force OTTER to be cautious–"

"The boat is leaving," said I, watching the smoke intensify and the bow wave rise. "Perhaps it's nothing."

"Perhaps Watson, but look: Gaines appears to be going back inside. Yes, I saw the flash of a windowpane. He's gone."

Within seconds, a thick stream of grey smoke arose from the cottage's chimney. It lasted perhaps half a minute, then ceased as suddenly as it began.

"Hmmph!" snorted my companion. "There could hardly be a more obvious signal than that, or a more *silent* one. I doubt if the guards in front are even aware of it. Yet if they are, they surely haven't laid eyes on the motor launch, which is fast departing to places unknown. And always Gaines can say he was only burning up some wastepaper!"

Gaines rejoined his companions on the hillside, and they all watched the boat make a wide circle seawards, then return back in the direction from whence it came. The men went inside the cottage, closing the door behind them. All was quiet again.

"I wonder if Cardwell and Miss Simmons are all right?"

"I would say the chances are good Watson. I'll wager the real action won't begin until later tonight. High tide will be at 9:13, and they'll want to arrive at least four hours before low tide if they come by sea ... I would say we can expect them around ten o'clock."

As usual, he was correct.

* * *

It was 10:27 when I heard the *snick* of the rifle bolt beside me. Fandango—who possessed the animal instincts of a true killer—had heard the running footsteps long before the rest of us. It was a runner from squad three, informing us of a periscope wake off Ballow's Wash.

"Splendid work!" said his commander. "Now not a peep out of anyone until you hear the first shot, clear?"

The runner, a man called, appropriately, "Legs" Thomkins, reaffirmed the instructions and flew away down the hill. We raised our glasses. In the moonlight, we could see the patch of white froth, scarcely two feet across and twice as high, that swam malignantly into the cove. Soon afterwards, the dark stalk of the periscope too was visible. Then, as the invisible vessel beneath slowed to a halt, the wake shrank, then vanished altogether. The black pipe advanced imperceptibly towards the shore. Finally, I saw it move no more. Then it slid down out of sight.

"The Hun has arrived," said Holmes slowly. "Now it's my guess that OTTER will attempt to lure Cardwell down here, or else take him as surreptitiously as possible. Therefore, it would be wise to send a runner to the second team, instructing them to follow the party down here to the wash, perhaps a hundred yards behind ..."

Ainsley agreed on the strategy, and one of our men sped down to relay the instructions. But before the message was relayed, the night came alive with gunfire and violence.

It began as I saw, through my glasses, the rear door of the Cardwell cottage open. Four men came from the lighted doorway, and began to make their way down the hillside to the cliff path a hundred yards below. All appeared quiet, as if the two cohorts had succeeded in luring Cardwell away from the cottage. As per our arranged plan, he was to go along with them, raising no objections, until he was brought to the head of the stairway to the Wash. At that point he was to fling himself aside and sprint for cover. However, to our dismay, we saw one of the silhouettes turn suddenly. At the same instant I could see several pinpoint flashes, and in the next moment could hear the faint popping of pistol fire. Then the figures were faintly illuminated by a series of bright flashes, followed by many loud echoing retorts. One of the figures fell; the remaining three scurried down the hill while the firing continued. No one said anything, but I'm sure we all had the same thought in mind—praying the man who fell wasn't Geoffery Cardwell. However, if Ainsley's men had indeed followed their instructions to the letter, there was little danger that he would be hit; they were told to protect the man with the bandaged head at all costs.

An explosion sounded to my right, and I saw Ainsley with the smoking flare pistol in his upraised arm. There followed a high whine and a faraway pop. High overhead hung a fiery red ball that floated slowly down. We ran down the hill to the top of the Eyrie Cliff. From the opposite side of the cliff wall came the sound of a heavy breech block working. The big machine gun was ready. I felt a sharp tug at my elbow.

"Watson look!" said Holmes.

There was a great roiling of seawater beneath us; a huge oblong patch of luminescence as the water boiled and frothed into white foam. Then the dark hull rose menacingly. The prow emerged first, an angular, predatory snout—the apotheosis of evil and destruction. The water flowed from the metal in bright streaks. Presently I heard the muted whine of an electric motor, and then the hollow groan of compressed air as the boat blew her tanks. It was a horrid, melancholy sound, a noise like a thousand death rattles. The conning tower appeared, straight and intricate with its tubes and rods thrusting upwards. The flare had burnt out by the time the boat surfaced. Furthermore, as Holmes whispered to me, the men in the submarine had obviously not heard the shooting. To their minds, then, all was in order. The boat lay still in the water. The only sound was the whine of the engines, which had been cut back. A squeak and a clang, and a circle of light appeared in the conning tower, soon to be blocked out by a crew member who scrambled up the hatchway. He was followed by three more men, who then walked briskly along the foredeck, past the deck gun to the bow, where they busied themselves inflating a rubber boat and sliding it into the water. Still the cliffs were silent; there was no sound from the cliff walk. I was amazed at the patience and stealth of the Special Detachment.

The moonlight was bright enough to clearly see the general outline of the cove and the stairhead, as well as the outline of the grey steel fish that lay below us. Presently we heard the sound of running feet on gravel, and saw the outlines of three men at the top of the stairway. One of them shouted in German, and was immediately answered by the crew of the submarine. What was said I do not know to this day, but I was distressed to see two of the U-boat's crewmen race to the deck gun and tear off its canvas cover, whilst the other two ran towards the main hatch for help.

Ainsley's pistol barked a second time, and seconds later a miraculous change had come over Ballow's Wash: the entire area was flooded with light as bright as day by a phosphorus flare. The men at the stairhead jerked round, alarmed. One of them held Cardwell round his neck, a pistol at his head. It was Abercrombie.

"Just as I suspected!" cried Holmes. "If we make a move, they'll kill Cardwell, and Mycroft will never forgive me–"

Abercrombie, by now exposed as OTTER, shouted to his pursuers on the path that he would kill Cardwell if they weren't granted safe passage to the boat. A heavy silence followed, during which time his free companion, Howarth, began descending the staircase as fast as he could.

"I repeat!" shouted Abercrombie, "let us pass or I'll blow his brains out!"

We could see the soldiers stop their pursuit. Abercrombie, hostage in tow, began backing down the stairs, unaware that there was anyone at his back save the submarine and its crew. I saw Fandango bring the rifle to his cheek. Then Ainsley fired another flare, and soon the fading light was again dispelled by light as bright as the sun, throwing stark shadows everywhere, and showing the two figures plain as day. The heavy rifle cracked, and Abercrombie grabbed his left ear as the bullet spun him round. As he whirled about in the instant before falling, I could see that half his head was gone. As he went over the rail Cardwell sprang back up the stairs shouting. He was none too fast either, for the next instant came the terrific pounding of the 75 millimetre deck gun, and the entire iron stairway was blown to pieces.

Perhaps the most curious of all the events as they swam by us at dizzying speed was the great commotion caused by thousands of shorebirds as they flung themselves into the air shrieking. Amidst the rifle and cannonfire, they whirled about everywhere, crying and beating their great wings, which further added to the chaos.

With Cardwell safely in the clear, our forces opened up with a fury that was unbelievable. As much as I despised our Hun foe, I couldn't help thinking at that instant how dreadful was his plight, stranded in a cove which bristled from every side with hostile fire. With a roaring boom, the 50 calibre machinegun commenced from the opposite cliff first strafing the conning tower and spitting two Germans into the sea, then sweeping the hull at waterline to tear open the ballast tanks.

The tracer bullets streaked downwards in the dark in thin white lines.

Our Lewis gun sent a stream of bullets at the bow of the submarine, sweeping the two men into the water, dead. The deck gun was now silent. But the fore-hatchway flashed open and new crewmen scrambled out to replace their fallen comrades. Truly one was forced to admire their courage and tenacity, their animal strength in battle. The sailors fired their Lugers blindly up at us, the bullets ripping into the rock wall beneath.

The U-boat was beginning to list to starboard; the armour-piercing bullets of the big Browning had apparently found their mark. I heard the whine of the motors increase, and the sound of the klaxon horn below decks.

"*They've given the command to dive!*" shouted Ainsley, and tore open the canvas haversack he'd carried with him. The other soldiers did likewise, and commenced flinging Mills bombs—which looked like miniature footballs—down into the wash. These exploded with ear-splitting roars, and in huge sheets of flame and flying metal. Tall geysers of water rose in their wakes. At first I was dumbfounded by this seemingly random violence, but then one of the bombs found its target and fell through the forehatch of the vessel. In the instant that followed, a blinding pillar of flame shot upwards through the opening, and a muffled explosion and visible wrenching of the boat told me of the horrendous damage done below. And it was impressed upon me then, as never before, how frail a craft a submarine is. For its defence and effectiveness lie in stealth and surprise, not in the strength of armour or armaments. Suddenly, the boat fell dark and silent. The list increased—the conning tower lay almost submerged, and the fierce-looking sea-dragon of moments earlier appeared pathetic—a feeble, crippled, pod-shaped hulk of burnt metal.

Heavy smoke issued from both hatches, and increaseed each second. Cries of "*Bitte! Bitte!*" reached us, and Ainsley fired a blue flare: the cease-fire signal. Four torn and blackened figures emerged from the main hatch, retching and coughing, their hands on their heads. Two of them were officers. They made their tortured way to the foredeck and sat huddled, like naughty schoolboys, upon the tilting deck, hoping we would not blow them to pieces.

As the last light of the blue flare faded away, the cove again grew dark. But shortly we could again see the terrified men huddled in the moonlight. Sounds from the head of the eyrie cliff told us that the second team had found its way to the beach despite the blown-out stairway, and was proceeding towards the wrecked boat.

Fandango stood up, raising his sniper's rifle. Ainsley shouted at him not to fire, but the Basque, without firing, swept his scoped weapon to and fro along the beach, as if searching for something. Then from the beach below a pistol spat in a tiny spark of flame. Fandango, with a groan, dropped his rifle and fell to his knees, clutching at his middle. I rushed crawling to his side, attempting to pry his hands away to examine the wound. But the next instant his hand flashed upward, the bright blade cut into the flesh of my forearm, grating on the bone.

"*Leave him alone doctor–he'll kill you,*" shouted Ainsley. We'd best wait 'til he passes out."

I crawled back to Holmes and Ainsley. The latter was beside himself, shouting into the cove. Who had fired the shot? The order was *cease fire*!

Holmes grabbed me by the arm and dragged me away.

"*Quick Watson, what a fool I've been*! Fandango is smarter than all of us. Don't you see he went *down* instead of up? Come on, we've got to warn them."

We raced madly round to the head of the cove. Having thought of everything, the detachment had even brought rope ladders. One of these was now hung from the twisted remnants of the old stairway, and down it we sped as fast as safety would allow. I noticed we were followed by Ainsley and the rest of the flying squad, who also realised their job on the clifftop was over. I thought sadly of the wounded assassin left alone to die on the rock, but my arm, spurting blood and throbbing with pain, told me there had been no choice, at least for the present. We ran along the beach; Holmes shouted ahead to the soldiers already there, but he was too late. I saw Mad Mike Higgins slump to the ground as the tiny pistol spat again, with the same tiny spark of flame shooting from its muzzle. The pistol sparked again, and another soldier dropped in his tracks.

"Drop your guns–all of you!" came a clear, high voice. In utter disbelief, I stared at the prim face, the neatly-parted brown hair, and the rimless spectacles of John Howarth, who held his revolver with both hands."

"Too late!" whispered Holmes in my ear. "None of us stopped to consider OTTER was *two* men!"

Hearing our approach, Howarth aimed the gun at Holmes' chest.

"I shall kill him where he stands," he said grimly, "If you do not do as I say!"

I squinted in vain for some sign of life from the opposite cliffside, but that team, like ours, had no doubt left its post and was rushing to join us. Reluctantly, the soldiers dropped their weapons in a clatter onto the gravel. Howarth, in perfect German, shouted to the huddled crew of the U-boat a hundred yards behind him. Soon I could see them standing on the tilted deck, heading for the gun! I returned my eyes to the traitor who crouched glowering at us, his small face filled with hate. I felt an unspeakable loathing for him.

One of the soldiers suddenly raised his right arm up, then flung it down. Howarth fired at Logan, and the "Lion of Leeds" fell to the beach, but not before delivering his missile. Howarth stared terrified at the dirk lodged in his side. Then, as if he knew escape was impossible, he desperately swung his pistol back towards my companion. The moonlight glinted faintly off his spectacles, making his eyes appear as tiny shining lights. The pistol cocked, and I sprang in front of Holmes desperately as he sank to one knee.

The pistol fired, but the shot was aimed at the sky, for at that very instant Howarth's head shot backwards with blinding speed, his back arched convulsively. The glare of the pistol shot illuminated his throat, which erupted outward in a horrid sea of gore and torn flesh as the bullet exited his neck and buried itself in the sand. The deeper crack of the sniper's rifle filled the cove and drowned out the snap of the small pistol. And looking upwards beyond the sprawled body, we could see the silhouette of the lone marksman on the cliff. Then the figure grew limp; there was the hard, dry clatter of the rifle as it fell from his grasp and struck the cliffside many times. Then the figure swayed forward with incredible slowness, and was gone. Shortly afterward came the faint splash at the base of the cliff. And so ended the life of *Fandango*, the brutal beast who lived only to kill, and as his last act killed yet one more. But in so doing, spared the life most dear to me.

Needless to say, with OTTER now totally out of the way, we made short work indeed of any further plans for resistance on the part of the German invaders. They were rounded up quickly and soon found themselves shackled together and heavily guarded in Helgeson's parlour.

Mycroft arrived by ten next morning. Naturally, he was shocked and grievous at hearing the news that both his aides working in tandem had been the party known as OTTER. His state of mind was improved immediately, however, when he was informed by Holmes and Ainsley that the Naval officer sitting chained before him was

none other than Hugo Von Luckner, known in the North Sea region
as "Orca," and brother of the illustrious Felix Von Luckner, about
whom so much is known it would be gratuitous to repeat it here.

"I can't wait to see Winston's face," he gloated, rubbing his palms
together gleefully. "The king of the wolf pack in our hands! And now
gentlemen, the best news of all: *America has entered the war on the Allied
side–*"

"It's high time, I should say," replied my companion irritably.
"Lord knows they've sat back on their haunches for the past two
years, watching us take a bellyful!–"

"But they've come *in*, Sherlock, and largely at Churchill's and my
urging, so let us take solace in that. Well, what of our casualties
here?"

We informed him that we lost four men to their ten, or actually
thirteen, if one counted the enemy agents.

"I most certainly *do*," he intoned with a wince, "I count them
double, nay, *triple* the others."

In the afternoon we returned a final time to Ballow's Wash. The
crippled U-boat had been hauled up, and the receding tide had left it
stranded on its side like a beached whale. Faint wisps of smoke still
issued from its hatches. The air was filled with the odors of burnt paint
and engine oil. A seagull perched nonchalantly on the tipped
periscope of the vessel, oblivious to the horrendous death and
destruction wrought the night before. But the evidence was all round
the place in abundance: the torn and twisted stairway, the craters of
blackened earth, the spent shell casings, the bloodstained beach, the
smell of cordite and the damp, earth smell of shattered rock. But the
birds cried and wheeled about as before, and we knew that soon the
Eyrie Cliff would return to its previous state.

Upon reaching the clifftop once again by the crude ladder, my
knees buckled. The excitement, lack of sleep, and loss of blood were
taking their toll on an old man. Furthermore, I was not yet fully
recovered from my collapse in London.

"And I came to the South Downs for a *holiday!*" I chuckled falling
into a wicker chair at the Cardwell cottage thirty minutes later. It
commanded a fine view of the sea, and I accepted the large whiskey
eagerly. "Some holiday, eh Holmes?"

"Ah my friend," said he settling himself in a neighboring chair,
"we're too old now for this sort of thing. I can scarcely remember a
more taxing adventure and, as I told you three days ago, there was
never one more important. Also, I almost lost my life. As typical of

you Watson, in a fit of foolish sentimentality and *bravado*, you flung yourself in front of me to take the bullet. Foolish Watson! But without such foolishness, such emptyheaded heroism, what would life mean? Needless to say, I am touched beyond words."

"You saved my brother's life?" asked Mycroft, leaning forward in his chair.

To this question I explained the truth, that I had simply acted out of impulse, and we were both saved by the crack marksmanship of a professional killer.

"This man Fandango sounds like a nasty fellow," mused Mycroft as he puffed on a cigarette. "Dead you say? Well, we shall decorate him posthumously ... and the others too."

"You see Mycroft, I was struck from the beginning by the acuity of Fandango's senses," said Holmes. "He was a true predator, in every sense of the word, and seemed to have the atavistic killer instincts and precautions to a very large degree. I know now that he was sweeping the beach with his rifle scope when he was shot by Howarth. The scope has light-gathering qualities, you see, that would aid even his incredibly keen eyes. His hunter's instincts told him something was amiss—a piece was out of place. If indeed Howarth were true, why would he run *down* the stairs instead of up, as Cardwell did? When one is in danger, one's impulse is to run for one's friends. Howarth's turning to the beach was a giveaway—but the sniper realised it before me I must admit, for my mind is rational, whereas his was intuitive, instinctive ..."

"Well Sherlock, you have indeed done well. And you too, Watson. Now as of seven o'clock this evening—two o'clock American time— all the world shall know of the United States' entering the war. President Wilson's speech to Congress and Declaration of War shall be in all the evening newspapers. In less than a month, there will be a review of the Allied fleet off Spithead. Churchill and I will be there. So will the both of you, by official order. So will Lloyd George. And so, gentlemen, will the *King*."

And with that proclamation, Mycroft Holmes finished his whiskey, walked out to the drive, and departed for London in his limousine.

EPILOGUE

Never fond of public appearances, Sherlock Holmes paced the hallway below in a fit of irritation. I could see him for brief moments as he passed back and forth by the foot of the stairway, his lean form hunched over with anticipation. He checked his watch nervously, then, coming to the foot of the stairs, placed his thin hand on the newell post.

"Get a move on Watson! The car shall arrive shortly, and you're not even dressed; what on *earth* is taking you so long? One would think fifty years of practice would suffice—"

"My hand is shaking Holmes. If I hurry, I'll cut myself for sure..."

"Well you can jolly well *stop* your hand from shaking. Do you want a dram?"

"I'll be down directly," I retorted, finishing with the razor and splashing water on my face. I dressed as quickly as possible, but the double cutaway suit and wing collar made progress slow. However, I soon joined my companion downstairs. Lighting cigarettes, we went outside to await the official auto that was to convey us to Spithead, and the ceremony.

"I say, the Douglas would hardly suffice for us dressed like this, eh Holmes?" said I as we passed the machine parked on the gravel path and covered with a canvas tarpaulin.

"These clothes are outrageous. Thank goodness we've only to remain in them for another four hours or so—"

"You don't plan to stay for the reception and dinner following? Surely that would be a *faux pas*, since the ceremony is in our honour."

"I confess you've got a point. And I suppose Mycroft will insist. Dash it, why did I accept this time?"

"You declined it once before; to do so again would be an injury neither King nor Country could bear..."

"Perhaps," he said vaguely. "Well anyway, it's certainly too late now: here comes our ride."

* * *

In less than two hours we were standing with Mycroft on the high bluff that overlooks Spithead, the traditional rendezvous for the British fleet. We were joined shortly afterwards by Churchill, whom we'd met previously on more than one occasion. The frigates came steaming past from the Solent, bound seaward for France. They paraded by in sublime majesty, during which time many salutes were fired from the shore. In a special canopied stall sat His Majesty, flanked by David Lloyd George and Colonel House, the American envoy. As the parade of warships neared its end, the Anthem was played.

Then the band struck up the *Star Spangled Banner*, and the stars and stripes rose majestically up its flagstaff to take its place beside the Union Jack. There was a great cheering and commotion from the huge crowd present, and then I saw them pointing and gesticulating towards the Solent once again. Soon the American naval vessels hove into view. We were awed by their size and numbers! Painted white, they slid by belching rolling clouds of smoke, their wide hulls bristling with heavy guns. The Yankee sailors lined the rails and turrets in huge numbers. They shouted and waved their hats at us, smiling and singing.

Truly the American might was an impressive spectacle.

"Thank God!" I murmured.

"My thoughts exactly," added Mycroft. "Let us all hope England's long nightmare is almost over. With America joining the fray the Huns cannot hope to last another year."

"See how eager they are," remarked Holmes cynically. "You can be sure they'll change their tune after a year in battle..."

"Certainly they will," replied Churchill. "Yet it does me good to see them over here: so proud, so strong, so brimming with confidence. I tell you America is a mastiff puppy. Here she is, frolicking in her youth, unaware of the awesome and terrible power she will one day become. And become a power she *shall*, gentlemen. *A power to shake the earth* ...Well, come along, you must prepare yourselves. Now remember both of you, when you've knelt at His Majesty's feet and received the accolade, you are to rise at his command and say: 'Your Majesty, by the Grace of God, Defender of the Realm and of the Faith, I, Sir–giving your full name–do most humbly give thanks.' And as for you, Watson, keep in control of yourself. You're entirely too sentimental and emotional, as I'm sure Mycroft has told you. Now for God's sake man, keep your eyes dry!"

We followed the portly form of Mycroft Holmes and his energetic and brilliant companion to a specially prepared lawn that was draped round with bunting. Two columns of crack troops stood at attention on either side: The Royal Lifeguards and the Coldstream Guards. Soon these were joined by another column I failed to recognise. They were big fellows, clad in khaki uniforms and wide-brimmed hats. At their waists hung huge automatic pistols. I was informed they were United States Marines, the first of hundreds of thousands of American troops soon to join us.

"I'm not at all surprised they've come," said Mycroft paternally. "In my heart, I always knew that America would do her duty. After all, they were British citizens for over a century. I would say we've trained them rather well."

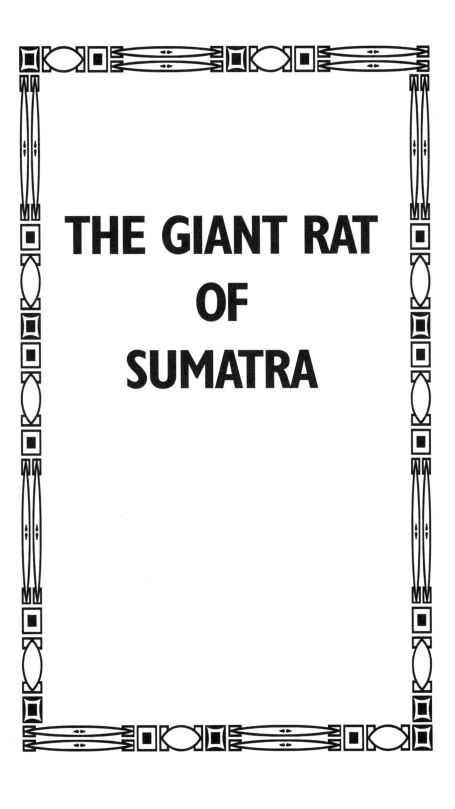

THE GIANT RAT
OF
SUMATRA

AUTHOR'S NOTE

When your eyes pass over these words, dear reader, I shall be many years in my grave. For a multitude of considerations, some of which will become apparent in the pages that follow, it is necessary to withhold publication of this narrative until after the passing of the people named therein. Accordingly, this manuscript shall lie in the strongbox of Barclay's Bank, Oxford Street Branch, London, until the year 1975, a round figure I choose arbitrarily with the assurance that, by then, the people who could be injured or offended by what follows shall have long since turned to dust. This I do ordain as a condition and procedure of my last will and testament, to be carried out by its executor or by his appointees.

John H. Watson, M.D.
London, 1912

I

THE TATTOOED SAILOR

The summer of 1894 was hot and dry and without noteworthy cases or events, save for the mysterious disappearance of Miss Alice Allistair which threw the Kingdom into shock and sorrow. On a midsummer holiday to India with her chaperone, she was abducted from a Bombay market without a trace.

Her father, Lord Allistair (whose name was, during the last half of the previous century, upon the tongue and in the mind of every British subject) secretly summoned Sherlock Holmes to his assistance. But weeks passed, and still no word arrived from the East as to the fate of his daughter. Early September found my companion restless, bored, and morose. A trip to Bombay, and a handsome fee paid by His Lordship were in the offing, but still Holmes paced and fretted, fretted and paced, and muttered interminably.

I must here inject the observation, based upon long experience, that for all the excitement of living with the world's most renowned consulting detective, life with Sherlock Holmes had its drawbacks. He kept odd hours, was often moody and uncommunicative and was, in his personal habits, untidy to the point of slovenliness.

It was early evening of September 15 of the year mentioned when, glancing at Holmes sunk in thought on the divan, I could bear the silence and oppressiveness of our flat no longer. Our quarters reeked of stale smoke and chemical fumes, and Holmes' insular behaviour and despondent attitude did nothing to relieve the situation. I rose and went over to the bow window, opened it, and allowed the balmy summer breeze to enter–dispelling the fumes and boosting my spirits.

"Lovely evening, Holmes. Perhaps you would care to join me for a walk?"

"I think not, Watson. I have enough to occupy myself for the present."

"The Bradley forgeries, or the Allistair case?"

"Both. The first is unimportant, and easy: if the clerk has a limp, he's guilty. I expect a solution at any moment. The other, more serious, one I am powerless to attack without evidence."

He gazed at the wall, and sank deeper into thought.

I returned to the window. The sky was the brilliant copper colour of the dying sun, fading to dark blue towards the horizon. The faint babble of pedestrians wafted upwards to my ears. Peering down, I could see the sheen of top hats and the lilt of parasols as the couples passed beneath. Their laughter enticed me. Where had they been? Where were they going? More directly: why were we imprisoned in our drab flat, away from it all?

"I say Holmes, just a short jaunt—enough to stretch the legs and mind, would be—*hullo*, what's this?"

Holmes shot a glance toward the open window. "Well Watson, what is it?"

The clatter of hooves and a pair of wildly veering carriage lamp had drawn my eye. In the fading light I could barely see the driver standing in his box and flailing at the horses with the utmost savagery.

"It appears to be a drunken cabbie. Poor beasts."

"Hardly a drunken cabbie. I'll wager it's an *ambulance*."

He rose from the divan and joined me at the window. To my utter amazement the vehicle, dashing past the street lamps below, showed itself indeed to be an ambulance; the markings on its side were unmistakable.

"You astound me Holmes! How could you tell it was an ambulance?"

"One can observe with one's ears as well as one's eyes. The ambulance, for obvious reasons, has a longer chassis than the four-wheeled cab. A hospital carriage, bouncing over cobble-stones, reveals itself by a curious deep rumbling in its timbers which the four-wheeler lacks. This particular sound is also emitted by lorries and dray carts, but given the hour and the vehicle's speed, we are left with the ambulance."

"Bravo!" I cried.

"But only half the puzzle it seems," said Holmes, as he leaned further out of the window and swept his eyes anxiously over the horizon.

"I have a strong suspicion that in addition to the misfortune in this neighbourhood, there is occurring at this very moment elsewhere in London a catastrophe of great magnitude, that we shall no doubt read about in tomorrow's newspapers."

This stream of inferences so stunned me that I remained speechless. Holmes observed the puzzled expression on my face.

"Come now Watson, you're a medical man and know ambulances: was there anything amiss?"

"No," I replied after some thought, "except that some unfortunate—"

"Tut, man! Not anything else?"

I shook my head.

"Let me enquire then, how it happens that you were unable to determine the vehicle's identity until you saw the markings on the door?"

Once again, as in so many instances during my long association with my friend, I felt embarrassment at having overlooked the obvious.

"The *bell*. There was no bell."

"Precisely. The warning bell carried by our ambulances was not sounded. This explains both the erratic path of the carriage—attempts made by the driver to avoid running down pedestrians—and the rather frenzied behaviour of the driver himself, both interpreted by you as being brought about by an excess of drink."

Holmes continued to scan the horizon and the streets below. He charged his pipe and, between staccato puffs of smoke, muttered to himself.

"Of course, there is always the question as to why the bell wasn't sounded ..."

"A new driver ..."

"No. The man's skill in handling the team and avoiding people shows that he is quite experienced. The walk that you mentioned earlier has suddenly taken on a new attraction. Let's be off."

"Of course, it's obvious," he remarked as we scurried down the staircase, "that the ambulance was bound from St. Thomas' Hospital."

"Hah! I'm afraid you're wrong there old fellow; you seem to slip a bit Holmes, if you don't mind my saying so," I said with some smugness. "Here I shall use your own methods against you. You seem to overlook Charing Cross which, although situated in the same general direction as St. Thomas', is considerably closer. Logic decrees therefore, that the wagon came from there, since all possible haste was necessary."

"Excellent Watson! Really, you quite outdo yourself!"

I was deeply flattered, for Holmes was not a man to shower praise willy-nilly.

"It's a pity you are mistaken," he added.

"What makes you so sure?" I retorted, somewhat piqued.

"Once again, you have failed to observe completely. Did you see how the driver plied his whip?"

"He was quite zealous."

"So much so in fact that you cried 'poor beasts.' Did you also observe the horses themselves as they passed beneath the street lamps? Their flanks were frothed with sweat. These two observations together force us to conclude that the horses had come from the *direction* of Charing Cross Hospital, yet a much greater distance. The point of departure was therefore St. Thomas'."

Once explained, the conclusion seemed simple.

"But you have done well in using logic Watson, because we see that the *illogical* has happened: instead of coming from the nearest hospital, the ambulance has come across town. That is interesting. Also the want of a bell arouses our curiosity. Perhaps we can fit these two pieces together. We know the driver did not neglect to ring the bell–he is too experienced for such an oversight. What does this leave us with?"

We were walking south down Baker Street towards Portman Square, but engrossed as I was in the puzzle the evening's beauty escaped me. I plied my brain to the questions Holmes had raised.

"The bell was then either broken or missing," I suggested.

"*Exactly!* Which indicates that this particular ambulance, being ill-equipped, was not intended for use. It was, then, dragged out of the repair shop at a moment's notice, and from the wrong hospital at that. Does this suggest anything to you?"

"Of course–all of the regular carriages were engaged!"

"Ah! But engaged for what purpose? Obviously they have hurried to the scene of some terrible calamity. I'm quite certain it is a fire. Why a fire? Well, what else could it be? Flood? Certainly not; the river is normal and we're in want of rain. Earthquake? Preposterous. Mass murder? In America perhaps, but never here. No, it is a fire that has occurred, and I–"

"What is it?"

I observed on Holmes' face the look of eagerness that told me of a new development at hand.

"See that crowd there by the kerbside? There's our ambulance too. I just saw Lestrade making his way into the centre of it, and I fear that this personal tragedy may have sinister overtones. Come on, hurry up! We want to arrive before the police make a total ruin of things."

We fought our way through the knot of curious pedestrians. Arriving towards the middle of it, I could hear Lestrade's gravelly voice barking orders to subordinates and onlookers alike. In the gaslight that was partially blocked by the crowd, I could see a dark form sprawled in the gutter.

It was obvious that Lestrade viewed Holmes' presence with a mixture of relief and annoyance.

"It beats me, Mr. Holmes," he remarked, "how you seem to materialise on the spot when there's been murder done."

"Murder," said Holmes, visibly quickening. "Watson, our evening stroll grows more engrossing by the minute. With your permission, Lestrade, I should like to examine the corpse."

When the crowd of onlookers was sufficiently dispersed, the three of us were at liberty to examine the body in detail. The victim was a middle-aged, powerfully-built man with thick, dark hair and beard and a swarthy complexion. The man appeared to be diving headlong into the street; his feet remained strewn on the kerb–his head and shoulders shoved forward into the paving stones. A pool of blood had collected on the pavement beneath the open waistcoat and blouse which Lestrade drew back. The cause of death was immediately apparent. A horrid gash, extending up the trunk from the waist to the left shoulder, and terminating in a series of smaller slashes, had brought a quick and brutal end to the victim. The wounds were so vast and grotesque that, despite my medical experience, I was shocked and repelled in the extreme.

"Not a pretty sight, if I may say so," said Lestrade. "But then murder never is, no matter the method."

"From these tattoos on his arms and chest and from the look of his clothes, he appears to have been a seafaring man," observed Holmes. "Has the body been moved?"

"Not to our knowledge," returned Lestrade. "The constable who discovered him is Roberts–a good man mind you–but for the life of him he's unable to track down one witness to this affair. The crowd drew him to the discovery. But as to what occurred, we are unable to locate one shopkeeper, resident, or passer-by who can give us the slightest account."

"That is odd, considering it is a natural evening to be outdoors. There are many people on the streets tonight. Given the nature of the wounds and the physique of the deceased, one must assume there was a struggle, at least an outcry. It is very singular that the event failed to draw anyone's attention."

Here my companion paused and looked, not without remorse, at the body sprawled beneath him in the gutter.

"Of course, since we have no living witnesses to aid us in our enquiry, then the dead man must tell the story."

Holmes then proceeded to examine the body to the minutest detail. He skipped nothing, examining his clothing, particularly the shirtcuffs and pockets, the torn waistcoat and ripped shirt, the boots, the tattooed chest (butchered though it was), and concluded by thrusting his nose into the dead man's whiskers and sniffing vigorously. The next instant he was gone, pacing up and down the street and puffing furiously at his pipe, glancing in all directions.

Having become accustomed to this sort of behaviour on the part of my companion, I fell into conversation with Lestrade, remarking how strange it was that no excitement had been aroused during the murder, and how odd it was that not a mark of identification, nor any personal possessions for that matter, was found on the body. The attendants having placed the body on a litter, I watched Lestrade conversing with several correspondents who had been waiting at the edge of the crowd. I was thus engaged when I heard Holmes calling to us.

"Up here Watson, Lestrade. Come up, this may interest you!"

Looking up past the glare of the street lamps, we caught sight of Holmes' angular face peering from the rooftop directly above.

"Take the second door there—the plain one, not the storekeeper's."

Leaving two constables to dispatch the ambulance, we clambered up the narrow and dingy staircase which led unobtrusively from the street. At the first landing we found Holmes waiting for us. He led us up another flight of stairs and then through a narrow door of crude wood.

"This is the stairway that leads to the roof. Lestrade, if you've your dark lantern, now's the time it would be helpful."

We found ourselves on a flat rooftop with a façade about three feet high on the Baker Street side, in front. Holmes, having taken the lantern from Lestrade, walked to a corner of the roof and let the beam fall upon a crumpled handkerchief.

"There's a piece of evidence for you, Lestrade. Perhaps you can smell the chloroform from here."

"Yes, so it is ..." mused the detective, somewhat chagrined at Holmes' astuteness. "But how the devil did you seize on *this* place?"

"Logic, my friend. Consider this: a large, muscular man in the prime of life has been brutally murdered with a dagger. The body is discovered on a busy London thoroughfare. Yet, in spite of these two things, no one seems to have witnessed the deed. To explain this, we must either assume that our citizens are deaf, dumb and blind, or we must seek a more rational explanation: that the man was murdered elsewhere and his remains deposited on the kerbside. But *how* deposited? A passing carriage would be a means, but it would be noisy and conspicuous. The absence of alternative explanations has led us to this rooftop where, as you can see, the evidence suggests the murder was committed."

To make his point, Holmes pointed to the façade top overlooking the street. It was splashed profusely with blood.

"But why the chloroform," I asked, "if the deed were done with a dagger?"

"The man was drugged into unconsciousness beforehand—hence the silence of the deed. The murderers, and I believe there were more than one, then waited from this vantage point until the street below was temporarily vacant, whereupon they hurled the body down into the street, then fled down the ladder which overhangs the rear of the building.

"It's my guess, Lestrade, that your men will find several broken ribs on the corpse to substantiate my theory."

"Well, Holmes," said I, as we descended the stairway, "things seem a bit clearer now, don't they?"

"On the contrary, Watson. What was cloudy at the outset is now murky. What before was merely unexplainable now becomes incoherent: *mad.* This latest discovery only lifts the curtain on what promises to be the most intricate and diabolical case we've handled in some time."

"Let me ask you, my dear fellow," he continued, "hasn't this rooftop killing raised some questions in your mind? Remember that just as the physician seeks the extraordinary, the unique, in making his diagnosis—so does the detective seek the illogical, the grotesque in guiding himself to the source of the crime. What *irrationality* have we indirectly witnessed?"

"That the man needn't have been stabbed–the chloroform or the fall would surely have killed him."

"Yes, there's that. But hasn't it occurred to either of you that the criminals, once having committed the crime, were placing themselves in jeopardy by *throwing the corpse down into the street for public display?*"

"Your point is well taken," admitted Lestrade. "In fact, the oddity had just occurred to me. The usual preoccupation of the murderer is *concealing* the body."

"But these killers have deliberately set the law after themselves and made their escape perilous by 'giving up' the body rather than disposing of it."

"Perhaps they wish the killing publicised to serve as a warning."

"I agree, at least for the present."

Lestrade and I followed him to the rear of the building, where Holmes examined the wrought-iron fire ladder and the pavement under it. The examination yielded nothing except a shred of dark blue wool which Holmes plucked from a projecting ladder bolt.

"Here's a piece of good fortune," he said turning it round in his fingers under the lantern beam. "At first guess I'd say it was from a Norwich mill, but closer examination is necessary to make certain."

Holmes was interrupted from his reveries by a great commotion in the street. The sound of police whistles and tramping boots brought us to the front of the building on the run. There we spied several constables waving their arms.

"Are they still on the roof?" cried one. "Fetch a calling trumpet will you? I–no *there* he is! Inspector Lestrade! We're wanted on the docks quick as a wink, if you please, sir!"

"The fire is a large one then?" asked my companion.

"Frightful! And spreading fast. I–" Lestrade stopped in midsentence.

"But how came you to hear of it? I myself was just notified by police wire. I heard no one else mention it."

"Do you mind if we tag along?" asked Holmes, avoiding the detective's question.

"Well, I suppose there's no harm in it. I say Mulvaney, is there room in that wagon? Very well, can you handle three more? That's a good fellow. Come on then, but mind, stay out of the way."

We swung aboard and settled ourselves on the benches of the open wagon amidst a dozen bobbies, who could talk of nothing except the great fire on the docks. I assumed they were exaggerating the calamity. But thirty minutes later, when I saw the eastern sky aglow and the Thames a ribbon of gold, I knew it was worse than any of us had feared.

The first indication of the fire's size was the traffic. Roads were clogged to overflowing; children ran shouting in all directions; barking dogs scurried in front of carriages and between flying hooves. Horses reared and cried. A steady stream of the curious flowed towards the waterfront—only to be met by terrified residents fleeing the area. And the glow in the sky grew larger, brighter, with each passing minute.

"The weather we've had hasn't helped, you may be sure," said Holmes out of the corner of his mouth, his eyes glued to the sky.

Countless times we were mired in a sea of people and vehicles. But fortunately, the bell on our police wagon *was* in working order, and it sang out mightily until my ears throbbed and ached.

"Stand to there! Give way for the police! You! Mind your reins I say!" shouted the driver, a burly fellow, obviously an expert. He handled the four sets of reins, and the eager animals they led to, with admirable skill. We dashed around corners at dizzying speeds. We clattered through alleyways. We flew along the streets. Above the pounding of the hooves and thunder of the wheels, I could hear the furious panting of our horses—a sound like a thousand giant bellows.

Presently I saw a ball of fire loom up behind a building and knew we were nearing the scene. At the same instant, there shot forth from a side street a fire engine, trailing plumes of oily smoke and drawn by six magnificent horses in glistening livery. We fell in behind, and the two vehicles raised a terrific din!

Onwards we flew, the crowds parted, and cheered us as we passed. At Preston Road we turned south, and continued until we were well within the Isle of Dogs. Here were the great wharves and quays: the maw that fed the Empire. Here too lived the working folk who took their livelihood from the maritime industries: sailors, pilots, stevedores, shipwrights, riggers ... and of course, tavernkeepers.

We sped out from between two huge warehouses, and a great and terrible panorama met my eyes.

To call it a fire would be an injustice. A slice of Hell, fetched up and planted on the river bank, would be a better description. The awesome power, the horror of it! Great fireballs leapt into the sky. Horrendous showers of sparks and glowing debris spewed upwards and drifted down to start new fires.

Three buildings were ablaze, and several more would shortly follow. They were huge. One giant in the centre seemed to be the source of the inferno. Even as I watched, a hole broke through in the roof and a pillar of flame, perhaps two hundred feet tall, erupted from the structure like a slender, malignant toadstool–its rounded head bursting outwards in a giant red ball. The flames lighted the ground for hundreds of yards around. A sea of faces, eyes upturned, surrounded us. Children in their innocence raced to and fro, shouting in the din. To them, it was merely an event to break the summer's tedium–they were blissfully unaware of the destruction being wrought.

Our van pulled up close to the blazing buildings. I jumped down, my face stinging from the heat. I could scarcely breathe. All around me firemen scurried and shouted. Three immense engines stood in a line, working furiously. The teams, despite their training, reared and pranced in the firelight, sending huge, grotesque shadows dancing over the pavement. The scene repeated itself endlessly into the distance: fire engines pumping and belching smoke, frantic teams being led away and tethered, men pushing hose carts, carrying ladders while their officers shouted orders through trumpets. Above it all rose the tremendous roaring, crashing din.

The one factor in the firemen's favour was the nearness of the Thames: drafting hoses were lowered over the quays into the limitless supply of river water. An enormous steam-driven "fire-float" was brought up alongside the docks and from its squat, barge-shaped hull spouted a stream so powerful that it shattered the wooden walls of the buildings to reach the flames within. Nearby, knots of men struggled as close as they dared and raised their hoses– but they were as pathetic as mice attacking a lion, and the streams of water had little, if any, effect. Hearing a commotion behind me, I was surprised to see a coal wagon approaching. I watched the curious irony of the firefighters feeding the flames at the base of the engines.

Police formed a cordon to hold back the crowd, and I saw Lestrade barking orders. Seeing him thus engaged prodded me into a painful realisation. Cursing myself for idleness, I dashed from Holmes' side and sped to the nearest constable.

"I'm a physician–where are the injured?" I cried and, having received his directions, fought my way to the rear of a brick building where, sheltered from the heat and din, a crude nursing station had been set up. At once I grew optimistic: there were very few casualties. Most of the people were suffering only from minor burns. Looking past them, I could see the reason for our "ill-equipped" ambulance of an hour earlier. Long lines of the carriages stood nearby in readiness, the horses stamping their feet with impatience. To my amazement, they weren't needed. The severely injured had already been taken away, and I busied myself with cleaning and bandaging the "walking wounded." Thank God, I thought to myself, that the buildings are mostly warehouses, which accounts for the few casualties. I was distracted though, by a sight and sound I shall never forget—and all my relief and optimism vanished in an instant.

There came to my ears a wailing sound, and I rose in search of it. In a dark corner alcove of the old building, huddled in a worn shawl, was a woman who clasped to her breast a tiny bundle. She looked up at me with a face that was not a face, and shrieked in a voice that was not a voice. She tore at herself in the agony of her grief—her face a shambles of torn skin and tears.

"Abbie! My Abbie!" she screamed, and fought off those who tried to calm her. Finally the attendants succeeded in placing the blanket-wrapped bundle in a carriage. The crazed mother clambered after, and amidst the dreadful sound of grief the sad procession departed.

It was some time before I could bring myself to return to my work. Seeing death almost daily, a physician becomes inured to most of it. The passing of an old man or hopelessly sick woman, these are part of the doctor's work and world. He recognises them as natural.

But the snatching away of a young life—the taking of a child who was perhaps two hours earlier laughing, sitting on her mother's knee with her evening sweet—the transformation of this creature into a tiny mute bundle ... this kind of death smites us with full force if even for the hundredth, the *thousandth* time. Pray God the day shall never come when I can accept it.

After several hours of tending minor wounds, I made my way, exhausted, back to Holmes and Lestrade. Although the fire had spread considerably, the huge plumes of flame had vanished. Instead there was a great glowing at ground level and the heat issuing forth had become yet more intense. The firemen had wisely given up on the big buildings and concentrated their efforts on saving neighbouring ones. The fire was now contained, and the din and excitement were abating, save for occasional tremendous crashes as walls and roofs collapsed. But still the great engines worked, and still the bands of men sallied back and forth, often carrying a fallen comrade. Wearied and depressed, Holmes and I arrived at Baker Street shortly before midnight. The roar of the fire, clatter of engines, and the horrific grieving of the mother still rang in my ears.

We sat for some time in silence. In a voice made dull by sadness, I related to him the incident of the dead child. He was deeply touched, and let out a slow sigh.

"There is so much suffering in the world Watson, and it is no accident, I can assure you, that most of it falls upon the poor."

"Certainly this is an evening we won't soon forget," said I. "I am exhausted, and yet I'm certain I cannot sleep."

"I confess I feel the same tension. Let us have some whiskey then, and we'll talk about the earlier occurrence."

So saying, he poured two glasses, reclined on the divan with his pipe, and assumed a far-away expression.

"It seems safe to conclude," he said at last, "that the man was a sailor ..."

"I'd certainly say so, from his clothes and appearance—"

"... recently arrived in London from Borneo or thereabouts ... and was, at the time of his murder, coming to see me."

"What!"

"I must say his death touches me more now, knowing he was seeking my assistance ..."

"How are you sure of this?" I asked.

"At this stage it's pure conjecture, but let us reconstruct the chain of events. As I have stated, the man was in or near Borneo not longer than six or eight weeks ago. This is revealed simply and unequivocally by a recent tattoo on his right wrist. It is Malayan in origin, and appears to be about two months old. Figuring on a sea voyage of about the same length of time, we know he had not been long in London. Fetch *The Times*. Let us see if by chance there has been an arrival from that corner of the globe recently."

Whilst I rummaged for the paper, Holmes curled up on the divan, drawing on his pipe.

"There are three within the last fortnight. The *Yarmouth Castle* arrived on Tuesday last from Foochow ..."

Holmes shook his head with impatience.

"The barque *Rangoon* put in the day before last, bound from Hong Kong ..."

"And the last?" he queried.

"The packet-trader *Matilda Briggs*—by Jove!—put in this afternoon, from *Batavia*!"

"That's our sailor's vessel! I see by scanning these back issues that there's been no other ship from there in two weeks. Our dead friend arrived this afternoon then. He must have had something of the utmost urgency to tell me. It is a pity that his lips are sealed for ever."

"How do you know he was bound here?"

"Picture this in your mind, Watson: a sailor arrives in port after a sea voyage of many weeks. What is the natural thing for him to do?"

"Go on a fling, I should imagine."

"It would seem so. But this fellow is a queer bird. He is not grogging down in Limehouse—no, he's up in the West End, in Baker Street. Why? I don't wish to appear vain my friend, but you know as well as I that I enjoy a considerable reputation in this city, and not only in the more proper circles."

"That is certainly true."

"It is entirely possible that one of my shadier acquaintances down on the docks referred the man to me. Also, I have what I think may be evidence to support this."

Holmes took pen and paper and drew the following marks:

// // /

"Do these marks suggest anything to you?" he enquired.

"Absolutely not—mere hen scratchings."

"The police think so too, no doubt. I found them on the man's right shirtcuff, evidence, bye the bye, that he was left-handed. He'd drawn them on with rough crayon of the type oftentimes carried by seamen. Like most sailors, he was accustomed to representing numbers with vertical strokes. Hence, we derive the numbers 2-2-1, or, if you please, 221 B, Baker Street."

"Extraordinary!" I exclaimed.

"Not really. The man obviously didn't bother to write down the name of the street: he could remember that easily enough. But he wanted to be sure of our number."

"Poor chap."

"He was dogged and ambushed one street away from his destination, which suggests that those who murdered him know of me. Otherwise why would they murder him here and not down by the docks?"

"They feared he would reveal his secret to you, and therefore did away with him."

"But not before removing all of his identification. Yet the throwing down of the body seems to have been done to serve as a warning to other confederates who would hear of this man's death. I fear it is a dark and vile conspiracy we are confronting, Watson: a band that will stop at nothing to protect its secrets. As tangled as the problem appears however, there is a thread that runs through it. We know that the problem is international; it is not confined to London but has roots either on board the *Matilda Briggs* or even in the Orient. Bearing in mind the man's tattoo, and the *Briggs'* port of departure, we see that Malaya keeps reappearing. Did you observe closely the wounds on the victim's body?

"They were severe in the extreme."

"Was there nothing unusual about them?"

"They were different from ordinary knife wounds, but I am at a loss as to exactly how they were different. I vaguely remember having seen similar wounds before ..."

"In Afghanistan, perhaps?"

I jumped clear of my chair in amazement.

"Holmes!"

"Don't be alarmed, I made a hazard and it proved correct. Afghanistan would have been the most likely place for you to have seen such wounds but not as likely as the Malayan archipelago. The instrument used on our sailor, if I'm not mistaken, is of Malayan origin. The kris dagger, as it is most often referred to, is a double-edged combat weapon with a serpentine blade, which is, as you have seen, capable of inflicting the most ferocious of wounds."

There was a pause as I collected my thoughts.

"You think then that he was killed by a Malay?" I asked finally.

"That is uncertain. I believe that the crew of the *Matilda Briggs* may be of some help to us in this matter. I'm afraid you will breakfast alone tomorrow, Watson; I shall be down at the riverside at an early hour. Who knows? Perhaps in some dingy lane or noisy grog-shop I'll find a piece of this puzzle. Did you notice the moon on our return? There's a halo around it; there'll be rain before dawn, which will aid the firemen. Get to sleep, you're as pale as a ghost. Goodnight Watson."

I bade my companion likewise and, as I prepared to enter my bedchamber, could not help but wonder at the way in which a lovely autumn evening had been so suddenly transformed into a night of destruction, mystery and havoc.

2

WHAT BOATSWAIN SAMPSON HAD TO TELL

I was awakened next morning by a blast of thunder and rain lashing at the window panes. Upon dressing and entering the parlour I saw the remnants of Holmes' hasty breakfast. I rang for my own and, while waiting, chanced to see the *Morning Post* strewn in front of the fireplace. My eyes fell immediately on the following story:

Warehouse Fire Claims 7 Lives

Preston Rd., Sept. 15: A fire of horrendous proportions last evening claimed the lives of seven citizens. The conflagration, which purportedly began in the maritime shipping warehouse of G.A. McNulty & Sons in Preston Road at approximately 6 p.m., raged until 3:30 a.m. this morning when it was finally extinguished by the 2nd and 4th fire brigades. A list of the dead follows in the next column.

The cause of the fire has not been established. Police have not ruled out the possibility of arson, and have requested the assistance of Scotland Yard.

All the victims were trapped in adjacent buildings. The total number of buildings destroyed is eight: five residential buildings and three commercial properties, including the previously mentioned one belonging to Mr. McNulty.

The article continued in greater detail, but it made me so heavy-hearted that I deferred and went on to the next page. Relief was not in sight, however, for no sooner had I turned the page than my eyes fell upon the following piece:

Baker Street Murder

London, Sept. 15: The mutilated body of Raymond Jenard, Able
Seaman of the cargo vessel *Matilda Briggs*, was discovered on the
kerbside opposite Curray's, the clothier, of 157 Baker Street. The
cause of death was a series of stab wounds.

Inspector Lestrade, of the Paddington District Station, has informed the Post that the deed appears to have been a street murder
with robbery as the motive, since no valuables, nor identification of
any sort, was found on the body.

Identification was made possible only by the assistance of Mr.
John Sampson, boatswain of the *Matilda Briggs* and a friend of the
deceased.

Mr. Jenard, who left no family, resided at 22 Preston Road, and
was considered an honest and kind fellow by the shipmates who knew
him well.

I was in the midst of my breakfast, which Mrs. Hudson had
brought up, when I heard a tread upon the stair. A moment later the
door opened, and there stood before me a wizened old sailor, his
hoary beard partially obscuring a wrinkled, ruddy face. The eyes
however, shone with a merry twinkle, as if the old man were
delighted at my surprise.

"I beg your pardon–" I said abruptly as I put down my cup.

"Mr. 'Olmes in, mate?" he rasped.

"No, he isn't," I replied with some indignation, "and I'll thank you
to knock when you come to a stranger's doorway, sir. Furthermore,
you're ruining Mr. Holmes' carpet."

His oilskin, glistening with rain, was dripping on the rug that was
given to my colleague by the Shah of Persia for recovering the
famous Delak Tiara. I knew Holmes wouldn't be pleased. The
strange, bent old man stood wheezing before me, swaying slightly as
if on a ship's deck at sea.

"Kindly state your business sir," I said in a clipped tone, "and be
off if you please; I am very busy this morning."

This was not true, of course, but I wanted to be rid of him.
Something in his stark manner unsettled me.

"'Ey mate–got a dram o' rum for a cold old man?"

"Certainly not! Now if you'll not state your business–"

"It's the murder. I've come," and saying this, he shuffled over until
he stood directly over me, "... to tell about the murder, don't you see ..."

I stared up at him with incredulity. He then bent his face down to mine and said, in a low coarse whisper: "You see mate ... I'm the one what *done it!*"

I sprang from my chair and, in a flash, had flung open the drawer to Holmes' side table. I had clasped the revolver handle when the cry of a familiar voice stopped me.

"Whoa, Watson! I fancy a joke can go too far!"

Turning round, I observed the old salt transformed as Holmes removed the false whiskers and putty.

"This is indeed one of my better efforts," he said chuckling to himself. "If my closest friend cannot recognise me so close, I am assured that the denizens of the East End were deceived as well. Ah Watson, a touch of brandy doesn't seem so outrageous after all, for I am chilled to the marrow."

"Really Holmes! It's a bit early in the day for pranks of this nature. I seem to have quite lost my appetite."

Indeed, I was still reeling slightly from the encounter.

"Then in all sincerity, I must apologise. I did not intend to make you the object of ridicule, nor to give you a fright."

His apologetic tone had a remarkable effect upon my recovery, and I managed to finish my somewhat chilled breakfast while Holmes removed the remnants of his masquerade, lighted his pipe, and settled himself before the crackling fireplace. Outside, the storm raged on; the rain fell in great sheets, and thunder burst incessantly above us.

"Well Watson, I see you've had a glance at the *Post*. Was there anything about the two news items, the fire and the murder, that caught your attention?"

I replied in the negative.

"Isn't it curious," he pursued, "that our sailor Jenard resided in one of the buildings that was destroyed by the fire?"

"I seemed to have missed that," said I, examining the paper again, "but it's a coincidence certainly."

"I fear not. I think rather that the two tragedies of last night are in some way bound together. You realise, of course, that the *Post* is in error."

"You mean as to the motive for the murder?"

"Obviously on that count. But I am referring to the fire. The article states that it began in McNulty's warehouse. By reading the article carefully, one sees that this could not have been so. The article is a self-contradiction of sorts."

I joined Holmes before the fireplace and, paper in hand, applied myself to discovering the discrepancy that he had found so obvious. Before long, however, my train of thought was broken by the appearance of Mrs. Hudson.

"Mr. Holmes, sir," she said, "there's a gentleman downstairs to see you."

"Did he give you his card?" asked my companion.

"No, sir. But he did mention his name."

"Yes?"

"Mr. John Sampson."

"Show him up immediately," said he, his face full of eagerness. "Quick Watson, stir up the fire while I pour a glass for our visitor. This is an extremely fortunate turn of events, for, if I'm not mistaken, here is a man who can shed much light on these calamities."

I busied myself with the tongs and bellows, and lighted a cigarette in anticipation of the arrival of Boatswain Sampson. His tread on the stair was slow and heavy.

Although John Sampson undoubtedly possessed the build and carriage of a boatswain, it was indeed a pale, harrowed man who appeared in our doorway. He was large, no older than thirty, with blue eyes and great curls of blond hair. Were it not for his temporary condition, I would suppose him to be a man of great strength and vitality. His countenance had a frank and honest look; he appeared a fellow who would grant favours and make friends. On the other hand, I fancied it would be imprudent to make an enemy of him.

For the present, however, he was visibly shaken, and seemed to weave before us in a fit of anxiety.

Holmes diagnosed the man's state as quickly as I did, and led him to a chair.

"Pray sit down before the fire, Mr. Sampson, and warm yourself. This is my fellow boarder and friend Dr. John Watson. You may tell him anything you wish to tell me."

The boatswain gave me a firm handshake and settled himself before the fire. Before long, the fire's warmth and the brandy worked their magic, and a touch of healthy colour sprang upon his cheeks.

"Mr. Holmes and Dr. Watson," he began in a shaken voice, "as you may have read in today's papers, I am the bos'n on the merchant vessel *Matilda Briggs*. It was I who identified the body of my unlucky shipmate Raymond Jenard late last night–"

"Indeed, we've been reading about it."

"I had intended to go to the police today, but early this morning I was knocked up by a Mr. Josiah Griggs, who strongly recommended I pay you a visit, Mr. Holmes."

"This man is a friend?" I asked.

"No, sir. In fact, I'd never laid eyes on him. He just stands there in my doorway, dripping wet, and says, 'Mr. Sampson, if it's advice and help you'll need, and you don't wish all of London to know about it, Sherlock Holmes is the man for you.' He seemed a trusty fellow, and one who'd bumped around the world a bit, if you know what I mean. So I took his advice, and here I am.

"First of all, you may wonder how I came to be at the city morgue last night at so late an hour. As you might guess, I was one of the many spectators at the dock fire last evening, for I live nearby, as most men of my calling do. While watching the flames, I suppose it must have been after two in the morning, I overheard several constables discussing a mysterious murder that had taken place earlier. When I heard them describe the victim, my suspicions became aroused, for reasons which will soon become clear to you. I asked the constables if the man were tattooed, and when they answered yes, I rushed over immediately in a cab. Sad to say, my suspicions were right.

"What first set me thinking was the fact that Jenard's own dwellings were ablaze—but he was not in the ring of onlookers, though I searched for him. But there is something else, something deep and terrible I fear, that had made me uneasy about Jenard's safety for some time ..."

At this point Sampson paused, as if he were too embarrassed to continue. Holmes said nothing, but remained settled back in his chair, eyelids halfway closed in scrutiny, his fingertips pressed lightly together.

"Now Mr. Holmes, I know you may think it strange that I suspected foul play from the beginning–"

Holmes nodded slightly.

"Were not the tale so strange, the circumstances so mystifying, I would tell you all without the slightest hesitation ..."

"Then do so," urged my companion. "I have found over the years that the only way to arrive at a solution to any problem is for my client to tell all, having complete trust in me and my colleague. You appear a bit shaken, but otherwise in sound health. I shan't think you daft if you relate to me the entire history of the past few months, omitting nothing."

Heartened by those words, Sampson leaned forward and began his tale:

"I have been aboard the *Matilda Briggs* four years. I signed on directly out of the mercantile service. This is my first position, and I've been happy with it up until the past few weeks. Naturally I don't want to give notice, but recent events may force me to.

"The *Matilda Briggs* makes a fairly regular run between London and Batavia. We haul freight and, now and then, passengers as well. There has never been a mishap aboard her, and nothing amiss until this last voyage. We'd loaded up in Batavia in the middle of July and were set to put out. We were delayed, however, by the arrival of Mr. Ripley, a missionary from the interior, who sought passage to London. This is often the way with cargo vessels, since any loss in time is offset by passage fees. Mr. Ripley seemed pleasant enough, and no doubt paid Captain McGuinness handsomely for passsage for the three of them—"

"*Three* of them?"

"Yes, sir, he arrived with two companions. His friend Mr. Jones, who apparently had been a sailor, and his man Wangi, a horrible wretch he brought with him from the interior. An ugly, heathen devil with a hump on his back ...

"Well, shortly after they came aboard, the three of them: Reverend Ripley, his friend Jones, and our Captain McGuinness had a long gam in the cabin. Afterwards, the first of the queer things occurs: the Captain calls us aft and announces that, as of that time forward, Mr. Jones is First Mate, replacing Armstrong. We were dumbstruck by this, since Armstrong's the finest mate in the packet trade. But the Captain's word is law, as you gentlemen may know. So there we were, stuck with the situation, you might say.

"But we got off all right, sailing with the tide that evening. There was a fresh wind up, and we fairly boomed along. It was mighty pleasant, except that Captain McGuinness seemed out of sorts, as if some strong spell were upon him. This was most unusual for him, such a pleasant man as he is.

"We soon entered the Straits of Sunda, and it was here that the second strange episode took place. Directly we left the straits behind us, Captain McGuinness gives the order to change course. Instead of proceeding along the usual route, which would take the *Briggs* just under the tip of India and Ceylon, he took the ship northwards. We were then running along the coast of Sumatra. When I enquired as to the reason for this change in plans, the Captain brushed me off.

'Oh Johnny,' says he, 'the Reverend Ripley has a final bit of business to transact before we make for England. He must make a quick stopover on the coast to visit his mission.' Informed it would only take a day or so, and realising it was for the good of the church, we obeyed willingly enough–though some of the crew were mad as hornets about it, they being in a rush to get home ..."

The boatswain paused to sip his brandy and light the cigarette I'd offered him, then continued.

"A day and a half later, the *Briggs* eased into a deep inlet halfway up the Sumatran coast. We dropped anchor in the sheltered lagoon. It was lovely enough: the inlet was fringed with palm trees and wide beaches, and the water was so blue and clear it hurt your eyes to look at it. We all stayed aboard whilst Ripley and Jones went ashore in the jolly boat. We frittered away the time on deck till they returned, which was at sunset. But rather than hoist anchor and be on our way, the Captain, with the passengers on each side of him, calls his petty officers aft.

"'See here men,' he says, 'Our good passenger, Reverend Ripley, thanks you for your kind patience. We will sail with the tide tomorrow morning and resume our usual course. In the meantime, Mr. Ripley has been kind enough to provide you and the crew with a treat.' So saying, the three of them hoisted a key from the after hold. 'Roll it forward men,' shouts Mr. Ripley, 'and let each have his full share!'

"Well, we all thought it was bully, and raised a cheer for Mr. Ripley and the Captain. I was whooping as loud as the rest, but noticed that Captain McGuinness looked anything but happy. Indeed, he seemed more worried than ever. This, and the fact that doling out rum is a strange custom for a reverend, should have set me thinking. But I was lost in the moment, as they say. Jones and I rolled the cask forward and what a carrying on there was that night! I've never been much for drink on account of my upbringing Mr. Holmes, and was also aware of my duties as boatswain. But Mr. Ripley, seeing I wasn't pitching in with the others, came forward to set me at ease.

"'Don't worry lad,' he says to me, 'there's nothing in this calm inlet can harm your ship. The three of us shall stand the watch tonight, so have your fun.' Of course, I must ask the Captain and he weakly gave in, saying we should all indulge the reverend in his kindness. So I joined in the merrymaking, and a real ripper of a party it was too. Considering the potency of the rum, and the amount of it, it wasn't long before the crew was senseless in the foc'sle—many of them unable even to find their bunks."

Here the boatswain paused for another sip.

"I had turned in ahead of the others. The only one to beat me turning flukes was Jenard, who I saw was fast asleep. Bye and bye— it was very late—I was awakened. I sat up in my bunk. Save for the drunken snoring of the crew, the ship was quiet. But then I heard it: the clanking of the aft windlass. The noise stopped, and I heard a distant thumping upon the deck.

"'Sampson!' a hoarse whisper cried, 'Sampson, are ye about?'

"It was Jenard. I answered that I was indeed awake, and was curious to know who'd been turning the windlass.

"'Let's be topside,' says I, 'and see what's what.' We made our way in the darkness of the foc'sle through the clots of men, lying where they had fallen in their stupor, and scurried up the forehatch. We'd heard stories of the Indian Ocean pirates you may be sure, but Jenard was a good fellow in a fight, and I've never considered myself a pushover. He was in the lead, and he'd no sooner popped his head up and looked aft when he ducked it down, saying: 'Something queer's up, Johnny, we'd better lay low.'

"Now I've never been a fellow to sneak about ferret-like, and considering my position as bos'n, it was my duty to render assistance if the ship were in any difficulty. So I led Jenard up the forehatch. It was a fair night, but black as pitch owing to a new moon. It was then that we spied a knot of men on the quarterdeck, leaning over the taffrail. A lighted lantern was all that made them visible, and we could scarcely hear their voices. As we reached the main hatches, we could see it was our Captain McGuinness, Reverend Ripley, and his two companions. They were talking excitedly in hushed tones, and were peering sharp out into the darkness.

"It was obvious they were waiting for a boat of some sort, and it was also clear they wanted none of the crew to know about their rendezvous. But curiosity had got the best of us, so Jenard and I slipped over the gunwale as quiet as cats. Our feet on the main channels, we crouched behind the deadeyes and shrouds. From where we hid, we could look out across the water, and had a clear view of the men on deck as well.

"Bye and bye, we saw a light twinkling far off on the water and drawing closer every minute. It excited the men a great deal, the evil Wangi especially, who fairly danced and spouted gibberish until he was hushed by a blow across the face from the Reverend Ripley. The light on the water was extinguished, and in its place, a triangular sail appeared. As it drew closer, we could see it was a lateen rig–a native boat, and swarming with the heathen devils!"

Sampson paused for another sip, and I observed that Holmes' face bore a look of rapt attention as he leaned forward in his chair.

"The boat, a sleek dhow trader, came up alongside, not forty feet from us, but, owing to the darkness of the night, we were invisible. The crew was a wicked lot, clad in white robes and turbans, their dark faces gleaming in the lantern light, and daggers in their sashes. A dozen of their number swarmed about the *Briggs*, then busied themselves rigging a jury derrick to the mizzen. I again heard the windlass turning and the clinking of the heavy pawls as they fell into place. It was then that Jenard and I noticed a large crate lashed to the deck of the native boat. It was a full yard high and deep, and the length of a man. It was of the stoutest timber and must have been of considerable weight, since the windlass was required to hoist it, by means of the heavy tackle, onto the deck of the *Briggs*. It was then lowered into the after hold, through the hatch on the quarterdeck. Throughout the entire proceedings, hardly a word was spoken by anyone, and the utmost care was taken to maintain silence. Having watched these strange events, and the manner in which they were executed, I was firmly convinced that our once-honest Captain was engaged in smuggling. It may surprise you gentlemen, but such activities are not at all uncommon, especially in the far reaches of the world. As the heathen crew was making ready to sail off, Jenard and I returned to the foc'sle.

"'Jenard,' says I, after crawling into my bunk, 'I think it best if we don't breathe a word of this to anyone. There's not much we can do in the middle of the Indian Ocean now, is there? When we reach London, I'll notify the authorities.' He agreed wholeheartedly, and, thinking the matter ended, we turned in."

John Sampson paused again, and the anxiety which Holmes had laid to rest welled up in him once again.

"It's here that the fantastic part of my tale begins," he said nervously. "Two nights after our episode, I was enjoying my evening pipe on the foredeck, as is my custom, when Jenard sought me out.

"'Johnny,' he pleaded, 'may I have a word with ye?' His eyes shone as if with fever, and despite his deep tan, I could see the pallor in his face. I begged him to tell me all that troubled him.

"'Johnny,' he cried, all a-quiver, 'would ye think me daft if I told you that I've seen a *monster rat?*'"

At these words, Holmes started visibly. In disbelief, we exchanged a quick glance. Holmes grew yet more attentive, leaning forward on the very edge of his chair. John Sampson continued his tale.

"So shocked was I at hearing this exclamation that I asked my shipmate to sit down and repeat it.

"'A rat, Johnny,' he said. 'A rat as big as all Creation!'

"Upon hearing these words, I naturally supposed the poor fellow to be ill. I advised him to get out of the sun, and was about to summon assistance, but he was so strong in his manner Mr. Holmes, and such a close friend, that this action seemed a betrayal. Seeing that nobody was within earshot, I asked him to tell me how he came about seeing this creature.

"He explained that he had observed Jones entering the after hold, which is below the officers' quarters, and reserved solely for their use, with a large bundle of food. Curious, he had followed the mate and seen him enter the stern locker. As the door swung open, he'd caught a glimpse of what he claimed was a monster rat.

"'I saw its face I tell you, peering out from the crate. It was a rat's face Johnny, as big as a keg!'

"Sitting there on the foredeck in the lovely evening, I felt that his tale was incredible. The *Matilda Briggs* had resumed her normal course and the morale of the crew, owing to the generosity of Reverend Ripley, couldn't have been higher. How strange then, to think of this ungodly monster less than fifty yards from where I lay and smoked my pipe! Yet he insisted that the creature was on board, and in so earnest a fashion that I felt bound to verify his story.

"That night, we concealed ourselves in the aft passageway shortly after midnight. At this time of course, the crew is either on duty topside or secured in the foc'sle, and since it is always dark below decks even with the paraffin lamps, concealing ourselves among the cargo was no problem.

"Presently, Jones appeared bearing a large bundle, which we supposed to be food. We watched intently as he unlocked the stout door that led to the hold and entered. He did not close the door after him, but paused to light a lamp. It was then, Mr. Holmes and Dr. Watson, when the lamplight filled the little hold, that I beheld the face of the giant rat."

John Sampson's manner became earnest, persuasive, as if he were eager to convince us of the validity of his amazing tale.

"It was a rat, gentlemen. Of that I am sure. I've been at sea long enough to know a rat when I see one. But its size! It had upright, roundish ears, a twitching, rodent snout–"

"You saw the entire animal?"

"No, Mr. Holmes, only the head, which peered out through a hole cut in the crate. A brief glimpse of the monster was all we were allowed, for the next instant Jones closed the door, and we made our way back to the foc'sle, full of fear and wonder."

"Is it not possible," I enquired, "that this 'monster' could have been a puppet contrivance fashioned from animal fur?"

"No, sir, of that I'm sure. It was not a puppet, nor the trick of a magic lantern. It was a live, breathing animal, for we heard it snort, and saw the eyes roll, the teeth gnash in a most horrible fashion! It was the most fearsome and repulsive object I have ever looked upon, for a rat is surely the lowest of God's creatures ... but a rat the size of a calf!

"Of course," the boatswain continued, "it wasn't very long before others of the crew had seen it also, and within two days the entire crew was paralysed with fear. No one would venture even into the aft passage, but clung tightly to the foc'sle except when on duty. Every rat on board was searched out and flung overboard, lest they somehow breed with the monster and overrun the ship. Never have I seen a body of grown men so gripped in terror. I cannot describe the relief we all felt when we made port yesterday. To a man, we cleared the ship, and most won't venture back, even though we've not been paid. There has been no talk of the monster on the docks, for fear of being ridiculed, or thought insane."

"The Captain McGuinness, the Reverend Ripley and the two other passengers, are they on board the *Matilda Briggs*?"

The boatswain's face darkened.

"The main purpose of my visit this morning Mr. Holmes, is that I was informed by Mr. Josiah Griggs that you might be of assistance in tracking down the killers of my friend. I have come in hopes that you will accompany me to the *Matilda Briggs*, for I am convinced that the people you have named are at least in part responsible for his murder."

"And you have decided not to leave the matter solely in your own hands. Mr. Sampson, I see that you have brains as well as stature, for such an approach would be unwise, even dangerous. Now let me ask you a question: did the *Matilda Briggs* stop at Gravesend?"

"No, sir."

"Thank you, you've been most helpful. Now we had best start for Limehouse. Come Watson, with Sampson here we should be able to gain access to the ship without delay."

We were met on the stairway, however, by Inspector Lestrade and two constables.

"Mr. John Sampson," said the inspector gravely. "In the name of the Queen, I arrest you in connection with the murder of Raymond Jenard. It is my duty to inform you that anything you say may be used in evidence against you."

Sampson said nothing as the iron bracelets were put on, but the look of astonishment and outrage revealed his emotions.

"Mr. Holmes, is there nothing you can do?"

"I'm afraid not at present, Mr. Sampson. I advise you to co-operate, and rest assured that both my companion and I shall be working night and day to clear you of this charge and secure your release. Lestrade, after you have delivered your prisoner, I would be obliged if you would secure a warrant and accompany us to the merchant ship *Matilda Briggs*, moored in Blackwall Reach."

"There's a fine bit of English justice," I said bitterly, as Holmes and I waited for Lestrade's return. "I must say, Holmes, I am surprised at your callous behaviour toward your client. The man comes to us, pours out his soul with the deepest trust and confidence, and at the end of this tale is hauled away to Clink Street. It's appalling."

"I am in total agreement, Watson, were it not for one fact: John Sampson is best off behind bars for the time being. I fear his life is in grave danger, and can think of no safer place for him than in one of Her Majesty's lockups. It was, in fact, with deep misgivings that Josiah Griggs recommended that he make the journey across town to our flat."

"Who the devil is Josiah Griggs?"

"Josiah Griggs, my friend, is the elderly, rather uncouth sailor who unwisely tried to fool my fellow lodger. Now then, here's Lestrade in a four-wheeler; fasten your oilskin Watson, for the weather, I fear, has grown worse."

3

THE SHIP OF DEATH

"I'm sure you're aware, Holmes," remarked Lestrade as he settled nervously into the cushions of our carriage, drawing on the double-claro Havana cigar that Holmes had given him, "that we can't hold Sampson forever. He was taken merely in connection with the murder, not charged as having committed it."

"Have you taken anyone else into custody? No? Then I pray that this excursion to Limehouse will put us on a new scent. What is your impression of the tale that Watson and I have related to you?"

The inspector was shaken by a fit of laughter so intense that he all but choked on his cigar.

"I must admit that my curiosity is pricked," said he whimsically, "but certainly it's without foundation. An amazing cover story, if you ask me."

"Nevertheless, one we can easily verify or repudiate; surely we shall track down other members of the crew. Let me ask you gentlemen, does this tale bring any others to mind?" Holmes sat with a twinkle in his eye, but the rest of his features bore a grave expression.

"Ah yes!" exclaimed Lestrade at last, "Five years ago, in eighty-nine."

"You mean the Baskerville business?" I interjected.

"The very same, Watson. Now if ever a tale had foundation, that one had, and yet to the casual listener it was merely diabolical nonsense."

"But the animal you shot to death on the Grimpen moor that night was still a hound," said Lestrade. "A huge beast, but a genuine one. The mere thought of a rat any bigger than a house cat is incredible.

Yet this man Sampson claims to have seen a rat as large as a calf. Impossible!"

"And yet the islands that comprise the Javanese archipelago contain some very interesting fauna," my companion continued. "As a matter of fact, according to Charles Darwin, insular animal populations, being cut off from the rest of their species, tend towards freakishness–especially insofar as size is concerned. The giant land tortoises of the Galapagos figure prominently in The Voyage of the Beagle. And Kodiak Island, in the Aleutian sea, is the home of the largest bear on earth. On the diminutive side, we have our miniature ponies on the Shetland Isles ..."

Lestrade knit his brow.

"I'm an amateur student of zoology, but I am aware that the islands of Java contain two unique species: one is a rare rhinoceros the size of a spaniel dog, the other is a gigantic lizard, named Komodo after the island it inhabits. Is it not possible, gentlemen, that the interior of one of these primeval specks of land plays host to a race of monster rodents?"

Then mention of the Devon tragedies of four years ago, and the speculation around Sampson's weird tale set my nerves on edge. Glancing out the carriage window, I could see coaches dashing through puddles and driving over the shiny paving stones. Working men in raincoats scurried about their business, slick with water and raw with chill. Though the hour was before noon, it was dark. It was hard to see, yet I could tell by the gradual decline of the neighbourhoods that we were on East Commercial Road, and approaching the Isle of Dogs for the second time in four and twenty hours. I lighted a cigarette and, for diversion, asked Holmes to explain the contradiction that he had found in the two *Morning Post* articles.

"You see, gentlemen," he explained, "it is natural for most people to assume that the fire began in McNulty's warehouse for two reasons. First, fires often begin in warehouses in the early evening: a departing stevedore is careless with his pipe. He leaves a spark behind which goes unnoticed in the empty building. Secondly, this type of building, being large and airy, burns more fiercely, hence people assume the fire started on the premises.

"But in this case, the fact that seven people perished in the blaze is remarkable as well as tragic. I discovered this morning that all of the seven dwelt in the residence at 22 Preston Road, the same residence as Jenard's. Considering the hour of the fire's inception, it is incredible to think that the blaze erupted in the neighbouring warehouse. The inhabitatants were obviously awake and alert at such an hour, most probably at their evening meal. Had the fire begun in an adjacent building, they would have been sufficiently forewarned to escape to the street.

"If, on the other hand, the blaze began in their own building on a lower floor, escape would be much more difficult. And yet, it would probably have been possible. What then, made escape impossible for these unfortunate victims? It was, in all probability, a combination of two things: a fire in the same building on a lower floor, and secondly, a fire that spread upward and outward with incredible speed and energy—"

"You are inferring then that the blaze was unnatural?" enquired Lestrade, leaning eagerly forward.

"I've no doubt of it. The blaze started in Jenard's quarters, and some substance, probably paraffin, was used to ensure a thorough job."

"Have you any idea what it was the arsonist wished to destroy?" I asked.

"If we had the answer to that question, we would be on the verge of a solution to the murder of Raymond Jenard, and perhaps the key to the puzzle of the *Matilda Briggs'* fantastic voyage. It is clear that this band of cutthroats gives not a farthing for human life, and they are a desperate lot indeed to sacrifice innocent victims who had obviously played no part in their foul scheme. Watson, I have never been more determined to reach the solution of any problem that has ever been laid before me. I vow to bring them to justice, not only to avenge Raymond Jenard, but for the sake of the seven innocents who by circumstance were swept away, including one in particular—Abbie Wellings, aged six."

A sigh escaped Lestrade's lips at hearing this poignant detail. I again recalled, as I have on innumerable occasions throughout the years, the torn face of the girl's mother as she clutched the tiny bundle in her arms. The revelation that the fire was deliberate sent hot rage coursing through me. I swore an oath of revenge, and knew I spoke for my friends as well, for their faces were full of fury. Truly, there were three grim men who disembarked from their four-wheeler at the banks of Blackwall Reach. Lestrade tugged at my sleeve as we walked towards the water. Looking back, the three of us could see a long plume of grey smoke and steam rising slowly up the river bank—the remnants of the previous night's disaster.

As our investigation with Lestrade was official, there was no delay in obtaining the assistance of Jennings, a customs house inspector who secured a launch for us. We descended the narrow stone stairway that led from the quay, with its gargantuan iron rings and bitts, down to the water's edge. Here we boarded the steam launch of the customs house. It was an open, wooden vessel with a small steam engine aft. It was fired by soft coal evidently, for thick oily smoke rose out of the chimney pipe. It was stationary and silent until we were all seated, then Jennings turned a small valve at the base of the boiler, and the engine took life. A flip of the flywheel and the steady chuffing and clanging commenced. We cast off, and churned our way into the inscrutable mist beyond. The visibility had not improved; Jennings minded the tiller with great care, and kept our speed down to a crawl. Before long, large masses loomed out at us, and we found ourselves passing under bows and transoms of sailing ships. Through the mist and rain, their upper spars were barely visible, which added to their ghost-like quality as they swung sullenly at their mooring cables.

Above the clatter of the single-cylinder jensen engine could be heard the shouts and curses of the sailors as they worked or gambled the time away. More than once from beyond the wooden bulkheads I caught the strains of a concertina. As we passed almost directly under the transom of a large barque I read in gilded letters: *Rangoon*, and recalled that she had arrived just a day before the *Briggs*, bound from Hong Kong.

Jennings again turned the brass valve and the engine's clatter ceased. A low groan of escaping steam and the chuckle of water were the only sounds to be heard. I cannot describe the melancholy I felt at this time. It was as if the engine's chuffing served to drown out the oppressiveness of the rain and fog, and now in utter silence we drifted forth into the grey mist.

"Keep a sharp eye out if you please," requested Jennings. "The *Matilda Briggs* lies dead ahead."

As if upon command, a dark, melancholy shape ghosted into view ahead of our bows. As we drifted closer, the shape became the dark, low hull of a packet trader. Perhaps it was her black hull, or the strange tale of violence that surrounded her, but she bore an aura of dread and foreboding.

Thrice we hailed her, but only the hollow echoes of our own voices responded.

"Jennings, has she her dockside clearance yet?" asked Holmes.

"Not to my knowledge, sir. There's been no preparation for transfer at all, sir. The Captain must apply himself, or send his mate if he's indisposed."

"And you have seen no one on this ship?" enquired Lestrade.

"No, sir. There has been no sign of life on or about her after the crew went ashore yesterday afternoon."

"The Captain and officers, do they remain aboard until the clearance is obtained?"

"Usually that is the case. I would be much surprised if she were deserted."

"We had best board her and see for ourselves. Over yonder, Jennings, the boarding stair."

The three of us clambered up the frail boarding stairway whilst Jennings minded the painter.

Seldom have I experienced a more ominous feeling that when I swung over the gunwale and planted my feet on the deck of the *Matilda Briggs.* She was a typical three-masted cargo vessel, around two hundred feet in length. What gave me pause was the dead silence, the desolation of the ship—deserted and swaying at her cable like a waif.

Hawsers creaked and groaned. The water slapped hollowly below us. Meanwhile, Lestrade scurried about, flinging glances over the entire deck. Holmes paced in methodical fashion, his keen eyes roving deliberately round him, taking in everything. Watching them, one had the feeling that the London police detective epitomised energy and thoroughness. Holmes, on the other hand, gave an impression almost of leisure. Yet, one could not help but be aware of the incredible force, the terrible power and energy of the mind that churned behind the keen face.

I drew my waterproof more tightly round me, for the wind and rain brought an unbearable chill. No other vessels were visible through the mist. For all appearances we could have been in mid-Atlantic, and there was a profound feeling of melancholy and desolation.

I paced the deck forward to the hatch that Sampson had described. From there, I looked aft to the quarterdeck. In my mind's eye I tried to picture the same scene in the middle of a tropical night, with scores of Malay tribesmen swarming like insects as they lowered the huge crate to the deck. I remembered the beast, and paused to consider: was it only the weather that caused me to shiver? Was that same monster lurking in its vile den somewhere below these very decks? I felt a hand on my shoulder and turned.

"Whoa, Watson! Did I startle you?"

I was looking into Holmes' face, the rainwater cascading off his cap.

"So you see—Sampson's powers of description are excellent. I might suggest he's got a touch of the poet in him. You were no doubt reliving in your mind the strange events of several weeks ago. Here are the very channels in which the pair hid themselves," said Holmes, leaning over the side. "In this tangle of rigging, with its shrouds and halyards, great coils of line and pin rails, they were hidden. But mind, what a view they had of the proceedings! Come down here with me, Watson—there—now, see that gaff on the mizzen? That's where the derrick was rigged. A block and tackle could then easily be lowered alongside to receive even a very large parcel."

We were called from our reveries by the tolling of a bell.

"Hallo! Anyone here?" cried Lestrade as he snapped the lanyard back and forth. He stood at the mainmast. At his waist, the brass ship's bell sang out mournfully.

"I declare Holmes," he continued. "This *is* odd ... surely someone must be about. Let's have a look below."

"Let us proceed then, but with caution," I warned.

Advancing onto the quarterdeck, we tried the aft companionway but found it bolted from within. Moving forward, we found the main companionway ajar. Sliding back the hatch, Lestrade bounded down, followed by Holmes, who was forced to stoop almost double. I managed to follow without much difficulty, and we found ourselves in some sort of narrow passageway, in almost total darkness. Suddenly Holmes shot back up the hatch. We heard his tread on the deck above. There was a heavy sliding sound, and, as if by miracle, the passageway was flooded with daylight.

"Well now, Mr. Holmes," remarked Lestrade as he returned. "I had no idea you'd been a sailor." He winked in my direction. "Next we'll have you swarming up the ratlines to mind the braces, won't we, Watson?"

"I accept your compliments, Lestrade. I think that the inspection of the *Matilda Briggs* will be a great deal easier with the skylight opened. Ha! You see? Look what we have here!"

He directed our attention to a tallow stub stuck onto a bulkhead timber just under the hatchway cover.

"A candle butt. So? I'll wager there are three score aboard this ship," I ventured.

"A safe wager, too, Watson. Yet even ordinary objects, when used

or placed in a certain way, can be suggestive. From what we see
before us, we can perhaps put together a chain of events which will
prove interesting."

After noting carefully the position of the candle stub on the timber,
Holmes plucked it delicately from its resting place and turned it
round in his hand. Taking out his pocket knife and pocket lens, he
shredded off a minute curl of the drippings which he scrutinised
under the magnifying glass.

"I say, Holmes," said Lestrade impatiently, "are you not exaggerating the significance of that bit of candle? There are surely more
important matters to investigate."

"I'm not so sure, Lestrade," observed my companion. Lestrade
waited in exasperated silence, stamping his booted feet against the
cold.

"We can say with reasonable certainty," Holmes said at last, still
turning the stub in his fingers, "that the *Matilda Briggs* has been visited
in the last twelve hours by a right-handed man of above average
height."

Lestrade and I stared blankly in amazement.

"Furthermore," Holmes continued in a montone, "he is unfamiliar with the ship, or at least this part of it. He undoubtedly used this
very candle in a curious manner, which will I hope clarify his
motives for visiting the ship. Also, he came in stealth, and wished his
actions kept secret—"

"Holmes! I never—" interjected Lestrade.

"And finally, he was obviously overcome with a tremendous
emotional burden—in fact, driven to a frenzy that was unendurable."

"Dash it, Holmes, enough of this quackery!" demanded Lestrade.
"I challenge you to substantiate this outlandish set of deductions. If
they make sense, I'll pay for your luncheon!"

Holmes' eyes sparkled. "Done, Lestrade! Where shall I begin?
Ah, yes, the simplest first. The man's height, you see is elementary.
The stub was placed on this timber, not either of the two lower ones.
Furthermore, observe how this corner of the chandler's bench sticks
out. You see, one must bend over it before reaching up to place the
candle—further evidence of the man's height."

"I suppose that's sensible enough," growled Lestrade, "but what
about the other theories? How do you know the fellow came in
stealth?"

Holmes pointed to a black object projecting from the bulkhead
less than a yard from where the stub was found.

"Of course, gentlemen, you know what this is. Quite so: a wrought-iron candle sconce. Although differing slightly in appearance from the ordinary sconce, the caked tallow drippings in the dish and the small pile of spent Lucifers makes its identity obvious.

"Now assuming the man was leaving the *Briggs* with a lighted candle in his hand, what more natural place to deposit the stub than in the sconce. Why not? Because he did not see the sconce. He'd extinguished the candle, you see, before entering the main passageway, and was forced to find his way out in darkness. Obviously, he did not wish to show even a candle light near the main hatch. Hence, he wished his visit kept secret."

"Remarkable, and yet simple," I mused.

"We can also see by the sconce's misuse that the man wasn't familiar with the vessel, or at least wasn't a crewman. If this were the case, he would have no doubt felt for the sconce in the darkness, since he would have been aware of its presence."

"Then explain how it is that the man is right-handed," demanded Lestrade.

"Very well, sir. Do you both observe how one side of the candle tip is much lower than the other? See how the drippings are clustered too on the opposite side of the depression?"

"Of course I see it," said the detective. "It's obvious that the man held the candle tipped to one side—"

"Yes. Now notice how the thumb has left a hollow in the tallow drippings. The hollow points diagonally downward. See how my right thumb nearly matches the hollow, yet switching the stub to my left hand—"

"It runs the opposite way from the thumb mark," I added. "It doesn't fit."

"Of course not. The man held this stub in his right hand, and at a strange angle too—I am hopeful we will find additional signs of the use he put to this candle."

"Holmes," said Lestrade, "I'll admit that you've indulged in a bit of cleverness here. And I'll further admit that what you say makes some little sense. But I'm dashed if I can see how a candle butt can tell you that the visitor was here within the last twelve hours. I'd be right obliged if you would explain this to me. And I'm sure Watson and I would both like to know what determines that the man was on the brink of mental collapse."

"Have you ever touched molten wax, Watson?"

"Now and then, but I avoid it if possible," I chuckled.

"Certainly you do. Molten wax is hot and painful. Yet here's a man who allowed wet drippings to cover his thumb, and evidently bore this pain without notice. Therefore, something of an enormous consequence was occupying his faculties. As for the evidence of elapsed time, I call your attention to this hallmark on the bottom of the stub."

With this, Holmes then turned the stub upside down to reveal the following hallmark embossed in the wax:

"It's the Broad Arrow," observed Lestrade, looking at the candle bottom closely.

"Yes, the mark with which government property is identified, from candles to cannon. This is a regulation Navy candle. These may be purchased at most marine supply house. These candles contain much whale oil, and are highly prized because of their brilliance. I've made a rather thorough study of candle tallows, as Watson can vouch for. Now a candle high in spermaceti is brilliant, but too brittle for use. Therefore, the makers of our navy candles have added a good dose of beeswax. The two blend together remarkably well, and produce a candle that is bright, yet long-burning and durable. Because of the addition of beeswax, this tallow does not dry to brittleness for some time. As you may have observed when I peeled at the drippings with my pocket knife, the tallow parted in a fine curl—it did not flake or chip as the body of the candle would have. Observe too the colour of the drippings: they are of a delicate pale opalescence, not the opaque white of thoroughly dried wax. From these characteristics, I deduce with near certainty that this candle was lighted not more than twelve hours ago. For your edification, Lestrade, I would suggest, once again, that the smallest details are often of the gravest importance. And now, while I contemplate my free lunch, let us proceed to the forecastle."

Leading an eager companion, and a somewhat irritable Lestrade, Holmes led us down the narrow passageway toward the bows of the *Matilda Briggs*. The odours of tar, hemp, and canvas were much in evidence. The huge oaken timbers creaked and groaned with dismal regularity as the ship rolled slightly in the current of the reach. For some reason, Holmes had departed from his usual detective habits. In the past I had grown used to observing him bent over like a strange old man, searching for footprints or a fallen object. Now, however, he held his head upright and seemed to scan the wooden beams and deckboards above.

Soon the passageway grew dark, and Holmes took Lestrade's dark lantern to lead the way. Far ahead was a dull blueish glow.

"The fore-hatchway," said Lestrade, pointing.

We passed under the hatch, which was bolted with a stout brass rod, and proceeded through a low doorway in a large, triangular room. The room was illuminated almost imperceptibly by a pair of heavy glass "bullseyes" set in the beams, but most of the crew apparently slept in bunks: the walls were ringed with them, fashioned from heavy timber and set one atop the other. What drew our attention immediately, however, was the untidiness of the compartment in general. While the sailors had evidently borne off their personal possessions before fleeing from the ship, the bunk mattresses and other ship's paraphernalia were strewn about and heaped in corners.

"Certainly not what I would call 'shipshape,' eh, Watson?"

"I should say not. It looks rather like the shambles of the Lower form dormitory after the last day of Spring Term. The lads have certainly cleaned out in a rush, as Sampson stated."

"There is probably an explanation for it," said Lestrade. "I'm confident that after we speak with the Captain–"

"Where *is* the Captain?" I asked.

"If he is aboard, we shall no doubt find him directly," said the detective in his most official tone. Despite his crisp manners, though, I had the feeling he wasn't really quite sure of anything–at least aboard the *Briggs*.

"Watson! Lestrade! Do come here! I believe I have found what I have been searching for–"

We turned and observed Holmes lying on his back in one of the upper berths. He held Lestrade's lantern on his breast, and let the beam illuminate the ceiling timbers of the foc'sle.

The detective and I, placing our feet on the edge of the lower berth, leaned over and, by twisting our necks into an almost impossible position, could observe, in script letters three inches high, the following words done in candle smoke:

"All is stairs and passageways
where the rat sleeps–
his treasure keeps"

"Well gentlemen," enquired Holmes, from the deep recesses of the bunk, "what do you make of this latest find?"

"It's some sort of poem or riddle," I speculated, "and appears incomplete."

"The man wrote the passage whilst lying in his bunk obviously. I think it's a warning. Notice that a rat is mentioned too," said Lestrade. "The question is: why would a man write a warning up on the timbers above his bunk? It's absurd."

"An excellent point, Lestrade. For whom is the warning intended, and what does it mean? Or does it mean anything? I for one think it means a great deal," said Holmes as he rolled out of the bunk and lowered his angular body to the floor. "As you may have noticed, I have been looking for this writing in candle smoke since I examined the stub in the main passageway. It is curious that we find it over the bunk of a crewman. It would be interesting to know which man occupied this bunk ..."

"It was Jenard's," I observed, pointing to a small metal plaque fixed with a pike to the head timber of the berth.

"Excellent Watson! I must confess I quite overlooked it, being so intent on what my search of the ceiling would reveal."

"This means Jenard wrote the words," I suggested.

"Certainly," agreed Lestrade. "He perhaps had a dire feeling with regard to his own life, and left this crude cryptogram here to warn others or implicate the party whom he feared."

"Your conclusions are logical with regard to motive, my friends, but if what we deduce from the candle drippings is true, this message was written within the last twelve hours. At that time, poor Jenard was lying stone dead in the city morgue, a shocked Sampson identifying the remains."

Lestrade and I pondered this twist in silence.

"Even assuming the evidence of the candle drippings is inconclusive, it is plain that Jenard, a left-hander, couldn't have written these words. You remember, Watson, the marking I observed on his shirtcuff?"

I replied in the affirmative, and explained Holmes' previous deduction to Lestrade, who grew still more confused.

"We know that whoever held the candle was right-handed. Furthermore, after lying on the bunk for a few seconds and tracing the message with my own hands—even allowing for my long arms, I can see it would be impossible for the words to be written with the left hand. That hand, you see, is on the inside and the proximity of the deck would render the task impossible for anyone save a contortionist. I think this chamber has told us all it can, at least for the present. There's nothing to be found in this bunk, nor in the single one yonder, which I assume to be Bos'un Sampson's. Let us then, work our way aft and examine the officers' quarters."

We made our way back through the dark passageway towards the vessel's stern. We passed the main hatch and, after a few steps, saw a faint gleaming which marked the after hatch. Passing under it, we came upon the termination of the main passage, which was marked by a cluster of doors.

"There are the officers' quarters," remarked Lestrade.

"Yes, but which compartment belongs to which?" I asked. Realising that our knowledge of maritime life was limited, Holmes sent me up to fetch Jennings.

"These two belong to the mates, or other petty officers," said Jennings, pointing to the two doors nearest us, one on each side of the passage. "The Captain's cabin, or main cabin, will be that one, in the centre furthest aft."

"And if the vessel were to take on passengers?" asked Holmes.

"The passengers would be berthed in either of these two cabins, the two mates doubling up in the other one."

We tried the doors of the two smaller cabins and found them locked. Proceeding to the main door, Lestrade rapped sharply. He rapped and hailed alternately, but there was no answer.

Trying out the latch, we were somewhat startled to find the door swung open without effort. I had seen a Captain's cabin only once before, on my return voyage to England aboard the troopship *Orontes*. That fleeting glimpse was during a spell of the enteric fever which had necessitated my leaving Afghanistan, so the recollection was somewhat foggy. However, glancing at the main cabin of the *Matilda Briggs* seemed to bring those distant memories sharply into focus, for the two cabins were similar. A low ceiling, slightly curved and set with heavy beams, several small windows set in the transom, a trim bunk bed and tidy desk, bookshelves laden with maritime tomes, all these could possibly been found in any sailing ship of the period. Dull greyish light filtered in through the windows and played upon the brass lamp that swung slowly from a chain over the desk.

The compartment was somewhat gloomy, but appeared to be in order; there was none of the untidiness that we had observed in the foc'sle.

"It appears that Captain McGuinness is preparing to take leave but has not yet done so," observed Holmes, pointing to a fully packed carpet bag near the bed. "We had best not touch anything here, Lestrade, until we speak with him."

"He is most likely in the hold, gentlemen. It is often the custom of the Captain and his chief steward to examine the cargo directly before unloading so as to determine pilferage or spoilage. If you wish, I'll go below and hunt him up."

As Jennings disappeared down a short ladder we seated ourselves and lighted pipes. In apparent disregard of his own suggestion, Holmes plucked a leather-bound volume from the shelf and began to search through it. His close inspection of the volume, which I assumed to be the ship's log, was interrupted only by an occasional grunt of satisfaction or surprise. After a few moments of this examination, he brought the volume over to us.

"See here," said he, showing us two pages from the log, "here's evidence enough that all is not well aboard the *Briggs*. Lestrade, I ask you to examine this handwriting—never mind what it says."

The detective duly scanned the large, well-formed script whilst I looked over his shoulder.

"Nothing too unusual, Holmes."

"Precisely. It is good handwriting. It was written in May, during the *Briggs'* outward voyage to the Orient. It is a strong hand, with distinction and some flourish. I would say offhand it indicates a person of strong character and generosity. Now, Watson, I'd like you to examine this specimen."

"It's clear that the mate wrote these passages. The hand is altogether different."

"Careful Watson—don't jump to conclusions. Do you see any similarities?"

"Now that you mention it, there is a marked resemblance in the lower case 'o's.'"

"Yes," interjected Lestrade, "and notice the curious tail on the letter 'y' when it completes a word. These could even be the same hand, and yet—"

"—and yet while the one is strong and steady, the later is weak, unsteady, without character," added Holmes. "I tell you, Lestrade, one day there will be a complete and legitimate science dealing with handwriting. Few things reveal as much about a person's character or emotional state as his hand. It is clear that James McGuinness wrote both passages, yet the later passage, penned only a few weeks ago, reveals that the Captain was on the verge of cracking under an intolerable strain. The log itself reveals nothing of Sampson's strange tale, if indeed there's truth to it. It is plain we shall have to depend on the Captain himself to–My God!–"

Holmes was interrupted by a sound I shall not forget for the rest of my days. It was a scream, or rather a high pitched, hoarse shriek that rang about the ship like the trumpet of Doomsday.

It lasted for what seemed an eternity, then ceased. We sprang from the cabin, almost tripping over each other in our haste. We had not gone more than a few feet down the passage, when the shriek sounded again–it was pitched still higher, and sounded even more terrifying.

"Down here!" shouted Holmes, and dove down the ladderway into the hold.

The hold was shrouded in total blackness. The three of us groped our way forward frantically. After much difficulty, we succeeded only in working our way into a blind alley. Bales and hogsheads formed high walls on three sides of us.

"We must take our time," insisted Holmes. "In my haste, I left the lantern behind. It is quite possible, I fear, to become lost in this labyrinth for days. Listen!"

A low, mumbling sound came faintly to my ears. After several seconds I recognised it to be a human voice. The words were not audible, but their tone suggested profound grief and agony.

Slowly, the three of us crept forward, feeling our way in the darkness toward the sonorous, dirge-like chanting. For it was a chant, and as we drew nearer the sound I recognised the words "Dear God, Dear God," being repeated.

After some time, I felt a ladder brush against me. Realising it was the same one by which we had entered the hold, it became clear to me that we had turned the wrong way upon entering. We were now heading aft, and a short distance ahead could be seen a dimly lighted doorway. I heard a metallic click from Holmes' direction and knew he had drawn his revolver. Lestrade and I followed suit.

"This is no doubt the after hold Sampson mentioned," said Holmes in a hoarse whisper. "Let us proceed."

An instant later the ship took a roll, and, as if to announce our arrival, the thick oaken door ahead of us slowly swung open with a terrible groaning of its massive iron hinges. The chamber within was small, perhaps built for the personal possessions of the Captain. It was not more than fifteen feet on a side, and was low-ceilinged. In the split second that I examined the chamber itself, rather than its contents, I was aware of large iron rings set in the wall timbers, these no doubt used to lash cargo securely. There was another door, quite small, at the far wall of the after hold. It was shut and bolted with a heavy timber.

The dismal chamber was illuminated dully by a candle. The candle was held aloft by Jennings, who stood in the doorway, frozen in terror. His blank gaze was fixed at what lay in the centre of the small room, sprawled in a heap. We entered the room quickly and calmed Jennings, who had ceased his mumbling. Holmes took the candle and examined more closely the corpse on the floor. The man was dressed to go ashore, and from his cap, which lay a few feet from the body, we guessed him to be Captain James McGuinness.

It was only after Lestrade had led the shaken Jennings topside with orders to summon additional men that Holmes leaned over towards me and asked:

"What of those wounds, Watson? Sure I have not come across the likes of this before. See here, all about his chest and throat. What sort of weapon do you suppose–"

"Holmes!" I shouted, rising, "Let's be off this ship at once!"

"Steady Watson!" said Holmes as he gripped my shoulder. "Watson, you're reeling ... there, hold on–"

But at that instant a claustrophobic fit came upon me, and I wanted nothing so much as to quit the dungeon-like bowels of the ship and breathe fresh air. Things went dim, and I was half-conscious of fighting my way somehow to the main hatchway, Holmes steadying me all the way. There I sat near the skylight until things came into a sharper focus.

"There, you're feeling better, eh Watson?"

I saw Holmes' eager face peering down into mine, as he steadied me with a firm grip on my shoulder.

"I lost control of myself, Holmes," I remarked bitterly. "I am truly sorry to have disappointed you."

"Think nothing of it, dear fellow. Perhaps it was the closeness of the chamber itself, as well as the contents. Tell me, were you not conscious of a foul stench?"

"Yes, certainly–a heavy animal smell. But as to what upset me–"

"I was going to remark that something upon the corpse set you reeling, and I know you well enough, my friend, to know that you aren't upset by a trifle."

"Holmes," I intoned solemnly. "You asked me what weapon was responsible for the wounds on the victim ..."

"Yes, that seems a puzzle. No knife could have—"

"No knife was used. The wounds upon the Captain's throat are teethmarks."

"You are certain?"

"I am positive. And what makes it all the more shocking and, if you will, mysterious, is the fact that they are no ordinary teeth."

"How do you mean?"

"The wounds weren't inflicted by fangs, as a large dog or cat would possess. Nor are they tusks, such as wild pigs have. They were, I fear, *incisors*—or, if we can give even the slightest credence to Sampson's tale, the *teethmarks of a giant rat.*"

4

RED SCANLON AT THE *BINNACLE*

Events moved quickly: Jennings was dispatched to the customs house, and within an hour the *Matilda Briggs* was swarming with inspectors and detectives.

A thorough search was made of the entire vessel. The cargo holds were examined, but yielded up nothing save the original cargo, which consisted of copra, raw silk, and small amounts of tea and tin. Holmes, Lestrade and I returned to the murder chamber and again examined the corpse. Despite his outward show of official confidence, Lestrade appeared inwardly shaken and confused. Holmes said nothing during our inspection tour of the after hold, but his face was full of the keenest interest and curiosity.

The Captain's body lay twisted on its side, as if he were trying desperately to escape. He had put up some resistance, as indicated by the condition of his hands and the flecks of blood on the sides of the chamber. The beast, whatever it was, that killed him, undoubtedly possessed great strength and incredible ferocity, for the man's neck was nearly severed. An indication of the animal's size could be roughly gauged from the crate that stood against the far wall. It was of the dimensions Sampson had described: six feet long by three feet high and wide. At one end, a hole a foot in diameter had been cut. It was through this hole apparently that the monster thrust his head. Holmes examined everything with the patience and thoroughness that were his hallmark. The musky odour that lingered in the small room suggested a beast had been quartered there, and recently. Yet no sign of the animal itself was found. The only interesting discovery we found in the after hold was a transom port, or "lumber hole" as I believe the sailors call it. It was a hatchway cut horizontally through the transom of the ship, and fastened, when not in use, by the small stout door, heavily bolted, that I had observed when first entering the hold. Jennings, who had by this time recovered from his shock, explained to us that this type of hatch facilitates the loading on of long pieces of lumber, even entire logs, that would not fit down the deck hatchways.

"Tell me, Jennings," enquired Holmes, "does the *Briggs* generally haul lumber?"

"I believe not, sir," was the reply. "To my knowledge, she has not hauled lumber under her present owner."

"Then this hatchway should not have been used for several years at least. It appears to have fallen into disuse, doesn't it Watson? Notice the heavy rust on the hinges, and the marks of discoloration on the wooden beams where they have touched the metal. Yet, I would call your attention, gentlemen, to three curious things."

Holmes swung the door open.

"First, note the ease with which the door swings. This is most odd for a heavy door not often used. Secondly, note the hinge joints: see how the rust, heavy as it is, is broken and chipped along each groove. Finally, through my lens, observe if you can the minute burring of the iron latch where it strikes the plate—and the shiny metal it leaves. Now gentlemen—one of these signs by itself could be accidental. Two could perhaps be coincidence. But the three of them together force us to conclude that this hatchway was indeed opened, and opened recently."

Engrossed, the three of us peered out the small doorway, which was large enough for a man to crawl through. The water seemed surprisingly close, certainly not more than six feet below us. We left the grim cubicle behind and returned down the boarding stair to the launch. Shivering by this time, we huddled on the cushions while Jennings got us underway.

"The question is, why was the portway opened?" said Lestrade, as he smoked in the bow.

"Obviously," I replied, "to enable someone, or *something*, to leave the ship unobtrusively."

"There are many questions that need answering," remarked Holmes as he lighted a cigarette. "Who was the night-time visitor with the candle? Did he murder Captain McGuinness? If so, how? To all appearances, the man was worried to death by a large beast. A giant rat? It is hardly believable, yet Sampson swears he saw such a creature. Certainly the after hold smelled of an animal. And there is no denying the teethmarks on the corpse. Ah, here we are at the quay. Mind the painter, Lestrade.

"Now, Lestrade, I'll allow you to live up to your reputation as a man of your word. I know of a lively little inn not far from here much frequented by sailors. It serves excellent beer, good boiled beef, and much dockside gossip. You needn't scowl, my friend; the prices are reasonable. Let us be off."

We left the iron gates of the customs house behind, and began a twenty-minute expedition through the labyrinth of winding streets and dingy lanes of Limehouse. The object of our quest was the *Binnacle* public house, an ancient, heavy-timbered establishment named after the enormous brass nautical instrument that stands near the doorway. It is located in Robin Hood Lane, and under its swinging, dripping sign we entered, descended four stone steps, and found ourselves in a low, narrow room that seemed to extend forever in a series of hallways and turns. We were shown to a table by a stout woman who had three mugs of the dark beer in front of us almost before we were seated. The ale was a refreshing bracer after our morning, and the beef and onions were a fine accompaniment.

"But of all the unanswered questions," pursued Holmes, "the most unexplainable seems to be the message above Jenard's bunk. It was plainly put there by our night visitor to the *Briggs*. We know the visitor was not of the crew, and the time of the visit was after Jenard's death. Yet, the visitor wishes us to believe it was Jenard who wrote the message. Why does he wish this, and what does he want us to take from the message?"

"All is stairs and passageways where the rat sleeps—" I chanted.

"... his treasure keeps ..." continued Lestrade.

"What's the treasure?" I asked. "Do you suppose that Captain McGuinness was engaged in smuggling?"

"It is certainly possible," said Holmes. "The message, though, seems puzzling in another regard. It mentions stairs where the rat sleeps ... I cannot recall any stairs."

"True—there were none, only passageways," I remarked. "Furthermore, we can see by the author's use of the word *is*, rather than *are*, that he is illiterate."

Holmes' thin lips curled into a hint of a smile at this observation.

"Yes, Watson, that is certainly the most logical explanation," he said, with a curious gleam in his eye.

At that instant our thoughts were interrupted by a great din of shouts and oaths emerging from the parlour bar of the inn. Leaving our table, we wound our way back to the front room of the *Binnacle*. There, in the low-ceilinged drinking room was a great commotion: a dozen or so sailors were clustered around one of their number who, soaked with rain, had apparently just entered the establishment. It was some time before the group settled down enough for their conversation to become intelligible. We caught a few phrases with the words "murder" and "*Matilda Briggs*" from across the crowded room. We drew closer to the group.

"... just before noon, so I heered it," said the sailor who had just entered. He was very large, with a bushy red beard and bald head. He had shed his overcoat, and stood at the bar, pausing in his narrative to drain the pint in a single gulp and slam the mug down upon the bar as a signal for another. The bartender, although complying with the request, was apparently too slow for him.

"Step to it, Alf, mind you hurry! Red Scanlon is thirsty and, from what I seen this mornin' will have me six or seven more before I leave ..."

He received his porter, turned away from the bartender without thought of paying and, aware of his captive audience, demanded tobacco and the best fireside bench before continuing. The knot of men leaned close in eagerness, and bore the look of fear and wonder on their faces, as Red Scanlon, obviously a master storyteller, went on:

"Well, the first I laid eyes on was old Jennings, slinking around the quay he was, and lookin' pale as death. So I says, 'What's up?' But he don't answer, don't acknowledge, and I sees three glum lookin' gentlemen followin' close behind—coppers most likely. Well, I knows now it's something bad, and most likely to do with the *Briggs* you see, because of ..."

At this point, the storyteller paused.

"Because of what?" several in the group demanded.

Scanlon eyed the questioners uneasily; his eyes lost their boldness and appeared to shift slightly. Two men in the group remained silent, as if they were aware of what Scanlon was referring to.

"Well now, Scotty, you wasn't berthed on the *Briggs*, now was you? Then o'course, you don't know ... but Winkler, and Thomas here, they know—"

The two men indicated shook their heads ever so slightly, as if to convey their wish to avoid the reference altogether.

"Are you by chance referring to the giant rat of Sumatra?" a clear voice enquired.

The huge sailor lowered his mug and peered uncertainly beyond the group toward the doorway where we stood. Through the dim light of the room, his eyes fixed upon Holmes, leaning nonchalantly against the doorway, for it was he who had asked the question. Scanlon rose and advanced with a catlike silence that was amazing for a man of his stature, and menacing.

"See here, whoever you may be ..." he began in a low voice, then hesitated as he inspected the three of us. "Why, by Jove, it's the glum gentlemen!"

"I am Inspector Lestrade of Scotland Yard," began our companion, but he was cut short.

"Now see here gentlemen," said Scanlon quickly, "if it's about that business, me and my mates here want no part of it. We don't know nothin', do we Thomas? Winkler? No sir, you see? Now if it's the same to you good gentlemen, we'll be poppin' off–"

"In the name of the Queen I must ask you to remain," commanded Lestrade, "and your two shipmates as well."

Now the entire group of seamen was staring sullenly at us, and I noticed, not without uneasiness, that one of them had seized the fireplace poker and was holding it firmly across his knees. The lively festivity of the *Binnacle* had given way to an ominous silence. As I felt the poisonous stares all round me, I realised how far indeed we were from Regent's Park, in distance vertical as well as linear. Lestrade, however, always the policeman, seemed unaware of our true situation and surged ahead in his most officious manner.

"I would recommend you don't resist," said he, shaking his finger at Scanlon. "Your boatswain Sampson had the good sense to co-operate. Now if you will–"

The men brightened noticeably at the mention of Sampson's name. It was evident, and not surprising, that they held warm affection for him.

"Then you've met Johnny?"

"Yes. Met and arrested him," continued the detective, blithely unaware that the group had risen and was forming a crude circle around us. "And I hereby warn you that if you fail to cooperate, you'll all soon be joining him behind bars. Now if–"

"Johnny in the darbies!" cried Scanlon, his face flushed with anger. He turned and addressed his followers. "Did you hear that? They've taken our Johnny off to jail!"

The outcry served as a sort of general signal to the denizens of the *Binnacle.* As the circle closed in, I remembered hearing the sounds of scuffing feet and the pushing back of chairs. As I braced myself for the broadside soon to follow, three words caught my ears. They were spoken clearly above the tumult: "Bully Boy Rasher."

The circle stopped moving. Scanlon approached Holmes and bent his face close to my companion's.

"Bully Boy Rasher," said Holmes quietly. "Have you heard of him?"

"You can bet I have—but what of it?"

"I knocked him out in a glove match two years ago, Mr. Scanlon. If your intentions are as I perceive, I would prefer an individual settlement rather than a general brawl."

Before the astonished giant could reply, a squealing, apron-clad figure dashed between the two men. It was Alf, the bartender.

"Mister 'Olmes, sir!" he piped. "It is you, ain't it? I'm sure if we'd recognised you sooner sir, there'd ha' been no trouble, such a friend of the working man as you are, sir. I'm sure our good friends here at the *Binnacle* haven't forgotten how you saved Chips Newcombe from the gallows, or cleared the young apprentice Smythe of the burglary charges against him—unjust as they were ..."

The mood of the people had changed miraculously; they now gazed with curiosity at this slender, well-dressed man who had acted so nobly on their behalf. Scanlon, half-mollified, inspected the narrow physique of my friend incredulously.

"You beat Bully Boy Rasher, London's top middleweight?"

"Aye, Red, and what a pretty fight it was! At the Crib Club, was it not, Mr. 'Olmes? Such as me aren't allowed there of course, but a pretty fight, so I heard."

"I might say, Alf," said Holmes, "that from appearances, I'd rather face three Rashers than this man before me."

These words had a most remarkable effect upon Red Scanlon, who unclenched his fists, took two steps backward, and looked at the floor.

"You all should know," Holmes said in a solemn voice, his eyes sweeping over the entire group, "that John Sampson was put in jail largely at my unoffical request. To explain this action, I think I need only ask you two questions. First, are you aware of the fate of Raymond Jenard?"

There followed a grim acquiescence.

"Secondly," pursued Holmes, "would any one of you wish the same fate to befall John Sampson?"

There was a vehement denial.

"Then I must ask for your forbearance for a short time, Mr. Scanlon. If you would be so kind, I would very much like to ask you and your shipmates some questions concerning the recent voyage of the *Matilda Briggs*."

The huge man considered a moment, then bade Winkler and Thomas to join us near the fire. He told the rest of the company to "shove off," which they promptly did.

With gentle prodding from Holmes, he related his personal history and the account of the voyage from departure until the night of the crew's celebration. It was alike in every detail to Sampson's account. Owing to his predilection for strong drink, his memories of that particular evening were somewhat hazy.

"There's not much I 'member, gentlemen, except that upon 'wakin' I felt that I'd been done over with a capstan bar, and right smartly, too."

"And none of you was aware of any commotion on deck during the night? Thomas, Winkler?"

They all answered negatively.

"When were you aware of something strange on board?"

"When we first caught sight of Jones sneaking food aft," replied Winkler. "Then, of course, we saw the rat itself—"

Here Winkler was rebuked by Scanlon and told to hush. Holmes filled in the narrative related by Sampson, however, and the three men grew confident. All had seen the head of the beast; all swore it was of a rat of fearsome size.

" .... and alike in every detail to a ship rat," said Scanlon.

"You have mentioned that Jones took food into the hold where the monster was kept. What did the bundle look like?"

"I can't tell you, sir," replied Winkler, "for they were always covered."

"They?"

"Yes, there were always two, both of them covered with cotton cloth. One was thrice the size of the other."

"That is interesting. What was your impression of the mate Jones?"

"A shirker, sir," he replied. "A real laggard, even for an officer."

"How about Reverend Ripley—did you gain any lasting impressions of him?"

"Now there's a strange one. Didn't seem to me he was much of a parson. Winkler here overheard him rip out a terrible cursin' one day below the decks, didn't you, Wink? Cursed the Captain terrible he did!"

Holmes' face sharpened. "Isn't it odd for a passenger to behave this way towards a ship's captain?"

"Of course, sir! But then, there were many strange things on the *Briggs* this last one out, weren't there boys?"

There was an agreement and a brief chuckle as the men pulled at their mugs.

"What does Ripley look like?" asked Holmes.

"A blondish, pale fellow—an indoors man if you know what I mean. And yet ..."

"And yet what?" I asked.

"O, I don't reckon it's of any account—"

"Pray tell me Mr. Scanlon: even the smallest details are of great account."

"I was about to say that frail and retiring as he was, he could be quick and agile on deck when the mood struck. Most often, it was in the form of leaping up to the quarterdeck to watch the petrels."

"He was fond of them?"

"Quite," interjected Thomas. "But he was most keen on the wee creatures, sir."

"The *wee creatures*?" Lestrade said in amazement. "What the devil are wee creatures?"

"Oh sir, the wee creatures that swim about everywhere. Sometimes in the tropics, they glow like a peat fire—practically read a gazette from the light they give off—"

"I believe, Lestrade, Thomas is referring to various plankton: minute larvae, crustaciae and algae that breed and flourish on the surface of the tropical oceans and prey upon each other."

"That's it, sir: them's the wee creatures. The Reverend Ripley busied himself by haulin' them aboard with a net he fashioned from cheesecloth and battens. On a calm day, we could see him at the taffrail, trailing the net aft like a ship's log. Queerest thing we'd seen in ages ..."

"My dear Thomas—that piece of information is indeed singular—and most welcome. In its own way, it throws considerable light upon the case. Tell me if you can, any of you, what did the Reverend Ripley do with the net and its contents after he hauled it on deck?"

"Oh that's easy, sir—that's the queerest part of all. He would sit on the hatch cover Indian-fashion and dump the net onto the boards. Then he'd watch and poke, and poke and watch as the wee creatures slithered and scratched over each other. All the while, he'd be picking out the choice ones and stuffing them into jars and bottles, which he'd carry down below."

"Aye, gentlemen," continued Scanlon, "and there was more than one of us thought the Reverend must be ailing—calling upon Weiss the cook to brew up his special chowder."

They laughed heartily—and Holmes almost grinned.

Lestrade grew impatient.

"Enough storytelling. We must find Ripley and his confederates. A thorough search of these neighborhoods will be undertaken immediately. All roads and railway stations will be closely watched. In the meantime, I assume that you will offer us every assistance possible in the way of information."

"They've already been most helpful," remarked Holmes, rising. "Especially concerning Ripley's pastime with marine fauna. We are looking for three men, together or separate; a nondescript white man, his valet—a Malay named Wangi, and a seafarer named Jones, who is of average stature and appearance. It would seem then, that the most visible is the Malay. I am familiar with several parts of London where such a man might hide, Lestrade, and will be happy to render assistance in that regard. However, there are two major questions still untouched: the whereabouts of the monster rat and the motive behind the multiple murders. Can any of you offer even a partial explanation?"

The three sailors replied in the negative. The only explanation that had occurred to them was that the rat was a fiend, an instrument of the Devil, and had returned to Hell as mysteriously as it had come.

5

THE HUNTER OR THE HUNTED?

In one of his customary fits of energy, Holmes left the inn directly the interview with the sailors was concluded, leaving us baffled and without the slightest idea of where to go next. Grumbling slightly, Lestrade paid the waiter and summoned a cab. At police headquarters we parted company; I went to my club where I spent a restive afternoon. Returning to our lodgings just before supper time, I heard the sobbing of a woman as I ascended the stairs.

Having prudently knocked, I was immediately shown to a seat beside a middle-aged woman, whose face was all but obscured by the lace handkerchief she held to it.

"John Watson, this is Miss Beryl Haskins, who has been kind enough to drop round for tea and a chat. There, there, Miss Haskins, your tale convinces me more than ever that the responsibility was not, could not have been yours ..."

"You have no idea, Mr. Holmes," she sniffed, "how painful it has been to return home alone—"

"I can well imagine."

"The Allistairs have been so kind, so gracious through it all. Lord knows how much they're suffering. I expected to be turned out—"

"Pshaw! Her Ladyship has spoken most highly of you. You are uppermost in their affections. Now Miss Haskins, I agree with them: a holiday is what you want. Do take the evening train to Brighton. I assure you we'll do our best to resolve this affair as quickly as possible. Now here's your cab just pulled up. Off you go now, and have a pleasant rest. *Au revoir.*"

The lady managed a weak handshake and apology to me and followed Holmes to the door. He returned to his armchair and, without waiting for my obvious questions, launched at once into the explanation.

"As you've no doubt surmised, Miss Haskins is in the employ of Lord Allistair. She has been in his service since 1875 when his daughter Alice was born. The two have been inseparable ever since: Miss Haskins was the little girl's governess and, more recently, had assumed the role of her travelling companion. She was accompanying Alice Allistair on her summer holiday when the girl was abducted. She is now departing for a much-needed rest for she has been, as you have seen, beside herself with remorse."

"If I recall the newspaper accounts, was not the companion—Miss Haskins—detained on a false errand whilst the girl was kidnapped?"

"That is correct: it happened, you'll remember, in a crowded Bombay market place. The girl was forced into a palanquin by two natives and borne off into the throng. No one has seen or heard of her in the ten weeks since ..."

"That's a long time to keep a hostage ..."

"It is. In fact, it is what worries me night and day. The outlook for her well-being is not bright, I'm afraid."

"But in once sense the great time lapse may be a good sign; perhaps it has taken the abductors this long to get her back into England. If this be true, then she is surely alive, since no one would waste so much time on a corpse."

"Excellent Watson! I must say the same thought has occurred to me. However, it's best not to be too optimistic. Remember; pessimists are surprised as often as optimists, but always pleasantly."

"After leaving the two of you at the *Binnacle*, I set off on a number of jaunts, one of which was a call at the Allistair residence in the Bayswater Road. Miss Haskins was not in when I called, so I requested the brief visit that just took place.

"I suppose you think it strange that I should continue on the Allistair case, devoid of evidence as it is, when we have our hands full with the present business—"

"You yourself said it promises to be the most difficult and diabolical one we've handled in quite a while."

"I've no doubt of it. This morning's events bear that out, surely. Yet the Allistair tragedy has its interesting aspects too. You know me well enough to realise that I generally have sound reasons for what I undertake, and pursuing two lines of inquiry at once may not be as outlandish as it sounds."

"Have you any theories?"

"Actually, yes. But they are too embryonic at present to warrant discussion. Ah–here's Mrs. Hudson with out supper. Despite our hearty lunch, I'm famished. Would you see to the door while I fetch a bottle?"

After our meal, Holmes snuggled into the divan cushions and put a match to the reeking bowl of his clay pipe.

"You see Watson, as conspicuous as the valet Wangi is, certainly the giant rat, if indeed it is flesh and blood, is extraordinarily visible."

"Not to say horrifying," I added.

"I concur. The mere thought of the monster scurrying through alleyways and over rooftops is appalling. And yet there's been no outcry–obviously no one has seen it. It is not aboard the Briggs, that much is certain. Has it been destroyed–killed and dumped into the Thames? Or is it caged in some cellar lair, ready to be unleashed upon selected victims, or upon the populace at large?"

"The thought alone gives me chills. When I think of the remains of the Captain–"

"Yes, it is grisly business. But where is the rat? Whether destroyed or taken away, there is the very real problem of getting the animal off the ship unnoticed–no mean task, for we are already familiar with the method of getting it aboard."

"In my opinion, Holmes, the rat hasn't been destroyed. All events indicate that Ripley values the beast highly, for whatever nefarious purpose. Otherwise why would he go to the great pains of smuggling it aboard the Briggs and caring for it throughout an eight-week voyage?"

"An excellent point. Yet he doesn't value it for circus purposes– that is to say for exposition, since if this were true, he would be anxious to attract publicity."

"Perhaps the animal has an innate value, perhaps for its fur."

"If the animal is a rat, Watson, I cannot see any value attached to it. Of course, it most probably is not a true rat. The largest rodent known is the Capabyra, a spaniel-sized aquatic animal that lives in Central and South America. It may be that the animal is heretofore unknown but in any event, it is capable of killing a man and–alive or dead–is no doubt within twenty miles of Blackwall Reach. If the monster is as fearsome and unforgettable as our witnesses have described, it should be difficult to keep concealed. It is my plan to continue the chase tomorrow. To that end, I dispatched two wires today. The answers that will arrive in the morning should be of value. No, Watson, I'll skip my whiskey and soda tonight and go directly to bed. Goodnight."

Next morning I was first to arise and before Holmes had descended into the parlour I had read the following telegrams which Mrs. Hudson brought up:

TRAIL ENDS AT BALFOUR LANE AND WHITE-CHAPEL ROAD–

–GREGSON

The above had been posted in London. The other was from Exeter and read:

YOU ARE CORRECT: NO ABSOLUTE PROOF
–MASON-JONES

Holmes was most interested in the first wire, and promptly set up his large Ordnance Survey map of London and Environs on his marble-topped table, and spent the first half of the morning poring over it. Although he was not a man to lose patience easily, I could tell by occasional sighs and mutterings that the problem was complex, even for his keen faculties. I left him alone.

"I shall stop by and call on Mrs. Redding, Holmes, and see how she is recuperating. I'll drop by Mortimer's on my return to pick up my pipe. Do you want anything?"

"Yes, Watson. If you would be so kind, get me four ounces of navy-cut–oh, and while you're at it, if you've the time, stop by the British Railways offices–the one in Oxford Street is closest–and fetch me complete timetables for Bombay and lines eastwards–also a list of depots, offices, and their addresses, will you? When you return, I should be most grateful if you would accompany me to the East End again if time allows."

I performed the errands. Mrs. Redding was recovering nicely from her bout of influenza. I bought the tobacco for Holmes and complimented Mortimer on my new pipe stem. I appeared at our quarters shortly before lunchtime, my arms overbrimming with pamphlets, maps, schedules, and office listings. These Holmes took eagerly, and spent another half hour poring over them, scribbling notes all the while. Finally, he took a blank notesheet and printed a lengthy telegram, which began "HAVE YOU OR YOUR STAFF ANY RECOLLECTION ..."

We left the flat, took our lunch at Marcinni's, and proceeded to Whitechapel Road. The intersection of that street and Balfour Lane was nondescript save for its general dinginess and proximity to the river. As there was no policeman or inspector there to meet us (I half expected there would be), we were left on our own, and Holmes glanced round himself and ambled vaguely about like a dejected urchin. I followed silently, peering into shop windows and through tavern doorways. We proceeded up Balfour Lane, thence in the other direction. We repeated this process in Whitechapel Road. At the end of forty minutes, Holmes leaned against a lamp post, assumed a jaunty air, and asked me if I had any conjectures as to why the trail of Ripley ended at that particular intersection.

"How indeed do we know it does?" I asked.

"Because upon my suggestion Lestrade has employed the rather commendable talents of two of Scotland Yard's most able sleuths."

"You mean MacDonald and Grimes?"

"Not exactly," Holmes chuckled. "I am speaking of Nip and Tuck, who have between them the most successful record in the entire organisation."

"Who?"

"Nip and Tuck are bloodhounds, Watson—the finest I've yet seen. I have no doubt they could give even Toby a run for his money."

I, of course, recalled Toby with fondness, the gentle mongrel (now deceased) belonging to Mr. Sherman, the Lambeth taxidermist. It was Toby's sharp nose that aided us in the capture of Jonathan Small, the peg-legged jewel thief.

"You see, shortly after we disembarked from the *Briggs*, Lestrade sent for the dogs; they cast Ripley's scent from his bedclothes. Nip and Tuck made a beeline from the quayside to this intersection, whereupon they stopped dumbfounded. Now Watson, what became of our Reverend Ripley? Did he vanish into thin air—dematerialise like a ghost? What is the answer?"

"The answer is simple: he boarded a cab."

"Ah! That is certainly possible. But why here, instead of at the quayside which the cabs frequent?"

"He no doubt had some business nearby—"

"Yes, Watson! Now it seems we are getting to it. What sort of business?"

"Let me see," I murmured, running my eyes over the various shop fronts and businesses, "If it was not the visiting of a friend—"

"Your point is well-taken: it is conceivable that Ripley could have been on a personal visit. If this is the case, our conjectures are difficult. However, let us for argument's sake assume it was a business errand. Do any of the shops catch your fancy?"

"The grocer's to buy food—no, no ... the *Wheatsheaf* public house— no, that would indicate a private meeting—here's one Holmes, the haberdashery. Perhaps he would want a change of clothing to aid his escape ..."

Holmes was growing impatient.

"Really, Watson, every business place can suggest a possibility. The trick is to select that establishment which presents the most likely possibility—or series of possibilities—and which will explain the greatest proportion of events. You have stated that Ripley boarded a cab. That is not a bad guess. However, we can see that there is no cab-stand nearby. Furthermore, the intersection is not a lively one; it would be a singular occurrence if a cab happened along just when Ripley would have need of one."

In a flash, it came to me.

"The livery!"

"Excellent!" beamed my companion. "Yes, I think that's where we should begin anyway."

Ballantine's Livery and Smith Shop was a few steps north in Balfour Lane. Underneath the large sign was printed: "Horses, Carriages and Wagons to let—Daily or Weekly Rates." We entered the establishment through a small doorway which led into a narrow hallway, the walls of which were lined with harnesses and horse collars. We could hear the whoosh of blacksmith's bellows, and occasionally the ringing of the hammer. Presently the hallway opened onto a large building set back from the street. Here were housed the stables, wagon yard and the smithy forge. A wiry man with knotted arms toiled at the forge, while further back, in the shadows, horses of every description stamped and switched their tails contentedly. Upon hearing the nature of Holmes' inquiry, the smith laid his hammer aside and led us back towards the street to where a tiny, cluttered desk stood. From a drawer in the desk he extracted a leather purse, pulled loose the drawstring, and poured a pile of gold coins into his calloused palm.

"I don't reckon what place they be from," said the smithy, "seeing the funny figures and scribbles on them—but I know enough about metals to recognise gold when I sees it."

"From India, or perhaps Ceylon," mused Holmes as he peered into the blacksmith's palm. "Is it customary for you to demand such a large deposit for your equipment?"

"He weren't renting—he were buying, sir. Bought my stoutest wagon, and a horse to match."

"Did he leave his name?"

"Oh no, sir, I didn't think to ask it. He paid for the rig in gold and was off."

"What time was that?"

"The day before yesterday. It was just before tea—about four. No, I don't have the name, gentlemen. As for his appearance, he looked a gentleman, with a thinnish nose and a fancy bearing. All in all, I would call him an ordinary gentleman."

"Was there anyone with him?"

"No sir, he was alone."

"Was there anything unique about the wagon?"

"Not really. It was similar to the one remaining at the back. A heavy dray wagon with enclosed top and sides, and a bolted doorway in the rear."

We had been returning to the rear building, and now stood near the remaining wagon, which Holmes examined with much interest.

"The wheels—are the rims of similar thickness, with the same type iron treads?"

"To my mem'ry, sir, they're twins in every respect. I bought the both of 'em from a retired stonemason in Hammersmith. He used them for hauling his tools and rock slabs—they're built like a fortress, as you can see ..."

"Lestrade and his crew would do well to have a look at this, Watson. What of the horse—anything special?"

"Twelve-year-old gelding, dappled. He's quite heavy—a perfect match for the wagon I say—I'll wager he's some shire blood in him for the height and weight he carries."

"Thank you, that is most helpful. Now Watson, let us borrow our noble defenders of justice, Nip and Tuck, if we may, and put them through their paces again.

"While we cannot be absolutely sure it was Ripley who bought the horse and wagon," pursued Holmes as we made our way towards the quay for the second time in two days, "we can be reasonably certain. That isn't bad for the present, and Lestrade and his men could spend their time far more foolishly than in looking for the large dapple horse pulling the mate to the mason's wagon."

"Do you intend to have the hounds follow the wagon?"

"If they could, they would be unlike any hounds in history. To cast a scent from a stable is impossible—but it seems more than likely that Ripley left the *Briggs* more than once—let us see if we can't find another trail."

It was a twelve-minute walk back to the Quay. The rain had stopped for some time, and the fog lifted enough to enable one to look out across the reach. There the tall ships rode. Some of them were being pushed and pulled about by squat steam tugs belching clouds of oily smoke. Some were moored at the quayside, and derricks and "donkey" steam engines were busily engaged in the transferring of cargo. The *Matilda Briggs* looked ordinary enough from that distance, except for her deserted appearance. Small groups of onlookers had gathered on the docks, and occasionally one would point and gesticulate in the direction of the silent ship. Word of the murder had spread.

After walking toward the customs house we spied Gregson with two gigantic dogs on long leads. It was my guess they weighed a hundredweight apiece.

"Hello, Mr. Holmes, Dr. Watson. It seems the weather is a bit brighter, eh? Still, finding another trail shall be difficult, I warn you, even for these two beauties, after all the rain we've had."

"Let's try our best, Gregson. I've a message for you first, however, concerning the first trail you discovered. Have you your notebook?"

Holmes related our recent visit to Ballantine's Livery, and furnished him with enough detailed description to set the detective fairly hopping with anticipation.

"If you don't mind, gentlemen, I'd much rather be pursuing this other line of investigation. Indeed, it is my duty. You may use Nip and Tuck here till you heart's content. Personally I believe it's useless. I'll send a man round to your flat this evening if convenient. They're no problem, I assure you. But mind, don't feed them the slightest morsel; they work best hungry and aren't worth a farthing with the taste of food in their mouths. Good day."

He dashed off, brimming with excitement.

"Ah, Watson, we are free to use our canine friends here at our leisure. I had hoped our news would send him off. A nice fellow Gregson, and competent, but the police are more often than not a hindrance to me. They are far better serving as messenger boys and lookouts. I wish them every success in tracking down the wagon. Now then, you take Nip—or is it Tuck?—oh, well, we'll handle one apiece. Have no fear, man, for despite their size, they're as placid as sheep, as you can see."

I took one of the sad-faced creatures and petted its domed head. It responded immediately by nuzzling and licking my hand, and whining softly.

"Quite right, Holmes, he's as gentle as a lamb. How then, do they attack criminals?"

"Ha! You are as ignorant as most of the public on that score, I'm afraid. Let us walk these two crime-fighters about a bit and see if we can't find another scent. In the meantime, I'll tell you something about them."

We cast the scent again, from the scrap of bedclothes that Gregson had provided us. The dogs whined eagerly and began trailing, nose to the ground, almost pulling me off my feet.

"The breed's ancestor, the St. Hubert's Hound, originated in the Abbeys of France, a descendant of the hunting dogs used since the time of Charlemagne. The name we English have bestowed, *Blood*hound, refers not to the animal's lust for blood, nor its penchant for following blood spoor, but rather—whoa! I say!"

Holmes and I spent the next several minutes attempting to persuade the dogs to pursue a course other than the one they intended.

"This is the trail Gregson found. If we find nothing else, we'll come back—where was I—oh yes, well, the name *Blood*hound is used in the sense that the phrase blood horse, or blooded horse is used, that is, to indicate strict bloodlines and long lineage—for the strain has always been much prized ..."

"Most interesting," I answered, fighting the leash.

"We have here a beast with the keenest nose in the entire animal kingdom, and the only animal, the only animal save man, Watson, whose testimony is considered admissible evidence in a court of law!"

"You don't say!"

"Quite so, and—hullo, what's up?"

The dogs stopped their forward motion and were confusedly turning round in right circles, whining shrilly and flagging their tails.

"Ah! What have we here, fellows? Eh? What's up? Have you found something, eh?"

After observing this behaviour for a few minutes I asked Holmes if it meant they had found a scent.

"Found and lost it, Watson," said he. "Do you observe anything remarkable about this portion of the quay? How does it differ from other parts of the area?"

"Not in many respects," I answered, looking about. "It does seem, though, that there is a gradual sloping to the water's edge here, instead of a sheer drop of several feet."

"Yes! Yes, Watson, go on—anything else?"

"No, I confess I cannot discover another distinguishing characteristic."

"Oh really? I can see something from here that is most remarkable. Do you see that smudge of greenish-brown substance yonder? There is something we should both be interested in."

I spotted the smudge some ten paces away, and went over to look closely.

"Axle grease!" I exclaimed. "But what of it? Surely there are quite a few dray carts running up and down this quay–"

"Yes, running up and down this quay no doubt. But *across* it?"

"I'm afraid that's quite impossible," I laughed. "You can see for yourself there's the water on one side, and the iron fence on the other."

As anyone familiar with the London Docks well knows, they are surrounded by high iron fences. The only gates are placed adjacent to the customs house. Thus, any comings and goings of either goods or persons may be strictly regulated by the officials.

"What you say is true. But notice the smudge itself. It was caused certainly by excess grease dripping off the front axle of some vehicle, then the rear wheel of the same vehicle running over the patch of grease and causing it to smudge."

"That appears to be the case," I assented.

"But we can both see that the smudge was elongated in such a way as to show definitely that the vehicle was bound in a direction *perpendicular* to the general flow of traffic."

"By George, Holmes, you are correct! That means the cart has been dumped into the river–we should have it dragged for at once!"

"Not so fast, Watson. We should examine all the possibilities."

"Yet you yourself have often stated that when the other possibilities are exhausted whatever remains, however improbable, must be the truth. I see no way in which a wheeled vehicle could clear the fence over there, unless it sprouted wings."

"Let us make certain," he cautioned, and left me with the hounds whilst he approached the fence twenty yards away. He inspected it carefully for a moment. Then, with a mischievous glance in my direction, he fetched it a powerful kick. To my utter amazement, an entire section of the wrought iron, perhaps eight feet square, fell away and crashed to the pavement with a tremendous clanging. For one of those extremely rare moments during my long association with him, Sherlock Holmes lost himself in laughter. Chagrined, I looked away and pretended to busy myself with the dogs. They, however, gave me the look of cold aloofness which told me I was a fool.

"The railings were filed through–that is obvious," remarked Holmes when I joined him at the fence. "This could be done in silence. Then the section was temporarily lifted away to allow a vehicle to enter, take on or leave its cargo, then leave by the same gap in the fence. The section was, as we have seen, then replaced. To passersby it was unnoticeable. A fairly remarkable feat."

"Even more remarkable when one considers it's impossible," I said. "To file through this fence must have taken well over an hour. Why weren't they discovered in this time?"

"A good point. But think a minute. This occurred the night before last. That night, you and I were not more than a mile from this very spot—"

"Ah yes, the *fire*! Certainly it was an excellent cover for them. They could have put on a circus at the quayside and no one would have noticed—"

"Right you are, Watson."

"No doubt the vehicle was the wagon that Ripley purchased from Ballantines."

"We can determine that easily enough in two ways. One, by comparing wheel tracks and axle length with the other remaining wagon that the smithy showed us. Secondly, we can take a bit of the smudged axle grease and compare it with the grease that is used at Ballantines. The two checks should give us a definite answer, which I am confident will be the same one you offered. This spot was selected probably because of the feature you noticed: the wagon could be backed down to the water's edge. Here, let us try something."

He took one of the hounds from me and led the animal down to where the first trail had ended. The dog again wheeled in tight circles, whining.

"Now Watson, bring your dog over here too. Now, lead him down to the water's edge, so."

We took the dogs to the very edge of the embankment. The next instant I was nearly knocked flat by the tremendous agitation of my leashed animal. As I whirled madly round like a top, spun by the leash as a boy pulls the top's string, I saw that Holmes, not as heavy as I, was having even more difficulty remaining upright. Finally, after much tugging and shouting, we managed to subdue the dogs somewhat. Still, they howled and gnashed their fangs; their eyes rolled upwards in their deep sockets, revealing the crescent of white underneath. They appeared both angry and terribly frightened, and pressed close to us, great ridges of fur rising along their backs.

Surprisingly, the dogs seemed eager to leave the spot, even pulling us swiftly behind them. However, the ridge of hackles along their backs remained, and also the deep growling in their chests.

"Seldom have I seen dogs so agitated," remarked Holmes a few minutes later. "Well, this seems to prove one thing, Watson: whatever the giant rat of Sumatra is, it is most certainly not a "puppet contrivance" as you once suspected. No indeed, my friend, it is a living, breathing beast, and one so fierce that its two-day-old scent is enough to send these two brave hounds into a frenzy!"

But he needn't have reminded me—I was aware of the beast's authenticity when I saw the gashes upon the Captain's throat.

"There remains only one more avenue of investigation with our canine friends, Watson. Let us see if we can't pick up another one of Ripley's trails, even though the police failed to do so."

We cast the scent time and time again, but without success. Finally, Holmes suggested that we go home to our lodgings and await the man who would return the dogs to Scotland Yard. We walked at a slow pace down the quay, past knots of onlookers staring wonderingly at the dark hull of the *Matilda Briggs*, past the customs house, and out through the tall iron gates. Holmes, in a pensive mood, declared he'd rather walk a mile or so than board a cab directly. So the four of us ambled on, the two *homo sapiens* apparently being led onward by two gigantic specimens of *canis familiaris*, the latter proceeding at a leisurely, sniffing pace.

Not far from the customs-house gates, we received a considerable surprise, for the dogs once again showed eagerness, flagging their tails and whining, and tugging at the leads.

"What have we here, my dear fellow? Could it be that Nip and Tuck have found something?"

It soon became apparent that they had indeed. They proceeded at first slowly, as if uncertain of a scent. However, after making steady progress for several hundred yards, they broke into a slow trot, and Holmes and I had difficulty keeping pace.

"We're off for the races it appears," said Holmes, gripping the leash with both hands, "let's see where it ends."

"This neighbourhood looks oddly familiar," I remarked.

Holmes nodded, and I noted that his face had become grim.

It was over before we even half-suspected it: the dogs crossed an alleyway, whirled about in a small dooryard, and crossed the street in a mad rush. We found ourselves standing under the swinging wooden sign, and staring with amazement at the huge brass pedestal topped with two iron spheres and the hooded compass. To our astonishment, we were back at the *Binnacle*.

"Well, well," mused our companion, and it seemed to me almost

an attempt at levity. However, his countenance certainly was anything but light. In fact, it was one of those rare moments when
Sherlock Holmes appeared lost. He stared keenly at the doorway to
the public house for some time, then glanced carefully all round us.
As the seconds ticked by, it became more and more apparent to me
that he had been taken completely off guard. Knowing the rarity of such
an occurrence, I became uneasy. I felt it necessary to break the silence.

"You were expecting the trail to lead elsewhere, were you not?"

"I must confess that I certainly was not expecting it to end here,"
he replied, with a flicker of amusement. "Surely you sense the irony,
the brashness, eh, Watson? Very few criminals would have the gall
of this Ripley ... very few—wouldn't you agree?"

Some fifteen minutes later we were packed into a four-wheeler
bound for Baker Street. Our friends Nip and Tuck (for which, to our
annoyance, we were obliged to pay half fare) were strewn between
our feet. Holmes, still not fully recovered from the surprise of our last
discovery, gazed out the carriage window.

"The cheek, Watson, the absolute *cheek*!"

"I don't quite follow you, Holmes."

"You don't follow me, but Ripley *has*," he snorted. "Don't you see?
He followed the three of us to the *Binnacle* yesterday. It is obvious
from the trail he left. Did you note how the dogs wheeled and paused
in the narrow doorway across the street from the pub? No doubt that
is where he ducked in to wait until we entered. So our missionary
friend is not jouncing over the countryside escaping in a wagon after
all, but here in London, dogging us ... which raises certain other
questions, which you've probably asked yourself."

"I have not been raising questions with myself, other than the most
obvious one, which is where did Ripley go after he left the *Binnacle*?"

"Into a cab, I'm almost certain. As you saw by the behaviour of the
dogs, he left no trail away from the pub. Therefore, he observed us
leaving the docks, followed us to the *Binnacle*, then departed by cab
after our luncheon was completed. But what is important is why he
followed us, not when or how. Are you familiar with Joshua
Hathaway's painting "Stag at Bay"? No? The painting depicts the
wounded stag making a stand against the yew hedge. The dogs are
closing in for the kill, yet half their number lie dead at the stag's feet.
I ask you, Watson, are we the hunters or the hunted? One thing is
sure: *the stag is not running*. Furthermore, there's the incredible
arrogance of Ripley ... the eagerness to battle wits with me ...
certainly that is an unmistakable hallmark—"

He seemed to drift into thought, and said nothing more until we were deposited inside our rooms. Mrs. Hudson brought up some knuckle bones, and the two giant hounds stretched in front of the fireplace, cracking the bones between their jaws whilst Holmes and I shared a pot of tea.

"Now let us reconsider the events *in toto* in the light of all we now know. The tale, incredible and implausible as it seems, does have patterns and a chronology that make sense, does it not? It is, quite simply stated, the smuggling of some sort of monster into London aboard a merchant vessel. Most of our observations flow *with* the current of this strange story–agreed?"

I nodded.

"Yet, there are three events which stand out as being grotesque– that appear, to continue my analogy, to be going *upstream* instead of down, do you agree?"

"There have been many strange occurrences in the past two days, but I'm not sure I can identify the errant ones," I replied.

"Then let me backtrack a little. The tale of John Sampson, while strange, has a certain logic to it. Likewise, the killing of Captain McGuinness, while horrific, is in one sense understandable."

"You mean because of the possibility that he wished to betray the pact, or wanted to escape?"

"Exactly. These can be considered downstream events in that they arise out of the basic plot, plan or whatever of Ripley and his confederates. But what of the fact that we were followed? Ah, that seems definitely in the upstream category, does it not? Yes, there is a counter-current running, and we must fathom it, or–"

"Or what?"

"Or we could be in a great deal of danger. I said from the outset that it was a dark and vile circle we were confronting. I say it again with even deeper respect. Now then, what of the other two upstream events? Another, I think, is the killing of Jenard. Why was Jenard killed and not any of the other crew–Sampson, for instance? If one of the crew was to be sacrificed for warning's sake, why pick a man as hale as Jenard, why not a little snip of a fellow like Winkler? And why not perform the deed on some dingy dockside, rather than Baker Street?"

"You said before that those who killed Jenard knew of you."

"Did I? Why yes, I recall it. Well, we seem almost to come full circle. Who sent Jenard in our direction, and why was he killed? What did he know that no one else does?"

There was a long pause.

"What is the third event?"

"The third event is the writing in candle smoke above Jenard's bunk. It is not only mysterious in its meaning, but by its very presence. What does its author wish to gain by it? Does he wish to throw us off the track, or onto—"

Here he paused, and soon the hint of a grin formed on his lips. Slowly, he reached upward and back with his left hand. I saw the grimy clay pipe in his hands as he filled it. Having seen this ritual countless times before, I realised he was no longer in our quarters, but perhaps slinking around the East End like a wharf cat. Since further conversation was useless, I spent the remainder of the evening with Tennyson.

6

DEPARTURE

Except for the release of John Sampson from Old Bailey, the next few days passed uneventfully. I busied myself with my practice and returned to Baker Street only to sleep, and then at odd hours. I seldom saw Holmes, and when I enquired into the progress on the case, received only a dismal grunt in reply. Assuming from these responses that all was not going well, I avoided him still further. Holmes could be distant and short-tempered when events frustrated him.

I noticed, however, that he was careful to bolt the door to our flat securely each night, and advised me to exercise caution whenever I left.

"Stick to the main thoroughfare whenever possible," said he, "and carry your pistol when you'll be out after dark."

I followed his advice, although with reluctance, for it dented my pride. But the recollection of the two mangled corpses was sufficient to keep me on the lookout.

On the fifth day my duties relented. My final appointment failed to arrive, and I found myself at Baker Street in early afternoon. I removed my coat and hung it on the tree. Holmes was standing in the bow window watching the leaves drift earthward in slow spirals. It was a bright, crisp autumn day and he seemed to be taking advantage of the clarity to scan the street in both directions. Behind him on the divan was the usual jackdaw's nest of papers including, from what I could gather from a quick glance, replies from various foreign offices of British Railways.

"Ah Watson! I see your last appointment was cancelled. I take it, then, that you are home for the day?"

"Holmes! How did you–"

"I'll tell you," he said mischievously, "only if you promise to accompany me to the Bayswater Road, to the residence of Lord and Lady Allistair."

"Certainly, I shall be glad to."

"Fine. Then let's set off. Shall we walk?"

"Now how did you guess that my last appointment had been cancelled?" I asked as we walked briskly across Portman Square.

"I didn't guess it. I inferred it. You are regular, almost Teutonic in your habits, Watson, especially your professional habits. I dare say that's why we get along so well, for I, as you well know, am the opposite. In any event, your professional life is well-regulated and organised to the core–"

"Yes, but my days differ widely. Sometimes I see twenty patients, sometimes four."

"Quite so. But always, Watson, always, you carefully write out your forthcoming appointments the night before in your pocket secretary. You sit in your chair with your right foot propped up on the coal scuttle–"

"Yes, that's true. I like to be organised for the next day."

"And always, you depart each morning with your secretary in your right breast pocket–your fountain pen placed inside it."

"How observant of you. Yes, I stick my pen inside to mark the place."

"You *return*, however, with your secretary in your left pocket, *sans plume.*"

"I suppose I do. After my last patient, I make final notes in my secretary, tear out the pages, and file them."

"But today, in addition to arriving home early, your pocket secretary and pen were in their "pre-work" positions, as I observed when you took off your coat. Ergo: your last appointment was cancelled. Now, see that forest of chimney stacks yonder? That, my dear fellow, is the house of the Allistairs. And two finer people you shall never meet. Come!"

Holmes' description was apt: the Allistair house at 13 Bayswater Road was indeed a forest of chimney stacks, and a sea of gables and cornices as well. The handsome red brick exterior was set off splendidly by an immaculate lawn and well-trimmed shrubbery. There was enough ivy about the house to provide a venerable feeling without seeming cluttered. I was impressed with its size as well as its beauty. The kidnappers were evidently well aware of the Allistair fortune.

"So you have remained in communication with the Allistairs. Have there been any developments?"

"Yes, as a matter of fact, and just about the time I expected, too. I must tell you at the outset, Watson: this won't be a pleasant call. In one sense, tremendous weight has been lifted from the Allistairs. In another sense, there is surely more pain to follow. I visited briefly with them this morning, and promised I'd return this evening with you. You can be of great assistance to all of us. Read this."

He handed me a wire which read: COME IMMEDIATELY–TERMS HAVE BEEN OFFERED.

"This is the first communication from the abductors to Lord and Lady Allistair?"

"Yes. I suppose one could take it as a cause for celebration but I must tell you privately, Watson, I fear for the girl. But let us go up, and for God's sake, be of good cheer."

We were shown through the front door by the butler, who, from his tense manner and sombre expression, evidently shared his master's distress.

Lord and Lady Allistair were seated on either side of a gigantic fireplace of carved stone. The high Georgian windows poured sunshine into the room, in which was displayed Her Ladyship's exceptional collection of rare china and porcelain. The sunlight on these objects lent a gleaming, cheerful atmosphere to the setting, but one glance at the couple was sufficient to convey the sense of anxiety that had overcome them.

Lord Allistair's appearance reflected his reputation. Tall, slender, around sixty years of age, he stood to receive us immaculately groomed and dressed despite the obvious emotional upheaval he was experiencing. His keen features were handsomely set off by a trim grey moustache and close-cropped hair. Her Ladyship remained seated, and one could only have admiration for her composure and cordiality at so trying an occasion. Only a few moments in their presence convinced me of their noble character and strong spirit.

A brief recollection of Lord Allistair's stunning career in government which, as the reader no doubt knows, was marked by compassion for the unfortunate, unrelenting pursuit of the corrupt, and zeal for progressive reform in all areas, only served to amplify my initial impressions of the man. The endowments, charities, and public works of his wife also came vividly to mind. As I took in the surroundings of the mansion, the thought struck me more than once that here indeed was a family of wealth and position that deserved every bit of it.

I was introduced as a trusted confidant, and was welcomed with a genuine warmth. Holmes and I seated ourselves on a luxurious sofa, which in turn was placed on an immense Persian carpet. The sunlight brought out the brilliant cobalt blue and deep burgundy red of its design and I couldn't help thinking that all in all, the room's size and appointments made our meagre Baker Street lodgings seem drab indeed.

"Gentlemen," began Lord Allistair as he leaned tensely forward over the coffee table, "as you know, this is the first communication we have received regarding our daughter's whereabouts or ..." he faltered slightly, "her well being."

He handed Holmes a sheet of ordinary paper. On it were two messages. The first, as is common with messages in which anonymity is essential, was constructed by the pasting of words and letters upon the sheet. The other message, however, was written in delicate long-hand in ink.

"Lady Allistair and I are certain that the bottom message was written by our daughter. It is her hand, sure enough, although it shows obvious strain and nervousness. Since the letter was postmarked yesterday morning, we know that she is alive, at least," said Lord Allistair.

"While we certainly share your optimism, sir," remarked Holmes, "we must not preclude the possibility, however unpleasant, that the handwriting was done some time ago, and merely posted yesterday."

The possibility smote the couple like a hammer blow, bringing an onslaught of sobbing from Lady Allistair.

Annoyed at Holmes' callous approach, I did my best to comfort them.

"I'm sorry," he said, "but it is a possibility that we must face, however remote. Here, Watson, what do you make of it?"

He handed me the note. The first message was short, clear and ominous: "£100,000 to be delivered in small bank notes from Strathcombe for the return of your daughter. Harm shall befall her if you summon help or fail. Further instruction await you there."

"Strathcombe is the country seat of Lord and Lady Allistair," Holmes informed me. "Evidently, the criminals feel safer in their plan by operating outside the city. The estate is in Shropshire, to the south and west of Shrewsbury, hard by the Welsh border. It is surrounded by nothing save craggy hills and great expanses of the Clun Forest. It is these rugged and desolate surroundings, perhaps, more than anything else, that have led the kidnappers to choose the place."

"Strathcombe was originally built as a hunting lodge, and is still used for that purpose," continued Lord Allistair. "It is remarkable for containing the only wild boar in the British Isles. In the seventies, a few choice specimens were imported from the Black Forest by Prince Albert. Since then they've bred and flourished, although still confined to the single wooded valley in which Strathcombe lies. But we don't frequent the place much, since we prefer the city. It is, as Mr. Holmes has stated, quite isolated, the nearest village being almost five miles distant."

I nodded and read the second message which was written by the young lady. It was simple and heart-rending: "Dearest Mother and Father, for the love of God, help me! I am unharmed physically, but can maintain my sanity scarcely another fortnight. Please do as you are instructed if you wish to see me again. Your loving daughter, Alice."

"The monsters!"

"Quite so. Knowing how you would react to this horror, Watson, and also knowing your sense of duty and your courage, I have brought you with me this afternoon in the hope, nay in the expectation, that you would render assistance."

"Of course I shall, Holmes, and I appreciate your trust and confidence. Lord Allistair, rest assured that I will wholeheartedly give any service that I can, small as it may be."

"We thank you, sir," said Lady Allistair, "Mr. Holmes has spoken most highly of you, and we can see he is a good judge of character." Flushing slightly, I waved off these compliments as best I could and awaited further instructions from my companion.

"Your practice appears to be flourishing of late, Watson—is it possible for you to leave London for a few days?"

I nodded.

"Splendid. Then you can be of great service to this distinguished couple by accompanying them to Strathcombe tomorrow morning. Your presence will be beneficial in two ways. First, you will, by your engaging personality and indomitable spirit, be a source of companionship and comfort. Secondly, and more important, you will serve as a chronicler of events to me and as personal bodyguard to His Lordship and Her Ladyship as well."

"Then you will not go?" I asked.

"I'm afraid not. As you know, there is another business afoot in London that requires my immediate energies; hence the need for your services. However, I shall be joining you all as soon as possible, perhaps in a few days, and certainly no later than a week. Is this agreeable to all? Excellent. Now, Watson, we shall return home where I will go over in detail with you your duties as intelligence gatherer and protector."

We rose from the sofa and made our way back to the hall. Holmes paused, however, at the antique French secretary which stood near the doorway. He glanced keenly at a pair of framed portraits that stood upon it. Each was mounted in an oval cardboard. One was the face of a beautiful young lady; the other showed a young man in full military dress.

"This is your daughter I presume," said Holmes.

The couple replied in the affirmative in voices scarcely audible.

"And this young man is your son? Yes, I see he is. As is so often the case with sons, he looks like his mother ..."

"Yes, that's young Peter," said Her Ladyship, smiling. "This is his third year at Sandhurst—"

"Ah, a military man, eh? So he's decided not to enter politics. I seem to remember reading about your son in the newspapers last year ... didn't he go to Eton?"

"Harrow actually."

"Of course, I remember now, and a preparatory school, in the North?"

"That's correct, the Malton School in Yorkshire—you've a good memory, Mr. Holmes."

"But mainly for unimportant things, it seems. Well, I hope to meet your son one day, and I'm confident we'll be seeing your daughter before long. Good day, Lady Allistair, Lord Allistair. I shall see you all off at the train station tomorrow. Adieu."

We walked back to our quarters. I noticed a keen smile on Holmes' face.

"Another piece of the puzzle seems to have fallen into place, Watson. It grows clearer by the moment."

If this were the case, it was indeed news to me. But, immersed as I was in my new role, I swept the "puzzles" from my brain. I had enough to prepare myself for, and not much time.

"Let's get down to the maps and instructions," I said, and quickened my pace.

The remainder of the evening and a good part of the night was spent in our chambers, where Holmes, with a survey map of the country around Strathcombe spread between us, explained precisely what I should be aware of, and where I was to keep close lookout. He had also obtained from Lord Allistair a large-scale map of Strathcombe itself, which showed the floor-plan of the house, and the surrounding gardens, grounds and outbuildings as well.

"As you can see, the house is not large, being of some fourteen rooms. It was, as we've been told, built as a shooting lodge rather than as a mansion. It dates from the time of Henry VII, although somewhat altered in later centuries, and is in remarkably good repair considering its age and infrequency of use. Perhaps the good condition of the house is due in part to its smallish size. In contrast to the house, though, the grounds are considerable, encompassing some 900 acres of meadow, woods and marsh. Furthermore, because of its history as a shooting lodge, the grounds are riddled with outbuildings. There is a stable house with stalls and loose boxes, a kennel with runs and huts, and gamekeeper's cottage, and the ruins of a mews, long since abandoned. The reason I pay close attention to all of this, Watson, is because I fear the kidnappers have chosen their site well. It is rugged, inaccessible, unpopulated, and possesses myriad hiding places and vantage points. It is no fool's errand you have volunteered for, my good fellow. The way is fraught with uncertainty and danger. You must be armed at all times and take no chances. Furthermore, you should communicate with me by telegraph daily. Your failure to do so will cause me to call out the militia, do you understand?"

"Perfectly. Bye the bye, considering your feelings on the 'other problem' here in London, I might give you the same advice."

"It would be well-taken, I assure you. Now the required amount of cash will be conveyed to Strathcombe in a strongbox which you will guard. In the event that the 'further instructions' come fast upon your arrival, it would be best not to try and contact me, as it would arouse suspicion. You remember from the note that Lord Allistair was *not* to seek help."

"Certainly. How then, will my presence be explained?"

"Quite simple: you are a distant cousin of Lady Allistair's, and you are joining them for a stay in the country. I doubt the criminals will see a connection, but if they do, you had best be prepared for the worst. Also, there is something else you should know: none of the household staff at Strathcombe knows the real purpose of the

Allistairs' country visit. For safety's sake, this is to be kept secret as long as possible."

"I understand."

"Furthermore, considering the emotional state of Lord and Lady Allistair, I need hardly mention that the dreadful business surrounding the *Matilda Briggs*–"

"You needn't fret about that–the tale of the giant rat of Sumatra shall stay locked in my bosom."

"Excellent."

I rose early the following morning and packed my grip. Extra items included a Webley-Smith revolver and box of cartridges, field glasses, and Holmes' split-bamboo fly rod, which he was gracious enough to loan me.

"I doubt if you'll have time to put it to use, but it makes your appearance more legitimate," he commented over the breakfast muffins, "and pray, don't forget the maps–you'll want to familiarise yourself with the surroundings as soon as possible. We'd best be off; the train to Shrewsbury departs within the hour."

Paddington Station was crowded; we trundled about for what seemed an age before we caught sight of the Allistairs boarding the second to last railway carriage.

"If they've followed my instructions, they have booked the entire compartment. This will ensure comfort, safety, and privacy. However, you should carry your pistol on your person, not in your luggage."

I did as he bade and clamboured aboard. Finding the compartment, I entered and was warmly received by my recent acquaintances. They appeared in better spirits. Whether it was the freshness of the morning, or perhaps the anticipation of the dreadful trial coming to a close, I cannot say, but they appeared almost cheerful, although the anxiety showed through occasionally. I pushed the carriage window down to bid Holmes goodbye.

"The very best of luck to all of you, including your daughter," cried Holmes as the train began to roll, "and mind, Watson, keep in touch daily, I'll be joining you when I'm able."

Then, it seemed to me very suddenly, he turned and plunged into the thickest part of the crowd and disappeared like a stone in water.

Almost immediately, I was aware of another man following him into the crowd. The glimpse lasted but an instant, due to our quickening speed, but he appeared intent, even grim, in his mission.

"Who might that be?" enquired Lord Allistair.

"I've no idea, but I don't like his manner I'm bound to say," I replied. "My friend has emphasised caution time and again—I only hope he heeds his own advice."

With this unexpected turn of events, the journey, of more than two hours, passed more slowly than it might have. My mind could not help dwelling upon the possibility that Holmes' life was imperiled. Accordingly, at the next stop, I disembarked and sent the first of my wires, albeit prematurely. It read, "Beware, you were followed this morning at Paddington."

Feeling slightly relieved, I passed the remainder of the trip in pleasant conversation with Lord Allistair and his lovely wife. The rocking of the carriage, and the soporific rumbling and clacking of the wheels soon caused Lady Allistair to doze, albeit fitfully, and Lord Allistair and I talked of Holmes' last exploits, and the assurance we both had that if anyone could set things right it was Sherlock Holmes. One thing he showed me, however, that returned some feelings of apprehension was a compact leather pouch. Upon opening it, I saw a sight which almost took my breath away: £100,000 in small and medium banknotes. I drew the compartment curtains and placed my loaded pistol on the seat beside me.

The remainder of the journey passed uneventfully, his Lordship reminiscing about his youth in the Cornish countryside, and his younger years in parliament; and I felt fortunate in having the opportunity to have become intimate with so illustrious a man. The country rolled by, and the meadows and pastures gradually gave way to dense forests and craggy hills. One saw fewer farms and villages, and less of civilisation in general.

"We are entering the valley of the Severn," explained Lord Allistair. "To the south, it is a sportsman's paradise. Clear lakes and deep woods abound there; the only open areas are rock-strewn meadows, and occasional clearings for farms and houses."

"The woods are very dense, are they not?"

"Ah, I can see you've never been to this part of England before, Dr. Watson. These are the finest forests in the land. They are primeval, and have been for centuries some of the favourite hunting grounds of English kings. They are mostly oak and beech. Some of the older trees, dating from the Middle Ages, are gigantic."

I was amazed to see trees with trunks the size of cottages, and limbs the size of trees. The woods had an eerie, fantastical quality; their size and grandeur defied belief—one expected them to be inhabited by goblins, witches and monsters.

Some minutes later, as the train eased to a stop, the faint clangour of the bell could be heard over the hissing of the steam and squeaking of brakes.

We gathered our things (most carefully, of course, the satchel containing the fortune in ransom money) and quit the compartment. I took the lead. I carried my grip and fly-pole with my left hand, my right hand casually thrust in my coat pocket clutching my revolver. While I didn't wish to cause the Allistairs any undue alarm, I knew that if the kidnappers wished to make an early escape with the money, the railway station, or nearby, was the logical place to lie in wait. However, the corridor was deserted, and we alighted on the platform without incident. Also, to my pleasant surprise, the only other disembarking passengers consisted of an elderly couple. Evidently then, we weren't followed from London.

We were promptly met by Brundage, the head of the household staff at Strathcombe. He was a middle-aged bald man with greyed temples and a dreamy, wistful expression. His meeting with the Allistairs was charged with emotion: there wasn't a dry eye amongst the three of them. I took this to be another good sign—the head servant was an old and trusted employee, and one with great attachment to the family. As he packed our luggage expertly in the landau, I glanced keenly about. The station platform was deserted save for several gossiping bumpkins whom I took to be farm labourers, and a lounging gypsy.

All in all, I was much heartened as we boarded the open coach and set off for Strathcombe, some eleven miles distant.

"We shall lunch at the *White Hart* in Rutlidge," called Lord Allistair to his servant as we set off.

Shrewsbury is a small but prosperous city, having a large business in tanneries, and is an outlet for the various minerals and timber taken from the countryside. We skirted a handsome park and rumbled through several narrow streets, each lined by the black-and-white timbered houses. Leaving the city, we caught a glimpse of the old abbey and castle, built in the eleventh century as a Saxon stronghold. Soon afterward, however, all traces of civilisation were left behind, and the road cut its way through more of the towering forests I had seen from the railway carriage.

The only break in this rugged and wild scenery was the hamlet of Rutlidge, which consisted only of a score or so of buildings, one of which was the charming country inn called the *White Hart.*

We had an excellent and hearty lunch of cold ham, creamed

potatoes, custard pie, and cider. Neither the innkeeper nor any of the guests, of whom there were several in the dining room, showed the slightest interest in us. Apparently, they did not even recognise the famous couple.

"We aren't well known hereabouts, except by reputation," explained Lady Allistair. "I doubt if there are a score of people round the countryside who could know us on sight. As we've told you before, we do not spend much time here, and when we do we keep pretty much to ourselves."

How ironic, thought I, that these kind, simple country folk go about their tasks blissfully unaware not only of the presence of one of England's foremost political figures, but of the ominous exchange that would possible take place within a matter of days.

"Get out!" I heard the innkeeper cry. He entered the dining room with a look of loathing on his coarse features. Looking beyond him, I saw a figure reluctantly slink down the dark hallway of the public house. As he swung open the door to leave, I saw it was a gypsy, whose earrings, slouch hat, and swarthy features were unmistakable. Furthermore, I noticed it was the same fellow who had been idling about on the railway platform. He ambled dejectedly out into the autumn sunshine.

"Sorry to trouble you," pursued the innkeeper as he passed our table, "but I fear I've lost all patience with that lout. He's been loitering about the place for two days."

"And you've never seen him before then?" I asked.

"Not that I can recall, sir, no. But they come and go, living off thievery and poaching. With their bad habits and ill manners, it's no surprise they're forced to keep moving. Oh, they're thick around these parts. They like the woods, for it enables them to hide from the law. There's plenty of game and fish, too, for them to live off of. Plenty of gypsy camps hereabouts, but I don't recall that shirker before, no sir."

The early afternoon sun was warm for an autumn day, and the four of us proceeded at a leisurely pace. The horse, who knew the way, kept at a slow trot, and Brundage soon forgot whip and rein. The autumn colors were just beginning to turn their rich reds and golds, and the aroma of damp leaves and fallen fruit was thick on the wind. The famous couple held hands together in the rear seat. It was obvious they were still deeply in love, and enjoyed showing affection to one another. To think that somewhere in the surrounding wilderness there crept villains who would stoop to an act so vile as the kidnap of their daughter filled me with rage and revulsion.

Soon we came out of the beech forest and ascended a long, gentle rise, the summit of which provided an excellent view of the entire countryside. Here there were few trees, owing to the great abundance of boulders and cliffs. As I looked back down towards the forest, I was aware of a slight movement along the side of the road. Without comment, I took the field glasses from the leather case and raised them to my eyes.

It was a man on horseback, perhaps a mile behind us. Though still in the woods, I could see his outline as he passed through the myriad shafts of sunlight that pierced the gloom of the heavy wood. For a brief second, he was entirely illuminated by the sloping rays of the sunlight. I could see that it was the gypsy. The third appearance of this character, travelling apparently aimlessly, yet in our direction, made me uneasy. Had Holmes observed him thus, I am sure he would have said that there was an ominous deliberation about the man—that although possibly only a coincidence, a coincidence was unlikely. The gypsy was following us. I was about to tell Brundage to reverse and confront the lout, whereupon I could threaten him with my revolver. However, I recalled the portion of the ransom note which warned of any involvement with the police or other parties. One glance at the Allistairs, so brimming with hope and confidence in me, and I realised this was a foolish course, however much I yearned for action. A few minutes later, we topped another rise. Again, I looked back. Even with the aid of the glasses, I was unable to see anyone upon the road. The man had vanished into the forest. Somewhat relieved, I returned the glasses to their case and, not mentioning the incident, sat out the remainder of the ride in silence.

Unlike most country houses with which I have been acquainted, Strathcombe was not set off in full view of passers-by. It had neither an open approach to the grounds, nor a high fence with elaborate gates. It was, rather, set halfway into a copse of tall trees that all but obscured the house and buildings. One did not approach it, but stumbled across it gradually, as if by accident. The gravel path turned, and we passed several of the outbuildings before the house itself came into full view.

With an expertise that had grown from long practice, Brundage swung the open carriage round and we alighted upon the stone steps that rose gradually to the open terrace in front. Ascending the steps, the three of us paused on the bricked terrace to admire the view. The terrace, enclosed by an ancient lichen-blotched stone balustrade, looked out over a broad valley, through which meandered a small trout stream. Clumps of willows abutted the stream, and the meadows on each side were bordered by woods. Save for the small outhouses, there was not another sign of civilisation to be seen—not so much as a farmer's cottage nor a church steeple. The dying sun cast a reddish glow in the West, and the setting seemed already to work a soothing spell upon the couple. Accustomed as I was to city noises, it was a pleasant change indeed to hear the myriad bird sounds—the mewing and twittering of the swallows as they crisscrossed the dusk on crescent wings, the trill of the lark and blackbirds.

Having been shown to my quarters, which consisted of a bedroom, dressing room and parlour, I unpacked my belongings and dressed for dinner.

After changing my clothes, I placed the map of the estate that Holmes had given me on the bed, and, by looking out of the double window, proceeded to orientate myself.

The house consisted of four large rooms downstairs surrounding a great hall. Upstairs were ten smaller rooms, at one time no doubt serving as individual bedrooms to accommodate guests. Now, however, these rooms were split into three suites, one of which I now occupied. My suite was in the left wing, in front, and commanded a splendid view of the main approach to the house. In the dimming light, I could barely make out the grey tower of the ancient lime kiln.

A motion caught my eye near the lime kiln. It was a man on horseback. Could it be the gypsy? Would he have the effrontery to follow us onto the very grounds of Strathcombe? I raised the field glasses to my eyes for a better view. The man was certainly not a gypsy: he had blond hair. I glimpsed him only for a moment, however, because he wheeled his horse quickly about, dashed over the meadow and cleared the stone wall in a prodigious leap. Whoever he is, I thought, he can surely handle a horse. Who was this man? I must remember to mention him to Lord Allistair.

Continuing to examine the grounds from my vantage point, I took in the meadows and deep woods beyond with a sweeping gaze. Holmes was correct; the kidnappers had indeed chosen their site with cunning. Hidden in the deep woods or on the rugged hillsides, they were secluded and safe. To search them out would require a score of men and horses, and hounds as well. Obviously, this course of action would spell disaster for Lady Allistair. Clearly, the criminals could remain safe as long as they wished. On the other hand, the close-lying woods and broken stone walls would allow them to skulk about close to the house itself without being detected. This would enable them to come and go as they pleased, to leave notes of instruction and, ultimately, to obtain the ransom. It is an old soldier's saying that "the unseen enemy is the most feared." I have always believed this, and standing at my window in the twilight in that desolate place I was profoundly convinced of the saying's veracity. To add further to my feelings of uneasiness was the evidence of high intelligence and assiduous planning behind the kidnapping plot. Already I longed for Holmes' presence and support. However, determined to fulfill my role as Holmes had described it, I assumed a cheerful, almost jaunty air and descended the staircase to meet Lord and Lady Allistair in the great hall.

Strathcombe's history as a shooting lodge is never so vividly pressed into the mind of a visitor as when he ambles about, glass in hand, under the innumerable mounted heads that stare balefully down from the high dark walls of the great hall.

"The vicinity is most famous for boar," observed Lord Allistair as he refilled my glass. "But there are fine stags hereabouts as well. We used to keep a pack of hounds to hunt them, but not in recent years."

My attention was directed to a massive head over the great hall fireplace. It was as large as the head of a colt, and was set off by curving ivory tusks as long as a man's fingers.

"That boar was brought down three years ago by Count Le Moyne during an official visit to this country. As a goodwill gesture, he left the head for our hall."

"It's immense. Surely there are not creatures like this roaming the woods?" I asked.

"To be sure, Dr. Watson. They may weight as much as four hundredweight. It's fortunate that Le Moyne is a crack shot, for it took two rounds at close range with a Holland and Holland double rifle to stop that brute. He wouldn't be alive today, I can assure you, if he'd missed with either barrel."

I gazed in awe at the head, frozen in a horrid snarl. Truly this was a wild stretch of country that lay round-about us, and the realisation made me feel further for the safety of Alice Allistair.

"If I may interrupt, sir," said Brundage, "Ian Farthway, the gamekeeper, tells me that there is another boar newly arrived in the river bottom. From the prints it leaves, it promises to be even larger than our present specimen."

"You don't say so!" replied Lord Allistair. "Then it must be huge. God forbid it has a temper to match its size. Perhaps our friend, Dr. Watson, would like to go after it."

"No, thank you," I protested. "Having been once shot myself, I am loath to take up firearms, except in defence."

"Well then, since I share the doctor's distaste for blood sports, we shall leave our wild pig to roam and root about the bottomland as he pleases."

"He shall never be hard to locate, your Lordship," continued Brundage, "as Farthway claims he leaves a curious print ..."

"Eh, curious print? What do you mean, Brundage? Explain yourself."

"Apparently, sir, this boar leaves a three-toed print instead of a cloven one. It's some sort of deformity, no doubt."

"On one foot, or all four?" I enquired.

"I don't know, sir."

"Well, it's a curious thing. And now, doctor, I believe Meg has announced the evening meal."

"Tell me about this man Farthway," I asked as we made our way upstairs, claret in hand.

"Our gamekeeper—knows the countryside like the palm of his hand."

"Is he a blond fellow—good horseman?"

"The very same—but have you met him?"

I then explained my brief glimpse of Farthway, and we entered the dining room.

Our dinner was pleasant, and only slightly subdued considering the enormous tension that the noble couple was striving to conceal. The partridges were excellent, served with a delectable orange sauce and accompanied by a choice bottle of burgundy. When the meal was over, Lady Allistair excused herself and repaired to her room. From the look on her face when she went upstairs, I foresaw a bout of crying. Saddened as I was by this, as a medical man I was aware of the purgative effect of tears, and felt it would help her sleep. After her departure, His Lordship and I seated ourselves before the dying fire. With his wife out of earshot, Lord Allistair's conversation assumed a harder tone, a tone that was, I felt, grounded in sober realism. Hearing him speak thus, I was aware of another side of this benevolent human being: one that showed his iron will and keen determination against long odds.

"God knows where they've hidden her," he said in a low tone, "but I think it best not to foray out after them—"

"No, by all means we must wait, if even for a short time ..."

"Quite. We should attempt a peaceful, if expensive solution to this.

The money is nothing; were it my life savings I of course wouldn't care. But if my daughter has been in any way harmed—"

He gripped the arms of his chair until his knuckles grew white.

"Steady, Lord Allistair, I have every confidence that she will be returned unharmed."

"Ah, were it so! I, however, have no illusions as to her grave danger. The only thing, in fact, that saves me from breaking down utterly is the numbness brought on by a too-lengthy wait."

I nodded in sympathy.

"But Doctor, there's another element working here. I can't help but feel that in addition to wanting money, the kidnappers seek a personal revenge against me—or my wife."

"How so?"

"Why was there no word about Alice for over two months? *Why*, when a short telegram—that could have been sent with discretion and safety—would have done so much to alleviate our suffering?"

"Ah, I see your point. And yet they chose not to send any message whatever until now—and so have kept you in misery these ten weeks."

"Who could have such a hatred of me? I have enemies as anyone in public life is bound to do. Yet I consider them political opponents—not personal ones."

"And you can think of no one in your past who would deliberately seek to hurt you?"

He knitted his brows in thought.

"No," he said at last.

And I wasn't in the least surprised. If I could think of any great man who had risen to power without making enemies, it would be Lord Peter Allistair. As I looked at the man who sat within a few feet of me, I was aware of how old he suddenly appeared. The renewed hope then, the warm optimism of our outward journey was a sham, perhaps a temporary show for my benefit. Clearly, these two people, noble in every sense of the word, were close to being permanently shattered by this experience. As I said goodnight to Lord Allistair, I renewed my resolve to do anything in my power to secure the safe return of Alice Allistair.

I was enervated by the journey and the nervous strain. But though I longed for bed, I sat down at his Lordship's study desk and penned the following wire to Holmes:

HOLMES: REPORTING DAILY AS INSTRUCTED. AR-
RIVED STRATHCOMBE SAFE. STAFF APPEARS LOYAL
BUT SURROUNDINGS FORBIDDING. NO INCIDENT EX-
CEPT FOLLOWED BY GYPSY. LETTER FOLLOWS–HOPE
YOU COME SOONEST. WATSON.

I sealed this message with instructions to Brundage that it be sent
in the early morning to Baker Street. And then, with a weary body
and heavy heart, I ascended the carved oak staircase to bed.

7

SOUNDINGS

Perhaps it was the sunshine that flooded my bedchamber, or was it the warblers and finches outside the window that so improved my frame of mind next morning?

Another reason, particularly apparent to me as a physician, is that the human soul is adaptable and resilient; we can go only so long in an anxious, depressed state before a voice from deep within us cries, "enough!" and we summon up from the depths of our spirit a strength and optimism we had not realised were there.

I dressed and joined my hosts for a hearty breakfast of scrambled eggs and fried trout, with plenty of toast and honey.

Afterwards, at my suggestion, Lord Allistair took me on a tour of the grounds. The morning was lovely, filled with the brisk air of autumn. I donned a shooting jacket and, following Holmes' strict instructions, carried one of Lord Allistair's seldom-used shotguns, a magnificent Purdey twelve-bore, at my side. I had made the suggestion of the tour deliberately, of course, because Holmes considered it imperative that I familiarise myself with the grounds and terrain, paying particular attention to any sites of possible concealment, or hidden approaches to the house.

"I'll show you the kennels first," said Lord Allistair, "since they're in the best repair, having been used until quite recently."

We strolled over the lawn to a low stone building with a slate roof almost entirely intact. Looking inside, I could see two low hallways and about a dozen runs. The building was slightly over a hundred yards from the house.

"The stables are still in use, of course," Lord Allistair continued. "I'll show you when we meet Wiscomb."

"He is your stable-boy?"

"Stable-boy and gardener both. He's been with us quite some time, even longer than the Brundages—a bit infirm nowadays—"

"Do you consider him reliable?" I cut in.

"Oh, entirely."

"I don't wish to pry," I continued, "but it would be most helpful if you could briefly relate the histories of your household staff."

"Ah, I feel the presence of our mutual friend, do I not?"

I admitted frankly that Holmes had given me certain instructions.

"Then of course, I'll do exactly what you wish. On our way round the place, I'll tell you everything I can."

So as we strolled across the grounds, our shadows playing across great stretches of lawn in the early sunlight, I was given a brief thumbnail sketch of each of the servants.

The Brundages had been with the family for more than twenty years, and distinguished themselves by superior service and loyalty. Clearly, we could exclude them as far as any sort of foul play was concerned. There were two maids: Julia and Betsy, Julia being Lady Allistair's private maid and Betsy serving guests and visiting relatives. Neither had served the household for long, but both seemed of good character. Betsy, however, was apparently in the midst of a lover's quarrel, and appeared upset.

"Is he a local fellow?" I asked.

"Who?"

"Betsy's beau. Is he from hereabouts?"

"Nobody knows, for we've never seen him. She goes off to town to meet him, and she never speaks at all of him, according to Julia. Now here are the mews, Doctor. As you can see, they are fairly tumbledown."

The building, almost roofless, contained two rooms (I supposed for different sized birds), but the walls were largely missing. For a place of concealment, the building was useless except at night.

The lime kiln, located towards the front stone parapet, was singular. Being twenty feet across, the hollow cylinder rose almost the same distance, and was approached by walking up the earthen wagon ramp that sloped up one side. An iron door was placed at the base, through which the rendered lime was removed. It had not been used for generations. We looked briefly at the trout pond and garden, and returned towards the stables.

"That leaves only Farthway, the gamekeeper," continued Lord Allistair. "We know less about him than the others since he's quite new, having been brought into our service less than a year ago. He's a superb gamekeeper. I sometimes think he's not entirely happy here though. He's a fast-paced young man, having served in the Black Watch. I can't help wondering if he doesn't get bored in his present job."

"You say he was in the Black Watch?"

"Yes indeed, and an officer to boot."

"You don't say! But doesn't that still require money?"

"Certainly. I think that's why he left. Of course it's pure conjecture on my part. It would never do to ask—"

"No, of course. So his family suffered a decline?"

"So it would seem. I believe the Farthways were once one of the most respected Scottish families. Well—for whatever reason, Farthway quit the service and joined us as gamekeeper."

"That seems odd, and surely a fall in station, wouldn't you think?"

"Certainly. But of all the applicants, he was the most insistent, and qualified, as you'll see. But as for his reasons—well, as I've said, we know very little about the man."

"I should like to make the acquaintance of this Mr. Farthway," I said.

"No doubt you shall in the near future. And now, here we are. Hello, Wiscomb, I see you've saddled our horses."

We were met in the stable yard by the elderly and somewhat uncouth Wiscomb. Upon taking note of his trembling extremities, and the colour of his nose, I assumed him to be a part-time drunkard, and thus Lord Allistair's statement that he was "a bit infirm" made sense. He seemed dutiful and obliging enough as he guided us into our saddle, yet what inner torment wracked him so that he sought solace in the bottle?

"Tell her Ladyship we shall return for luncheon," was all Lord Allistair said as he adroitly wheeled his horse about and plunged across the sparkling lawn.

I followed him as best I could, and after a brisk trot, we'd cleared the near fences and started off across the meadow. This portion of the grounds was well-kept grass, but in less than two hundred yards the meadow gave way to a deep forest of ancient oaks and gigantic beeches, the latter towering over a hundred feet. We pursued our way directly into this natural labyrinth, following ancient narrow paths that criss-crossed infinitely into the deep recesses of the wilderness. The old trees formed a canopy above us, and, the ground being free of undergrowth, one could see between the massive trunks for quite a distance in any direction. Lord Allistair informed me that during Strathcombe's time as a hunting lodge it was the custom for mounted hunting parties to pursue game through the woods at full chase.

"And we've never been the only ones to take game from this country, Dr. Watson," added Lord Allistair as he cantered by my side in the gloom. "I must admit to being somewhat lax about the poaching. You see, these woods have long been the temporary home of woodcutters, poachers, gypsies and, I'm afraid, occasional felons of every description who've grown used to taking game from the vicinity. They take it both by gun and snare, and without regard to season."

He reined in, and pointed down.

"Evidence of their comings and goings can be seen here, and even more clearly in the dried mud of the river bank ..."

The loam of the forest floor was heavily marked with recent prints, both of horse and man. Lord Allistair, in a discursive mood, continued:

"Strathcombe, as the name implies, is a broad river valley cut through deep forests and steep hills. Although there are remnants of stone walls bordering the park and gardens, there are no formal boundary arrangements; people and animals are free to come and go as they please."

Needless to say, this last confession worried me a great deal. As confidant and guardian to this couple, how could I possibly oversee their safety with countless transients and ruffians trespassing their borders?

"As you can see, Doctor, the terrain is decidedly to their advantage. The maps Mr. Holmes and I poured over last week are unfortunately correct: there are numerous dips and rises, copses and stone walls within close reach of the house. Even a child, if he wished, could approach the house in secrecy—especially after twilight. Now the reason for this jaunt is for me to show you two places of considerable interest: the Keep and Henry's Hollow."

"They are nearby?"

"Oh yes—the Keep is three quarters of a mile to the east." After twenty or so yards, we came to a slight break in the forest. Lord Allistair turned in his saddle and raised his arm. "There it is." He pointed to a towering crag of rock that rose skyward with steep sides. It did in fact resemble an ancient castle keep, at least in profile.

"From its summit one can get a bird's eye view of the entire estate and the country around. Years ago it was our custom to post a gamekeeper there to watch the hunt and spot stags. He would then, by means of waving flags mounted on long poles, signal the hunt as to where the game was to be had."

"How is it approached?" I asked.

"There is a precarious footpath that winds round it to the top. The summit is bare save for a few clumps of bracken and several wizened pines that sprout from crevices in the rock. Just below the summit is a flat outcropping of rock under which is a small cave, large enough for several men to sleep in, sheltered from the elements. There, can you see it?"

Up near the craggy peak I could barely see a ledge of rock and a dark depression underneath. It must have been hundreds of feet above the woods. Considering the present circumstances, I definitely did not like the look of it.

"And the other place?"

"We are headed for it now." Lord Allistair pointed with his riding crop straight ahead. "Henry's Hollow lies less than two miles down this path."

"What sort of place is it?"

"A very interesting one, I can assure you. If the legend is true, it is an historical site. But whether the tale that surrounds the place is truth or fiction, Henry Hollow is an eerie place, as I'm sure you'll agree. It is the one thing about coming to Strathcombe that the new visitor remembers most."

We trotted along the faint path that was marked with tracks of other horses, and deer as well. Twice Lord Allistair paused and pointed to other cloven tracks that were massive, and sunk deep into the hard-packed loam.

"Wild boar," said he. "But not the monster one that Brundage mentioned."

The horses, catching the scent of the wild pig, shied slightly and needed no urging from us to continue our jaunt at a rapid pace. So we rode on through the forest. The horses' feet rustled the fallen leaves; woodpeckers hammered against the huge trunks, and jays flew shrieking overhead.

"Ah, jays and crows are the watchmen of the forest. None can enter without the announcements you hear."

I was amazed at the distance the crying of the birds carried, reverberating through the moss-covered trees for hundreds of yards. The gloomy forest seemed to stretch away infinitely.

"Do you see it?" His Lordship asked a few minutes later.

"I don't see anything out of the ordinary," I confessed, peering into the dimness ahead. Shafts of sunlight pierced the gloom at random intervals, but even with this illumination I could see nothing remarkable.

"Let us draw a few feet closer," he said.

Never shall I forget the eerie spell which came upon me when I finally realised that I had been staring at Henry's Hollow for the previous ten minutes. Even as I write these words, I can once again feel the tremor of excitement that comes when witnessing something unique and grand.

Not thirty yards ahead was a line of immense oak trees, each with a trunk as wide as a carriage. The distance between the trunks was only slightly greater than their diameters. Their massive lower branches, each as big as most trees, interlaced to form a barrier as stout as the strongest castle walls. It was then I realised that the line of trees was not straight, but circular. We dismounted and, leading our horses, approached the ring of giants.

Lord Allistair and his horse passed through first. I followed and joined him on the edge of a ridge, and gazed with wonder and amazement at the depression in the forest floor: an oblong-shaped hollow resembling an amphitheatre, some two hundred yards long and perhaps one hundred feet deep at its centre–the whole surrounded at the rim by the palisade of huge trees whose branches all interlocked in frozen majesty.

"So this is Henry's Hollow ..."

"Quite so. You are probably supposing it takes its name from this earthen hollow. However, there is another story of the name's origin, and it is linked with the general legend of Henry's Hollow which, by the way, historians now regard as true.

"This place is named after King Henry IV. It is said he camped here with his troops on the eve of the battle of Shrewsbury in 1403. As anyone can surmise, this spot is an ideal camping place, and, if need be, an effective defence works, too. Now obviously these trees were planted long before even Henry's time, perhaps by druids or other forest folk who made this natural dell into a defensible, sheltered home.

"It is remarkably well-hidden, too, especially considering its size."

"Follow me down, Doctor," said His Lordship, and we wended our way, horses in tow, down into the centre of the strange place. There were oaks in the hollow as well, and under their protective arms the troops of Henry IV must have slept in preparation for the great battle against the Welsh rebels almost five hundred years ago. In my mind's eye I could picture them squatting or lying about on rude beds of ferns and leaves, their helms and armour glinting in the firelight as they ate and sang to summon up courage for the ensuing fight.

We wandered about under the trees and stopped in a small clearing towards the very centre of the dell.

"Supposedly, King Henry constructed a crude forge on this very site by building a fire in the base of a hollow tree. Some still think this weird place took its name from the hollow tree rather than the depression in the earth. According to legend, Henry had the forge constructed to re-temper his sword. With it he vowed to kill Owen Glendower. But as we know, he failed in this, although he slew Harry Percy, called Hotspur, and displayed his body to the people of Shrewsbury as proof of the deed. The rebellion was crushed. Since then, Henry's Hollow has changed little, if at all. No one lives here permanently, but because of its isolation it has attracted vagrants, felons and ne'er-do-wells of all descriptions for centuries."

Upon hearing these words I scanned the rim of the hollow uneasily.

"Perhaps it is best if we return to Strathcombe," I suggested, and unslung the shotgun from my shoulders.

"You are quite right, my friend. It's nearly noon, and I don't like to leave Lady Allistair for long these days."

We led the horses up toward the rim. We were almost to the ring of oaks when Lord Allistair paused.

"I forgot to point out these caves in the sides of the hollow," he said, "they are all round the place, dug in amongst the roots."

To my amazement, I saw numerous holes in the sloping bank of the dell. Drawing closer, one could see they were tunnels dug out between the roots of the large trees. The roots no doubt acted as joists and rafters, holding the soil together and thus preventing collapse. They seemed to wind into the earth for some distance, but as we were both anxious to return to the Lodge, I cut my inspection short.

We left the hollow and returned to the forest path. In less than half an hour we were at Strathcombe, but two things occurred which I must relate, although I did not mention them to Lord Allistair.

The first was the unmistakable odour of woodsmoke in Henry's Hollow. It was faint, and had the dank and musty smell that comes when a fire is doused with water. But it was evident nevertheless.

Someone was living in Henry's Hollow. Somewhere, among the giant trees and dismal hillside caverns, was lurking a fugitive, or an enemy. Was this person, or persons, warned of our approach by the jays and crows?

The second thing was even more alarming, and was observed in the twinkling of an eye. Upon our return journey I chanced to look once again at the high walls of the Keep. The rock was bright grey as the sunlight struck it. I remember musing on what a charming place its summit must be—what a pleasant spot for a picnic lunch. The midday sun made the rock ledge and the cave beneath even more noticeable. I was about to turn my head when I saw it: a pinpoint flash of light coming from the dark mouth of the cave. It lasted no more than half a second. I am sure His Lordship did not notice. I of course knew instantly what it was; my days as an artilleryman had taught me to recognise the flash of field glasses in the sun. Someone was watching us.

8

NEW HOPE AND A PUZZLE

I decided to mention neither the odour of woodsmoke nor the reflection on the Keep to Lord Allistair. He was bearing up well under the tremendous strain, but I had a feeling he was near the breaking point; more bad news could severely tax him.

As we approached the house, we were struck by the silence and deserted appearance of Strathcombe.

"This is odd. Usually one sees some of the staff at work, especially on so pleasant a day."

We drew closer and with each passing second, my apprehension grew. Before we'd even reached the stable yard, we were met by Wiscomb, who came hobbling at top speed from the house waving his arms wildly. He was followed almost immediately by Lady Allistair, who appeared as distraught as the manservant.

"Something's amiss!" whispered His Lordship under his breath.

"Peter–Peter!" cried the Lady as she ran towards us. As she approached, it became obvious that whatever had occurred, it was cause for happiness; her face was joyous.

We dismounted and Lord Allistair ran to his wife, caught her in his arms, and bent over close to hear what she had to say. After a few seconds, he turned round and shouted.

"Alice is safe! There's a note inside that proves it so!"

I followed the jubilant couple inside and watched as Lady Allistair plucked an envelope from the mantelpiece.

"Where did you find this?" he asked Lady Allistair.

"Meg found it this morning on the terrace balustrade directly after you and Dr. Watson left. It was weighted with a brick."

"It's amazing, and shocking—the ease with which they placed it there," he added and, his hands trembling with emotion, opened the envelope and extracted what appeared to be a sheet of newsprint.

"It's on the front page of the *Manchester Guardian*," he exclaimed, "this morning's edition. Ah! See here, Dr. Watson, her note is penned directly on the margin, thank God!"

A brief message, in the same handwriting I had observed in the living room of the Allistairs' in London, was penned on the right margin of the newsheet. It was obvious that the newspaper proved that early that morning Alice Allistair was alive and well. As can be imagined, this crude epistle had a marvellous effect on all of us—Lady Allistair in particular, who wept with joy.

The message read: "My dearest Father and Mother, I am safe for now. I am assured of prompt release to you if the total ransom, in amount and form previously indicated, is paid upon request by those who hold me. Instructions will be forthcoming shortly, and must, upon pain of my death, be obeyed to the letter. I am unharmed and well, and joyous in the knowledge that I shall soon be with you both.

The note was signed, as before, "Your loving daughter, Alice."

"They have kept their word so far!" cried Lord Allistair, beaming. "Pray we can get through these next few difficult days—then our sufferings will be over. Come, let's have some sherry."

Our spirits raised, we gathered in the conservatory, which was really an extension at the back of the central hall, with huge windows on three sides. It was, in contrast to the rest of Strathcombe, bright and cheery. We seated ourselves in front of these windows and awaited Brundage, who soon appeared with a silver tray laden with bottles and glasses. Lady Allistair again picked up the sheet of newsprint with her daughter's writing on it. Tenderly, almost lovingly considering the blessed news it had brought, she fondled the page of newsprint and read and re-read the message of hope written a few hours earlier. She held the paper as one would hold a book, and inclined her body forward slightly in a posture of deep concentration. The strong rays of early afternoon sun streamed down upon her from the tall windows behind.

"Well, this is indeed encouraging," said His Lordship, draining his glass. I could see before me the weight of weeks of worry lifting visibly from the couple.

"Since it's this morning's paper," I offered, "instead of last evening's, your daughter and her captors must be hereabouts. I venture they're not more than ten miles distant. You see my friend Sherlock Holmes has taught me—"

I was struck by a most curious sight.

"Yes, Doctor, what were you saying?" asked Lord Allistair.

"I was saying ..."

"I say, Doctor, are you all right?" Her Ladyship asked, putting down the paper.

"Fine, thank you," I replied. "But pray, don't put the paper down just yet. Please hold it as you were a moment ago.

"Like this?" she asked.

"A little lower, please," I instructed. "Just above the tray—"

Her Ladyship did as instructed, and brought the paper down to within a few inches of the silver serving tray that sat upon the coffee table.

"Now this is most interesting," I pursued. "If you'll excuse me, I would like to remove the sherry bottles for a moment, and leave only the tray ..."

The couple looked at me as if I'd lost my reason, but I proceeded to remove the bottles.

"Now see how the sunlight comes strongly down through these windows at this time of day," I said, the excitement growing in me.

"One would expect so in a conservatory," said Lord Allistair, not without a touch of irony.

"... and strikes the paper full force, as you see. Now Lord Allistair, look down at the tray."

He followed my instructions, and a look of amazement grew upon his face.

"Good God—look at those tiny sparks!"

Reflecting off the shiny silver were many small pinpoints of light, resembling a miniature constellation. I took the sheet of newspaper from her Ladyship and held it up to the light. The tan translucence of the newsprint was pierced by a score or so of tiny pinpoints of bright light.

"These tiny holes were made by a pin or a needle," I said, "and they appear to be arranged somewhat symmetrically. Also, they occur only in this one section of the page and nowhere else."

"They seem to be arranged in rows," continued Lord Allistair, who was looking over my shoulder, "and are placed sometimes singly and sometimes in pairs. Now that's a queer thing, Doctor. What do you make of it?"

"I can't make anything of it," I replied, "except their arrangement is certainly not random—they must have some meaning. Here—

you'll notice that all these pinpricks are spaced within this single short article entitled "Foreign Investment." Let us first read through the article."

The article, if it could be called such, was a mere "filler" piece used to round out the column. It was a scant two sentences in length, and ran as follows:

"LONDON–The Home Office today announced a joint production agreement with Belgium. It involves the manufacture of internal combustion engines."

"The article is unimportant, surely," said Her Ladyship after reading it. "It's simply one of those snippets tacked onto a column for appearance's sake."

"Perhaps, but if my long association with Sherlock Holmes has taught me anything, Lady Allistair, it is that things that appear trifling are often not. It is possible that these small pinpricks in the paper were deliberately placed there to convey something."

I then briefly related the events, and the apparently nonsensical message surrounding the "Gloria Scott" adventure. Upon hearing of the dire fate proclaimed by that message, Lady Allistair once again fell into a fit of depression and worry over her daughter's well being. Enraged at myself for having unwittingly shattered the calm that had so recently descended upon her, I tried to allay her fears by assuring her that the tiny holes in the paper were probably without meaning.

"You are not a good liar, Doctor," said Lord Allistair. "I agree that there is some meaning to these strange marks. However, we know Alice is well. There's no reason to assume that they carry bad news."

And so saying, he instructed his wife to retire to her room for a short nap while we adjourned to his small study. Soon a pot of coffee was brought in, and we sat smoking before the fire, attempting to decipher the meaning, if any, of the tiny pinholes in the paper.

"We miss your friend terribly at times like these," said Lord Allistair. "No doubt he is capable of arriving at answers to puzzles like this one?"

"If it is penetrable to the mind of man, it is child's play to Holmes," I replied. "But since he is not here, then we must proceed as best we can. Let me shut the door to insure privacy, then we shall, with the paper on your gaming table, set ourselves to the problem."

The short piece looked like this with the pinprick marks filled in with pen dots:

LONDON—The Home Office today announced a joint production agreement signed with Belgium. It involves the manufacture of internal combustion engines.

We stared at the words and markings for some time, each advancing his own hypotheses.

"The most obvious explanation is of course that the pinpricks point out letters in the article either directly above or below them," advanced Lord Allistair.

"Yes, I think we can both agree on that. But why are some marks above the letters and others below? Also, why are some pricks paired while others are alone?"

"Let's first spell out the letters that are indicated regardless of the position or number of marks," he suggested.

We spelled out AJOTPRIASWHNSEATREEBE.

"There's no meaning whatsoever in this hodgepodge—except that the word seat is spelled," said I. "I take it we can dismiss this message."

"I have it!" he cried, jumping up from the table. "The various pinprick positions and number indicate different words. See here: let us take the single dot on top first. Tracing the letters where this dot appears, we will have the first word, or a word at least, of the code."

Following this scheme we arrived at the word ATRA.

"Is that a word you know of, Doctor—perhaps in Latin?"

"No. However, let's go on to the next set of markings which would logically be the single dot underneath the letters."

Following thus, we arrived at the word WARE.

"Still no sense to it. And the next word?"

"P-I-S-S-E-T-B-E-." I spelled aloud, and wrote PISETBE next to the other words.

"I suppose it's useless," said Lord Allistair. "There must be another key to the puzzle. Or else, like as not, there's nothing to it."

"Let us try the last group: the double dots underneath ..."

To our utter amazement, the dots spelled JOHN.

"That's more than coincidence surely, Doctor. Now the question is—if this is indeed a word, why then aren't the others?"

We tried re-arranging the letters of the other "words" in the event that they appeared out of order, but still could make no sense of them.

"All we know is the message is from John, or *to* John. But who is John?" I asked.

"No one in this household ... unless—"

"Unless what?"

"Unless it's you: John Watson."

"But that's absurd!" I cried. "Nobody in these parts has ever heard of me. Besides, what have I to do with the return of your daughter?"

"Nothing directly. But perhaps those who hold Alice aren't aware of this. Perhaps they see you as a threat to their plans."

Upon thinking about this for a moment, I decided to reveal to Lord Allistair what I had seen earlier in the day.

"Someone was up on the Keep watching us you say?" he asked incredulously. "But if that is the case they, whoever they may be, were aware of your presence even earlier, because the letter was awaiting us upon our return."

"Quite so! I confess I'd forgotten it. Dash it! I wish Holmes were here."

"But since he is not, we must continue with our search for the wisest course of action."

"Lord Allistair, if I am in any way endangering the return of your daughter, I must leave at once—"

"Nonsense. If I were convinced of that, I would of course insist that you depart. It is extremely unlikely that this is the case. Furthermore, Mr. Holmes' instructions were, as we can both recall, quite strict: you are to remain at my side until his arrival. So be it. In the interim, we shall continue our quest for this message within a message. The more I brood upon the matter, the more convinced I am that these tiny pinprickings are the work of my daughter."

"Why do you say that?"

"First of all, because they are meant to be discovered upon close inspection but not noticed casually. As a matter of fact we were very fortunate to have noticed them at all—thanks to your keen eyes and our silver serving tray. No, it was definitely done secretly and perhaps hurriedly—a message within a message. Who else could wish secretly to convey a second message but my daughter? Secondly, there is the mode in which the message has been executed: a needle or pin as you have suggested. Does a man carry these about? Not usually. Furthermore, note how precisely the pinpricks are placed: not one out of line and no tears in the paper. All the more difficult when we consider the fragile texture of newspaper, the small type, and the speed and secrecy with which the message was transcribed. Do you, a surgeon, think yourself capable of this?"

I replied that I wasn't sure; the precision was extraordinary.

"And you begin to sound like Sherlock Holmes," I added.

"I'm surprising even myself," he laughed. "But I know that Alice is very good at needlepoint, and would therefore have the skill to do something like this, and in a hurry as well."

"It's a pity we cannot decipher the message. I think the best thing to do is summon Holmes as quickly as possible. So I shall ride to town this afternoon and dispatch a wire to that effect. All indications point to events coming to a head imminently."

He nodded his head slowly.

At this point, we were interrupted by a gentle knock from Brundage, who informed us that Betsy, the upstairs maid, wanted a word with us.

"Can't it wait, Brundage?"

"She is quite distressed, sir. It is partly at my recommendation that she has come, Your Lordship."

"Very well, show her in."

Betsy appeared, visibly trembling. Her eyes were tear-stained and her face was contorted, evidently from a recent and lengthy bout of crying. Upon seeing her condition, Lord Allistair rushed to her side, put his arm around her, and led her gently to his chair and sat her down, all the while speaking in soothing tones. I was much struck with his fatherly compassion for her, and was once again reminded of his compassion and concern for his fellow man, no matter what their station. After a few moments of this kindness, the girl grew more composed.

"My Lord!" she entreated, breaking out into fresh sobs. "God have mercy on me. I shall hang for what I've done!"

"What's this? There, girl, it cannot be that bad. Now tell me and the good doctor what it is you've done, or haven't done, that's got you so upset. There, there."

But she grew uncontrollable once again, and it was only after several more moments and two sips of brandy that she was again able to continue.

"Is your distress in any way related to the finding of the letter on the balustrade this morning?" I asked.

She hesitated for an instant, then nodded quickly, her eyes brimming over with tears.

"Did you see who placed it there?"

"I placed it there!"

Shocked at this admission, we both plied her with questions in rapid succession. Was she one of them? Where were they? Was

Alice truly unharmed? But to all of these she was unable to answer, so distraught was her state. Finally, following Holmes' example in instances of this sort, I convinced her that whatever secrets she held from us, it was better to reveal them.

"Betsy, both His Lordship and I realise that you have come to us of your own volition. Whatever difficulty you are in—no matter how serious—it will not be made better by your silence. We are on your side and wish only to help. Now please, tell us everything about how you came to be involved in this."

"Oh please, sir—you must believe me! I was never involved with them directly, I swear it! It was Charles—"

"Who is Charles?" asked Lord Allistair.

There was a pause, and the girl fell silent, looking shamefully at her hands, which were twitching in her lap.

"We were to be married," she said quietly.

"Is this the young man you have been seeing in town?"

"Yes, My Lord. I'm in love with him, My Lord."

"And he with you?"

"I was so sure of it until recently. Oh he's so winning in his manner, and generous. I only hope nothing ill's befallen him!"

"You must begin at the beginning, Betsy. When did you meet this man, and what connection has he to the abduction of my daughter?"

"I met Charles Compson three months ago at the Shrewsbury Fair. We were attracted to each other almost immediately, and it wasn't long before we were seeing a lot of each other. He works as a tanner in the village, and always dreams of being rich enough to buy his own tannery in Australia. He's always talked of somehow raising the capital, and the two of us would marry and set off to make our own way. Well, happy as I've been here, My Lord, the dream has had a certain appeal, if you can understand—"

Lord Allistair nodded.

"Things have been marvelous up until a few weeks ago. At that time, a change occurred in Charles that has perplexed and bothered me ever since."

"What sort of change?"

"He seemed secretive, as if he were holding back. Three nights ago, he asked me to meet him in the village. We met at the public house there, and he confided that he'd got the opportunity to raise the money needed to fulfill our dream. Of course I was overjoyed, never dreaming for a moment it would end like this."

She bit her lip and fought back a recurrence of her sobbing.

"He said that I must first promise not to tell anyone what it was that he would confide in me. I promised, and he revealed that he had been in contact with two gentlemen who knew the whereabouts of your daughter. He made it clear that they weren't the ones who had taken her, but merely knew her whereabouts ..."

Lord Allistair and I exchanged a momentary glance, half disgust and half pity, that a poor innocent country girl should be so cruelly deceived.

"Charles told me that all I had to do for my part was keep a sharp eye out round the house to see who came and went. I was also to watch for any strangers or friends," she continued, looking up in my direction.

"Charles said that when the time came for the release of Lady Allistair, these observations would make things go more smoothly. For his part in helping with the release, Charles was to be paid handsomely; enough money for passage to Australia and several tanneries.

"Early this morning, before the break of dawn, I met him at the foot of the village road to report your arrival, Doctor. He handed me the letter, saying I was to place it on the stone balustrade and call attention to it. 'It won't be long now, Betsy darling,' he told me, 'the young lady is safe and sound and, thanks to us, will be delivered up to her parents quick as a wink.' So I did as I was told, and now ..."

"And now what?"

"I fear harm may have come to him."

"To Charles?"

"Yes, he was supposed to meet me at two, and he was not there. It's not like him to miss appointments, My Lord."

"Where was this meeting to take place?"

"Where we usually meet: at the foot of the town road."

"Now Betsy, we are going to try and help you. But first there are a number of important questions we are going to put to you. You must answer them completely and truthfully if you expect any mercy on our part concerning your involvement in this foul scheme— whether deliberate or accidental."

She indicated that she would comply totally.

"First," said Lord Allistair, "to your knowledge, is my daughter unharmed?"

"From what I hear, she is."

We both breathed a sigh of relief.

"Have you any knowledge of the contents of the envelope handed to you this morning?"

"Yes, My Lord. It was a handwritten note from the young lady."

"And anything else?"

"No, My Lord."

Lord Allistair and I exchanged a quick glance. In all probability, neither Betsy, Charles, nor the kidnappers themselves knew anything about the second message done in pinpricks.

"Have you ever seen the 'gentlemen', if such they can be called, that your friend Charles referred to?"

"No, My Lord, never."

"Did he tell you anything about them—what they look like, where they are staying?"

"No—nothing. Except that they cannot be far away, since I know Charles goes often to speak with them, and returns to his lodgings in the town."

"Is there anything else you can remember that may be of use to us? Anything you can do to help us is to your advantage as well as ours."

"I am sorry," she said at last, "but I cannot think of anything. You both must believe me, gentlemen, I never thought I was engaging in anything that would in any way endanger Lady Alice. I am sure Charles feels the same way—"

"Does he?" asked Lord Allistair sternly.

"Oh, I am sure of it! And that is why we must find him. I'm so afraid ..."

"You are convinced in your own mind that he is in trouble? How do you know he hasn't fled with the others?"

The poor girl lowered her eyes again, as if ashamed to admit that the possibility might in fact be true. Her face trembled slightly, and after some time she spoke.

"Because he loves me," she said in a barely audible voice.

"I must tell you that you have behaved foolishly, Betsy. And there's a possibility you have been cruelly used as well. However, you have been a good servant. We know you didn't enter into the pact with bad intentions. You must leave us while we decide upon the best course of action. Kindly wait in the kitchen. We will send for you shortly."

The poor girl departed, and left the two of us to determine her fate. "I'm afraid she has been taken advantage of," he said. "And her young man, this Compson, seems a bumpkin as well. No good can come of it."

But Lord Allistair called her back a moment later, and she reappeared, still shaken.

"Betsy, so that we can find this friend of yours—eh, what's his name again?"

"Charles, My Lord. Charles Compson."

"Yes. Can you give us a brief description of him?"

"Of course, My Lord. He's medium height, sandy air, a big moustache."

Lord Allistair paused.

"That description may fit many people hereabouts. Is there anything particular only to him?"

"No, My Lord, unless it's Clancy."

"Who is Clancy?"

"His Kerry Blue terrier, My Lord. They're inseparable, are he and Clance. Go just about everywhere together—have for years. Yes, My Lord: where you'll find Clancy, you'll find Charles not far off."

She was again dismissed, and Lord Allistair and I were left to ponder this revelation.

"I can't help wondering," I said slowly, "to what extent her revelation of me will jeopardise the exchange."

"Hardly, if at all. She doesn't know your real purpose here. I'll give Betsy's description of this Charles Compson to Farthway, the gamekeeper. He'll then keep a sharp lookout for him throughout these parts. If you're going to send a wire, Doctor, you'd best get started. Do you want a horse or carriage?"

I selected a horse and, placing my Webley in my coat pocket, started off on the nine-mile trip. Ian Farthway was to start an impromptu search for Betsy's man, and I was to keep my eyes peeled as well along the road. Lord Allistair and I had agreed that should Betsy find Charles of her own accord, she was to tell him that I had departed for London. In this way, it was thought, the kidnappers would feel less threatened and the exchange could be handled more smoothly.

Seldom have I been in gloomier spirits than when I wheeled at the outer stone fence and swung away towards town. The sun was gone behind a gathering cloud bank, and what had appeared bright and cheerful earlier now seemed gloomy and still. I made my way at a medium trot down the first long slope and entered the woods. There was no sound save the clip clop of the hooves upon the road, and in the stillness it seemed ear-splitting. I recalled the gypsy who had followed us earlier, and the strange events of the morning. The letter from Alice Allistair was an optimistic sign, to be sure. And yet, of all the events of the past two days, it was the only cheering note. The smoke in Henry's Hollow, the watchman on the Keep, the puzzling message within a message, and the league between the maid and the abductors, all pointed to the utter encircling of Strathcombe by unseen forces, and their deep penetration into our defences. And the gypsy: was he simply a lout, or was he, too, in the employ of the criminals? So overwhelmed was I at the sudden and foreboding turn of things that I was convinced it was time to summon Holmes. For if any man could devise a productive strategy against these ruffians, it was clearly he.

The forest closed around me, and it seemed to grow darker by the minute. I spurred the horse onward, keeping my eyes about me. The visibility was poor, and the great trees of the forest loomed out as if to devour me. I was thankful I'd brought the Webley, and hurried on toward Rutlidge, four and a half miles away.

I arrived there in less than forty-five minutes, dashed straight to the telegraph office, and sent the following wire:

EVENTS MOVING SWIFTLY–REQUEST YOU COME AT ONCE. SPIES IN THE HOUSE AND THE ENEMY EVERY-WHERE. WILL WAIT FOR ANSWER. WATSON.

I had thought it best to wait for a reply so as to have some news to tell the Allistairs upon my return to Strathcombe. I was obliged to wait for well over an hour for his answer—much longer than I anticipated. This struck me as curious, since Holmes had promised to remain within a few minutes' walk of the nearest telegraph office. Finally it arrived and read as follows:

SHALL ARRIVE ON TOMORROW'S TRAIN 1:30 P.M. SEND CARRIAGE. HOLMES.

Thank God, Holmes was on his way! But what else could transpire within the intervening time? I shuddered to think. As I opened the door to leave the office, a thought struck me.

"I say," I asked the key operator, "have you seen a gypsy hereabouts in the past day or so?"

"I certainly have. There was a vagabond in this very office late last night, enquiring about a wire."

"What did he look like?"

"Tall lean chap with a hook nose and a scarf tied round his head."

That didn't sound like the gypsy I'd seen, but I did not rule out the possibility that the two could be in league. In fact, this was most probably the case.

"What sort of wire was he enquiring about?"

"He wished to know if there had been any messages to Strathcombe, the Allistair estate."

A tremor passed over me.

"And what did you reply?"

"That it was none of his affair, and to leave the premises."

"That's a good man!" said I, tossing him a half crown. "Goodnight!"

Needless to say, the appearance of the second gypsy made a dismal situation seem yet darker, more ominous. There was obviously a band of them, and they appeared to be well organised. The thought crossed my mind that careful planning and close communication weren't marks of these wandering, lazy, hot-blooded folk. Yet this group seemed to be an exception. I swung into the saddle resolved to keep silent about this development–at least until Holmes' arrival.

It was past nightfall when I struck the forest road. It looked still more dismal and ominous, and I passed through it at a brisk trot. My horse, for some reason, displayed a nervousness that was unnatural for a seasoned hunter. I sympathised with her, because some sixth sense inside me said all was not well, and I had best reach Strathcombe soon. Accordingly, I took her to a canter, and then to a gallop.

It was with a deep sense of relief that I topped the final rise and saw the few twinkling lights of Strathcombe ahead. I looked behind me. There was no sign of anyone. I hadn't been followed and help was on the way. Evidently, Alice Allistair was safe and unharmed. Surely, then, things weren't all that bad. Hopefully, within two days the trial would be over, and Holmes and I would be free to take two days of fishing at Strathcombe and then return to London, perhaps to continue our hunt for the giant rat of Sumatra. In lighter heart, I proceeded past the outer stone fence.

I was abreast of the lime kiln when I heard the howling of the dog.

9

CONFLUENCE

A chill shot through me at the sound. In the deep recesses of
my mind I could feel a dark blanket of dread drawing ever
closer.

My horse shied and whinnied at the eerie sound, and raced eagerly
to the stables. It seemed to have suddenly grown much colder, and
I longed for the parlour fire.

"Who goes?" cried a shrill voice as I approached the stables.

"It is I, Dr. Watson."

"My apologies, Doctor," said Wiscomb, as he made his way
feebly from the stable door. "I am unused to riders arriving at this
hour."

He appeared slightly the worse for drink, and his hands trembled
as he took the reins. "It's got right chilly, eh Doctor? And there's
something else, too, about tonight. I've the feeling something's up.
Can't put my finger square on it, but there's something in the air,
someth—"

"There, you hear it!" said I. "It sounds closer now."

"Ah, the dog. He's been at it all night. Chase 'im off four times
already I have—"

"What does he look like?"

"Oh, smallish, wire-haired. There! He's comin' back. I'll give 'im
what for—"

"Hold on!" I cried. "I'll go outside and see to him on my way to
the house—no need to bother."

He relented, put down the crop he'd picked up (I assume to teach
the dog a lesson) and ambled off to finish dressing down the horse.

It had indeed grown chilly outside; as I left the stable building I could see my breath, and the wind had quickened as well. I was halfway to the house when the howling commenced once more. Looking to the head of the drive, I observed a small dog hurrying to me. Forty feet away, it paused, whining. I knelt down and stretched out my hand.

"Clancy!" I called, and instantly the dog sprang forward with a joyous yelp. Upon reaching me, however, and sniffing my person, he again backed off, looked slightly confused, and resumed whining. He then paced to and fro, occasionally proceeding in the direction of the drive, then returning. It was plain the animal had lost his master. Considering Betsy's earlier concern, I didn't like the look of things.

I entered the hall to the sound of sobbing. Julia, the maid, met me in the main hallway.

"Good evening, Dr. Watson. Lord and Lady Allistair are waiting for you in the library. We are so glad you have returned sir—"

"Julia, may I enquire who is crying?"

"It's Betsy, sir, afraid for her man."

"He has not turned up yet?" I asked.

"No, sir."

I entered the library to find Lord and Lady Allistair in a semi-darkened room, pacing nervously to and fro. They greeted me with visible relief. The relief turned into delight when I told them that Holmes would arrive the following day.

"Shall we meet him at the train?"

"Brundage can do that—he requested a carriage. He seldom—hullo, who's this?"

I was surprised to see a shadowy figure emerge from the doorway and approach us. As he neared the fireplace, which was the primary light source, I could see that he was the tall, blond man I saw on horseback the first night at Strathcombe.

"Ah, I remember now, you have not met. Farthway, this is Dr. Watson, second cousin to my wife."

"How do you do, sir," said Farthway coolly. He had the air of dash and daring about him. At first glance, he seemed frank and open enough, yet there was a coolness, a hesitation, that set my guard up slightly.

"What is it, Farthway?" pursued Lord Allistair.

"Your Lordship, I understand from several of the staff that you and the Doctor rode deep into the forest this morning."

"That is correct, but I cannot see how this concerns you, Farthway."

"I beg you pardon, Your Lordship, but I feel it concerns me in a personal way, since the woods are dangerous now."

"How do you mean?" I demanded.

"There are a good number of vagabonds about, sir," he replied, still looking at Lord Allistair. "And there is the big boar in residence along the river bottom."

"And no doubt you have also some knowledge of the letter delivered to us this afternoon?"

Farthway nodded. Lord Allistair hesitated a moment, as if undecided whether to reprimand or praise his gamekeeper.

"Very well, Farthway. Thank you for your concern. But I must remind you that it is my decision entirely to enter the woods or avoid them. As a matter of fact, we shall no doubt be going there again tomorrow, and would like you to act as guide."

"Very good sir. Will you shoot?"

"No," answered Lord Allistair after an inquisitive glance in my direction. "You may go."

But as he turned to depart, I called him back.

"Mr. Farthway, from what I have seen and heard of you, you handle a horse very well, and a gun, too, I understand."

"Thank you. I endeavour to give satisfaction to my employer and his guests."

"Are you engaged tonight?" I asked.

"*Tonight*, sir?"

"Yes. Could you find your way about in this countryside in the dark?"

Farthway hesitated, his keen features working in the firelight as he attempted to look beyond my simple, and no doubt perplexing, request.

"I'd venture to say," he answered at last, "that I could find my way about blindfolded—anywhere you'd care to go but—"

"But what?"

"I don't think it would be advisable to venture out tonight, sir," he said nervously.

"Why not?"

He shifted, and his eyes refused to meet mine directly. "I just don't think it advisable," he said.

"Could it be, Farthway," I taunted, "that you fear for your safety?" and I saw his eyes flash with anger.

"I might remind you, Dr. Watson, that I have spent a good many of my years defending the Empire all over the globe, often in the face of hostile fire. You have, in all probability, spent your time quite differently. It is for your safety I fear, not my own. But if you are determined, I shall have the horses ready in twenty minutes."

With this, he turned like a Prussian on his heel and departed.

Meantime, Lord and Lady Allistair had been standing by, apparently thunderstruck at my request.

"You are not serious, I hope. I take it your request was a form of humiliation for him—and well deserved, too, I might add," said Lady Allistair to me.

"Quite an outburst for a gamekeeper. I may have to sack the man, good as he is."

"No doubt he is regretting his shortness with me already," said I, "yet I was, and am, entirely serious about venturing out tonight. From all accounts, the one man to accompany me is Ian Farthway.

I then briefly explained the episode of the lost dog to them. Although they showed some concern for Betsy, it was obvious that, in the light of recent revelations, their concern and affection for her was not infinite. Moreover, their concern for me was paramount. At some length, however, I managed to persuade them both that Betsy's difficulties were in some way connected with their own.

"So we really must go and look about the place," I said, "and though I challenged Farthway, I achieved my end, for it is imperative to have his services this evening, even if it was necessary to taunt him into it."

"Then if go you must, for God's sake be careful. I'll have flasks of coffee and brandy brought up for you both. Remember your pistol, sir, and do as Farthway says."

"Thank you, Lord Allistair."

It was a sullen Farthway who met me, horses in hand, at the foot of the terrace steps. I presented him with his flask and he grunted a reply. As we mounted, I noticed he had the familiar fowling piece slung over his shoulders, yet somehow it looked heavier.

"Holland and Holland double rifle," he replied shortly when I asked him about it. "Not a fowling piece. This can stop an elephant. Now Doctor, would you mind telling me why you've proposed this nocturnal jaunt?"

"Here comes the answer, I think," I replied.

At that exact moment, Clancy, the terrier, came round the drive whining and wheeling in tight circles. I simply told Farthway that the dog's master was missing, and perhaps the animal could lead us to him. It seemed as if some of the daring and excitement of his earlier career was returning to the ex-soldier. With a keenness that bordered on enthusiasm, he started down the drive at a brisk trot. The small dog led the way, alternately yelping and dashing ahead into the darkness, then, less sure of himself, returning in our direction in the same whining, turning fashion as before.

"It seems to me I've seen this dog before," said Farthway after a quarter hour's ride. "Is his master a loutish fellow, leather apron, walrus moustache?"

"That sounds like him, a tanner's apprentice named Charles Compson. Was he often about?"

"I've seen him on the main road here a dozen times during the past few weeks. A simple fellow—always the little terrier was at his heels. The man has not been seen?"

I retold Betsy's story, but only mentioning their love affair and eventual plans to emigrate to Australia. I mentioned nothing of Compson's supposed involvement with the abductors. We hurried on down the road in the darkness. In my haste, I'd forgotten a lantern, and quietly cursed myself. However, I realised too that a lantern enables one only to see immediate objects; it is useless for seeing distances at night. Perhaps it was just as well I'd not brought one. We were headed not towards Rutlidge but rather in the opposite direction—towards the Welsh border. The dog was alternately running and trotting now, and his howling increased in intensity. That sound, with the hollow clatter of our horses' hooves along the cold road, sent chills through my body. The night, having grown even more overcast, was dark as pitch. Nothing was visible save occasional glimpses of the small dog as it flitted gingerly between the horses.

"I must say," he offered at length, "that I was a bit short with you, Doctor. I apologise."

"You needn't worry yourself over me, Farthway. But your remarks to Lord Allistair could have more serious consequences."

"Ah, but what does he know of the dangers that lurk about here? He and the Lady come here twice a year at the very most. It would not surprise me in the slightest if he were to get lost in his own woods some day—"

"You speak in a tone of contempt for him," I returned. "For a man of his stature, that is surprising. And for a gamekeeper and employee your tone is offensive."

"I did not wish to give that impression. Quite the opposite is true. I came into Lord Allistair's service more out of admiration that for any challenge and excitement this job would offer me which, as you can see, isn't much."

"Until recently."

"Aye. And therein, Doctor, lies my concern. The woods are always full of thieves and brigands, but now they are more dangerous than usual. I reacted tonight out of concern, not insolence."

"Tell me, don't you ever fear for your own safety if they are as dangerous as you say?"

"No, sir. There's no one that knows this country as I do. I can lose anyone in these woods, sir, quick as a wink. I know every dell and copse in the Clun Forest, from Henry's Hollow and the Keep clear over to the Clee Hills and the Wrekin."

"You were born here?"

"I was born in Glasgow, but moved to Ludlow as a boy—so it was here I spent my youth. I daresay that there's none know this country better than Ian Farthway."

"I understand that until recently you were with the Black Watch."

"Indeed I was."

We continued for some minutes in silence.

"Why don't you ask me why I left the regiment, Doctor?" he asked.

"Well I ..."

"Come now, you're probably dying to know. The truth is, I was forced to retire from the service for the same reason I moved to Ludlow as a boy, as a young man: lack of funds."

I said nothing.

"You see, my family, for all its veneer of respectability and wealth, has had more than its share of drunkards—the worst of which was my late father. In his short lifetime, he managed to squander our family's remaining fortune and ruin our name in Scotland. So I headed south and took a workingman's job, saving all the money I could. My stint with the Black Watch was enjoyable, and I was a good soldier, but the money ran out, so here I am. I tell you this because I harbour in my soul some resentment for those who've never done an honest day's work."

"Are you referring to me?" I bristled.

"No. Neither you nor His Lordship. But I suppose my temper gets up when I see Strathcombe, and think of the life I might have had if my forebears had been more prudent. Well, I've said enough."

And so we rode on, following the lively gait of the little terrier. But I could not help wondering about this young man. Even considering his financial situation, why was he content at being a common gamekeeper when his record and personal bearing suggested he was capable of greater things? Why was he distant and aloof, even with his employer? And finally, where did this young man go to on his fine stallion? Where did he spend his time between sunrise and sunset? More particularly, where was he bound the evening I arrived, when I saw him clear the stone fence in a magnificent leap? These questions specifically, and his mysterious manner in general, concerned me. But clearly, there was urgent need of his talents that night, so I decided to put aside my suspicions for the time being.

After perhaps twenty minutes, the dog grew noticeably more nervous. Suddenly he stopped altogether and, nose to the ground, made his way to the edge of the road. There, he slowly lifted his head and peered into the tall forest that began less than twenty yards away. A low growl began in his throat. It rose higher, louder, then ended in a terrified shriek as the dog bounded back in our direction and cringed between us.

We tried to urge the horses forward in the direction in which the dog had gazed but they too, as if taking a cue from the smaller animal, refused to proceed further. Even Farthway, with his tremendous skill as a horseman, couldn't budge his mount. They snorted and whinnied, then reared, but no amount of spurring or oaths would move them.

"We'd best dismount, Doctor," said he, "and approach on foot."

But no sooner had we left our saddles than the horses turned tail and broke for Strathcombe at full gallop.

Farthway, sensing that this turn of events cast some doubt on his abilities as gamekeeper and horseman, let out a string of oaths that was remarkable indeed.

"Well, there's no retrieving them now. We may as well go and have a look—we'll be walking back anyway," I said.

Farthway unslung the rifle and I drew out my Webley and cocked the hammer.

The terrier had stayed with us, as one would expect of a dog, particularly of the terrier breed. It was frightened, however, and seemed even to regret that it had led us to the dreary place. We left the road and walked slowly through knee-high bracken until we were at the forest's edge. The dog, barely leading us, would never venture more than a yard or so ahead without looking round to see for certain that we were close behind. It was quiet now, as if afraid of disturbing some sleeping monster. The only sound it made was a barely audible deep growl that always changed to a shaken whine. I placed my hand on its neck, and could feel, through its wiry fur, the little pulse pounding wildly.

"Have you a light?" I asked, after gazing at the ominous wall of trees. "No? I have only a pocketful of matches for my pipe. We should feel our way forward in the darkness then, and save our light for the end of our mission–if there is one."

As we strode cautiously into that looming black mass of the forest, I was overcome by one of those peculiarities of life known as *déjà vu*. Where and when had this occurred before in my life? In a few moments I remembered, and grew all the more wondrous at how strange a thing the mind is, for the instance in my youth that had brought on the *déjà vu* occurred when I was only seven, and through I could not have thought of it more than a dozen times in my thirty or so intervening years, yet there was the incident called up from the murky deep, and recalled clear as a bell. Soon after my seventh birthday, my mother took me on a journey to France, and we boarded the night ferry at Dover. I remembered clambouring up the gangplank, hands clutching at my mother's dress, towards an enormous black shape that was the ship. Since the gangplank seemed to terminate in the very centre of the ominous mass, it was terrifying indeed. I had the dread feeling that we were about to be swallowed up by the huge dark thing, and never were to see the light of day again.

But as I was terrified as a boy, I must admit that approaching the looming mass of the forest that night in the wilds of Shropshire (even considering my age, my companion, and the fact that we were armed and capable men), the same feeling of dread crept upon me. For just as a small boy has his fears, he also has his mother, in whom he may invest boundless quantities of wisdom and courage. And so when he becomes a man, while he is the more capable and strong, yet he no longer has the all-protecting figure to watch over him and he realises that he is entirely on his own. So it seemed to me to be a bob for a shilling: we never can shake off the anxiety that dogs our heels from the cradle to the grave, and is always ready at a moment's notice to clutch its icy fingers round our hearts.

We had slowed to a snail's pace, owing to the blackness and the tangle of trees and branches. We could feel the terrier slinking between our legs and hear its frenzied panting for, so terrified was the animal now that no other sound emerged from it.

"You see," said Farthway in a low voice. He raised his arm and pointed into the darkness. "There's a clearing yonder–can you see the gleam of pale stone?"

I confessed I could see a patch of faint grey, but nothing else. As we drew nearer, however, I could see it was a clearing made by outcropping stone, on which no trees could grow. Drawing still nearer, I could see that the outcropping, as is common with formations of the sort, projected from the earth at an angle, and had almost the appearance of a miniature Gibraltar. After several minutes we came into the clearing but, even though it was an area devoid of trees, the darkness was complete. We walked twice around the rock, which was about sixty feet long, without noticing anything amiss. At its highest, the projecting rock rose in a wall almost perpendicular–a miniature cliff ten or twelve feet high.

"Clancy!" I called softly, for it was he, and only he, who could show us the way.

But the dog had vanished.

"When did you last see him?" asked Farthway.

"I remember him at my side just as we saw the clearing," I replied, "and can't remember seeing him since."

Then there came to our ears a low crying sound. We were almost positive it came from the dog–but from which direction?

"It seems to come from nowhere," said Farthway.

"And yet from everywhere ..."

"It seems nearby ..."

"But far away as well."

Again we cocked our ears. Again, the sound came. It was not more than ten feet away.

"Doctor–above you!" said Farthway in a hoarse whisper.

We had been standing under the cliff end of the rock. I looked upward and in the darkness could see the faint moving silhouette of the small dog's head as he peered down at us, whining.

"There Clancy–how did you get up there?"

"He must have walked up from the other end of the rock–but why would he venture up there?"

I took a match from my pocket and struck it. Its first flash momentarily blinded me, but once the flame had steadied, I held it up as far as I could reach. Clancy's alert face came into view.

"Good God!" cried Farthway in horror.

Just as he shrieked, I uttered a cry of terror as well. We both saw it.

At the dog's feet, projecting over the edge of the rock and placed as through delicately shading the flame which I held aloft, was a human hand.

We stood for some seconds transfixed by the mute horror of it. The terrier, as if bidding us to ascend the rock, began barking. We stared in disbelief at the hand, whose delicate appearance, palm downward, fingers curved slightly, lent a mocking irony to the scene.

"Oh Lord, Doctor," whispered Farthway as he drew near me. "I've seen many a horrid thing, and scores of corpses too, but this is truly frightful."

I had struck another match, and still we stared.

"Well, there's little doubt as to whom the hand belongs," I said. "Poor Betsy's apprehensions have proven justified, I fear. How did the wretch come to be up there? I cannot help wondering how the dog ..."

"I remember seeing a gentle slope of rock on the other side. If we go round this way, we'll run into it."

Again in darkness, it took my eyes some time to grow accustomed to the dim light. At length, we came upon a wide crevice in the rock, through which ran a ramp-like path of gently-sloping rock. This we trudged up without difficulty, yet neither of us was eager to reach the far precipice, aware of the grisly scene which awaited us. As we neared the edge, I could see the blurred movement of the terrier as he skipped round the dark object that lay outstretched on the pale surface of the rock. I was amazed, drawing nearer, at the huge size of the object–it appeared several times larger than a man. The projection was perhaps nine feet wide, and the prone object took up a full half of the width.

"It is huge, Farthway. Was this fellow a giant?"

But before he attempted to answer my question, he was already at the body, kneeling over it. I was somewhat surprised to hear him utter a long sigh of grief. Could this cocky lad by a softer sort underneath? Was the bluff and bluster merely a show? Or, perhaps in a more sinister vein, was this sigh some contrived part of his personality, put on for my benefit? To be sure, this fellow was an enigma–far different from the frank and simple gamekeeper one usually finds in the English countryside. Capable as he was, I was a long way from putting my total trust in him.

"Strike a match Doctor," said he, his voice full of gravity, "and you shall see his true size."

I did so and, leaning over, saw a sight that fairly took my breath away. Farthway too, iron-nerved as he was, gave a gasp, followed by a low moan. The dog lay down in silence beside the remains of his master, his head resting wearily on his paws. The reader will understand the double shock that smote me when I explain that my overestimation of the man's size was due to seeing what I thought was a huge dark object. What I was actually seeing, in the half light, was a body amidst a dark sea of blood: blood as I have never seen it, and pray God never shall see again for the sake of my sanity. It spread out from the corpse in pools and rivulets. It had stained the paws and legs of the dog. It was everywhere, in ghastly profusion. The man lay face downward at the very far edge of the rock. His hands were flung outwards from the body, the one, as the reader knows, protruding even over the edge. From the behaviour of the dog and the large moustache, it was obvious that the man was Charles Compson. He appeared to have fallen violently forwards as if having tripped while running at top speed.

But the shock and revulsion that smote like a hammer blow and fairly set me reeling off the rocky projection, was the manner of the man's death.

"Good God in Heaven," I gasped, "the giant rat!" For upon looking at his neck and back for only an instant, all the horror of the death chamber of the *Matilda Briggs* came racing back through my soul like an express train. Looking round me at the silent forest in a frenzy of apprehension, I realised I had come upon the confluence of two great tragedies. The episode of the *Matilda Briggs* and the trial of the Allistairs were in some nefarious way connected. The centre of all the seemingly disparate events—the vortex, as it were—was not Limehouse, nor even London, but the deep and forbidding forests of Severn.

Even as I spoke the dreaded words to Farthway's astonished and confused face, I could picture in my mind's eye the fugitive pursued by the monster. Totally spent, did he seek this outcropping of rock as a final haven from the beast? Stumbling through the forest—the creature at his heels making god knows what horrid sound—did he stumble across the small hillock, and, in desperation, scale it in the hope that the thing would be unable to reach him? I was recalled from these ghastly speculations by Farthway, who was shaking my shoulder.

"There! You've burnt your fingers with that match, sir—what about a rat? What rat could do this?"

But I waved him off.

"Tell me, Farthway, from what you see before you, how did this poor wretch meet his end?"

"He was running from something—that much is clear. He ran up this slope hoping that whatever was chasing him would not follow. But he was followed, and brought down and worried to death right on this spot. A boar could do this perhaps, but only if wounded—or mad—"

Working our way back down the narrow incline, we found ourselves once again at the edge of the trees. I peered back at the slanting monolith with a shudder. Were it not for the little dog, how many months or years would pass before anyone would have discovered the grisly object on its summit? Hidden from the road in the midst of deep woods, surrounded for miles by wild Shropshire hills and forests, it was indeed a lonely spot to die.

"Here's the spot to look if it's tracks you are searching for," said Farthway.

Only a few moments' search was needed before we were both kneeling down next to a clear set of enormous tracks. We examined them at length using several matches in the process. Farthway, for all his experience and expertise, was plainly confused.

"I've seen these tracks only once before," he said finally. "It was on the hard-packed soil of the forest path near Henry's Hollow. I saw only one print clearly. It had three toes, but I assumed it to be a deformity of sorts, and that the other footprints would appear in the normal cloven patterns of a forest pig, had I been able to see them. Clearly though, it is evident that all the feet of this animal are different from a boar. In fact, they are different from any animal I have ever seen on three continents."

"I see that some feet bear three toes, but others appear to bear five. Is this possible?"

Farthway assumed a puzzled expression.

"It is possible because we have seen it, sir. But other than that, it is the most extraordinary thing I've seen in years."

"There are two beasts, then?"

He shook his head.

"It would appear so. But I've never seen the likes of any of this before. The tracks, too, are huge—much bigger than any boar could be. What sort of animal is this?"

"Ah! The more I see evidence of it, the more bizarre and fearsome it becomes! Come, Farthway, we've a long walk back, and must then ride to town again to summon the authorities. Thank God Holmes arrives tomorrow—"

"He is coming tomorrow?" he asked quickly.

"Yes, he wired—" I stopped at mid-sentence and stared at the man. "How do you know of Holmes?"

"What do you mean? He is a friend of yours?" he answered

nervously.

"You responded as if you'd heard of him. Yet, I have been most careful not to mention him in any company save the Allistairs. Now how came you to hear of him? Answer up straightaway now, or it'll go hard with you!"

He remained silent for some time, obviously undergoing some kind of inner struggle between telling me all and holding back.

"I have nothing more to tell you, Doctor," he said at last. "I'm afraid that if things go hard with me at Strathcombe, then so be it."

Considering the ability of the abductors to plant spies in the Allistair household, and apparently come and go about the place as they pleased, this stance by Farthway set me very ill at ease indeed.

"I urge you to reconsider. Your silence will be interpreted as an admission of being in league—"

"Such an interpretation would be unwarranted and foolish. I am in league with no one. Furthermore, I am most anxious for the well-being of all the Allistairs—hence my concern for both of you earlier this evening when I'd found you had visited the Hollow. Now please, you must not question further, Doctor. As you have said, there is much to do and little time."

So saying, he turned and struck out in the direction of the road. I was about to follow, but remembered the one who had brought us to the eerie place. I retraced my steps to the top of the stony precipice. There was poor Clancy, just as we'd left him. I urged him to come away from the dire spot, but no amount of calling would suffice. When I attempted to pick him up, he growled and snapped at me. So I left him there at his dead master's side, his head on his paws in grief. I descended the rock, and started on the long, cold walk back to Strathcombe with a man whom, for several reasons, I did not wholly trust.

Never before, in all my years with Sherlock Holmes, had events rushed so ominously and inexorably toward some dark and puzzling *finale*. And never before was I so alone.

10

THE VORTEX

I cannot convey in words the relief that coursed through my soul when, shortly after three on the following day, I heard the rattle of the landau in the drive and spied the angular face of Sherlock Holmes, who was perched upon the rear seat.

I was, however, much surprised that he should choose so public an arrival. Surely this formal approach to Strathcombe in broad daylight flew in the face of the warning to the Allistairs that they should seek no help. It seemed to me that he was tempting fate, but so glad was I at his arrival that I decided not to raise the issue. Holmes had come, and I could breathe a bit easier.

"Well, well, Watson," he observed as he climbed the terrace steps, "Brundage tells me that things have been cooking here at Strathcombe since your arrival—"

"Boiling over is more the word—dash it, man, it's good to see you!" I blurted as I wrung his hand. "Brundage has told you about last night's occurrences?"

"The death of young Compson? Most unfortunate. And how's the girl?"

"Off to her relatives. It was all I could do to keep her sanity. But Holmes, I must mention the manner of the man's death—"

"Worried to death?"

"Precisely. An exact duplicate of the McGuinness murder, but how did you guess?"

"Let us just say that for some time I've suspected the abduction of Alice Allistair and the giant rat of Sumatra were connected. No doubt this surprises you. You are also probably surprised that I am showing myself in this rather bold fashion, since the abductors have decreed that Lord and Lady Allistair should act alone. I have my reasons for this too, but shan't explain them now."

"As you wish ..."

"Now you haven't, I hope, mentioned anything of the rat to the Allistairs–"

"Absolutely not; you needn't fear on that score."

"Good."

"Lord Allistair is waiting in his study. There is something of the utmost importance we must discuss."

After a warm greeting from Lord Allistair, and a cup of tea, Sherlock Holmes listened attentively to our story of the message within a message. He sat at the felt gaming table, turning the piece of newsprint round and round in his hand. He even inspected it under his pocket lens.

"Turn up the lamp, would you Watson?"

"What do you make of it?"

"I would say first of all that your optimism is well founded. If this is indeed Alice's hand, then your daughter is presumably alive and well. The matter of the coded message is, however, more difficult. To all appearances, I would agree with you, Lord Allistair, that this was written–or rather pricked–by your daughter. By running your fingers over the pinpricks, you can feel the bumps are on the front side. Thus, the needle or pin was plied from the back. This was done with extraordinary skill, and just the sort of talent a seamstress would develop. I congratulate you on a fine bit of deduction."

Lord Allistair beamed with pleasure as he refilled his cup. Surely, Holmes' arrival had a miraculous effect on the man.

"Furthermore, since the natural mode of executing such a message would have been to stick the paper from the front, we can assume that Alice was being closely watched and was forced to resort to the awkward tactic of punching out the holes from underneath. In this manner, if the paper were resting in her lap, her hand, plying the needle, would be hidden from view beneath the paper."

Lord Allistair could contain himself no longer. He rose from his chair and paced frantically about.

"You see? You see what a clever girl she is? Ah, there's none like her in all the kingdom I tell you!"

Holmes smiled, paused, and continued.

"Perhaps this also explained why she confined the message to the single short article. If she moved her hand about, it would attract attention."

"Now as to the message itself. Can you decipher it?"

"I'm afraid gentlemen," he said after a cursory glance, "that I cannot tell you what it says."

"But Holmes," I protested, "surely you can decipher it if you spend the time and effort. You have solved far more difficult puzzles and codes than this in the past. The Dancing Men and the Musgrave Ritual certainly were more taxing."

"Well, this one is quite difficult, I'm afraid," he said, and idly tucked the paper away into his breast coat pocket.

"Holmes! This is most unlike you. With your love of the mysterious and complex, this cavalier attitude is surprising indeed. When you say you can't tell us–do you mean you can't–or won't?"

"I mean ... well, hello, Lady Allistair, this is indeed a pleasure."

She greeted him cordially, but unfortunately she had relapsed, after her brief reprieve from anxiety, into another fit of depression. This was occasioned by the death of Charles Compson. While she didn't know the man, Betsy's grief was contagious. Furthermore, the violent manner of his dying had sent new ripples of dread through her.

As I saw her enter the study, I couldn't help thinking that, glad as she was at Holmes' arrival, she was still worried lest our presence in some way endanger her daughter. Sympathetic as I was to her dilemma, my total faith in Holmes' prowess and judgment assured me that the present course of action was the only one. Holmes saw her to a fireside seat, drew a chair near to her and, as I had so often observed in the past, displayed a most sympathetic and reassuring bearing towards her.

"There now, Lady Allistair. It's been most difficult for you, and for such a long time too. I have two distinct feelings: first, I am confident that your daughter is safe. Secondly, I have a strong feeling that the trial, hard as it has been, is drawing to a close."

His words had the desired effect, and it wasn't long before she managed to regain her composure. I could see that Holmes had no intention of returning to the subject of the coded message whilst she was in the room. So, confounded though I was with Holmes' casual attitude towards it, I decided to let the matter drop–at least for the time being.

"And now," concluded Holmes after his cordial welcome, "I'm afraid there's some grisly business to attend to. Watson, did I hear you mention that you'd informed the authorities about Mr. Compson?"

"Yes. Directly Farthway and I arrived here last night I sent Wiscomb to town with the news. I've no doubt the local inspector is at the scene this very moment."

Holmes' face darkened.

"Then we'd best be off, and in a rush too—you know very well what the 'local inspector' is capable of doing to even the most rudimentary evidence. Would you care to come along Lord Allistair? No? Well, perhaps it's best if you remain here. Now Watson, let's find this Farthway fellow before we depart; he should be of some assistance."

We found him in his cottage, hovering over a curious-looking lamp on a table that stood before a bow window. I noticed that the window looked out directly toward the house and driveway.

He and Holmes shook hands cordially, although I fancied I saw a shade of suspicion or cunning cross his face. He agreed at once to go with us, and promptly pulled on his riding boots. The walls of the tiny cottage were covered with various hunting trophies, mostly heads of fox masks and stags. On a dresser against the far wall lay an officer's sabre, the scabbard of which was brilliant silver bound in gold. Near it stood the tall shako of the Black Watch. I could not help being impressed. As we turned to go, I again noticed the lamp.

"Holmes," said I, "isn't that a semaphore lamp? I seem to recall seeing one like it earlier—you remember, aboard the steamship Rob Roy, in connection with the adventure of the Curious Boatman—"

"Yes, it's a semaphore lamp," replied the gamekeeper hurriedly. "I took it off a derelict in Bantry Bay and keep it as a souvenir. Should we be off?"

Holmes flicked the brass lever on the lamp's side and the metal shutters snapped open and shut with a brisk clacking sound.

"Quite a signaling device, eh, Watson?" remarked Holmes as we left the cottage. "Now we're to take a carriage—ah, there it is waiting at the foot of the drive."

I shan't bother you, dear reader, with all the details of our grim expedition. Suffice it to say that we located the fatal site once again but only because we spotted the small terrier Clancy at the roadside. I thought at first he'd sensibly given up his lonely wake, but when we reached the outcropping of rock and climbed it, the corpse was gone. I heard Holmes curse sharply under his breath.

"Now, Holmes, surely we can't expect the constables to leave the body out in so desolate a place as this—decency dictates that it be gathered up for proper burial—"

With a grunt of disappointment, he whipped out his pocket lens and set to work scouring the rock and its surroundings. He seemed to find nothing of interest save the great bloodstain, which he examined closely. He descended the rock and walked thrice around it until he stopped near the forest's edge. I could hear him mutter an exclamation.

"The animal, whatever its identity, is enormous. Have you seen these?"

"Yes, last night in the dark. Do you know the identity of the animal? Is it indeed a rat?"

"I'll repeat what I said in the carriage with Lestrade a fortnight ago, Watson: it could be some strange animal not yet known by civilised man. I think that possible. Certainly, we now know, by a multitude of means, that it is an animal–no puppet or optical trick as we suspected upon hearing Sampson's tale. Mr. Farthway, judging from the diameter of these prints, and from the depth of the impression, how much would you guess this animal weighs?"

"Between five and six hundred pounds at least."

"And I, no novice on the subject of footprints, would concur. With a beast like that at his heels we can see why young Compson was so anxious to climb this rock."

The journey back to the house was swift. Farthway sat in the driver's box whilst Holmes and I sat in the landau's rear seat, smoking and talking quietly. I made it plain to Holmes early on that I viewed Farthway with some suspicion, and related his background, along with other recent events which had formed this unsavoury opinion in my mind.

"And I might as well add, Holmes, that I didn't like the look of that signaling lamp he has in his cottage. They can be seen for miles, can they not?"

"Really, Watson," said Holmes impatiently as smoke burst from between his lips in short puffs, "you're acting like the town gossip–"

"But he also knew you were arriving this morning–yet I'd not so much as mentioned your name, nor had Lord Allistair for that matter–how came he to this knowledge?"

Holmes visibly started at this revelation. He fixed his eyes on the back of the gamekeeper, only a few feet from us, who blithely minded the reins without the slightest show of suspicion or concern. Obviously, he could not hear a word we said, for we were talking *sotto voce* and the clatter of the horse and coach obliterated every trace of our conversation.

"Well, that is interesting. I shall remember to have a private talk with Mr. Farthway directly we reach the house."

"Come to think of it, there's something else I remember too," said I, as I leaned forward and asked, in a loud voice, "I say Farthway, who of the household staff informed you of our journey to Henry's Hollow yesterday?"

I had evidently caught him off guard. The question seemed to both puzzle and annoy him.

"I, ah, cannot recall exactly sir."

"You cannot recall?" I persisted. "That is strange, considering it was only yesterday. When you recall, will you let me know?"

I sat back in the carriage and chuckled to myself.

"Neither Lord Allistair nor I breathed a word of our ride to Henry's Hollow to anyone," I said. "This fellow has a lot of information he has no business having. I say—oh well, here's the house behind those trees. See the chimney stack? I suppose the two of us and Lord Allistair should have a lengthy, private chat."

"Capital, Watson. Let's begin after dinner."

And so we did. Lord Allistair had Brundage build the fire up and, as we sat before it with our brandy, he closed the door and bolted it.

"Dr. Watson is correct, Mr. Holmes. Neither of us mentioned our little expedition. How came Farthway to know of it, and your arrival here as well? I must confess this makes me uneasy. We are in violation of the instructions. Considering the manner in which they've been known to deal with those that cross them—I'm thinking of this poor Compson fellow—I am beginning to fear the worst."

"While I fully understand your concern, Lord Allistair, I am afraid we're bound to our present course of action. If I were to depart now it would raise as many suspicions as my arrival. Furthermore, to dismiss Farthway, as you and Watson seem intent upon doing, would only rouse his anger if he is one of the confederates, or diminish our friends if indeed he is loyal."

This point impressed us both. Based on my long association with him, my inclination was to follow Holmes' judgment. We decided to wait it out.

"And now, let me hear more about this place called Henry's Hollow."

We described the place at length, and I mentioned the traces of woodsmoke I had smelt there. Holmes plied us with many questions—how large was the hollow? What of the hillside caverns, how many were there, and how large? Did we see any other traces of recent habitation in the strange place? Would it be possible to conceal horses there, or possibly a cart? Lord Allistair answered all of these as best he could, and we concluded our session after he drew a rough sketch of the place for Holmes to keep. It showed the relation of the Hollow to Strathcombe with regard to distance, direction, and forest paths, and indicated points of interest in the Hollow as well.

"If you don't mind my saying so, Holmes," I remarked as we went upstairs for the night several hours later, "you seem to have lost some of your old zeal."

"Really?" he replied with irritation. "What makes you say that?"

"Did you have a private conference with Farthway?"

"Yes, right after our meeting in His Lordship's study. While the two of you played billiards, I visited his cottage again. We had a lengthy discussion. Here Watson, come into my room for a minute."

I followed him into a room similar to the one I occupied. This one, however, looked out directly over Farthway's cottage. Holmes seated himself and relighted his pipe.

"It's not like you Holmes, to cast puzzles aside as you did the coded message. Furthermore my observations of Farthway seem to have been quite accurate, even valuable, yet you seem to take his proximity to, nay, *involvement in,* this business almost casually–"

"Do I? Really, I hadn't thought so. It is just that I am more careful, less emotionally charged than others of my acquaintance."

Sensing this barb was aimed at me, I rose from my chair and began pacing up and down the room before the window. Through its ancient glass I could see that twilight was fading.

"Did you observe the Allistairs at supper tonight? I've never seen two gloomier people. Obviously our presence here is reassuring to a certain degree, but deeply troubling to them in another. Holmes, we must *do* something!"

He rose also and placed a steadying hand on my shoulder.

"Good old Watson, always the man of action! Always drawn at full-bow ready to spring forth to render assistance. But we must wait till the ransom demand is delivered. To do anything else at this juncture would be imprudent, even disastrous. No doubt the tension is telling on you, as it is on all of us. Has it really been just ten days since we found Jenard's body? It seems like an age ..."

"What have you learnt of Farthway?"

"Ah! First, he was informed of your visit to the Hollow by poor Betsy, who overheard you discussing the jaunt shortly before she entered Lord Allistair's study."

"That could be true," I admitted at last, "or it could be otherwise."

"Still, we must accept it for now. To stir things up here, with regard to Farthway or anyone else, could have dire consequences. We must play the waiting game, Watson. Our success in the case, and the welfare of Alice Allistair, depend on it. But wait, I can perhaps set your mind at ease a bit—is the door bolted?"

I went over and bolted, then returned to my chair. Holmes drew his close to mine.

"As you know, it is often my custom not to reveal all I know about certain cases until my theories can be borne out by events. Now in this case, I have for some time suspected a link between the kidnapping of Alice Allistair and the bloody events connected with the *Matilda Briggs.* The reasons for this are many, but suffice it to say that, so far, my suspicions have proved correct."

He went over to the window.

"As for what will soon transpire out in that wilderness, I have my theories too. But it is a deadly business, and if we are to have a prayer of success, you—and Lord Allistair as well—must follow the kidnapper's instructions exactly and without question. Will you do this?"

"You know very well my faith in you, Holmes. Yes, I give you my assurance that Lord Allistair will comply as well."

"Excellent. Then get to bed. I'm sure that tomorrow we'll need all the strength we can muster. Goodnight."

It would be incontrovertibly demonstrated the following day how true his warning would be. As I left his quarters, I heard the clap of thunder overhead.

I retired soon afterwards, pausing beforehand at my window to sweep my eyes over the dark landscape. A light rain had followed the thunder—the type of drizzling shower that may last for days on end. Drawing the covers about me, I listened to the rain upon the windows, and soon drifted off.

I awoke in the dead of night. A sound in the hallway—perhaps a stealthy tread—had set me bolt upright. The sound was ever so faint, but I had not been sleeping soundly, and so was sensitive to the slightest disturbance. After drawing on my trousers, I went to the dresser. I opened the face of my watch and felt the hands. It was shortly after three. Without a sound, I entered the hallway and cocked my ears. All was quiet. I stood motionless in the dark for several minutes, but could hear nothing. Assuming it was only my nervous imagination, I turned to re-enter my room. But as a last-minute thought, I decided to look in on Holmes. A very light sleeper himself, perhaps he had also heard the noise.

I rapped softly on his door and waited. Hearing no reply, I opened his door and approached the bed. Imagine my surprise and distress at finding him gone! Moreover, his bed had not been slept in. Had Holmes himself been kidnapped, or lured away on a false errand? I let out a low curse. Was there no relief from this anxiety? How ironic, thought I, that just as Holmes arrives and things seem on an even keel at last, he disappears at the hour of greatest need!

But I reconsidered a moment. Reflecting on my friend's unique constitution and strange regimen, I decided it was quite possible he'd gone for a midnight walk. I succeeded in fooling myself in this way for a few minutes. Then two things shook me back to reality. One was Holmes' earlier urging of the need for plenty of sleep. The second thing was an event which sent me reeling with apprehension. Standing near the window I chanced to be glancing out over the grounds. Suddenly the curtains in the cottage widow beneath flew open; a dull glow fanned out from the window onto the ground. In the dim light, I could see a pair of hands upon the brass signaling lamp I had seen earlier. In the next instant, there shot forth from the cottage a beam of incredible brilliance. As bright as the headlight on a locomotive engine, it cut through the night like a white knife as far as the eye could see. The next instant, all was black again, and my eyes were seeing streaks and spots in the beam's absence. Thrice more it flashed, and there was a long pause.

As soundlessly as possible, I threw up the sash, thrust out my head, and peered in the direction the beam had pointed. Winking in the distance, at the very edge of the great forest, was another light–far less brilliant, but plainly visible. When it had finished its message, the light below me shot forth again. I noticed it was made even more visible by the drizzle that caught itself in the glare. After several flashes in quick succession, the lamp ceased; the curtains were redrawn. As I turned to dash from the bedroom, I heard the slamming of the cottage door and the rush of feet on the gravel drive.

Then this explained Holmes' absence! He'd obviously seen the flashing signal from his bedroom and left the house to investigate. Disappointed that he'd left without me, I paused only long enough to snatch up my revolver before plunging down the staircase.

I left by the front door. Barefoot, I slipped silently down the terrace steps and round the drive to Farthway's cottage. The door was unlocked, and the cottage was empty. The gamekeeper's bed, too, was undisturbed. Then Holmes had heeded my suspicions; he had stayed up waiting for Farthway to signal his confederates.

The odour of hot metal sent me over to the window. I flicked the lamp's lever, but it had been extinguished. A thought struck me: should I relight the lamp and set it flashing? A false signal might foil their plans. On the other hand, any misleading on my part might endanger Lord Allistair's daughter, so I left the cottage, closing the door behind me.

Ambling down the drive in the dead of night, I felt as dejected as an orphan. Obviously, Holmes had left in pursuit of Farthway—no doubt it was his tread I'd heard in the hallway. But why had he gone alone? Why, after all the adventures we had shared, had he chosen to complete this one without me? Did he fear for my safety? Did he think me unfit? I was disappointed, and more than a little hurt, by his actions.

Since sleep was out of the question, I continued to walk the grounds. The old timbered lodge, scarcely visible, loomed up ominously through the trees. I stopped at the stables; they were silent save for the drunken snoring of Wiscomb. I entered, and walking past the stalls, heard the swish of horsetails and thumping of hooves. The animals snorted at me, but became calm when I spoke to them. There seemed to be no horses missing. So the chase, wherever it was occurring, was on foot. I returned to the terrace where I sat on the balustrade for almost an hour. But nothing happened. There were no sounds except the usual night-time ones: the sighing of the great trees overhead, the hooting of owls and din of crickets. The rain continued to mist downwards. With a chill, I realised I was clad in nothing except my trousers and nightshirt, and longed for the warmth of bed. I made my way wearily back to my room and, after a lengthy bout of conjecture and worry, fell asleep.

I was awakened with a start. A shadowy figure was kneeling at my bedside.

"Hsssst! Watson! Up man, up!"

It was Holmes, dressed in a dripping waterproof. His face bore the keen look I have long associated with impending action.

"Holmes, thank God you're safe! But where the devil were you last night, and why didn't you rouse me?"

My voice must have shown irritation, for he gripped my shoulder earnestly.

"Steady old fellow. There's no time to explain it now. Take my word that what was done was done in your best interest—"

"Did you catch Farthway? Where—"

"There, there!" he interjected sternly. "Now you mustn't ask, really you mustn't! Farthway is gone and I've returned safe. Now there's the end of it. We must concentrate on the matter at hand: *the demand has arrived.* The money is to be carried by you and Lord Allistair—"

"By *me*?" I said, getting groggily out of bed. "Surely there is some mistake. No one in these parts knows of me."

"You aren't mentioned by name—but come! Everyone's downstairs waiting."

With that, he departed, and it was only after several minutes that the full import of his words struck me. I must confess I had not planned on being the actual courier of the money. A confidant, yes, but an actual *participant* in the exchange! That I hadn't counted on. Furthermore, the choice of Lord Allistair as courier also puzzled me. I could of course understand the villains' wanting his wealth, but requesting his personal delivery of it was nonsensical. Upon reflection, I realise that I should have been suspicious at the outset, as events were later to prove. My heart thumping madly in anticipation, I went downstairs into the great hallway.

It was a tense scene that greeted me there. Lord Allistair, a non-smoker, was pacing wildly to and fro in the hallway puffing frantically on one of Holmes' cigarettes. His wife was seated on the leather bench, still as a wax figurine save for her hands, which trembled in her lap as she wrung them. Brundage stood with the tea tray near the door. The breakfast upon it was untouched, even unnoticed. Holmes, exuding torrents of smoke, muttered to himself as he peered through the lattice windows. For the first time I noticed his appearance. His trouser legs were torn and muddy, especially about the knees. His face was lined with tiny cuts and scratches. Obviously, his nighttime chase had taken him through the woods and thickets. The fine rain beat on the windows with scarcely a sound. The silence was broken only by the hall clock, which struck at the hour of seven.

Holmes approached solemnly and thrust a note into my hand. Like the first note from the kidnappers, this one was composed of letters pasted upon a notesheet. It read:

> LORD ALLISTAIR—You shall carry the required sum to the oak ring. You shall be accompanied by the man who rode there with you earlier and no one else. You shall come unarmed. My manservant holds a knife to your daughter's throat. You imperil her life if you fail.

The last portion of the note was particularly ominous—made even more so by the absence of any written message from Alice.

"So there you have it," said Holmes dryly.

Lord Allistair, called from his intense reverie by the sound of Holmes' voice, came forward to greet me.

"How are you this morning, Doctor? Eh? Well, I'm a bit shaken too, I'll admit. The note seems clear enough; we're to return to Henry's Hollow. It's strange, though, that they should have included you—"

"They've seen us together no doubt. I shall be happy to go with you and shall try to be a stabilising influence."

"I can't help thinking ... perhaps the coded message was meant for you after all ..."

"We haven't the time now to puzzle over it."

"You must remember this, Doctor: you're not bound to go. If you'd rather not—"

"Nonsense, Lord Allistair! I am bound to go, and in more ways than one, not the least of which is my affection for you and your family. Let us be off then. You have the money I presume ..."

He pointed to a pair of leather saddle pouches into which the notes had been transferred. These I slung over my shoulders after donning my heavy coat. Upon seeing us make ready, Lady Allistair sprang from her bench and clung to Lord Allistair in a fit of worry.

"Oh dear God!" she cried. "What if I'm to lose you both?"

We comforted her as best we could. Then Holmes and I left them alone for a few minutes while we talked on the terrace outside. How different Strathcombe looked early on that drizzly morning compared to the peaceful, sun-washed retreat of two evenings earlier! The terrace stones were slick and shiny with rain. The wind stung our cheeks and ears. It was dark.

"There, I don't like the look of that!"

Holmes pointed towards the stream that ran through the meadow and willow clumps. A heavy mist was rising from the wet bottomlands of the valley. An ominous pale grey colour, it crept towards the woods on either side.

"Where was the note found?" I asked, to change the subject.

"Tied to this very door-knocker, wrapped in oiled paper. Brundage discovered it less than an hour ago. It was evidently left during the night. Ah! I hear His Lordship coming. Quick Watson, listen carefully to what I have to say—"

He grabbed me by the shoulders and peered intently into my face.

"You must know, dear fellow, that you are embarking upon a dangerous errand. Not only dangerous, but possibly fatal, despite all that I can, and will do to help you. Do you understand?"

"I do. And I accept the risk. What will you be doing in the interim?"

"I cannot say. First, because to reveal my plans to you might jeopardise everyone's safety. Secondly, though I have a few notions as to what will transpire, I am not yet fully certain. Will you trust my judgment?"

"Implicitly. As I always have."

"Then Godspeed to you, friend. If all works well, we shall by tonight have freed Alice Allistair and caught the villains who have taken her and murdered others. Shhh! Not a word!"

Lord Allistair strode onto the terrace looking remarkably composed. But whether it was composure or contained vehemence, I couldn't say.

"Whatever the outcome, gentlemen," he said grimly as we walked to the stables, "the conclusion is at hand. Thank God for that at least."

Wiscomb had our mounts ready. They pawed the gravel as he held the reins. I flung the pouches over the flanks of Lord Allistair's horse, and mounted my own. Although none of the staff save Brundage and his wife were aware of the ransom demand, Wiscomb could sense the import of the moment.

"God bless you, sir," he said softly as he helped Lord Allistair into his saddle.

"Thank you, Wiscomb. You are to go to the house now and remain there; Brundage has strict instructions for everyone, Farthway included."

"Farthway, sir? Farthway has gone."

Lord Allistair turned sharply in disbelief.

"Gone! Gone where?"

"I don't know sir. He's not in his quarters."

I glared at Holmes and shook my head slightly. This certainly was not an auspicious beginning. But Holmes met my stern glance with a blank, resigned expression.

"Well, we shan't worry over him," said His Lordship, and we started off down the drive together. As we headed towards the mist in the valley, I looked back at Holmes, who raised his hand in farewell.

It is at this point that the memories of the horrific occurences at Henry's Hollow cause my pen to shake, my brow to grow damp. It is many, many years later that I write these words, and though the recollections of the trial should have faded and dimmed with time, yet they seem in some perverse way to grow more vivid.

We made our way into the drifting mist. As we ascended the opposite side of the valley, it seemed to cling and follow us into the forest. It swirled amongst the tree trunks. It crawled and floated up the slopes; it flowed languidly down into the dells and hollows of the woods.

If the forest seemed gloomy on our previous trip, it was fearsome now. The nearest trees were easily seen–the oaks with their rich brown bark, the beeches with their blue-grey metallic sheen–but after only a few yards, even the most massive of the trunks were faint. Beyond them lay a pale grey curtain that was impenetrable.

As unnerving as the mist was the utter silence of the woods. No jays shrieked and cackled. No songbirds trilled. The only sounds were the thump of hooves and faint patter of rain upon the leaves.

After twenty minutes we paused while Lord Allistair examined the path.

"It's much more difficult to find one's way in this fog," he said. "In normal daylight I have landmarks enough to guide me–but now it's a labyrinth. Pray to God we're on the right path and haven't missed a turn. What a tragedy to lose my daughter because we cannot find the place!"

"No need to worry yet, Lord Allistair. See that curious bent tree there? I remember that from the day before yesterday–it came just before you showed me the Keep from a small clearing–"

"Yes, I do remember it. You've a keen eye, Doctor. Henry's Hollow lies not far ahead."

After several moments (it seemed like hours) we stopped on the path. Through the mist, I could barely recognise the strange symmetry of the oak ring some yards ahead. We waited for a shout, a whistle. None came. Proceeding still further, going as slowly as possible, we at last arrived at the rim of oaks. Peering down, one could see only the uppermost branches of the trees in the hollow, for they were above the low-lying mist. Beneath us the grey earth fell gently away into the swirling vapour. There came to my ears a faint rustling sound.

"Stand to!" a voice called.

Not twenty feet away, a shadowy hooded figure emerged from behind a trunk and approached us.

"Don't move," the figure cautioned, and strode catlike by us back to the trail over which we had passed and disappeared.

This behaviour only served to heighten my anxiety. But after a few minutes, I divined the reason for it. I turned my head to Lord Allistair and whispered.

"He's listening on the path to be sure there are no others."

He nodded in agreement. How fortunate that we had obeyed the instructions! Once again, I couldn't help but wonder at the careful planning and painstaking execution of the diabolical plot. There was certainly, at the centre of this evil web, a man of monstrous cunning and deliberation.

The figure returned and strode silently round us. He was dressed in black from head to toe and carried a pistol. The hood covered his entire head, and as can be imagined, increased the chimerical quality of his appearance.

"Open your coats."

We obeyed, and the figure seemed satisfied that we were unarmed. He beckoned us to follow him and led us down into the hollow. As we guided our mounts down the slope, the air grew heavy with the thick, dank smell of matted vegetation and wet earth. There was another odour, very faint, that was almost musky. Our guide stepped behind a tree and emerged carrying a lantern, which he held aloft as he walked before us. The mist formed a delicate halo round the lamp, which I assumed was being used as a signal since it was utterly useless to guide us.

We passed the chimney tree which marked the approximate centre of the hollow. We were then proceeding to the far end of it—the portion that Lord Allistair had not shown me.

We proceeded one behind the other along a faint track that wound between the trees. As we made a turn in this path, a breeze coming from the far end of the hollow sprang up and smote us head on.

Our horses stopped in their tracks.

There were a few seconds of silence. Then Lord Allistair's horse snorted twice, the thick streams of vapour shooting from its nostrils. It whinnied sharply, its head bobbing up and down. My horse stretched its neck forward and brought its nose up. It grunted, stamped its feet, and began to back up. The breeze freshened still more, and Lord Allistair's horse wheeled and bucked. He fought to stay in the saddle, and deftly brought the animal towards me. It rolled its eyes so that the whites showed.

Alarmed, our guide ran back to us and, clutching at the horse's bridle, gave the order to dismount. Puzzled, Lord Allistair complied, and I followed. As instructed, we tied the animals together to a small tree and proceeded on foot, Lord Allistair carrying the saddle pouches. I looked back to see them huddled together, flank to flank. They stamped their feet and pawed the earth, and their ears pointed in our direction, turning and twitching.

I need not relate the effect of this incident upon me. Suffice it to say that the previous incidents of this sort of behaviour on the part of horses and dogs gave me an inkling of what could be waiting for us at the far end of the hollow. My knees turned weak, and I felt a tingling in my limbs. So as not to alarm my companion, I managed to control the terror that was beginning to well up inside of me.

We came at last to the far end of Henry's Hollow. I heard the sound of falling water. During my initial visit to the place, I assumed that it was elliptical in shape and similar on all sides. I was in error, however, because although roughly the shape I had imagined, the far side of the hollow was not a sloping, dish-shaped depression but a deep gorge, bounded by a perpendicular cliff of layered limestone.

This precipice rose some thirty feet, and was topped by an oak ridge as was the rest of the rim. Upon reaching this sheer wall, we turned to the left and descended a step path that led us to a small clearing in the shadow of the cliff. From the rocky wall spurted a miniature cascade, the sound of which had been audible for some distance. The clearing was covered with ferns and moss. I imagined the sun never shone in this place, so tucked away was it in the dankest, gloomiest part of the hollow. At the far end of the clearing I saw a glow from a campfire. In all probability, this place was the source of the smoke I'd detected earlier. The mist in the clearing was as thick as the heaviest London fog. From the splashing sound of water, I surmised that the tiny waterfall fed a pool at the base of the cliff. From this pool the mist seemed to waft up in thick clouds.

We made our way into the clearing. After a few steps, I could see the campfire. Stretched out next to it was a pair of shiny boots—the firelight flickered off them. As the wraith-like cloud of mist was borne away, I could see the man who lounged by the firelight. The wide-brimmed hat, drooping moustache, dark complexion and earrings were unmistakable. It was the gypsy who'd followed us the day of our arrival. We drew still closer, and the dark-shrouded figure who had guided us to the dismal lair stepped close to the seated gypsy and whispered into his ear. The gypsy, in turn, whispered back.

"Bring the money forward," said the hooded figure in a low, measured monotone. The two men examined the contents of the pouches for several minutes. Although they did not count all of it, they seemed satisfied that the ransom was complete.

"My daughter!" shouted Lord Allistair. I could see the perspiration on his brow—the throbbing arteries of his neck and forehead. He had clearly waited long enough. "Where is my daughter?"

The gypsy drew a revolver from his loose coat and pointed it at Lord Allistair's breast. His companion did the same, and pointed his gun at me. The gypsy made a sign and his companion commenced speaking.

"Your daughter is safe. You shall see her for a few minutes when I have her brought forward. Now listen carefully to what I have to say: you have apparently kept your word. You have come as instructed with the required amount of money. This is good. You shall see in a few seconds that we have kept our word: your daughter is safe. Not only is she safe, but she has not been harmed in any way.

"But there remains for you, Lord Allistair, one final task which you must accomplish before we release your daughter to you. Failure to complete this task will result in her death—"

"What is it—in the name of Heaven! And why was I not advised of this remaining duty earlier?"

The figure paused and, in an explanatory tone, continued.

"In order to secure our safe passage from this country, we need additional hostages."

"I refuse."

The gypsy beckoned to his companion, who bent over close to receive more instructions. I thought it odd that the gypsy, obviously the leader of the two, did no talking. The possibility struck me though, that there could be a language problem. In any event, the hooded figure continued as spokesman.

"If you refuse, we cannot guarantee the safety of your daughter. You must know that we will keep the hostages only long enough to escape. They will be released unharmed shortly thereafter."

"How can I be assured of this?"

"You must trust us to keep our word, as we have done thus far. Look here ..."

With this, he cried out in a language I had never heard before—nor since, for that matter. Almost immediately, two dim figures appeared in the mist behind the fire. All we could see of them was their silhouettes, but one appeared to be of medium height, the other short and crooked.

"Come forward slowly," said the hooded figure, and Lord Allistair and I approached the two men and the fire. After a few steps, it was apparent that the pool fed by the waterfall lay directly behind the campfire. The two figures were standing on the opposite bank.

"Father!" cried an anguished voice, and at the same instant there strode into the firelight a spectacle that I shall never forget. I remembered the portraits of Alice Allistair; there was one at the Bayswater residence, and another at Strathcombe. She was stunning in her loveliness—yet the sad creature that stood waving in the mist before us bore little if any resemblance to her pictures. Her features drawn as if in incredible pain and anguish, she appeared to have been crying for weeks on end. Her bosom heaved and shook, and she had the captured, frightened expression on her face that I had observed before only on the faces of the inmates of prisons and asylums. One glance at her told me of the torture and confinement she had endured these two months, yet I was certain it was even far worse than I had imagined. Lord Allistair dropped to his knees with a low cry.

"Oh Father—" she began, but was cut short by the other figure that leapt forward from the grey fog. It was remarkable for its ugliness. He was a hunchbacked Malay—no doubt the same one Sampson had mentioned. His appearance was hideous: a thick, greasy face, an ugly, twisted gash for a mouth, a nose like a blob of glazier's putty. The whole face was enclosed by a muslin turban, stained with grease and dirt. The small eyes danced in his gnome-like head. The stunted arms twitched, and the thick lips trembled in excited babbling.

But these observations were secondary. The object that held our attention was clutched in the wretch's right fist, and directed at the throat of the lovely girl. It was a dagger, and one glance at its blade, glinting in the firelight, was enough. Recalling the ghastly wounds inflicted upon Raymond Jenard, I was convinced that but a few strokes of this weapon were capable of rending flesh in the most gruesome manner. The blade was a foot long, and wound its way to and fro from hilt to tip in a zig-zag fashion, like the path of a crawling snake. I heard a gasp from Lord Allistair, and turned to see him leap forward toward his captive daughter.

"Halt! No further!" shouted the gypsy, bringing his revolver up and cocking the hammer as he did so.

Lord Allistair paused, then drew back. The gypsy glanced at me for an instant, then turned away. But it was too late, he had cried out, and in perfect English. Furthermore, the voice was faintly familiar. I had heard it before—somewhere.

"Are you all right, Alice?"

"Yes, Father. Oh, thank Heaven you've come! I–" but the poor girl, choked with sobs, was unable to continue.

Heartened by the appearance of his daughter, Lord Allistair considered for a moment, then spoke.

"Who are the hostages?"

The hooded figure pointed in my direction.

"This man, and the man who arrived yesterday," said he.

"I cannot do this. These men are my guests. As a gentleman I cannot–"

"For God's sake man, do it!" I shouted. "They want the two of us only to make certain a general alarm isn't raised until they're safely away. Is this not so?"

Both men nodded.

Lord Allistair looked at his weeping daughter, then at me.

"You must understand Doctor, how torn I am–"

"Nonsense! Go! Fetch him at once! You must hurry–we've come this far–there's no stopping now. They have kept their word; therefore I don't fear for myself. Now there's the end of it: you must be off!"

He turned towards the kidnappers.

"How shall Alice be returned to me?"

"One of us will follow you back to the house with her," said the hooded figure in a carefully rehearsed speech. "We shall be far behind you, and hidden. When we see that the second hostage is well upon his way here, we shall release your daughter in the vicinity of the house. She will find her way home from there."

"Very well," said Lord Allistair after some reflection.

"But mind," continued the masked man, "any divergence from the pre-arranged plan will spell her death."

"This is most repugnant to me," said Lord Allistair. "But I see I have little choice in the matter."

"I shall guide you to your horse. But first, I must fasten your companion to the tree with these."

While the gypsy held his pistol on Lord Allistair, the other approached, carrying a pair of heavy iron shackles of the type used on prison ships. Realising total cooperation was the only sensible course, I complied readily as he bade me sit on the ground, my back against a small beech tree. He then drew my arms behind me round the tree and shackled my wrists together. Being bound in this fashion made me most uncomfortable in many ways. However, sensing that my predicament was most painful to Lord Allistair, I avoided his glance and pretended to make light of the matter as he left the clearing, led by the hooded guide.

Just before they disappeared into the grey vapour, he turned and looked at his daughter.

"Never fear, dearest," he said hoarsely, "all will be well."

And then, with a glance at me, added, "I am terribly sorry, Doctor ... you must—"

"Nonsense," I quipped, as jovially as possible. "The sooner you complete your errand, the sooner we're together again. Now off you go!"

They departed, and a short while later the guide returned. After an exchange of nods with the gypsy, he led Alice Allistair from the clearing. I noticed as they passed me that she was sobbing softly, and that her hands were bound behind her. She whirled in an instant, her eyes fixed upon me with a look of guilt, and dread. She cried out:

"Oh, Dr. Watson. I tried—"

But she could not finish; a hand was clapped over her face, and she was half-led, half-dragged, from the clearing. Enraged, I swore an oath, straining at my bonds. But it was useless. Confined as I was, I could not even rise to my feet. Ominous thoughts raced through my brain. Then the coded message was sent by Alice Allistair, and it was meant for me! I remembered Holmes' casual dismissal of the message, and cursed him under my breath. How could he have been so careless, so foolish? But I was interrupted from these thoughts by a peal of laughter. Turning my head, I saw that an enormous change had overcome the gypsy.

No longer lounging idly by the fire, he was convulsed with laughter. The laughter was not normal. It was explosive—maniacal. He shrieked, he giggled, he sobbed with laughter. He lolled on the ground; his arms and legs twitched.

The hunchback, seeing this fit overtake his master, ran from the clearing and returned instantly, bearing a tin cup. The gypsy gulped down its contents, which I assumed to be spirits of some sort, and grew calmer. He stood up, paced about, and mopped his brow with a colourful handkerchief. Then he approached and, stopping not ten feet away, leaned toward me.

"You must excuse the outburst, Dr. Watson, but I've waited so long ..."

An icy chill pierced my chest at these words. The voice caught, and stayed in my ears. It was a voice I knew, and was associated with unpleasantness.

The gypsy drew still nearer.

"You know my voice? Come come, Doctor, can't you recall it? I am sure your clever friend Sherlock Holmes would remember in an instant ..." but he was taken again by a fit of laughter. Wailing, he caught at his sides until it subsided. As he made a tremendous effort to control himself, I observed the unmistakable symptoms: the trembling in the extremities, the perspiring, the wild-eyed stare, the raving, convulsive laughter. It was quite apparent: *the man was mad.*

"Who am I, Dr. Watson? Eh? I see by your puzzled look that you don't recollect. Do you need some help?"

With this, he drew up to me and, in an instant, had torn off the gypsy disguise. What I saw caused things to weave and whirl about, then grow dim. I was speechless with awe: the face looking into mine had come forth from the grave.

"Impossible!" I gasped. "You are dead!"

Again, a change came over the man. The raving maniac was replaced by the cold, calculating machine I has so often observed in earlier times.

"No, Doctor," he said in a voice that was barely audible, "no, I am not dead. Though people have thought so for some time."

I listened spellbound, the terror growing in me.

"My presumed death made my escape easier," he went on soothingly, "and still protects me. The only reason I shall reveal all to you is because I have the assurance–nay the *certainty*–that neither you nor Sherlock Holmes will live to see tomorrow's sun."

THE BEAST IN HENRY'S HOLLOW

"Stapleton! So you are the villain behind this nefarious scheme!"

"Ah, but you may as well know my name: Rodger Baskerville! Though I have traveled under many different guises, that is my true name. And Baskerville Hall my true residence!"

"That is debatable, to say the least."

He struck me across the face. Then, as if alarmed at his lack of self-control, he caught his fist up and held it to his breast. He rocked to and fro on his haunches, his head flung back, eyes half closed.

"I am excitable lately," he groaned. "The strain, the strain has been intolerable. If you knew of the planning, the waiting ... Ah! But it shall be over soon. Oh, Dr. Watson! Although I have reason to despise you and your foul friend, I admit that the death you are to suffer is a *horrid* one!"

A fluid panic overtook me and turned my limbs to water. My hair stood on end.

"What's this? Do I detect the look of fear upon your face, eh?"

He rolled his head backwards and, staring straight up into the grey sky, shrieked with laughter.

"Oh, this is delicious. Truly delicious! Already the long wait is well worth it."

The fit seized him again, and he was convulsed. Finally, he managed to calm himself, and proceeded in the soft, soothing voice that so characterised the Stapleton of my acquaintance.

"I trust you are impressed with the planning and execution of this venture—you should be. It is the product of intense thought and firm discipline. You should know at the outset Dr. Watson, that I have also planned your death. Your death, and the death of Sherlock Holmes.

In a sense I regret killing you, since you are obviously a dupe and a simpleton, and kept by our 'friend' only because you are a toy to feed his pride. However, Sherlock Holmes has wronged me deeply, and must be punished. Part of his punishment is death, but the other part—"

And here he paused for emphasis.

"—is watching *you* die before him."

"You beast!" I cried. "You are mad!"

"*Stop it!* Stop it, Doctor!" He screamed. "Now we'll have no more of such talk, do you hear?"

He stared down at me in a fit of rage. I remained silent and after another pause, he continued in a low voice.

"I am excitable, true. But who wouldn't be as he sees the genius of his plan unfolding? Who wouldn't be agitated as the hour of sweet revenge draws closer?"

He paused to light a cigarette. The hollow was entirely silent save for the splashing of the tiny waterfall behind me.

"Ah, I bask in the euphoria of it! At this very moment Sherlock Holmes, supposedly the finest mind in Europe, gropes his way through this fog, unaware that he comes to meet his death! And as the lamb strays towards the wolf, I shall tell you a story. Would you like that? Yes, of course you would! We have almost an hour, and no doubt you are anxious to hear of my brilliant evasion from the Grimpen mire ..."

It is a mark of the madman to indulge in fantasies and grandiose delusions. So Baskerville regarded his every thought and action as divinely inspired. But I noticed his eyes wander and glaze slightly as he fell into his narrative. The liquor was taking effect—aided, no doubt, by the nervous exhaustion that was clearly overtaking him. It is enervating to rave and shriek. Also, now that the battle was won, the passion that had kept him going at fever pitch for the past weeks was quickly fading. My only hope of escape, however faint, was to keep him talking—to feed his delusions. In this way, I hoped, he would be enfeebled by the time Holmes arrived. What would happen then was in the hands of fate.

"Yes, I'd be delighted to hear your story. And pray, don't leave out a word. I must admit you've won, Baskerville. You are a devilishly clever chap—"

"Indeed I am! And so, let's have no more talk of ..."

He looked furtively sideways and continued in a whisper.

"... *madness* ..."

"It was sheer genius the way you eluded capture on the moors. Everyone thought you'd perished in the mire—"

"Idiot! Did it never occur to you that I had an escape route planned beforehand? Hah! Holmes was fortunate enough to see through my little scheme, but even he was too muddle-headed to foresee the possibility that I had prepared for everything. Well! As to what happened—"

Drawing yet closer, he sat cross-legged, facing me, on the dank earth—the mist swirling in spirals about him. A languid expression on his face, he began his tale. Seeing that he sat nearby, I made one supreme effort to break free my shackles with the hope of swinging my arm round and catching him on the temple with the chain.

"Don't waste your energy, Doctor. It's useless, I assure you. Those chains can hold a Shire horse—now, ah yes, the flight from the moor ..."

"We found Sir Henry's boot at the edge of the path. We assumed you dropped it in flight, then sank into the bog—"

"You assumed that because I wished you to assume it; I planned for it. When I heard the pistol shots through the fog, I knew the hound was dead and my plan had been discovered. I left my house and ran to the old tin mine at the centre of the bog, dropping the boot on the way deliberately. Once at the mine, however, I picked up a haversack I had hidden there for just such an eventuality—for as loutish as your friend Sherlock Holmes is, I had respect for his tenacity."

"How decent of you—" I interjected sarcastically, then winced in expectation of another blow. But engrossed in the tale that extolled his prowess, he ignored my comment.

"The haversack contained a blanket and tins of food, enough for several days. Now the brilliance of my planning, Dr. Watson, was in the forging of another path, unknown even to my wife, which led from the tin mine out onto the moor in the opposite direction. Had your friend been more careful, less flushed with his apparent success, he would have noticed it. But as fate would have it, he did not, and assumed I was dead.

"By the time you arrived at the abandoned mine, I was miles away. Tramping the countryside by night and sleeping in rocky crevices during the night, I made good progress. On the third day, I took a chance and entered a small village. I bought a newspaper and was delighted to discover that I was dead. You've no idea, Dr. Watson, how easy it is to get away when it's widely supposed that you are lying at the bottom of a bog. I made my way northward, heading for

Yorkshire since I know that country well. But on the way I entered
the valley of the Severn, and there I fell in with old King Zoltan and
his gypsy tribe. They were generous people, and asked no questions.
I adopted their dress and habits, and joined their caravan as it wound
its way through the hillsides and forests. Having been raised in Costa
Rica and the son of a native mother, I was naturally congenial to their
fiery temperament and romantic ways. King Zoltan adopted me as
his son, and so my disguise was complete; my escape from England
assured."

The mist was thinning, and more of the clearing was now visible.
At its far end, beyond the shallow pool, was a wall of rock. In this wall
was a small cave, the entrance of which was a dark crevice. From this
narrow fissure I saw the Malay emerge. He hobbled from it on his
stunted legs and made his way to the fire, which he built up. This task
completed, he scurried back to the burrow in the cliffside, gathering
the folds of his filthy robe about him. I watched as Baskerville
stretched his legs, and, leaning casually back on one elbow, continued.

"Perhaps you already know that this ring of oaks, and the hollow
within, is a favourite stopping place for gypsies. Into this very place
our caravan entered in the early winter of '89, just a few weeks after
my flight from the moors. We camped here for the winter, living off
the game we shot or captured in these forests. During our stay we
frequently saw shooting parties as they ventured forth from
Strathcombe. I was impressed with the wealth of the estate. When I
heard the owner was none other than Peter Allistair, I was shocked
to the core, and overjoyed too, for I had long sought to repay him for
his insolence–"

"Lord Allistair? What did–"

"Never mind," said Baskerville with a wave of the wrist, "it
happened long ago, before even the hound, but I could never forgive
him for ruining me. I had planned to kill him some dark night, but
realised the risk was great, and the punishment too swift ..."

I sadly recalled the ten weeks of anguish suffered by Lord Allistair,
and was only too well aware of the effectiveness of Baskerville's
torture. But what had Lord Allistair done to deserve this? Clearly it
was not in his character deliberately to wrong any man. My thoughts
were interrupted as the man before me continued his gruesome tale.

"But as fate would have it, I had no time for vengeance. In the
spring, the old king died. His people carried the body to the bottom
of one of these grisly caves and buried him. When I learned that the

band was to head south, I decided to depart. With a purse full of gold, a gift from King Zoltan, I continued northwards until I came to Liverpool. There I signed on a ship bound for America.

"It was during the voyage to America, Dr. Watson, that the memories of my frustration crept to the foreground. For weeks, I could think of nothing save the humiliating defeat I suffered at the hands of Sherlock Holmes. Such a brilliant plan, and foiled by an amateur meddler! It was then that the seed of my hatred germinated and began to grow. It grew with each passing day. And as weeks flowed into months, it became—"

"A passion," I interjected. He glanced at me nervously.

"You could call it that," he admitted, "and why not! What normal man, deprived of his rightful inheritance after months of careful planning, wouldn't seek revenge? However, I knew it was best to stay out of England for several years to give added credence to my death, and to let events fade into the past.

"After landing in America I worked my way across that continent, finally arriving in San Francisco. There I signed aboard a Russian sealer, and spent the next 15 months in the Bering Sea. In that frozen waste, there was little to think about save my hatred for Sherlock Holmes and the revenge I sought. My next ship took me to Santiago, where I met the man who is now carrying Alice Allistair to—"

His tale was interrupted by a sound. It came from the crevice in the rock wall. It was a sound I had never heard before, and it froze the very blood in my veins. It was an animal sound, and began in a series of snuffling grunts, then rose to a deep growl. Finally, it resolved itself into a piercing squeal that echoed off the craggy walls of the ravine in hideous cacophony.

"Good God!"

Looking back, I can scarcely remember saying those words, for my entire soul was seized with a fear so intense that speech was difficult, and thinking almost impossible. The memories swam in my tormented mind: the mutilated body of Captain McGuinness— the gory remains of Compson—

I struggled frantically to escape the bonds. I lunged my body forward a half-dozen times until my limbs ached, my wrists bled. My heart thumped madly, so that my entire chest shook. My stomach had the formless, quivering sensation that comes only with the deepest dread.

"There, there, Dr. Watson! You'll injure yourself! You *shall* be injured, I can assure you," he added darkly, "but all in good time.

Now you must sit and listen to my story—there's a good chap. Wangi!"

The heathen shuffled from the mouth of the cave and approached. He held a strange object in his hand. It was a wooden rod with an iron hook fixed to its end. I recognised the object: it was a mahout's goad, used to drive elephants. The hook was red at the tip.

"So our friend is misbehaving? He is impatient, eh, Wangi?"

The wretch grinned and babbled, revealing a loathsome mouth of broken and stained teeth. He struck the goad against the ground repeatedly, convulsed with guttural laughter.

"Ah, he is hungry, no doubt! Here Wangi—see how our poor hostage trembles in every limb. No, Doctor, the beast is entirely captive until we release it. He shan't emerge from his lair until Mr. Holmes arrives to take his place beside you ..."

The misshapen servant hobbled back into the cave. Almost immediately there came a dull thumping sound, and then another animal scream—this one yet longer and louder than the previous one. Though entirely strange (and therefore, all the more terrifying) to my ears, it resembled elements of other animal sounds: the snuffling which began the eerie cries resembled the snorting of a horse; the growling was deep and pervasive, like that of a tiger. The grotesque squeal that terminated the cry resembled the sound a pig makes as its throat is cut. It was made still more fearsome by the fact that it issued from a tunnel of rock, which amplified it—then resounded from the cliff walls in a shattering cadence.

As the sound faded from the hollow, so my sight and senses drifted away. I was propelled into a sea of swirling darkness.

In my swoon, which was short-lived, I dreamed I was drowning. This was no doubt due to the fact that, upon waking, I could scarcely breathe for all the spirits Baskerville had poured down my throat in efforts to revive his victim. I gagged and choked on the harsh rum. Nevertheless, it brought me round.

"There now, Doctor. Your friend approaches and time grows short. How am I to complete my marvellous tale if you won't stay awake?"

I nodded my head in weak resignation and he continued.

"It was early in '93 when I met Jones in Santiago. He had jumped ship from the *Meeradler*, a Prussian nitrate barque, and they were scouring the docks for him. Accustomed to pursuit, I helped him elude the officers. We struck up an immediate friendship, and consequently decided to sign on the *Dunmore* bound for Bombay. As I have mentioned previously, Dr. Watson, my desire for revenge was beginning to occupy a large portion of my thoughts. The long journey to India was no exception. It was my original plan to sail from India aboard a ship bound for London. Once in port, I could easily arrange a way to kill your friend and disappear, as I had so successfully done before. But as fate would have it, another opportunity presented itself in Bombay in the person of Alice Allistair, who was on a holiday there—no doubt you know all this—with her companion. Quite naturally, the local newspapers reserved ample space on their pages for coverage of her visit to Delhi and Bombay. It was thus through the newspapers, and gossip at fashionable tea rooms, that Jones and I were kept abreast of her every appointment and destination.

"I related to Jones my exploits with Zoltan's gypsy band, and my first-hand knowledge of the Allistair fortune. Together, we planned a daring and brilliant abduction of the Allistair girl which you no doubt read about—"

"All England read about it. It has been one of the most infamous crimes in recent years."

"As I have stated previously, I had a personal reason for wanting to abduct this particular girl: Peter Allistair had wronged me long ago. And so, by kidnapping his daughter, I could extract not only a fortune from him ... but pain as well ..."

Here he lost himself in a maniacal chuckle, and I reflected upon Lord Allistair's earlier suspicion that the terrible suffering inflicted upon him and his wife was deliberate and personal.

"What has he done to you?" I cried. "What could he have possibly done that would warrant such atrocious behaviour on your part?"

"That does not concern you. Suffice it to say that he deserved punishment. The look upon his face today tells me he has indeed suffered—and so my rewards are doubled. But time grows short; I'll return to my narrative. We decoyed Miss Allistair's companion, a certain Miss Haskins, on a false errand. With her disposed of temporarily, we then thrust the lady into a palanquin and then, several streets later, into a delivery cart. The cleverness of the plan lay in remaining in the city, rather than attempting cross-country flight. We hid in a ramshackle working-class section of the city, hard by the Fort. Typically, the city and environs swarmed with British troops and Sepoys. Typically again, they looked everywhere but near the fort! There we remained safe for over a week until the uproar subsided.

"Here also, Doctor, I may as well make a confession: genius that I am, I had miscalculated the effect of Lady Alice's abduction upon the military and populace at large. Obviously, it makes no sense to take a hostage in India for ransoming in Britain. It was my *original* intention to obtain the ransom money in India through an intermediary. In this way, of course, the whole business would have been completed in a matter of days."

"You've no idea," I interjected, "the misery you've caused! You may kill me, perhaps even Sherlock Holmes as well, but I swear to you—you shall pay for all you've done!"

"That could not be helped. And it's you, my friend, who shall pay, not I. In a matter of hours, Jones and I shall be on our way to Liverpool, where we'll catch a ship for Rio de Janeiro, there to spend the remainder of our lives in luxury ..."

"And Wangi?"

"As for our humpback friend, he has served us well. However, he is noticeable, to say the least. Very much so. His presence would hamper our leaving ..."

He placed his hand on the pistol butt that projected from his belt.

"I'm afraid this is poor Wangi's last day on earth—ah! To warn him is useless—he speaks no English, as you've noticed. Now, to return to our adventures ..."

I received his plan with incredulity. Obviously the unfortunate wretch, misshapen and heathen though he was, had been of enormous help, yet he was to be killed and cast aside without remorse.

The progression of his insanity had clearly made Baskerville a beast. Where there had been intelligence, there was now only animal cunning. Always a cold man, even the last vestiges of civilised behaviour had now fallen away, leaving a stark, vicious brute who killed as mechanically as a viper.

"Our miscalculations made one thing clear: we could not hope to ransom the lady in India. Bombay had been sealed as tight as a drum, which was easy, considering it is situated on an island. Troops were everywhere—they swarmed in the streets and on the roads; trains and ships were searched; all bridges were watched; the alarm had been raised.

"Now, as you may have heard, the abductors were described as natives: Jones and I deliberately disguised ourselves as Hindis. With the teeming millions of the fellows overflowing the city and countryside, and not a hair's difference between them, it's no wonder the authorities were frustrated. But as a pair of English journeymen who

ambled about Bombay, we attracted no notice whatsoever. Lady
Alice remained humanely, but safely, confined in our quarters.

When we realised that it was necessary to obtain the ransom
outside the country, the problem of exit presented itself. As I
mentioned, to attempt to smuggle Lady Alice from the port of
Bombay was out of the question. However, we observed in the
course of our many ramblings through the city that trains to the
interior and eastern ports weren't carefully inspected. It was a simple
matter therefore, to obtain tickets for the two of us to Madras, with
provision for the carriage of a large ship's trunk—"

"Monsters!" I cried. "To imprison her—"

"Quite so, Doctor. It was distasteful. I can assure you, though, we
had no other option. Trapped as we were in Bombay, surrounded by
troops and search parties, we had only three choices. The first was
to free the girl and flee, in which case she could describe and identify
us. This course of action was suicidal. The second option was to flee
with the girl to another port city, as we did. The third choice was to
kill her. This was most odious; besides which, it made ransoming
impossible. So we selected the second alternative. Lady Alice was
drugged to a deep sleep and placed in the trunk, carefully altered to
allow for ventilation. This was the only instance we were obliged to
resort to the use of drugs. As you saw for yourself, she has been well
treated these twelve weeks."

He paused for another smoke. So entranced was I at this casual
narration of horrendous deeds that, for the moment at least, I forgot
my plight and the strange cries from the cavern.

"Our darkest moment was the loading of the trunk onto the
baggage carriage. If they'd opened it, we'd have been hanged for
sure. But our appearance as well-to-do British citizens, and a
handsome sum handed to the baggage clerk, was enough and we
were off. The journey to Madras takes just over four and twenty
hours. We rocked over the rails, and the countryside shot past us:
great oceans of red earth dotted with scrub and thorn trees, bullock
carts, buffalo, and camels. And mostly, of course, hordes of brown
men wrapped in robes, with wizened faces and bony limbs.

"Once arrived in that steamy port city, we again found humble
lodgings and set the young lady free from her confinement. She had
weathered the journey extremely well and recovered almost immediately, except of course, for the long bouts of weeping ... The next
few days were spent along the waterfront searching for a vessel
bound for London. We found none, and were about to set off for

Calcutta, when we spotted an Arab dhow making her way towards the quay. She was a coastal trader—one of thousands in the Indian Ocean. They roam about, taking on and discharging crew and cargo as they bounce from port to port along the coastlines of Africa and Asia.

"She came up to the quay and made fast. Larger than most dhow coasters, her decks were piled high with cargo: hides, copra, spices, hemp, coconuts. Her crew came from every corner of the globe: Arabs, Malays, Negroes, Hindis, Chinese. We knew that these men, if such they could be called, were a desperate lot. For the right price, they would do our bidding and ask no questions.

"The captain was a fierce Arab named Harun Sarouk. He sat on the sun-drenched deck while his heathen crew tended the huge sail. He puffed on his hookah, crosslegged on a pile of hemp while his humpbacked Malay servant, the same one who's in that cavern yonder, fanned him with a palm frond. The boat had come from Zanzibar by way of Ceylon. It would depart in two days for Batavia. Sarouk would take us, and our passenger, if we paid him well.

"We set sail two nights later, and the trade winds took us eastward with great speed. After six days, we stopped at Kutaradja, at the head of the island of Sumatra, for the natives there had a wondrous animal that they'd captured in the jungle ..."

He let his voice trail off to a whisper, and reclined with a smirk upon his face. My eyes moved to the fissure in the rock. It was dark and silent.

"... a most wondrous and horrifying monster: a *giant rat!*"

Again, I was recalled to horror, and my face became damp with perspiration; my limbs shook.

"It sounds incredible, does it not?" he taunted me in a soft voice. "Yet it is real, and, as you may have seen, quite capable of gnawing a man to death ..."

Once again, I made a frantic attempt to break free. All my efforts were futile and only revealed that I had strained my muscles and done great damage to the scar tissue of my old bullet wound. The deep throbbing in my shoulder told me it would never be the same. However, since I had not long to live, what did it matter? Baskerville watched my struggles idly. He reached for a long stick and, turning on his elbow, poked the dying fire. He turned back to me with a leer.

"You thought the hound fierce? You were afraid of it? Then I must tell you Doctor, that compared with the creature you will see emerge from that cavern, the hound was a toy, a *play thing!*" He began to quake in his passion, but was interrupted by Wangi, who had emerged from the burrow and sat squatting at the edge of the clearing.

"Hsssst!"

Baskerville turned toward the savage, who drew his grotesque dagger from the folds of his robe. The warning sound came again from between his thick, gnarled lips, and he leaned forward, pointing upwards.

I heard behind me, and to my left, the faint sound of rustling leaves. A twig snapped, and the measured cadence of footfalls came to my ears. The Malay weaved in a crouch, holding his dagger in an upraised fist. But the greater change came over Baskerville, who visibly shook with anticipation. The strain was showing. Eyes bulging, he snatched the pistol from his belt and drew back the hammer. The footfalls grew nearer. I strained to turn my head, but try as I might, I was unable to look behind me at the approaching figure.

"Fly Holmes! Fly!" I shouted at the top of my lungs. "He means to kill us both!"

In a rage, Baskerville pointed his weapon at my breast. I closed my eyes, mumbling a snatch of prayer. But the bullet never came. When I opened my eyes, I saw that he had resumed his former stance: eyes staring madly into the mist in the direction of the footsteps, pistol held in both his trembling hands.

"Come forward, Sherlock Holmes!" he shouted triumphantly. "Come! Come join your friend ..."

The sounds grew closer, and at last I glimpsed the familiar slender figure through the swirling grew vapour. The silhouette advanced slowly, with incredible composure and deliberation. The sight filled me with remorse. I was aware, as Holmes surely must have been, of the risks involved with his profession. But to see him brought low by such a beast as Baskerville—it was too poignant. The figure halted, and I heard the calm voice ring out.

"I shall go no further until my friend is released."

"Then Mr. Holmes, you shall die where you stand," said Baskerville in a quavering voice, "and your friend shall die slowly ..."

After a pause, Holmes advanced into the clearing.

"Dammit man, have you no sense! Turn and fly, I beg you!" I shouted, my voice hoarse with the effort. "There's no saving me, Holmes, and Miss Alice is delivered safe. Turn and be off!"

"If you fly," warned Baskerville, "Alice Allistair shall die a lingering and lonely death. Mark my word! She is by now tightly bound in the bottom of Strathcombe's lime kiln. She is helpless and silent, I can assure you. If you do not comply, her parents shall never learn of her whereabouts. However, if you accompany us as hostages, we shall leave instructions here to effect her rescue. What say you, Mr. Holmes? Do your friends live ... or die?"

Before I could again cry out a warning to my companion, I saw from the corner of my eye a pair of dusky hands whirling about. Barely half an instant later, I felt the suffocating sensation of a heavy cloth fastened tightly about my lower face. So intent was I in watching Holmes' approach, I'd failed to notice Wangi sneaking round behind me. In a flash, I was silenced. Then it occurred to me that Holmes must have arrived unexpectedly early; I was to have been gagged before so as not to warn him of Baskerville's gruesome revenge.

"Your friend has no trust in me, Holmes. But you are a fairly intelligent man. I am sure you will do what's right ..."

"I obviously have no alternative ..." said Holmes in a resigned tone.

I shook my head to and fro till my head ached and my ears rang. I kicked and screamed, but all that issued was a muffled moan. Baskerville had planned his revenge as only a twisted, tortured soul was capable. Seeing my dear friend led to his slaughter was more than I could bear. I fought to hold back sobs of rage and frustration.

"I'm terribly sorry, Watson," he said softly and advanced towards Baskerville, who held the pistol pointed at his heart. Never taking his eyes from Holmes, he stepped backward and caught up another pair of manacles. Wangi crept behind Holmes, dagger in hand.

"As soon as Jones arrives, we'll fasten you to that tree yonder. Then, when we've prepared our flight, you shall join us. When we're safe from this vicinity, you shall be released.

"I know your history too well, Baskerville," Holmes interjected, "to doubt for a moment that you desire my death. I am under no illusions as to what you plan for me. But I ask you, in the name of all that's decent, to free my friend ..."

He had come to the hollow then, knowing he was to die, in a valiant sacrifice for me. He had come with the same aplomb, the same steadfast resolution, that he had shown as he walked the narrow ledge of the Riechenbach Falls to meet Moriarty. His words tore at my breast. When all was said and done—in the final hour—there was no truer soul, no more gallant companion, than Sherlock Holmes.

Baskerville's trembling quickened; the manacles he held clanked and rattled from his spasms. He said nothing.

"And where's your friend, Jones?" Holmes enquired slyly. "Was he not to return post haste? Has he forgotten you? Has he fled?"

"He would be foolish to do so!" blurted Baskerville. "The ransom is taken! Our flight is set!"

Yet for all his braggadocio, a wave of uncertainty crossed his face. His entire body twitched with nervousness. It is said that partners in crime never trust each other. The doubtful flicker on Baskerville's face showed me the saying's truth.

"You are right, Baskerville. I have no desire to see my friends perish at your hand. Keep me, therefore, and free the Doctor ..."

The villain approached, shackles in hand.

"I'll set your friend free as soon as you allow us to place these on your wrists. I cannot allow both of you to be free at once ..."

To my horror, Holmes was taken in by this promise. He advanced toward Baskerville, arms outstretched.

"Since I'm to die, and your escape is assured, would you consent to satisfying my curiosity?"

"What is it?" snapped Baskerville with a twitch.

"Will you admit to killing Raymond Jenard?"

"Of course!" said he with a wave of the hand. "He had to die! He discovered that Alice Allistair was aboard ..."

"And McGuinness, and Compson?"

"Yes, yes!" he screamed. "Now ..."

Baskerville raised the manacles to Holmes' outstretched hands. With mounting dread, I watched as he placed the first iron band round Holmes' delicate wrist and snapped it shut. The metallic click had a chilling finality. Keeping his pistol out of reach, yet pointed at Holmes' breast, he took the free end of the shackles and led Holmes toward a smallish tree, similar to mine and not ten feet away. Thrash as I might, Holmes paid not the slightest attention to me and allowed himself to be led, timid as a sheep, in the direction of the tree. The deformed Malay crouched behind him with drawn dagger. Clearly his situation was hopeless. Soon he would be joining me, awaiting the emergence of the giant rat from its lair. The irony struck me like a hammer blow: here was a man of brilliance, dedicated to helping those in desperation and destroying evil wherever he found it. This very man was to die an ignoble and hideous death: gnawed and worried to death by a giant rodent! Hopefully, the beast would be so fearsome that we would faint dead away at the sight of it, and so be spared the worst of the agony.

But apparently the strain was too much even for Holmes. Suddenly he clasped his free hand to his chest, made a mild coughing sound, and doubled over. Stunned, Baskerville drew back and gazed in amazement at the slender, bent frame as it wheezed and choked.

The Malay showed confusion in his coarse features, and Baskerville drew close to Holmes and stretched out a hand to steady him.

It happened in an instant. I never cease to be amazed at the sudden bursts of speed and strength my friend is capable of. One moment he was bent double, and apparently on the verge of fainting. The next instant, he had dropped to a low crouch, grabbed the gun in Baskerville's hand, and was beginning the high, wide arc with his right fist. He straightened his body as he swung, and the blow had the force of every muscle in his body. My eyes could not follow it. The blow caught Baskerville on the tip of his jaw.

Holmes' advantage was only momentary, however; in a flash the Malay sprang like a panther from behind. I saw the wicked blade descend and heard my friend's sharp cry. The blade was raised again, and I closed my eyes, for I knew the second wound would be fatal. But before Wangi could drive the dagger home, there came a muffled explosion and puff of blue smoke. The wretch grabbed his middle and fell in a writhing heap upon the ground. The two men rolled over and over, locked in a death grip. The revolver, still smoking, was held in Baskerville's hand. Holmes' long, thin fingers were clasped round his wrist. They struggled fiercely; their breathing grew loud and rapid. As they rolled about, I could see the dark stain on the back of Holmes' coat growing larger as each second passed. Not a heavily built man, it wouldn't be long before his strength left him. Yet still he struggled, and seemed to get the best of Baskerville. There was a sudden flurry of motion, and I saw the glint of the pistol as it flew from Baskerville's hand, aided no doubt by Holmes' iron grip. A small splash told me it had landed in the pool.

At last the men parted, both on the verge of unconsciousness. Baskerville was reeling from the tremendous blow Holmes had dealt him. Holmes, having lost much blood, grew paler by the second. But clearly the villain had the edge, for as time passed, his condition abated, while Holmes' worsened.

Baskerville looked round for help, but it would not come from his gnomelike servant. The Malay, tangled in his white robe, flopped and writhed grotesquely on the earth like a giant flounder out of water. Still clutching at his stomach, he worked his mouth in silent gasps. There was no sound from his lips, only trickles of blood that ran down his chin. I couldn't help but pity the poor wretch. He was dying a macabre, brutish death, one that seemed oddly befitting a man of his cruel and bestial nature.

As a last resort, Baskerville staggered to the side of his fallen accomplice and seized the dagger. Twenty feet away, Holmes stared back. It was the first, and last, time I observed a look of fear on his face. Too weak to run, he had no escape. He glared at the serpentine blade of this kris, the instrument that had gravely wounded him, and was now to kill him. Baskerville lurched forward. Even in his exhausted state, the prospect of final revenge caused his shoulders to shake with laughter. Holmes dropped to his knees. He reached round to grab at his wound. His eyelids flickered.

Ten feet away Baskerville, knife raised, made a final lunge. For an instant Holmes dropped his head, staring at the ground. Then, as Baskerville seemed to hover over him like the Angel of Death, his left hand made two tight circles in the air. The chain whirred. Holmes staggered to his feet, swept his hand wide, and the whirling manacle caught Baskerville on the ear with all the force of a mace and chain. He dropped senseless and Holmes, pale as a ghost, hobbled over to where I sat chained to the tree. He tore the gag from my face, clapped his hand to my shoulder.

"Watson!" he panted, "Can you ever forgive me ..."

"Holmes! Behind you!"

Baskerville was moving. With all the persistence of Hydra, he refused to succumb. He crawled towards the fissure in the rock. Holmes, realising the danger immediately, rose to his feet in pursuit. But after two steps he fell, and could not rise.

"... I have not the strength ..." he said weakly.

Baskerville disappeared into the cave. Wangi lay motionless. Holmes stirred his legs slowly, like a child awakening from deep slumber. The mist was rising. Now a great deal of the high rock wall was visible. I could see almost to its summit. The hole in the cliffside glared at me like a monstrous eye socket. All was silent. Perhaps Baskerville had fainted ...

Then it began: a series of thumps, then the animal cry. Behind the snuffling growls, I could hear a crazed cackle as Baskerville goaded the beast into a frenzy. The reader may think that by this time I was inured to horror. However the opposite was the case: I was in a state of complete emotional collapse. As the raucous cries bellowed from the cavern, my vision grew dim. All things grew dark and blurry, save for that thing upon which my eyes were riveted: the mouth of the cave.

Holmes slowly raised himself up on his elbows and stared likewise. He tried to bring his knees under him in an attempt to stand, but it was useless; the strength had oozed from him. His fingers clutched the earth and pawed it idly.

"... I am so ... tired, Watson ..."

Baskerville cried out twice. But his shouts were soon obscured by a series of sharp squeals. All was silent for a moment. Then the guttural grunting and snuffling was heard again. The sound seemed to change: it grew less sonorous, higher. The beast was drawing near to the entrance of the cave. I heard too the scraping of feet on earth and the crunching of small stones.

In an instant, I was looking at it. It took my breath away, for never have I seen a sight so foul, so horrid, as that face which peered from its burrow. The huge nose twitched, the rat ears turned in small jerks. The small eyes rolled. Holmes groaned in horror and disbelief. It was immense. The head was almost two feet long. It grunted and growled. Sniffing the air, it came to focus on the prostrate form of my friend. No doubt it smelled his blood. Then, horror of horrors! It squealed in rage, popping its jaws and revealing enormous incisor teeth!

Holmes, the colour drained from his face, stared transfixed at the monster. It lunged forward, yet something held it back. It was then that I noticed the hawser round its neck. It was as thick as a man's wrist. The animal snapped its head back and tore at the rope. It paused for a moment to glare in our direction, and I saw the cable was half gnawed through. In a moment, it would be free.

"Goodbye Holmes ..." I said with an air of resignation.

The monster lunged again. With a crack, the cable broke. It bounded into the clearing, a gigantic grey-black creature. It paused for a moment, then ran at Holmes, head down, jaws open.

"Holmes! Holmes! Dear God!" I remember shrieking. But my senses again grew dim. In the swirling darkness that descended around me, I could yet see the huge monster—maddened no doubt by the smell of blood—grasp Holmes' shoulder with its huge teeth and shake him. The tiny eyes rolled in frenzy, and the rat let forth a guttural squeal of rage. I also heard, dimly and as if from a great distance, Holmes cry out in pain. The next instant he was hurled over onto his back. He flung his fists desperately at the huge head and gnashing teeth, but they had little effect. He would not last more

than half a minute. Overcome with fear and sorrow, I fainted dead
away.

12

RECOVERY

I was brought around by an enormous crash that resounded through the hollow and seemed to shake the very earth under me.

I opened my eyes to see Holmes miraculously still alive, pawing feebly at the monster, which suddenly jerked upright and spun in a tight circle, biting at its own flank. Shortly thereafter, the creature seemed to be mysteriously propelled backwards by an invisible jolt, and the next instant came a second explosion. In the ringing silence that followed, I heard the metallic sound of a breech working. There came, too, the sound of footsteps above me. A shower of pebbles fell into the pool. I looked up and could see through the mist the outline of a figure at the cliff's edge. Could it be Jones?

There came a dull thump as the animal was spun about and flung down, then a third and final crash. It twitched twice, then lay still. A small hole in its side poured forth great rivulets of blood. I then had an inkling of who the figure on the cliffside was. But when I again looked up, it was gone.

For perhaps a minute, there was no sound except the waterfall. Baskerville was somewhere in the dark recesses of the cave either dead or maimed, for it was apparent by his cries that the rat had attacked him. Wangi was beyond help. My immediate concern was for Holmes.

I cannot describe my relief when I saw him thrash about, heard him curse, and saw him draw himself up into a sitting position.

"Ah Watson, how utterly foolish of me! I should never have undertaken this plan under–"

He paused to groan and reach for his shoulder.

"–under these conditions ..."

"What plan? Do you–"

But I was interrupted by a small man scurrying into the clearing with blinding speed. He rushed to Holmes' side and knelt over him. Dressed in a macintosh and felt hat, I could not recognise him until I heard the familiar, intense voice.

"All you all right, man?"

"I might live, but no thanks to you, Lestrade," said Holmes dryly. "I'll keep–unfasten Watson and use the shackles to secure our friend in the cave." He inclined his head in the proper direction.

Lestrade extracted a huge ring of keys from his coat pocket and was at my side in no time.

"Ah, standard Naval issue, these. I have a key right here–have you free in no time, old man ..."

I fairly bubbled over with questions. How long had he been nearby? Who was the figure on the cliff? Did Holmes arrange it all beforehand? My questions were unanswered, however, because as soon as I was released Lestrade dashed to the mouth of the cave and disappeared.

Upon being freed, my first duty was to tend to Holmes' wound. I took off his coat and shirt. Fortunately, Wangi had dealt him a glancing blow; the blade had entered the right shoulder directly from above–parallel to the spine. But it had been deflected outwards by the shoulder blade. Consequently, a good deal of muscle tissue had been severed (which accounted for the heavy bleeding) but no organs were damaged. I made a crude pressure bandage and sling from his shirt. Holmes was able to stand, but just barely.

"By Jove, look Holmes!" I said, pointing to the hillside.

Ian Farthway entered the clearing carrying his rifle. He walked straight to the dead animal and kicked it twice. Satisfied, he joined us, his face full of apology.

"You needn't bother to explain, Farthway," said Holmes. "The heavy mist made things impossible. I shall never forgive myself for placing Watson in this predicament!"

"You were stationed up there all along?"

"Yes, Doctor. Unfortunately, the mist made all of you invisible. I was unable to get a clear shot until the beast was almost upon you–"

"Holmes! What is this thing?" I enquired as I walked unsteadily towards the animal that lay frozen in death. Holmes, leaning on Farthway, followed slowly. The animal was strange indeed. While its head looked like a rat's, save for the size, the body resembled a pig.

Were it not for the men it had killed and the horrific start it had given us, one could almost say it had a comical appearance.

Holmes stood between us; we held him up.

"There's your giant rat, Watson: *Tapirus Indicus.* The Sumatran tapir, a nocturnal pachyderm whose nearest living relative is the horse. See here ..."

He knelt at the side of the strange beast and pulled up the fleshy snout, revealing huge yellow teeth.

"In tooth structure, it is almost identical to the horse. Note these incisor teeth, Watson, which you so astutely identified aboard the *Matilda Briggs* by the wounds they left."

"Then it must be vegetarian. Why did it attack humans?"

"We cannot be sure. In nature it is a shy beast. It feeds at night along jungle riverbanks, avoiding people altogether. But in the hands of a warped personality like Baskerville, heaven knows what it could become ..."

"He seems to have a talent for training diabolical creatures. This animal then killed out of rage, not for food. But why did Baskerville bring it with him? What was the purpose served?"

"I shall tell you all at length, Watson. It's the very least I owe you, having endangered your life and sanity. However, I am still slightly fuzzy ..."

He grew suddenly heavy in our arms, and we set him gently on the ground. A cry for assistance came from the cavern, and Farthway hurried off to help.

"Once again my apologies, dear fellow. When I warned you of the possible danger involved, I had no idea ..."

"I understand. Now let me fetch some water."

"I had of course arranged for double coverage for you," he continued between sips. "Farthway above you and Lestrade in the hollow. As luck would have it, neither could help. Whilst Farthway was foiled by the mist, Lestrade probably had trouble with Jones—"

"You didn't interfere!"

"Oh yes we did. But here's Lestrade himself to tell us. Well, Lestrade, you have our friend in tow?

The two men carried Baskerville into the clearing and laid him down. He was in a light coma. He moaned and shook as a child does in a nightmare. That word seemed to be an apt description of what his life had become. His wounds, which I examined, were minor, but the head injuries Holmes had given him could have severe consequences. But considering the condition of the man's brain, I doubted they could have anything but beneficial effects. I looked down and shook my head slowly.

"He'll never stand trial."

"Why so?" said Farthway. "We all heard his confession. Mr. Holmes asked him the questions deliberately—"

"Much as I would like to see him hang, no physician or judge of any competence would rule him fit for trail or sentencing. The man's in the final stages of insanity. No doubt he's been suffering for years, but the strain and anticipation of this episode sent him over the edge."

"My opinion, while non-professional, concurs with yours," said Holmes. "He's bound for Bedlam, not Dartmoor ..."

Baskerville began to stir and moan. Lestrade, always the professional, slipped a pair of handcuffs on his wrists.

"I shall send for a wagon in town," said he, "but first we must track down Sampson—"

"No need, there he is yonder. And look at the cargo strung on his back!"

The boatswain, with his rolling sailor's gait, strode easily down the hollow with Jones flung across his shoulder like a sea bag. Reaching us, he dumped the man unceremoniously upon the ground like a load of rubbish. The man didn't move. He'd been beaten severely round the head, and a glance at John Sampson's flayed knuckles revealed the source of his injuries. Sampson did not speak, but continued to glower at the two unconscious villains who lay sprawled on the earth, only a few feet from the grotesque monster.

Remembering the Malay, I bent over him, and was immediately conscious of a human stench that was more noxious than the animal one. As I suspected, he was dead.

"What has happened to Alice Allistair?"

"All is well, Watson. Lestrade and Sampson intercepted Jones and the young lady directly they left the hollow. There was a bit of a chase, which explains Lestrade's absence from our predicament. The girl is now safely in Strathcombe, engaged in a joyful reunion with her parents."

And so our sad and ragged procession wound its way out of the dreary place, leaving behind two bodies: one of a misshapen brown man whom fate had cast far from his homeland, to die in a dank pit at the hands of the white men he served; the other, a strange and timid creature of the jungle streams who, in the hands of a madman filled with hate, had become a ferocious killer.

The trek through the forest tired us more than we anticipated, and it was a relief indeed to see Brundage waiting at the meadow's edge with a carriage and team. Baskerville's limp form was deposited on the floor, to be followed by Jones. Holmes, who had taxed himself far more than he realised, fainted with the attempt to climb aboard. We laid him on the front seat whilst I, supported by Lestrade, rode in the back. While I had lost no blood, I must admit that I was badly shaken, and the ride to Strathcombe is hazy in my memory.

As he was borne through the great hall, Holmes awoke momentarily to witness the fruits of his endeavour: the heartwarming spectacle of Lord and Lady Allistair, in a state of complete relief and rapture, embracing their daughter on the sofa. Holmes' lip trembled, and for the only time I can ever recall, I observed his eyes fill, and a tear cross his cheek.

We were half-carried upstairs, and spent the better part of a fortnight recovering. With the help of Meg's rich stock broth, mutton chops, and stews, washed down with quarts of Ludlow ale, we recovered quickly. After slightly more than a week upon our backs, we were once again ready to venture out of doors.

13

THE POOL

I awoke. The willow boughs sighed above me. The stream chuckled over and along the moss-covered banks. A titmouse pranced amongst the roots of the trees, pausing now and then to whistle. Hearing a sonorous clamour borne from afar by the wind, I turned my head to see a long skein of geese winging its way over the horizon.

"Drat!" cried a voice.

I rolled over on the grass and back into the sunshine. The sun had shifted while I slept. The warmth felt delicious on my back.

"Oh blast!" came the voice again, and I heard a great splashing commotion.

"Watson, my casting arm appears to be ruined. That heathen devil Wangi! I must say the world is none the poorer for his departure ..."

"Exercise is the best thing, Holmes. That and staying in the sun. My, it's uncommonly warm for October!"

I raised myself up on my elbows and watched my companion working his fly rod in the midst of the pool. Painful as the operation was, he displayed extraordinary skill. The line swung to and fro in long loops. It rolled and swung about in great circles, with a delicate hissing sound. In a final stroke, he laid the line down upon the swirling water, and the tiny coloured float drifted gaily past a boulder. Instantly, there came a great flurry of splashing water, and I caught a glimpse of the brilliant iridescence of the trout as it struck at the fly.

"Ha! There's number three, and a big fellow! It's a pity Lord Allistair doesn't make more use of his trout pool–but perhaps more fortunate for me."

While he played the fish, I reached over the bank and drew the bottle of Barsac from its resting place in the shallows. Its sweet, heady aroma was overpowering as I drew the cork and filled glasses.

Holmes scooped his prize up in the landing net and struggled ashore. After cleaning the fish with a skill and precision that would have done credit to any surgeon, he filled the body cavity with damp moss and placed it on a cool rock next to the others he had caught.

I drew out my watch. It was one fifteen, and the garden party was to begin at two.

"Now, Holmes, you promised. We've just enough time for you to keep it."

"Very well, dear fellow," he sighed as he seated himself on the bank and took a sip. "I shall tell you all."

"It seems incredible to me that you knew not only the identity of the kidnapper, but his plan as well. It's as if you read his very thoughts ..."

"I daresay I did, almost. But there's no sorcery involved, simply keen observation and careful deduction. But where to begin? Well, the beginning will do, eh? Now Watson, it's always been my practice, in examining any crime, to separate the singular features from the ordinary ones. For it is the unique, the grotesque elements of a case that lead to its solution. No doubt I've mentioned many times before that the most difficult cases are those that lack these distinguishing features.

"Now let us consider the case of the giant rat of Sumatra in this light. As you may recall, my curiosity was pricked at the outset by the strange disposal, or shall we say "non-disposal" of Jenard's body. This flaunting of the murder deed was incomprehensible to me, at least early one. But this I knew and so stated to you: those who killed Jenard knew of me; the fact that he was put to death a street from our lodgings was certainly more than coincidental. So we have the throwing down of the body, which was really a flinging down of the gauntlet by Baskerville: an invitation to do battle. You know enough of the man's character and personality to see how this brazen act would be not unnatural for him."

I nodded my head in agreement.

"Secondly, the fact that whoever killed Jenard knew of me meant that *I* was involved somehow, directly or indirectly, with the deed.

"With Sampson's tale, my curiosity was sharpened still further, as no doubt yours was also. Considering the date of Alice Allistair's disappearance, and that part of the globe in which the *Matilda Briggs* was sailing, could not there be some connection? It was a remote possibility, but still a possibility.

"And now would be as good a time as any to explore the question of *why* Baskerville took the bother and expense–to say nothing of the *risk*–of buying and transporting the animal itself, the giant rat, halfway around the world."

"He was intrigued by animals. He also had an infamous talent for transforming even gentle ones into killers," I said.

"Yes, but there's a deeper reason behind his initial decision to buy the beast and stow it aboard the *Briggs*, Watson. Shortly after listening to Sampson's fantastic story, I did some reading up on rats at the British Museum. To my astonishment, I discovered that although people in general have always loathed them, the most passionate hatred of rats is displayed by sailors. This exists throughout all written history, from the time of Odysseus to the present. This is perhaps magnified by the fact, simple and unavoidable, that there is no escape from rats at sea. Man and beast are locked together in the ship and must share each other's company, no matter how unpleasant. But I digress ...

"Baskerville, and we must never underestimate his cleverness, realised that the tapir he saw on the beaches of Sumatra resembled a huge rat, especially its head. If he could only secure this animal aboard ship and give the crew the *impression* that it was a giant rat ..."

"They would be terrified!" I cried. "They would avoid that part of the ship altogether!"

"Precisely. You see, Baskerville was keenly aware that it would be difficult, if not impossible, to keep his hostage in the after hold for six weeks unnoticed. She might cry out. Jones or Wangi might leave a door ajar, and she would be seen. Furthermore, how to explain the food that must be brought to her? You see, Watson, how the presence of this "giant rat" was a perfect mask for the real crime?"

I nodded my head slowly. Surely, to quote an old phrase, there was "method in his madness."

"When did you determine the beast was a tapir, and how did you come to know this?"

"I was nearly certain of the animal's identity early on by a process of elimination. I knew the animal was huge, and resembled a rat, in the head at least. After some research I struck upon the Sumatran tapir. For a time I admit I was put off the scent by the complete unanimity of the authorities on the tapir that it is a placid and nocturnal herbivore. But I have since found evidence that the recent catastrophic explosion of Krakatoa, an island off the Sumatran coast, has had an extraordinary effects upon the habits and behaviour of many animal species throughout the area. The tapir is not found in captivity, so it's no wonder that superstitious sailors took it for a giant rat. Since Baskerville was anxious that the head be seen, but not the body, we can assume that he indeed wished everyone aboard the *Briggs* to think there was such a beast on board."

"Then why was it taken aboard in secrecy?"

"As you've probably suspected, Alice Allistair was in the crate along with the rat. Not in the same compartment, of course, because they had partitioned it. But she was swung aboard with the monster, and confined in the same dingy hold with it for the entire voyage. You recall Winkler's mention of Jones 'sneaking food aft'? Remember the food was in two bundles, one thrice the other's size?"

"Of course, the large bundle for the animal, the small one for Alice. Lord, to be shut up with that beast for eight weeks, the horror, the cruelty of it!"

"Quite so. She was no doubt in terror every second of the long voyage. It is remarkable she still has her wits. Surely a girl of lesser character would have succumbed long ago—"

"She is not yet fully recovered," I said in a professional tone.

"I can see that. Well, to return to our investigation. Upon visiting the *Matilda Briggs*, I uncovered two pieces of evidence which gave further credence to my embryonic theory: the candle stub and the message in candle smoke. Simply stated, both together told me that someone posing as Jenard—but definitely not Jenard—was giving us a clue as to the nature of the real crime behind the so-called giant rat. In a hasty, almost childish, bit of verse—"

"All is stairs and passageways where the rat sleeps, his treasure keeps—"

"yes, now it's painfully obvious that the first three words, minus the middle and final 's', spell Allistair—"

"By Jove, it never occurred to me!"

"Well it did to me," he remarked with some scorn. "In any event, the message gave a good deal of weight to my supposition that Alice Allistair was, or had been, aboard the vessel. The crucial point is that someone was attempting to give the impression that Jenard had written the words as a warning to the world. Both yourself and Lestrade interpreted the words this way. However, we knew by the candle butt that Jenard couldn't have written them. Why then, was the message written at all?"

Holmes paused to refill his glass.

"Barsac, the sweetest of the Sauternes ... it's almost cloying ..."

"Dash it Holmes! Get on with the story!"

"Someone wished to cast me onto the scent of the Allistair kidnapping, yet wished to do so as Jenard.

"You see, if Jenard had intended to give warning of the rat, why not do so plainly? Clearly, the cryptic warning was meant to arouse my interest, for whoever wrote it was certain I'd decipher it. Evidently that person knew me well. In short, Watson, I suspected a trap, an ensnarement aimed at *me.*"

"You knew it was Baskerville?"

"No. I didn't even suspect it could be him until after our luncheon at the *Binnacle.* You'll recall that both Scanlon and Thomas mentioned 'Reverend Ripley's' fascination with petrels and plankton ..."

"Yes. I thought it curious you were so interested in that ..."

"Details, Watson. *Details!* Of course you remember Baskerville's naturalistic bent, especially his fondness for collecting butterflies. Well, I had an inkling it could be him, since who else should wish to ensnare me? Moriarity is dead for several years, and others who have vowed my death are behind bars. I sent a wire to Exeter, and the reply I got was 'no absolute proof.' No one then, had found Baskerville's body. He *could* still be alive. Considering the general cunning of the man, I went on this assumption. It would be natural for him to plan an escape if things went wrong. Besides, who would be a likelier candidate to train a giant rat than the man who had trained the giant hound?"

"The pieces certainly fit."

"But where was this rat? It was not still aboard the *Briggs.* Had it been killed and dumped into Blackwall Reach, or somehow smuggled into London? When our trial led to the livery stable, and we there discovered that a large wagon had been bought, my suspicions grew that the animal had been slipped ashore. Remember the gold coins paid to the smith? They were Indian. Thus another link was established between the abduction of Alice Allistair from Bombay and the *Matilda Briggs.*

"The filing of the iron fence, the splotch of grease upon the quay, the frenzied behaviour of the hounds—all of these told me of the loading of the rat onto the wagon in the early hours of the morning."

"But how did the rat—the tapir—get from the ship to the quay?"

"The tapir is an aquatic animal, similar in this respect to the hippopotamus. It was a simple matter, after the tapir had finished with McGuinness, to open the lumber port, drive the beast down into the water—there being only a six foot drop—and guide it to shore as it swam alongside the *Briggs'* dinghy."

"Then they loaded it into the wagon," I said, "at the low point of the quay, made their way through the fence, replaced the cut section, and headed along the side streets ..."

"But you remember, Watson, when we strolled about with the dogs, that I mentioned the 'upstream events', things that appeared implausible. The first was, as we've discussed, the disposal of Jenard's body. But you also might recall the fact that Nip and Tuck showed us that the *three of us had been followed* to the *Binnacle* from the *Briggs.*"

"I remember. You stated that this was not normal behaviour for a criminal—to pursue the pursuers ..."

"No, not normal for the average criminal. But when I considered the effrontery that this criminal was displaying, I was convinced it was Baskerville; it could be nobody else."

"This brashness seems a hallmark of his," I admitted. "I remember in the earlier case he even impersonated you ..."

"... but *why* did Baskerville follow us, perhaps even into the inn, if not to determine for himself that I had taken the bait, that I had become so engrossed in the case that I would follow it *anywhere*?"

"Ah, and from this point you knew it was a trap!"

"Certainly. Hence my apprehension, and warnings to you not to leave our flat unarmed."

"And what were Baskerville and his henchmen doing in the interim?"

"After determining that I was indeed on the case, as hooked, you might say, as those three trout, he departed the city in the wagon, leaving Jones behind—"

"For what purpose?"

"To deliver the ransom note to the Allistairs' residence, for one. Also to keep an eye on the both of us and report developments to Baskerville, who was settling himself into Henry's Hollow, preparing for the ransoming and our execution ..."

I shuddered.

"It was Jones, of course, who followed me at Paddington. I remained in London, by the way, only long enough to give the impression I was remaining in the city. Actually, of course, I lost him soon thereafter and later in the day returned to the station where I caught the 2:45 to Shrewsbury—"

"You were out *here* then?"

"My dear Watson, where else would I be? Back at our flat playing my fiddle whilst you face the danger alone? I made Shrewsbury my headquarters. Any wires you sent to me in London were re-routed by Lestrade's men back to me, thence to you via the city office–"

"Then this explains the delay in messages," said I. "Were you ever in the Rutlidge telegraph office?"

"Yes, now that you mention it. On the night of your arrival–"

"And were you not dressed as a gypsy?"

"Quite so, good for you, Watson! Yes, it was quite a game of cat and mouse with Baskerville. You see, I knew I had to be on the scene to get the necessary information. Yet, if any of them discovered me near Strathcombe when I was supposed to be in London, the game would have been up in an instant–I was forced to be extremely furtive, and adopted the gypsy dress ..."

"I can understand your secrecy with Baskerville," I said in a hurt tone, "but why was *I* not informed?"

"Simple: neither you nor Lord Allistair is a good actor, Watson. This is because deceit is not in your natures. To apprise you of my plans would have rendered them useless. Your actions would have given us away in an instant. Baskerville would either fly or kill the girl. It has been a nerve-wracking business. But I was hereabouts as much as I dared, keeping a lookout. Incidentally, it might interest you to know that it was I who was watching you from the Keep. Never at any time were you more than a mile from us–"

"Either Farthway or myself. We kept in constant touch, even after my 'official arrival' at the lodge. This explains the semaphore lamp too. A capital idea of Farthway's, don't you think? His cottage being directly below my room, and the lamp pointing towards the forest, it was thus a simple matter for Lestrade, Farthway and me to be in constant communication ..."

"This grows wearying," said I, reaching for the bottle. "So Farthway was your cohort, and our guardian. This explains his odd behaviour–"

"Yes, his early morning jaunts, his knowledge of your visit to the Hollow–for he followed you there and back–and his irritation that you'd exposed yourself to danger."

"... I must apologise to him ... I take it then, you sought him out early on, before even out arrival here."

"Yes indeed, for I heard of his courage and reliability–not to mention the marksmanship to which we owe our lives."

"Ah. And you wisely summoned Lestrade and Sampson too. The boatswain behaved most admirably—doubtless because he was driven to avenge his dead friend."

"But despite the help I had, I was unable, unfortunately, to prevent the death of this Compson fellow—"

"You couldn't be everywhere at once. Now tell me the particulars about what occurred the night before our ordeal."

"Our night-time errand, as you may have surmised by now, was a last-minute reconnaisance of the enemy's camp. I was fairly certain the exchange would take place in the Hollow, but a final check was necessary to make sure. We did creep close enough to see the campfire, and the manacles set out in readiness."

"Why did you not seize them all then?"

"Are you forgetting the girl? No, we could not attempt anything by force with her confined in the cavern—"

"Yes, quite so. But how did you guess the note was to be delivered at dawn?"

"I knew Baskerville would try to spring his trap as soon as possible after the quarry was within range. Because of this, I deliberately made my 'arrival' as obvious as possible. Brundage met me at the train, unaware that I had merely taken it down the line a stop—in the dead of night—and back again to Shrewsbury at lunchtime. No doubt one of the confederates saw my arrival as well and passed the word.

"It was no surprise to learn that the ransom note was delivered within hours after my arrival. Once Baskerville learned I was on the scene, he acted at once."

"It did strike me as curious that you arrived in so noticeable a fashion, almost in defiance of the warning note."

"The caution to the Allistairs not to seek assistance was clever of Baskerville. For, much as he wished me to come out here, he realised that any note he sent without the standard warning would lack authenticity. He went on the assumption that if my curiosity were sufficiently aroused, I'd come anyway."

"So you came openly to show him his lure had worked."

"Yes, I wanted to indulge his sense of his own genius and cunning: to make him feel he'd outwitted me. This, incidentally, was another reason I didn't leave London directly, but played the waiting game."

I paused momentarily to wipe my brow.

"Your explanations have proved most illuminating. But I still have a number of questions. What about the fire in Jenard's lodgings?

And, were you ever able to decipher the coded message sent to us on the ransom note?"

"I'll answer these questions as we walk up to the house. We mustn't be late for the garden party."

Holmes packed his fish into the creel, slung his rod over his shoulder, and we walked up the sloping meadow towards Strathcombe.

"Before Lestrade carted him off, I had a long talk with Jones. He was most co-operative. It won't save him from the rope, I'm afraid, but he'll swing into eternity in a somewhat better frame of mind. The story Baskerville related to you before my arrival at the Hollow is accurate. The kidnappers smuggled the girl from India in the manner described. By the way, Watson, I was aware of their flight across India. My questions to the British Railways offices proved fruitful.

"Once they had Alice aboard the *Matilda Briggs* and bound for home their problems seemed over. McGuinness bent to their will, and they had the giant rat to protect their secret. Shortly before arriving in London, however, one crewman, Raymond Jenard, discovered the real secret in the after hold. We'll never know how he found out, for he didn't even have the chance to tell his good friend John Sampson about the captive lady, Sampson being engaged elsewhere.

"Jenard, upon going ashore, vowed to notify the authorities. However, he decided to grab a pint at a waterfront tavern before-hand. There, he asked the barkeeper for advice. This barkeeper knows me well—I am bound by oath not to mention his name or the name of his establishment to anyone—and recommended that Jenard walk across town to see me. Is this clear so far?"

"Perfectly."

"But as fate would have it, Jones was lounging over a mug in that same establishment, not ten feet away and hidden behind a pillar. He heard the barkeeper say, "Yes, lad, my friend Sherlock Holmes is the one to seek. You'll find him at 221B Baker Street—he's the one to tell about the captive lady ...""

"Instantly Jones crouched down in his chair to hide from the departing Jenard, who failed to see him. Just before he reached the door, he turned and said, "Even if I am unable to reach this man, I have it all written down in my diary—" patting his sea bag as he says this. As soon as Jenard was on his way, Jones sped to inform Baskerville that Lady Alice had been discovered."

Here Holmes paused to catch his breath. Though his wound had practically healed, the injury manifested itself in early fatigue.

"Leaving Alice bound in one of the cabins–they didn't worry about the crew since they'd fled the ship–they went to Jenard's rooms where they expected to intercept him. But he'd already left, headed for our flat. His sea bag was there, but not the diary. They assumed he had the diary with him. But what if he'd hidden it in the flat? Surely Jenard, knowing the true secret of the *Matilda Briggs*, must die. Eventually, the authorities would search his rooms. What if the diary were hidden there? It is at this point that a spark of Baskerville's madness boiled to the surface. Since they hadn't time to search the rooms for a diary that *might* be there, he decided to set them afire. And so, in a rage of frustration, without regard or even a warning to the other inhabitants of the building, the paraffin lamps, and spare containers also, were emptied onto the rugs, furniture, and curtains–"

"You needn't complete the story," I interjected. "You and I know too well the outcome ..."

"Before the flames had scarcely begun to flicker, the three of them were in a hansom racing for Baker Street, all eyes peeled for Jenard. They tracked him down only a few blocks from his destination, and lured him into the clothier's doorway. This was accomplished by Baskerville, who, in a disguised voice, called for help. As might be expected, Jenard responded to the call as any decent citizen would. Once inside the doorway, the three of them set upon him. The use of the chloroformed rag–another tie with Baskerville and his butter-flies, by the way–ensured a quick and silent end to Raymond Jenard.

"It is interesting to note, Watson, that had they followed their original plan and merely left Jenard's body on the rooftop, they would probably have succeeded.

"But standing there on the rooftop peering down at Jenard's body, something happened in Baskerville's twisted brain. As is character-istic of a fine mind gone awry, Baskerville fancied himself a genius. He perceived the way to accomplish *two* ends at the same time: the recovery of the ransom money *and* revenge against me."

"Of course!" I said. "He then deliberately mutilated the body and, at the right moment, threw it down onto the kerb to entice your curiosity–"

"Quite. He was throwing down the bait, and a gauntlet of challenge as well. Of course, you and I know the ultimate irony: I had already been summoned secretly into the affair by Lord Allistair himself. Had Baskerville discovered this, he would have been driven over the brink much sooner, I'm sure. Setting the trap for me was Baskerville's nemesis, for he allowed me to establish the links that led to his identification. Had I not known it was Baskerville at the centre of the web, I'm certain I would have advised Lord Allistair to pay the money and be done with it. They, at least, Baskerville and Jones, would no doubt be *en route* to South America at this very moment."

"He carried his evil one step too far, and so was undone."

"After fleeing down the rear ladder they returned to the *Briggs*. It was always their intention to do away with McGuinness. But now the plan changed somewhat and became bolder. Now the 'rat', which was to have been killed and dumped unceremoniously into the Reach, was to do the deed.

"Just before the weird party quit the ship in the midnight darkness, Baskerville was seized with yet another idea: a warning message, supposedly penned by Jenard, that would connect the kidnapping and the mysterious giant rat of Sumatra. Thus, he crept forward in the darkness and, with the candle butt we discovered, wrote the bit of simple verse that was to guarantee my entrance into the case."

"And from that moment on, it had Baskerville's mark on it in every detail. Now, for the final question: the message done in pinpricks."

"Pshaw! Don't tell me you haven't yet deciphered it—"

"I regret I do not possess your powers, Holmes," I said sarcastically. "I am merely mortal."

"There, there, old fellow," he chuckled. "I remembered to bring the message with me. Here it is in my fly book."

He opened the fleece-lined pouch and, from amidst scores of tiny feathered hooks, drew forth the message as copied by Lord Allistair and myself. He seated himself on the grass and spread the paper before him:

> LONDON—The Home Office today
> announced a joint production agreement
> signed with Belgium. It involves the
> manufacture of internal combustion
> engines.

"A simple code, although by saying that, I'm not in any way detracting from Lady Alice's cleverness—not to mention courage—in sending to you. Your basic supposition that the dots point out letters of words is correct. Your error was in failing to recognise that, due to the brevity of the article, Lady Alice was forced to run through it several times to spell the message. Thus, a word may carry through into a different dot structure."

"I'm afraid I don't follow you."

"In other words, the differing dot placements do not indicate separate words, but the number of times Lady Alice 'ran through' the article to find letters ..."

I scratched my head in bewilderment.

"Here, let me show you," said he with a touch of impatience.

"Your first word, counting the single dot on top as the 'starter', was ATRA, is that not so?"

I nodded.

"You then assumed the second word to be spelled by the single dot underneath, which yields WARE. The other words were PISSETBE and JOHN. Since only John is a word, the others are then parts of words. In short, they are parts of a message strung together. If we string these in a line, we get this: ATRAWAREPISSETBEJOHN."

"I can make nothing of it. Dash it man, it's not as simple as you say!"

"I forgot to mention that you made two errors in attempting to decode this. The second was assuming that the next word was formed by the single dot underneath, rather than the double one on top. Following this template, we interchange the WARE and PISSETBE, to get the following: ATRAPISSETBEWAREJOHN."

I stared vacantly at it for a few seconds before the message jumped forth: A TRAP IS SET BEWARE JOHN.

"What an ass I am!" I cried.

Holmes made no comment.

"I certainly owe Alice my deepest appreciation. She is clever indeed to have thought up this cryptogram at a moment's notice. I take it you knew the message all along."

"Yes. But of course to tell you of Baskerville's trap would have altered your behaviour; he could sense trouble in an instant. No, indeed. For my plan to work, which it did just barely I'm ashamed to say, it was necessary for you to be in the dark on all counts. I have never regretted anything more in my life, Watson, than putting you through that trial in the Hollow. You are visibly greyer in the temples, if you haven't noticed. I can scarcely look my old friend in the face without a twinge of guilt."

I stared at the ground for a moment before replying, for my throat had caught that curious tightening ache that comes in times of deep emotion.

"There ... there was absolutely no other way ..." I managed at last. "We all did our best."

We finished the walk in silence, since any additional words would have subtracted from the moment. Finally, Holmes resumed.

"On the bright side, of course, there's Lord Allistair's generosity toward us."

"Generosity? My dear Holmes, rich as the man is, his gifts border on the foolhardy!"

As he threw his head back in laughter though, I could not help but recall the dark side of the adventure's conclusion. It was a sad and tragic spectacle, and will haunt my memories till the end of my days. I can still call up the picture in vivid detail: Rodger Baskerville strapped to a leather pallet, soaked through with sweat as he thrashed his head and shrieked. In his ravings he'd bitten through his tongue, and his cheeks were flecked with red froth. As they slid the pallet into the van he began to call Holmes' name. They drew the steel door shut and locked it, and the wagon began its tortuous journey down the road. But even as it drew further and further away, I could still hear issuing from the tiny barred window in the steel door the ringing voice of the lunatic: "Holmes—no walls shall hold me!"

"There, there, Watson, try to think more pleasant thoughts! His suffering has probably diminished with time."

"You've read my thoughts!"

"No, I've read your face. You were staring down that bend in the road where we last saw the asylum carriage. Your face bore a look of hatred, then, as might be expected of a physician and man of your character: pity."

"Perhaps it should have borne the look of fear as well. You recall his boast of escaping. If any man could devise a means of escaping the stoutest walls, it is he."

"True. But happiness in life consists largely of refusing to worry about matters over which one has no control."

We had by this time reached the low stone fence, and entered at the gate. We could see, at the far edge of the green expanse, several long banquet tables covered in gleaming linen. A score or so of servants hurried to and fro bearing silver trays and steaming dishes. A line of carriages stood in the drive, with more arriving by the minute. We seated ourselves on a stone bench, and presently saw coming towards us a handsome and heartwarming sight.

"Ah Watson, it takes no great brain power to fathom the reason for Farthway's presence at Strathcombe, does it now?"

"Certainly not," I replied. "Well, I'm terribly happy for them both."

Arm in arm, Alice Allistair and Ian Farthway made their way slowly towards us. The lady's step was still a bit unsteady, but Farthway's strong arms and noble bearing were a tremendous reassurance. The tender glances they exchanged were further evidence of a bond that had existed for some time and showed no sign of diminishing.

Alice Allistair was fast on the mend–as each day passed she had grown more and more to resemble the lovely creature I had seen in the family portraits. With help from all of us, she seated herself on the bench.

With genuine gratitude and admiration, I wrung her hand in thanks for her clever coded message. She brushed off the string of compliments with becoming modesty and folded her hands in her lap.

"Now Ian, you mustn't scold me," she said in mock anger, "I've been waiting to tell these gentlemen all they wish to know–no please, all of you, I implore you, you must let me speak. To keep this tale locked in my bosom is to let it gnaw at my soul. I must, and shall, tell you all."

And so the young lady, hand in hand with the man who had done so much to secure her release, related the weird and horrible tale of her abduction, which was alike in every detail to the one I was forced to hear while bound to the tree in Henry's Hollow. Her journey had grown more frightful as time progressed, for the captivity in Bombay, while unpleasant, was devoid of horror. Likewise the confinement aboard the train and trip across the Indian Ocean in the Arab trader.

"The terror did not begin until we landed in Sumatra, Mr. Holmes. There Baskerville and Jones had a long meeting which I overheard. To my amazement and horror, I learned I was to be quartered with a mad beast the natives had trapped in the jungle!"

Here she paused to compose herself and receive a reassuring glance from Farthway.

"It was not long before I discovered that it was a tapir, a usually shy animal that lives on a diet of river plants. But it seems that this animal was exceptional–perhaps a descendant of some vicious strain, for it had killed several natives who were bathing in the river."

"This has occurred with hippopotamuses too," interjected Farthway. "There have been rogue hippos that have killed scores of people out of sheer malice, though they are also vegetarian and usually shy ..."

"Then I can assure you, Ian, this animal was a rogue. His savage temper was not improved, I might add, by being trapped in a staked pit and lashed in a crate. Add to this the weeks of cruelty and abuse from Wangi ..."

Holmes and I exchanged glances. Being forced to endure eight weeks in close proximity to this creature, it was no wonder she had been in a distraught state.

"But why," I asked her to change the subject, "did Jones and Baskerville appear in Batavia without you—with the Malay instead?"

"They explained the necessity of this to me before they departed. Recalling the difficulties of sneaking me from Bombay, they were not eager to repeat the experience in the port of Batavia—for the Dutch are notorious for their stringent cargo procedures—"

"So I had suspected," observed Holmes. "There was a great risk that you would be discovered, Lady Alice—particularly since they would be forced to enter *and* leave the port in order to place you on the *Briggs*. No, they were clever indeed to arrange for the midnight rendezvous up the coast. In that way, the port authorities could be circumvented altogether and the transfer made—"

"—the only remaining witnesses were the crew, whom they drugged with liquor ..." I added.

"It was all carefully arranged," explained Alice, her eyes growing damp. "I was left in the care of that savage group of men—with only the promise of gold as a pledge of my safety ..."

"What a dreadful man!" I said.

"For their part, they took the wretch Wangi along as a guide and hostage both—"

"Hardly an equal exchange—" snorted Farthway.

"The three of them made their way in a small *proa* southwards. We were to follow in a few days to a pre-arranged meeting place down the coast. They had little difficulty in locating a ship departing for England. Having bent Captain James McGuinness to their will by threats and bribes, they were in complete command of the *Briggs* from the instant she left the docks of Batavia ..."

"You needn't continue your painful narrative, Lady Alice," said Holmes, rising. "The rendezvous and the transferring of cargo we know of through John Sampson. The voyage, with all of its pain and horror, we can only imagine. Now here come your parents out onto the terrace. Do let's go up."

We walked up the garden path to greet the Allistairs, who had just strode down the terrace steps. Certainly the spirit rules the body, for with the return of Alice and the lifting of the enormous emotional burden shared for so long, they appeared years younger.

"I suppose the only thing that still puzzles me," mused Lord Allistair as he settled his wife into a garden chair and sat down next to her, "Is the personal desire for vengeance against me on Baskerville's part. Did you by chance ever discover his motive?" he asked his daughter.

"No, not specifically. He only said you'd wronged him years ago ..."
His Lordship knitted his brows in concentration.
"I cannot recall it," he said finally.
"He wouldn't tell me, though I asked him," said I. "I suppose we'll never know."

A gentle cough came from Holmes' direction. All eyes focused on his gaunt form, slung nonchalantly in the wicker chair.

"It is just possible, Lord Allistair," said he in a soft voice, "that you have overlooked an event which occurred twelve years ago ..."

Lord Allistair sipped at his port, the same quizzical expression on his face.

"That would have been in eighty-two. Ah, I see it now! It was in eighty-two that Cavendish was murdered in Phoenix Park—surely this has something to do with Home Rule and Parnell—"

"No, sir. It is more personal. In eighteen-eighty-two your son Peter was nine years old ..."

Instantly, the puzzlement left Lord Allistair's face.
"Mr. Holmes, may I see you alone for a moment?"
"Of course. But perhaps you wish to let the matter drop altogether."

After a momentary struggle within himself, Lord Allistair faced his wife with a candid and frank expression.

"Elizabeth, there is something you must know that up until now I have not told you—"

Farthway and I rose to go, and I was dumbstruck by Holmes' arrogance and callousness by remaining seated.

"Please gentlemen, stay!" said Lord Allistair, raising his hand. "You, Doctor, especially, have the right to know the events that led to the endangering of your life. Now, dearest, you needn't look so alarmed—what I am about to reveal I am ashamed of, but it is not something that would come between us.

"Now, Mr. Holmes, there is more than one side to this story, but having seen you work, if only briefly, I am assuming you are in command of all the facts—"

"That would be a safe assumption, Lord Allistair."

"Then let me begin by telling all of you," and he swept his arm in a circle as he spoke, "that while innocent of the crime itself, I am guilty of protecting the guilty party, and so am guilty as an accomplice."

We stared with incredulity at him. Was this man, who had so distinguished himself in the public service, about to tarnish his glittering career?

"In the year mentioned, my son Peter began his second year at the Malton School in Yorkshire, which was run by a man named Vandeleur—are we not thinking along the same lines, Mr. Holmes?"

"Yes sir, we are. And by the way, I cannot tell you how delighted I am that you're—"

"Making it public at last? Hah! It should have been done years ago, in an honest and forthright manner. I owe you yet another debt, sir, in bringing this to my attention. Thank you for your offer to keep the matter quiet; but upon even a moment's reflection, I can see that if my word's to mean anything, I must tell all—"

"As I knew you would—"

"Well then, a little way into the term, you can imagine my surprise when I was informed by the headmaster—this Vandeleur fellow—that my son had cheated in his exams."

There was a short silence as we absorbed this detail. I saw Lady Allistair wince.

"Since I was unable to leave London at the time—the Irish crisis I mentioned was at its height—I wrote to Peter and asked him if the charge were true. He answered that it was. I was of course mortified to learn the charge was true—but gladdened that Peter had voluntarily confessed. Well, as most of you can surmise, the cheating incident would mean that Peter's chances of attending Harrow, or any other decent school, were shot. I was distressed that such a foolish incident—and I say *incident* because Peter is a generally honest fellow—that such an incident should ruin his life."

He paused to sip his port, and, in a reflective tone, continued.

"But just as I resigned myself to it, there came a letter from Vandeleur, informing me that, for a certain sum of money, he would keep the matter quiet ..."

"I say! The leopard doesn't change his spots, eh Holmes?" I said, for I remembered "Vandeleur" well.

"Well I, of course, was revolted by this offer, tempting as it was. But what sort of man would make such an offer? Not a man who should run a boys' school, I concluded. Therefore, I engaged a professional acquaintance of mine in the area to look into the school. Were there any irregularities? How was the place financed? This sort of thing. In less than a fortnight, he'd uncovered enough malpractices—I needn't elaborate—to send Vandeleur to jail for a long, long time. You see, I wasn't the first person he'd tried to wring ..."

"And so you, through your agent, approached him with the evidence," said Lady Allistair.

"That is correct. Realising he was caught in his own web, the man fled, the matter of the cheating was forgotten, and nothing of the incident surfaced until now. I deeply apologise, dearest, and to all of you as well, for having kept it secret."

"I remember your explaining this part of Baskerville's past to me," said I. "This, then led to your questions about young Peter and his schooling at the Allistairs' London residence."

"Yes. When I heard of the Yorkshire school, the last piece in the puzzle had fallen into place. For as driven by money as Baskerville was, he was driven even more by hatred and revenge. Well, the time has come to put aside all unpleasant things. Let us talk of the future. Mr. Farthway, am I given to understand that you'll be seeing quite a bit of a certain young lady, yes? Well, that is good news. It should interest all of you that John Sampson has been promoted by the Oriental Trading Company to be first mate aboard the *Matilda Briggs*."

"Splendid!" we cried, and raised our glasses.

"I'm afraid we must retire to the Hall to greet our guests," said His Lordship rising. "You're free to join us, or amuse yourselves in any way you please until luncheon. Come dearest, up we go."

We hadn't long to wait, that was obvious. The servants, at an ever-increasing pace, filled the long tables with an array of food that staggered the imagination: partridges in plum chutney, skewered rack of lamb, cold cracked lobster, asparagus in lemon sauce, chilled turbot, fresh baked breads and pies—the list was endless. All this was to be accompanied by three white wines and four reds, iced cider, local beer and ale, and an array of fine brandies.

"What shall we all do then?" asked Alice. "We've only a little while. Shall we go—oh Beryl! There's my dear Beryl—come Ian, you must meet her, you really must!"

"Well, there'll be another tearful reunion. I'm sure Miss Haskins' recovery is almost complete. I can see the holiday in Brighton did her a world of good. No, let's not go in, Watson. Nice as they are, I'm sure that most of the people don't have much to say that's of interest to me."

"I agree. What shall we do then?"

"Ah, look yonder, under that Chinese elm. Is that not a croquet field?"

"So it is, how about a match?"

So after a few minutes of practice, during which the air was filled with the gentle clacking of wooden spheres and mallets, Holmes approached the home stake.

"Watson, I shall take the yellow, and you the red ... so. Now then, old fellow, shall we toss for the first hit?"

POSTSCRIPT

Over the strong objection of my modest friend Dr. John Watson, I have taken the liberty of inserting this brief note at the conclusion of the adventure that has come to be known as "The Giant Rat of Sumatra."

As mentioned in passing in the last chapter of this manuscript both Watson and I were given cheques by Lord Allistair upon the safe return of his daughter. The sum shall not be named, but suffice it to say that it made the earlier cheque given to me by the Duke of Holdernesse* seem paltry indeed. I invested my share in a variety of ways, some of which, I am loath to admit, hardly reflect the acumen portrayed in so many of Watson's stories.

What I wish to make public in this postscript (again, over the protestations of my friend) is the investment Watson made with the lion's share of his gift.

If you enter the halls of a great London hospital and amble about, before long you'll come to a small wing, newer than the rest, devoted exclusively to the treatment of children suffering from burns. A small brass plaque affixed to the wall at the entrance reads "Dedicated to the memory of Abbie Wellings, who died in the fire of September 15, 1894." The person responsible for the construction and maintenance of this facility in John H. Watson, M.D. In addition to providing the major part of the funds required, Watson also prevailed upon a large number of friends, myself included, for donations. I confess that of all my investments, this particular one allows me the soundest sleep, and pays the most bountiful dividends.

I make this statement because, after years of having my praises sung, I feel it is long overdue to repay in kind. Good old Watson!

S.H.
Sussex, 1912

*given to Holmes at the close of *The Adventure of the Priory School*

NOTES FOR GIANT RAT OF SUMATRA

Chapter One

Page 174   " ... the point of departure was therefore St. Thomas's."
We are assuming here that ambulances would only be dispatched from the larger hospitals. If this is the case, then the two hospitals named (Charing Cross and St. Thomas's) are appropriate. However, there were many hospitals closer to 221B, including various "lying in" hospitals that no doubt dispatched carriages.

Page 174   " ... we were walking south down Baker Street towards Portman Square."
Fine, but if the body is discovered south of the flat, and the hospital lies also to the south, how then could the ambulance "dash beneath" the window at 221B?

Chapter Two

Page 187   "Holmes ... settled himself before the crackling fireplace."
The fireplace at 221B was designed primarily for coal, yet there are instances in the canon that refer to logs being burnt in it. Besides, what's the use of a fireplace that doesn't crackle?

Page 190   "Instead of proceeding along the usual route ... We were running along the coast of Sumatra."
Just ten years earlier (in 1883), the volcanic island of Krakatoa literally "blew its top" in the Straits of Sunda. The explosion was probably the greatest in the history of the world—even more tremendous than our nuclear blasts. The sound was purportedly heard hundreds of miles away.

Page 192   "But then I heard it: the clanking of the windlass ..."
The *windlass* is a large winch, secured by a huge wheel with a notched edge. The *pawls* are actually ratchets that fall into the notches, thus preventing the drum from reversing. But usually the windlass is located forward, on the foredeck, not aft. We must assume that the *Briggs*, being a cargo vessel, had several windlasses for the loading and unloading of cargo.

Chapter Three

Page 198   "On the diminutive side, we have our miniature ponies of the Shetland Isles ..."
Holmes is in error, of course. While Darwin's assertions are true, the Shetland pony is the result of deliberate selective breeding. Its small size was desirable for working in mine tunnels.

Chapter Five

Page 226   "Yes, Watson, if you would be so kind, get me four ounces of navy-cut."
According to the majority of references, Holmes generally smoked "shag," an inexpensive tobacco that was strong and harsh. However, like most pipe smokers, he probably liked to switch tobaccos now and then. Navy-cut, invented by a sailor, is a tobacco blend obtained by twisting leaves of tobacco into a cable, then slicing into thin sections. The result is a strong, slow burning smoke of pungency that Holmes would certainly have enjoyed.

Chapter Seven

Page 263   "According to legend, Henry had the forge made to re-temper his sword. With it, he vowed to kill Owen Glendower ..."
Henry IV and Glendower were of course, real people, but the "legend" of Henry's Hollow is entirely fantasy, as is the Hollow itself.

Chapter Eight

Page 269   "The most obvious explanation is, of course, that the pinpricks point out the letters in the article either directly above or below them ..."

This "code" was invented—or at least implemented—by Sir Arthur himself. During the First World War it was used to communicate news to British prisoners of war. A book would be sent to the prisoner with the pinpricks commencing at a pre-arranged point. By selecting the letters indicated, the prisoner could then be truthfully apprised of the war's progress.

Chapter Nine

Page 284   " ... I tell you this because I harbour in my soul some resentment for those who've never done an honest day's work."
"Are you referring to me?" I bristled.
Why is Watson so defensive? Could it be that he harbours some doubts about his career? Why is it he seems to have so much free time? But are we not thankful for his lagging practice? Do we not offer prayers up daily for it? On another note, aren't we also thankful that the young Southsea physician (Dr. Doyle) found himself idle and so began *Study in Scarlet*?

Chapter Ten

Page 295   "The Dancing Men and the Musgrave Ritual certainly were more taxing."
The Dancing Men would be puzzling indeed to Holmes in 1894, since he did not even solve the case until 1898!

Page 300   "I quickly opened the face of my watch and felt the hands."
How else is Watson to tell the time in the dark? Luminous dials weren't invented yet. Note his watch is not a hunter's watch with metal face that must be opened to read the time, but rather has a plain glass crystal that could be raised to insert the winding key. We know Watson's watch had a winding key because it is clearly described at the opening of *The Sign of the Four*, when Watson gives Holmes the timepiece to examine to test the validity of the deductive method.
To tell the time in the dark, all Watson had to do is prise up the glass crystal, and orienting the "12" by feeling for the projecting stem, then feel the two hands. It was no doubt a delicate task, but one which could easily enough be mastered with sufficient practice.

Chapter Eleven

Page 324   "The captain was a fierce Arab named Harun Sarouk
..."

The name is as nonsensical as those Doyle gave to the Agra
confederates in *The Sign of the Four*. Harun is an Arab name. Sarouk,
as many readers may know, is a type of Persian carpet.

Chapter Twelve

Page 335   "There's your giant rat, Watson: *Tapirus Indicus.*"
Of all the elements in this story, the identity of the giant rat is the
most controversial. Many readers have told me that the choice of the
Sumatran Tapir as the villain is unwise. The animal, they say, is timid
and herbivorous, and would never attack man.

While this is true, I would remind them that the hippo, also timid
(usually) and herbivorous, has killed thousands of people along the
rivers of Africa. Furthermore, using Holmes own method of apply-
ing the principle of Ocam's Rasor, I ask them: *what then, can the
animal be?* Even the biggest rats cannot exceed two feet in length.
Baring-Gould mentions *Rhizomys sumatrensis* in his *Annotated Sherlock
Holmes*: the great Sumatran bamboo rat. But even this monster grows
only a foot and a half in length–hardly "giant" enough to be
fearsome.

I needed an animal as fierce as Baskerville's hound, and an animal
that was truly *giant*. The tapir is logical because it somewhat
resembles a rodent, is truly giant, and has the proper dentition.
Moreover, its range is restricted to Sumatra and the surrounding
islands.